KWAME
MBALIA

STAR WARS

THE LAST ORDER

LOS ANGELES • NEW YORK

Printed in the United States of America
First Edition, October 2025
1st Printing
FAC-004510-25294
ISBN 978-1-368-06561-0
Library of Congress Control Number on file
Reinforced binding
Visit the official Star Wars website at www.starwars.com.

To all the troopers out there—
it's never too late to join the Resistance.

CHAPTER 1

Coy Tria had to deliver a message. It was the only thing he had to do before he could climb aboard his ship, pray the old freighter didn't jam its fuel lines or wedge its heat vent shut, and return home to the silence of the family's tea farm on Myoca. He'd spent nearly his entire life on the arid planet, all seventeen (sixteen and a half, if he was being honest) years. If he closed his eyes he could almost smell the fragrant leaves as the wind swept through the rows of bushes yet to be harvested. It was nearly time—it had to be—and his father and grandfather would no doubt be tuning the equipment and hiring droids to prepare for round-the-clock work during First Bloom. Everything would be organized.

Neat. Tidy. Nothing like the jungles of Ajan Kloss, with its muggy heat and disrespectful weeds. Some member of the Citizens' Fleet he'd turned out to be. A glorified messenger boy, really. He hadn't wanted to fly the family freighter to the jungle moon in the first place, even after learning it was the home of the Resistance, but his grandfather had suggested it. Insisted, actually.

"A leaf alone cannot brew a tea, Coy-son," his grandfather had wheezed, sitting on his gardening pad as he did every morning, pruning back rows of tea bushes. "You must represent the family and go. Liberation is not a solo quest."

It didn't make sense then, and it didn't make sense now. Despite his grandfather's words, Coy hadn't even fired a shot during his short stint in the Citizens' Fleet, much to his dismay. He almost wanted to go on at least one adventure before settling into the family business, just to make it all worth it. Be a hero, save a friend, fall in love . . . something. But now it was over and reality was on the doorstep. It was time to go home.

First he had to deliver a message.

Coy stood a short distance away from the loading ramp of a cargo freighter, waiting for whatever meeting was being held inside to conclude. The sun's heat seemed to hover over only him, and he just knew he was getting looks over his rumpled appearance. He'd only been standing there for a few seconds, but already the back of his jumpsuit was damp and condensation pooled on the respi-vap near his waist. The device that helped his weak lungs breathe looked like it had been dunked in a pond, and he was sure his forehead was glistening. Totally unprofessional.

Suddenly the doors at the top of the freighter's ramp hissed open. Booted footsteps echoed down the ramp as an older human in fine regalia punctuated with a cape (A cape! In this humidity!) argued with a golden protocol droid about something. Neither noticed Coy until he stepped into their path, and their conversation halted.

"It appears you have a message, General Calrissian," the droid said.

"Yes?" the older human said, raising an eyebrow.

"Apologies, General," Coy said, clearing his throat and extending a datapad. "Communications delivery from the latest arrivals."

General Calrissian took the datapad but kept his eyes on Coy. The general's gaze swept over him, and Coy could see him linger on his sweat-stained collar and the dust on his boots. He straightened, and the general smiled.

"Relax, son," Calrissian said. "At ease. Comms tech duty?"

"Uh . . . yes, sir."

The general nodded. "We've all been there. Last batch of the day, with a cold drink waiting. What part of Myoca do you call home?"

"Iensi Plateau," Coy said, stunned that the general knew about his home planet. "Loe Province."

"Good tea from there. Need to see about shipping some to Cloud City when the dust from this venture settles."

"Yes, sir," Coy said, dazed.

As the general turned to the datapad, Coy hesitated. Technically his duties were completed and he could head back to the temporary base camp and wait to be relieved. Then it was getting a quick bite to eat, loading up, and taking off for Myoca. He still had a couple of things to pack, and some correspondence to write. The sooner he could get that taken care of, the better. And yet . . .

"Sir?" he said, speaking before good sense could tell him better.

General Calrissian looked up, eyebrows raised.

Coy flushed. "It's just . . . well, my grandfather would have me strung up by my harvest boots if I didn't invite you to come visit. After the harvest, that is. It's when the flavor is freshest and a joy to share with others, if I can be so bold."

Calrissian smiled, speaking as his eyes dropped to the

datapad and he scrolled. "Been a while since I've been to a First Bloom. I might just take you up on that. Soon as I—" He paused. His face tightened and his brow dropped until he was practically glaring at the datapad. Suddenly his head whipped up and his eyes, narrowed and laser focused, pinned Coy in place. "Who gave you this?" he asked, almost snarling.

Coy gulped. "Um, a pilot. Sir. One of the rescue ships."

Ever since the Battle of Exegol, Resistance ships had been sweeping the area to look for survivors, helping refugees from nearby First Order–controlled territories, and building connections for the future of the galaxy. It wasn't uncommon to stumble upon victims of slavers or pirates, as well, and standard procedure was to bring them in for questioning and processing. That was what Coy thought the latest arrivals were, rescued survivors. Apparently he was wrong. Very wrong.

"Have you read this?" the general asked.

"Well, I—"

"Have you read the message on this datapad?"

"No, sir. I . . . it said 'classified.' "

Calrissian's face softened for a second, though he stared at the datapad as if searching for answers the tech couldn't provide. Coy took the moment to let out a shaky breath and compose himself. He was about to turn and flee, and sorely wanted to, but the years of living with his grandfather and the manners surrounding the family tea farm rooted him in place.

"If I may," the droid was saying, "I'm sure Resistance leadership will want to speak with this pilot and gain more information."

"They're gone," Coy said, staring at the ground. When he looked up, he stiffened. Both the droid and General Calrissian were staring at him. He hastily continued. "The pilot, that is. They're gone. They said, 'The brass is going to want to see this immediately.' Then they handed me the datapad, swapped ships, and took off on another sweep." Coy paused, thought back for a second, then nodded. "They also spoke to an officer and said, 'Shuttle says it came from the Sardich system. Don't know how it drifted this far off course, but it did.' "

He paused because the droid seemed confused and the general looked furious. "The pilot said all that?" General Calrissian asked.

Coy nodded.

"Word for word?"

Again, Coy nodded.

The general glanced at the droid, then turned and stalked off along the trail through the jungle of Ajan Kloss, cape fluttering behind him. Coy watched him go, confused. The droid trundled up beside him to offer apologies and explanations.

"Oh, dear," it said, "you *must* forgive him. I think he took that message personally. I wouldn't worry about it. Soon enough, the moment will come when the two of you will be inseparable."

General Calrissian reappeared around the bend ahead. "Son!" he shouted back. "With me!"

"Oh," the droid said. "It appears that moment is now."

So much for firing up the family freighter for a smooth launch, Coy thought, trudging down the path after the general.

▮▮▮▮▮

The Resistance base on Ajan Kloss was really a collection of ships, caves, and forest clearings repurposed into a semi-orderly arrangement. As many meetings and planning sessions were held under the shade of the enormous broadleaf trees and curling vines as were held in the briefing rooms of General Leia Organa's temporary command ship, the *Resilience*, but what others affectionately called the *Tantive V*. So Coy was surprised when General Calrissian marched into the cave that hid the *Resilience*. He angled toward a collection of Resistance personnel clustered around a young man wildly waving about a cup of something brown. Coy recognized him, along with the olive-skinned man with wavy hair and a pilot's helmet tucked under one arm.

"Just taste it," the young man with the cup was saying.

"Finn," the other man warned.

Finn held up his hands in mock protest, accidentally sloshing some of the liquid in his cup onto his shoes. "What? You don't trust me? Just try it, Poe. I promise, one sip and I'll leave you alone."

Poe Dameron let out a huff of frustration, then snatched the cup from Finn and took a swig. Seconds later he was bent over, hands on his knees, coughing and retching while Finn stared at the cup in confusion.

"What backwater, filthy, muck-loving pond did you scoop that from?" Poe shouted in between bouts of retching. "That's disgusting!"

Coy wrinkled his nose. He could smell the faintest hints of mint and spice, and he was pretty sure the charred collection of twigs Finn pulled from the cup *used* to be tea leaves, but now . . . now it was an abomination.

"It's awful!" Poe continued. "It's—"

"I made it," Finn said, sniffing the cup.

Poe retched one more time, then straightened and took

the cup back. "Oh," he said, then took another sip. "It's not bad."

General Calrissian led Coy up to the laughing group, many of whom saluted before dispersing like farmhands caught lounging behind the collection barn during harvest time. Only Finn and Poe remained, and it was the former the general approached. Poe saw him first, however, and straightened.

"General Calrissian," he said.

"Poe." Calrissian nodded before turning to Finn. "I need you to read this." He handed over the datapad and waited while Finn scanned the reports. Poe peered over his shoulder, lips moving as he did the same. Coy shuffled his feet, still unsure as to why he was included in this briefing, if one could even call it that. He was used to the meetings his grandfather ran—up at dawn, huddled around a tractor, rows of tea bushes assigned and collector droids activated. No nonsense, no foolishness. Here . . .

Finn's face grew serious, then furious. "Is this accurate?" he asked in a low voice.

General Calrissian turned toward Coy, who started, then nodded. "Yes. Yes, sir. Straight from the pilot running rescue operations in the sector."

"Lieutenant Worlens," Poe muttered. "As solid as they come."

Calrissian was still looking at Coy. "Tell them what you told me."

So Coy repeated word for word what the pilot—Worlens—had said about the shuttle's origin system, and Finn flinched so hard Coy nearly stumbled over his words.

"You're sure about that," Finn said. "Sardich system."

Coy nodded, practically babbling beneath the heated glare of the Resistance leader. "Yes, Sardich system, not sure how it drifted this far off course. Word for word, sir. What's going on?"

But Finn was already turning to the general and Poe, the furious expression on his face morphing into one of concern. Or worry. What could possibly be so concerning that the leaders of the Resistance were driven to such a state? Coy preferred not to find out. In fact, he was seconds from discreetly slipping away—he was off duty, after all—when the group huddle ended and Finn stalked toward the front of the cave, heading for the starfighter landing zone with Poe and General Calrissian close on his heels.

"General D'Acy?" Finn said.

"In a meeting with other planetary heads," General Calrissian replied. "Only us."

"We need Jannah," Finn said. "She'll have information we might need. I'll comm her and head to that shuttle."

"And the kid?" Poe asked.

As one, they all stopped and turned to find Coy slinking in the direction of the storage lockers lining the interior of the cave. He'd hoped to gather his belongings and get back home, where he fit in and no one stared at the respi-vap when the dust got too bad or the humidity seized up his filaments. But under the gaze of those three, he froze.

"He's in it now," Calrissian said, and Finn nodded.

"Sorry, kid," Poe called out. "But you're glued to our hips for the foreseeable future. This is need to know and you know, so we need you."

Finn motioned for Coy to join them, and when they were all together and heading for the shuttle that had started this whole affair, Finn leaned in close.

"Want to try a sip?" he asked, holding out the cup.

▮▮▮▮▮

Apparently, being in the know didn't necessarily mean knowing everything all the time. Hours later, Coy found himself sitting on a supply crate, sipping a steaming cup of caf, wondering if he could convince the Resistance to order a shipment of tea from the family farm. He was working out the details of the contract in his head, figuring out hypothetical delivery schedules, when the door to the shuttle in front of him hissed open.

The shuttle had, to put it gently, seen better days. Coy wasn't sure if it was older than the family cargo freighter, but this craft had definitely been through worse. Scorch marks lined the starboard hull, while one of the stabilizing thrusters had been melted to a twisted hulk of metal. Whatever the passengers inside had been fleeing from, Coy knew it had been a close call.

A young woman a few years older than Coy appeared in the entranceway. Tall and slender, with dark brown skin and eyes that danced as she smiled at him, she wore a Resistance officer's jacket tied around her waist. She pulled her curls back out of her face and motioned for him to join her. Coy, of course, recognized her—she was the other *traitor*, the other defector from the First Order. That was what Siles, the comms tech Coy often shared shifts with, said. Coy just knew her as the person who dealt mostly with the orbaks, the four-legged tusked creatures that had been brought back from Kef Bir. Jannah. That was her name.

"Come on," she said, flashing a smile that robbed him of words. "No sense in you waiting out here in the heat."

Coy nodded, not trusting himself to speak. He was all left feet when it came to beautiful people. Besides, he still wasn't sure what his role was, other than a potential blabbermouth kept in check. Better to be silent and mysterious than open his mouth and put his foot in it.

He also wasn't sure why he'd been asked to wait while the others swept the shuttle and examined the contents. Was it illegal drugs? Some smuggled good from an endangered planet? Whatever he was about to observe, apparently it was safe enough that he wouldn't put himself—and, more important, the family freighter—at risk. He'd just pop in, follow orders, and then hightail it back to the familiar drudgery and routine of the tea farm.

So when he stepped into the shuttle, he wasn't prepared to be assaulted by an array of odors. His sense of smell was overloaded by the stench of unwashed bodies, burnt electronics, and—distressingly—the metallic scent of blood.

Coy was so overwhelmed that he almost didn't notice the others. Generals Calrissian and Finn were there, along with Poe and Jannah, but they weren't the only ones inside the shuttle. It was a standard evac shuttle, a rough tube-shaped vessel packed with thrusters at one end designed to get the occupants as far away from the launch site as possible, as fast as possible. Twenty-odd passengers could fit in the harness seats lining the interior, but only a third of them were currently filled. Besides Coy and the Resistance leaders standing in the center of the shuttle, seven others were in the harness seats.

They were all children. Thin, dirty, traumatized children, all wearing similar skinsuits. Uniforms.

Well . . . Coy squinted. The one in the middle was closer to his age, and actually maybe a few years older. She had her arms around a boy and a girl on either side of her, comforting them, and Coy realized nearly all the children were crying. The older girl in the middle lifted her head, and her eyes met Coy's; he flinched. She had no tears welling up, no streaked face or anything like that. All he could see was hatred and rage. Pure defiant rage. She turned her head to whisper to a youngling on her right and her hair shifted, revealing a symbol on the collar of her skinsuit. A symbol that was on all their collars. And that was when he made the connection.

"What's going on?" he asked. "Why are these children wearing First Order uniforms?"

Finn, who was walking by with a stack of blankets, nodded at the children. "Later," he said. "Poe and General Calrissian are going to get them cleaned up, fed, and into something comfortable."

Coy turned to grab some ration bars, but Jannah shook her head. "No," she said. "You're helping us."

"Helping? Helping with what?"

Finn held up a finger as General Calrissian, in a smooth low voice, coaxed the children up and out of their seats, most nearly falling asleep on their bare feet as they trudged out of the shuttle and into Ajan Kloss's afternoon sun. Several of them cried out, whether in surprise or joy was hard to tell, at the sight of the towering jungle plant life. Finn and Jannah followed and stopped just outside, huddling together to have a whispered conversation, leaving Coy alone.

Or so he thought.

Not all the passengers left. The older girl remained behind, still watching Coy.

"May I have something to drink?" she suddenly asked. Her voice was husky and echoed in the silence of the shuttle, and Coy jumped, startled, because he hadn't expected her to sound . . . well, like that.

"Of course," he said, and was halfway to the door when he realized he didn't know where to find what he needed. Luckily he saw an extra ration bar and canister of water near the emergency supplies Finn had found, and he brought both plus a blanket to the girl. She took them, nodding her thanks, while never breaking eye contact with him. It was unnerving, and Coy flushed.

"What's your name?" he asked, trying to sound authoritative and bold. Maybe this was what Jannah meant by helping.

She studied him. "Niila."

"Nah-ee-luh?" Coy sounded out.

A quiver at the corner of her mouth happened so fast he almost thought he'd imagined it. "Yes. Niila."

"Coy," he said. "That's, um, my name. Coy Tria."

"What do you do, Coy Tria?" Niila asked.

"What do you mean?"

She gestured toward the shuttle exit, where several ships in the starfighter landing zone could be seen. "You are a part of the Resistance, yes?"

It sounded different when she said it, this girl he'd never met before but who knew what that statement meant and what sacrifices came with it. It was nothing like the derision Coy's father had injected into the word when he learned of Coy's grandfather's decision. Nothing like the resignation and apathy he himself felt when he spoke about it. No, Niila said the word with reverence. With care, as if the title itself—Resistance—imparted some additional power when used to describe a person. Yes, he was with the Resistance, and he could feel his spine straighten for the first time in a long time when he associated himself with the group.

"I am," Coy said. He hesitated, then felt like he needed to clarify. "But only recently . . . I just joined. With the Citizens' Fleet."

"Oh," Niila said. Her head cocked as she studied him. "That must've been something, the battle above Exegol."

"It was . . . terrifying."

"The fighting?"

"The suddenness. To be surrounded by ships flown by people like me, not soldiers or fighter pilots, just cargo haulers and transports, maybe a smuggler or two. Then seconds later, to see those same ships ripped apart into shrapnel, no warning. Just . . . lightning in the dark. But . . ."

Coy's voice trailed off. He was shaking. He realized this was the first time since landing his family freighter after the Battle of Exegol that he'd talked with anyone about what it was like up there. Being all alone, nothing but his shaky breath and the alerts from the navicomputer breaking the eerie silence as he watched ship after ship torn apart.

A hand touched his arm, and he looked down to see Niila with an eyebrow raised. "But?" she repeated.

Coy let out a shaky breath. "But if you asked me, knowing what I know now, would I do it again? Leave the farm in the dead of night and fight alongside a group of people I've never met before in my life? I'd do it ten times out of ten. Because it was the right thing to do. Terrifying or not."

He stopped, suddenly feeling like he was talking too much. But Niila either didn't notice or didn't care. She nodded, as if what he'd said was perfectly normal and acceptable. As if he'd passed a test.

"The right thing to do seems like it is always terrifying," she said softly.

It was. The devastation, the destruction, the near fatalness of that race toward Exegol, and then the battle. It had driven a new appreciation for the calm restraint of growing tea leaves and harvesting them, the care and precision one had to apply in their cultivation.

And yet . . . a bit of thrill lingered. The knowledge that he had been a part of something, something bigger than his assigned row of bushes, or the team of farmhands that mocked him because of his respi-vap when they thought he wasn't listening. Bigger than the farm, or even the whole planet of Myoca. It was the galaxy, after all, and its very freedom. He had to be honest with himself—somewhere, deep down within his core, he longed for that sort of adventure again, and looking at Niila, he could tell she knew that about him, as well.

"Yes . . . it was something." He cleared his throat. "I'm sorry, I'm flapping my lips when you've been through so much. Granddad always said I could talk up a storm. Where are you from? I mean . . . before . . . um, before this." He pointed at the shuttle, then winced. That could've been handled with a bit more grace. It sounded like a line from a sappy holodrama his grandfather liked to watch. Not like she and the other kids had just gone through a terrifying experience or anything like that.

"That's what we're going to find out," someone said behind him. Coy turned to see Finn, his eyes hard as stone. "Come on, they're ready."

▮▮▮▮▮

The interrogation—Coy couldn't pretend it was anything else—took place within one of the *Resilience*'s officer briefing rooms. The rectangular space boasted the same ivory walls that covered the rest of the ship, while a large viewscreen flashed information that constantly updated the longer he stared at it. A large conference table took up the middle of the room, and that was where everyone had gathered.

Coy was out of breath as he paused in the doorway, tugging his shirt straight and taking a second to compose himself. He'd had to ferry several messages to petty officers, a distressed quartermaster, and even a droid with an attitude before he could rejoin the group as more ships landed and departed from the steadily growing base. That meant more logistics needed to be coordinated, so by the time he managed to return to the briefing room, Niila had been given a change of clothes and a chance to eat. She looked calm, maybe a little resigned, at her seat on one side of the table, while Jannah looked furious. General Calrissian frowned, and Finn wore a cold, calculating expression.

"—and you're positive about the timing?" Jannah asked.

Niila nodded. "Once the security controls went down, there was a lot of confusion. I grabbed who I could and found the first shuttle that didn't have any guards nearby. I wish I could've done more, but . . ."

Her voice trailed off, and for the first time since Coy had seen her, Niila's composure broke. She quickly cuffed away a tear with the back of her sleeve and hid her expression. Coy leaned over to the elder general with a questioning look.

"What's going on?" he asked.

"Trouble," Calrissian answered. "Those kids on the shuttle? They weren't refugees. They were recruits. First Order recruits."

Coy's heart skipped a beat, and his breath quickened so much his hand automatically fell to the controls of his respi-vap, twirling the dial until the invisible hands around his chest loosened and he could breathe normally again. General Calrissian noticed his panic and placed a hand on his shoulder.

"Easy, son. Take it easy."

Coy nodded, slightly embarrassed at his panic, and when he felt he could speak, he made sure his voice was low and controlled as the interrogation continued in the background. "But the First Order is done, right? They lost! We won . . . right?"

Calrissian shook his head slowly. "If there's one thing I learned from the last empire that was defeated, it's that tyranny doesn't just fade away into the sunset. It crumbles, but some pieces are slower to disintegrate than others. And the misinformation network those bucketheads ran was top notch, as much as I hate to admit it. There might be entire divisions of them still operating like business as usual for the foreseeable future. The job of the Resistance isn't over."

Coy stared at the general in disbelief. He thought once the Battle of Exegol had been won, things would . . . well, maybe not go back to normal but be different. Be better. But to learn that there was more work to be done, more danger, more struggle . . . it was a lot to take in.

Finn began to pace the briefing room, arms folded and jaw clenched so tight his words barely squeezed between his lips. "Tell us about the orders you saw."

Coy flinched from the fury in the words. But Niila nodded, licked her lips with the slightest hesitation, then spoke.

"I only saw a part of them before the security protocols kicked in and wiped the drive, but what I did see was a list of troops and when they were arriving."

"How many troops?" Jannah asked.

"Two, maybe three?" Niila said.

"Squads?"

She shook her head. "Battalions. The ones you see here . . . they were in my squad. That's how I was able to get them so fast. We were already together."

General Calrissian made a sound of disgust in his throat. "Battalions of children. Troops of kids. This isn't an army, it's a slaver ring. What's next?"

"We were training, preparing for the war. The real war. That's what he called it."

"He?" Finn asked.

"The major."

Before Finn could dig deeper, it was Jannah's turn to pace, and her face twisted with concern. "You mentioned the troops were supposed to arrive. Where? The shuttle flight records are corrupted—we need coordinates to trace back to where you came from."

Niila shook her head. "I can't remember. The communications were a bunch of planets and sectors and . . . I just don't . . ."

Jannah sat down in a seat across from the refugee, taking both of the other girl's hands in hers. "I know it's hard. You've done something incredible just getting you and the other members of your squad away and safe. I know how difficult it must've been. The terror you must have felt."

"You do?" Niila whispered.

"She does," Finn said from across the room.

Jannah squeezed the girl's hands. "I just need you to try and remember a location. We can take it from there."

"I don't know," Niila said, rubbing her forehead. "The major didn't share much. Just motivation and the promise that the new troops would help us win the war."

"This major," Finn said slowly. Everyone turned to look at him, but he was staring at the ceiling. No, beyond it, into the very stars themselves. He held a datapad in both hands, the white of his knuckles the only sign of the tension inside him. "What was his name?"

Niila hesitated. "He just liked to be called the major."

Finn dropped his gaze to her, and she flinched.

"Gohl," she said. "Major Gohl."

CRACK!

The datapad's screen shattered beneath Finn's hands. Jannah met Finn's gaze, and they seemed to have a conversation with their eyes. Then, almost as one, they turned to

General Calrissian, who also seemed to understand what was happening. He sighed and stood.

"Guess I'll head over and see what ship's available," he said. "Can't take the *Falcon*. That baby's more of a flying advertisement than the billboards in Cloud City. Need something no one's seen before and no one will suspect."

Coy cleared his throat, and to his astonishment and before he could actually think about what he was about to say, he spoke up. "I have a ship," he said. He looked around at the others in the room. "Who is Major Gohl?"

YEARS EARLIER

CHPTR - 2

They always began the day like they ended it—in dedication. Not to themselves. Not to each other. To a purpose. To conviction.

To order.

Like a parent gently waking up a child, the mantras began just before they woke up. Each bunk in the barracks was equipped with integrated speakers, and the words of affirmation and commitment to their cause caressed them to consciousness. Then they dressed in their armor in silence, lips moving soundlessly when a mantra needed repeating.

"There is a sickness in the galaxy."

First came the body glove, the all-black skinsuit worn beneath the armor, a further reminder that even beneath the armor they were the same. No matter their physical differences or origins, there was only the Corps. The mission.

"We are not the cure—we are the hand that delivers it. Not the medicine, but the doctor."

From the bottom up, the boots were next, followed by the gaiters and greaves. Each piece was tested to make sure movement and articulation were smooth.

"The First Order is not a family. We are more."

Thigh, butt, and groin armor followed. Their addition was quick, routine.

"We are the same. We are of a singular mind. Without stability there is unrest. Without dedication there is corruption. Without order there is chaos."

The chest plate was the biggest piece to put on, but once in place, the shoulder pauldrons, bicep guards, and vambraces for the forearms quickly came next. After that were the gloves, and everything was complete save for the last piece. The helmet.

"The you is dead. The I is dead. There is only we. You were discarded. I was abandoned. Your parents didn't want you. I was betrayed by my government. You are nothing. I am nothing. But we . . . we are strong. We are united. We are one."

The helmet slid over the head, and for a moment there was nothing but the darkness of oblivion. And then the display winked on, sight was restored, and the others in the room moved into position. Each stood in front of their bunk, armored, stormtroopers, as the last of the mantra finished and identification tags popped into view.

FN-0926

FN-1312

FN-2199

FN-2000

FN-2187

FN-2489

"We are the First Order."

The ending lines of the First Order mantra echoed in his ears as FN-2187 began his final lap. Physical fitness was the first item on the schedule for not only today, but every day. No matter what rank you were in the Stormtrooper Corps, PF was nonnegotiable, and it was always held at the start of the day, though instructors could mandate extra PF as needed within reason.

We are the First Order.

His boots thudded against the training room track. In front of him, behind him, shoulder to shoulder, his fellow cadets ran in unison. He loved it. Looked forward to it. Being a part of something. They were all around the same age, sixteen or seventeen, nearly done with their training as recruits and ready to launch into their first missions. It was past time. They were ready; he could feel it. They all had the same passion, sharing in goals and objectives. PF showed it. No other mandate except to finish. To keep going for as long as possible, because his effort, and that of the others around him, meant something. Centimeter by centimeter they pushed forward, together.

But he wanted more. He couldn't shake that hunger.

"Time!" an instructor barked as they crossed the finish line. "Thirty seconds to catch your breath, cadets!"

FN-2187 slowed to a walk, remaining in formation as the group moved to the next portion of physical fitness. It was habit by now, which he was sure was the point. To train until everything became instinctual. Until you could rely on any trooper you encountered because both of you were extensions of the same body. He wished they had a few more laps yet, if only to drive this nagging feeling from his mind.

We are the First Order.

"Slowing down in your old age, Eight-Seven," someone said behind him. "You're slipping."

He ignored it. Technically, conversations weren't prohibited while in formation, but they weren't exactly encouraged, either. Also, he knew who was speaking, helmet voice modulator or not. You grew to learn distinctions in speaking patterns and voice inflections.

You can't disguise being a jerk, Fifty-Five, he thought.

They left the track for a separate wing of the training complex. Large gray plasteel cubes were stacked in towering formations, simulating an urban cityscape. Later in the day, holoprojectors would convert the colorless environment into a bustling city, or a town center, or the interior of a space station. Whatever the training instructors needed it to be to hone the cadets' skills for their eventual missions. For now, however, it was a simple obstacle course and the objective was clear.

"Listen up, cadets!" a voice boomed over speakers hidden in the walls and ceiling. "As you can see, the rest of PF is dedicated to something very special. The course you see in front of you is your standard obstacle and endurance test. You will complete three laps."

The speaker cut out. Murmurs gathered in the ranks. Eight-Seven waited. There was more. There was always more.

Sure enough, the speaker crackled again. "You will complete three laps while avoiding the instructors posing as insurgents. Cadets who do not complete the course will have to retake it before they will be allowed to continue with the rest of their day. Cadets who complete the course will be granted privileges during their upcoming leave. Cadets who complete the course *and* acquire an insurgent's comlink will find themselves at the top of the list when it's time to consider specializations. Understood?"

"YES, SIR!"

Oh, he understood. Eight-Seven squeezed a gloved fist tight. Advance through the course. Get a comlink. Don't be last.

A shoulder jostled his. "Watch yourself," whispered the same cadet—FO-7155.

Eight-Seven ignored him again. He stretched, preparing for the course. Another cadet moved up next to him, mirroring his movements: FO-1103.

"Ignore him," she said. "Someone's a little nervous."

"Over an obstacle course?" Eight-Seven thought that was ridiculous. It was the same course they'd run since they could walk. Sure, the height and difficulty may have ramped up, but it was nothing to worry about.

"No, not the course. The instructors. Word is they're

looking for squad leaders and specialists, and Fifty-Five wants to be one. Seems like too much hassle for me."

Eight-Seven didn't acknowledge that. She could be right; she could be exaggerating; she could want the same thing. But when he glanced up at the observation booth high above, near the ceiling, more than the usual number of observers mingled there. The normal gray uniforms of the training instructors could be seen, but there were more. A flash of red. A hint of chrome. He swallowed. The potential to be top in the queue for specializations *and* squad leader?

"First sections up!" The command came from one of many speakers hidden around the course. There were cameras, too. They were always being watched.

"Next sections up!"

Mountain trooper. It was what he wanted. What he felt he should be doing. Snowtrooper meant freezing cold temperatures, which he didn't—willingly—do, and squad leader felt like too much responsibility. He had his own skin to worry about; adding two to three others was a recipe for failure. But a mountain trooper, at least according to the sims he studied almost every day, meant hiking through forests, patrolling near waterfalls. . . . It was almost a dream.

Eight-Seven chewed on the possibilities as he and the other cadets waited their turn to start the obstacle course.

On missions, orders filtered down the chain of command like bantha droppings. Squad leaders took orders directly from captains and passed them to their troops. Meanwhile, the specialist troopers took on additional training and were relied on in key situations. Both options meant more responsibility.

"Next sections up!"

Someone whimpered nearby. Through the helmet vocal modulator it almost sounded like static. When Eight-Seven looked up, he saw FO-7155 hovering near a smaller cadet, who was doubled over, clutching their sides.

"I *said* don't get in my way," Fifty-Five hissed.

"Next sections up!"

The next group of cadets started the course, leaving Eight-Seven standing at the front of the queue. FO-7155 turned to look at him as they both waited for the signal. Someone moved up on his right, and Eight-Seven saw FO-1103 limbering up out of the corner of his helmet but ignored her. There were no teams or squads during this obstacle course. Only the finish line.

Fifty-Five continued to stare up until the moment his group—and Eight-Seven's group—was called to the starting line.

"Go!"

They took off, shouldering aside stragglers and heading for the first obstacle, a wall twice as high as they were. Eight-Seven took it in a scrambling leap, flipping over and continuing to run without breaking stride.

Right on his hip were 1103 and 7155. The latter snarled, a harsh garbled sound, and smashed the smaller cadet into a wall.

Eight-Seven ran on.

Being a specialist meant extra responsibility, yes, but there were also benefits. Rank had its privileges. And its immunities. Separate training facilities. Enhanced nutrition allotments. Suddenly winning the race was starting to look more and more attractive.

CHPTR - 3

"I never thought I'd say it, but I'm sick of sunshine."

TZ-1719 didn't respond. She stooped at the base of a brick retainer wall, ornamental bushes crowding in on either side of her. A line of delicate flowers grew in the cracks of the brick, tracing the seams to form geometric patterns framed in bright petals of various colors. She studied them, noting the way their petals strained for the sky but dwindled in the crowded shadow of their neighbors. The strongest, the most colorful, navigated their way through twisted and tangled stems to claim their space. One had fallen to the ground, and she picked it up, tucking it away in her armor.

The entire retainer wall on this level bloomed in gold, while the levels above and below—smaller and larger in size, respectively, like a tiered cake—had walls covered in emerald green. There were seventeen levels in total, each covered in rare trees, imported shrubs, and flowers and serviced by an army of droid caretakers that puttered about, plucking weeds and pruning stems.

No blood. No hasty graves. No screaming.

"Boss, you hear me?"

1719 stood up and carefully stepped back from the wall to the path and brushed her gloves together. A bronze plaque mounted on a stone too clean to be real described the different plants on this level, and a phrase caught her eye.

"Boss?"

She keyed her mic, not bothering to check who was speaking. Only Clamps complained this much, this often. "What is it?"

"How much longer do we have to guard empty vacation palaces for the obscenely rich?" Clamps asked. He was above her, supposedly keeping an eye on servants' entrances near the top levels. Palace owners and their guests entered on the ground levels, where the rare plants couldn't be disturbed by the backwash of ship engines coming and going.

Another voice chimed in. "They're not empty. The droids are inside."

Clamps groaned. "I consider that empty, Twelve."

"Plus this is better than the *Scarab*," the other voice continued. "At least everything down here is new, and not abandoned."

"Cut the chatter," 1719 finally said. She shouldered her riot shield and grimaced—blasters weren't allowed on Hadne 3, as the owners were worried about damage to the contents of their precious palaces. The tropical moon was a collective venture jointly owned by several intergalactic corporation executives looking for a retreat space away from the city-planets where they normally did business. Instead of mansions, giant garden palaces dotted the landscape, each costing billions of credits to build and millions to operate and care for year over year. Apparently, the owners included a handful of galactic VIPs important to the First Order, and so blasters were stowed on the drop ship before they disembarked. Not that she minded.

Blood-soaked decks. Alarms blaring. Screaming. The coldness of space dragging her down as a hand grips—

"Boss, you good?"

Clamps's question pulled her from her thoughts. Memories of their last battle didn't intrude on her waking hours as much anymore, but they still happened from time to time.

"Good," she answered. "Check the next level. I'll join you shortly."

"On it."

1719 snorted softly. Another squad leader would've railed their subordinate for answering with anything but a regulation response, but Clamps had been in the trenches with her during the Merchant Uprising. He'd seen the blood. He also never questioned any of her orders, and she knew he would follow her to the end. It was actually, when she thought about it, a little scary, that devotion. It wasn't what she'd imagined. Her fingers on her right hand twitched as she remembered her last session with Captain Phasma before she was given the position of squad leader.

"Your aim and stamina have improved," the silver-armored captain had said as 1719 gasped and lowered her bow. "Your focus, however, is a concern. The ability to maintain accuracy, command, and tactical awareness under pressure is a core necessity for leadership in my ranks, trooper, and I will be looking for significant gains upon my return. Captain Shikra will be monitoring your progress, and I expect a stellar report."

"Yes, Captain," 1719 had murmured, still in awe at the promotion.

Now some of the luster of leadership had been rubbed away, especially as Clamps continued to complain. She missed her bow, and the calm before the bolt was loosed. It was a struggle to find that while on patrol, and she resolved to work on it. Later.

"Boss," a new voice said over the comm.

"Go," 1719 answered.

"Unregistered flight on scanners heading in your direction, approaching from the south. Small craft, it looks like."

"From the *Scarab*?"

Clamps snorted. "Not unless it's a rusty garbage bucket."

"No," the other voice continued, ignoring him. "This one's different. And no weapons on initial scans."

1719 pulled out her quadnocs and turned to scan the surroundings. It took her a minute, but she eventually spotted the gleam of a ship's hull cutting through the lavender sky. She traced its path as it descended, marking the location of a garden palace several klicks away and sending it to the rest of her squad.

"Twenty-One-Four," she said into the mic.

"Yes, boss?" TZ-214 answered.

"Any itineraries filed for the owners of the marked location?"

After a second: "No, not for several weeks yet."

"They're rich. Do they file itineraries?" Clamps muttered.

It was 1719's partner on this level of the palace, TZ-1212, who answered. "Yes, actually. The environment on this moon is carefully monitored so that unnecessary fumes and exhaust don't impact the sensitive flora imported at cost."

" 'Imported at cost,' " Clamps repeated in a mocking tone.

"Stow it," 1719 said. "Twelve, Clamps, you're with me. Twenty-One-Four, make sure no one else lands while we go check out the visitor."

A chorus of affirmatives echoed over the comm as she prepared to join Twelve and descend to ground level the old-fashioned way. The stairs cut into the corner of the walls, allowing them to traverse levels without having to enter the palace at all. But she paused and glanced back at the plaque mounted on the fake stone, then keyed a private channel.

"Twelve, can you translate something for me?" she asked. "I don't have the right language loaded."

"You got it, boss," Twelve answered.

She sent him a picture of the inscription, then waited.

"Ah, got it." He read off the phrase, then pulled up the translation. "Apparently it's not a local dialect, but one from the planet where those small flowers are imported from, and it's just their name. They're called Carpet of Paradise, and apparently they're really expensive, on account of how difficult it is for them to take root when away from their native soil."

"These seem to be doing fine," 1719 remarked.

"Well, if you *can* get them to take root, everyone seems to agree they're hardy little jewels."

Carpet of Paradise. She nodded. Appropriate, but its wording in the native dialect had more of a ring to it.

"Jannah al Sajada," 1719 whispered.

"What's that, boss?"

"Nothing," she said. "Let's go greet our visitor."

▮▮▮▮▮

"Why do they call you boss?"

The question came from TZ-1212—or Twelve as Clamps called him, and the name had stuck. He was new to the squad, a replacement for the sour-faced but dutiful TZ-1604, the only casualty from the squad during the Uprising. His replacement hadn't exactly been welcomed from the outset. But it was hard to be cold to a teammate on a paradise moon, and 1719 had encouraged Clamps and 214 to include him in more things, and he was gradually becoming useful.

Now she thought about his question. "Just something to

call me, I guess," she finally said. "Squad Leader is too formal, and Seventeen-Nineteen is a mouthful."

"Just like—" Clamps started to say on the team channel, right before 1719 kicked him off and rolled her eyes.

"As I was saying, it just happened. Clamps started it."

Twelve kicked at a rock. "He gives out all the nicknames, huh?"

"Be thankful. TZ-Sixteen-Oh-Four was Socks because Clamps said his feet had an odor strong enough to strip metal."

"Why's he called Clamps?"

The smile faded from 1719's face and she straightened. "Come on, we need to check out this newcomer."

Blood-soaked decks. Alarms blaring. Screaming. The coldness of space dragging her down as a hand grips her wrist, pulling her aboard. "I got you, boss. I got you."

The unknown ship had docked on one of the landing pads reserved for the palace owners, away from the sensitive plant-covered terraces but still close to the ground level. Sheltered from the elements, the pad was connected to the palace via a bridge that doubled as the roof of an aqueduct responsible for bringing water from the underground pumps to the palace irrigation system. High walls disguised as fake cliffs protected the area from the unwelcome eyes of neighbors, though any sort of noise that disturbed the eerie stillness as 1719's squad crept toward the ship would've eased her worries. As it was, she couldn't shake the feeling that something wasn't right.

"Twenty-One-Four," she said, "put a probe droid as high as you can over that ship and still make out details."

"You sure, boss?" came the reply. "Orders were no blasters or—"

"I know, but I'll beg for forgiveness if necessary."

"Copy that."

She nodded at Twelve and Clamps, and the two troopers split off to flank the ship on either side while she approached from the front, nearest the cockpit. It was a sleek monster, she had to admit. Two wings bristled with laser cannons, and a singular missile launcher was mounted beneath like the stinger of some territorial insect.

"*Roc*-class starfighter," Twelve muttered, more to himself than the rest of the squad. "Rare. Expensive, too. Maybe we're getting a field promotion?"

Clamps approached and tapped the hull with his gloved knuckles. "Don't jinx the mission. *I* think a senator forgot something during their last soiree. Or an employee is sneaking a joy ride trying to impress a date?"

The ship was empty. Whoever was inside when it landed had already entered the palace. Clamps's guesses could be true, maybe. Still . . . it was possible he was wrong and someone who wasn't supposed to be here had broken into the palace. While her squad was supposed to be patrolling, no less. No, she had to be sure. She hefted her riot shield and started walking to the hidden entrance tucked beneath a two-story fern around the corner.

"Boss?" Twelve asked. "We're not supposed—"

"I know," 1719 said.

Even Clamps hesitated. "Are you sure this is—"

"Not one bit," she said.

Only 214 didn't comment, instead choosing to send the compact probe droid ahead to scout. By the time 1719 got to the entrance, the droid had bypassed the keypad and the security systems. She nodded at the ocular lens. "Thank you."

"Sure thing, boss."

The interior of the garden palace boggled the eye. It was designed to, with curving pathways through vaulted atriums, dining nooks open to the outside, and more ornamental plants placed specifically to draw in the visitor. White stone so brilliant 1719 thought lights were embedded within competed with trailing vines from automated planters that drifted lower or higher in the room depending on the time of day. Bedrooms were made to look like jungle retreats, and steam-filled baths were carved directly into stone floors. Each room they exited was outdone by the one they entered next, and it was beautiful, if overwhelming.

It was also completely empty.

"Where are the service droids?" Twelve asked. The short boy hefted his riot shield nervously. His cautious nature and the fact that he was gentle at heart had caused him issues as a cadet during training.

"Where's the pilot of that starfighter?" Clamps muttered.

1719 wondered the same. They'd progressed through the first three levels unimpeded. 214 was directing the droid, remotely scouting ahead, and the two floors above had been reported clear, as well. Yet 1719 couldn't shake the feeling that she had missed something. Something obvious.

She stopped in the middle of a sitting room with a small stream trickling through it. Fish and an amphibious lizard swam beneath their feet as 1719 remained still for several seconds. Then she turned, shook her head, and began retracing her steps.

"We're leaving," she said.

Clamps and Twelve looked at each other. "Boss?" Twelve asked.

"We wasted too much time here and we've got a patrol to

finish. And I'm not trying to explain to a senator—or worse, to Captain Phasma—why we broke into a palace without authorization. Twenty-One-Four, set the table and meet us at the landing pad. We'll take a ride to the next palace, finish the patrol, then report back."

"Roger," came her reply.

Clamps hesitated, like he wanted to say something, but 1719 brushed past him and he sighed and fell in behind her. They took the turbolift to the ground floor, not worried about stealth this time, and exited the palace to make their way to the landing pad.

"Not your standard patrol according to regulations, trooper."

The voice came through the comm, but it wasn't anyone from their squad. 1719 stopped, blocked by a masked figure on the pathway between her and the landing pad. She hadn't heard anyone approach, nor had 214 alerted them. Where had they come from?

Someone stepped beside her. Clamps. "How are you on this frequency?" he snarled. "Identify yourself."

The newcomer tilted their head but didn't answer.

"I said—" Clamps began, stepping forward.

"Hold!" 1719 snapped.

"Boss," he began, but she shook her head.

"Twenty-One-Four," she said. "Ship info?"

"Oh," came a sheepish voice. "Right. Um—*Roc*-class starfighter, as Twelve said. It . . . oh. Um. Boss, it has a high security clearance."

"How high?"

"So high I need security clearance to identify the security clearance."

1719 nodded to herself. That explained how their comms had been breached—it wasn't a breach. The newcomer wore a tattered cloak that obscured most of their form, and from a distance it looked old and worn, but 1719 had trained enough, especially under Captain Phasma, to recognize synthetic polyweave when she saw it. Special forces?

"Registration?"

214 took a second, then cleared her throat. "Major Chetachi Gohl, First Order Security Bureau."

The newcomer clapped their hands. "Impressive. I'm still slightly disappointed that you allowed your squad to be ambushed this easily. If I could get the drop on you, imagine what terrorists and separatists could do, not to mention your run-of-the-mill street gangs."

1719 didn't say anything.

The cloaked agent paused. "I didn't ambush you, did I?"

She shook her head. "When we couldn't find any evidence

of you in the palace, I realized we'd forgotten one place that's easy to overlook, especially when we're standing on top of it."

"The aqueducts," Clamps and Twelve said, realization striking them at the same time as they both immediately looked at the ground beneath their feet.

"Still," the newcomer said, "you were taking quite a risk."

"Twenty-One-Four?" 1719 said.

The squad's shuttle transport lifted into the air from behind the palace. Their fourth member had it on autopilot as she leaned out of the side door, a long-range laser rifle with an outlandish scope attached pointed in their direction.

1719 shrugged. "I know the patrol briefing said no blasters, so we'd blame any damage on you after we took you out and reported back."

The newcomer laughed, and their hood fell away to reveal the rest of a synthetic mask that covered the lower two-thirds of their face. Bright amber eyes twinkled as they watched 1719, amusement crinkling their outer corners.

" 'Set the table,' " they said. "A code phrase. Clever."

She nodded. "Prepare for guests—"

"At the landing pad. As I said, clever."

Clamps looked between the two of them, figured out no violence was forthcoming, and leaned on his riot shield. "So if you're not here to shoot at us, why exactly are you here?"

The newcomer began walking back toward their starfighter, still speaking through their comms as they climbed into the cockpit. "I was sent to observe you. Captain Phasma spoke highly of you to my superior."

"Major Gohl?"

"Correct. My job was to watch you and report back."

"And?" 1719 asked.

"And that's what I'm going to do." The starfighter's engines roared to life as the stranger saluted them through the cockpit canopy. "But if I were you, I'd hightail it back to base to receive orders when they come in."

The starfighter lifted into the air, nose and stinger pointed at the sky, and shot off, backwash whipping up dust and leaves in miniature cyclones. 214 landed the shuttle transport and hopped out, joining the other three squad members just as Clamps turned to Twelve.

"This is why you never jinx the mission," he said.

CHPTR - 4

Get a comlink. Finish the race.

FN-2187 pushed himself.

Halfway through the course, in the middle of the second lap, they encountered their first major obstacle. Up to that point they'd scaled walls, crawled beneath blocks cut so the jagged edges stabbed and scraped, and pulled themselves through crevices that threatened to crush them, to squeeze their soft insides out of their armor. They'd hopped over pillars and scrambled up ramps, jostling and shoving and lashing out if other cadets got too close.

Still they ran on.

Eight-Seven could feel the beginnings of fatigue creeping

into his limbs. His arms felt heavier and heavier with each step, and with each pump he coaxed his body for more speed. His chest burned, every breath like hot nails clawing to escape through his skin. But he needed more. Cadets dropped around him as exhaustion overcame their fear of failure, but others were catching up. Their hands grabbed at his armor, but Eight-Seven shrugged them off and scaled the first wall for the final time. That pauldron was his, and a hungry smile stretched beneath his helmet.

He dropped down on the other side of the wall, then slowed to a stop.

An instructor wearing shabby robes over their uniform and a hood that threw half of their masked face into shadow stood in the middle of the corridor. Up until now the obstacle course had been free of human interference, but it looked like that was about to change. Eight-Seven didn't recognize them. Short, with spider-thin limbs and a fighter's crouch that didn't allow for an accurate read on height, they wore a mask that covered their lower face and connected to a green flexi-brace on their right shoulder. A small droid with a counter display built into its face hovered in the air over the shoulder wearing the brace. Eight-Seven did recognize the stance the instructor was in—standard close-quarters combat readiness—and the weapon in their hand.

A resonator mace.

The club-like weapon, capable of extending two additional energized prongs so it resembled a short electrified trident, thrummed. From the way the instructor twirled it as they launched into an attack, they knew how to use it.

Cadets began dropping down beside Eight-Seven, his pause allowing them time to catch up. They took off, some sparing him a glance before sprinting on, others paying him no attention, eyes on the instructor.

Thrum.

Thrum.

Two cadets, two swings of the mace, two bodies collapsing to the floor, writhing in agony. From the corner of his eye, Eight-Seven watched FO-1103 run by, and before he could shout a warning, the instructor lunged forward. The mace crackled through the air before exploding in a shower of sparks, thudding against 1103's chest armor and sending her flying backward.

The other cadets scattered, shouting in alarm. Some returned to the wall they'd just hopped over, interfering with the cadets trying to clear it. Others tried to swerve around the instructor. Eight-Seven held back, studying the pattern of attack.

Thrum.

Thrum.

The mace arced through the air, descending just over Eight-Seven's shoulder to crack the helmet of the cadet to his right. A few cadets tried to go on the attack, no doubt looking for a comlink to steal. All were quickly dispatched, left in a groaning pile of smoking armor. The instructor loomed over them, then slammed the mace down repeatedly until no one moved. Silence fell. Eight-Seven retreated a step, then surveyed the gathering crowd of cadets.

Thrum.

Thrum.

Two clumps of cadets split off, one group heading left, the other right. Eight-Seven waited, counted to three, then took off in a sprint.

The instructor leaped and twirled, mace sparking as it collided with armor. At the last second Eight-Seven swerved to the outside, closest to the wall, keeping several others between him and the silent instructor.

Thrum.

Somehow he made it through. Eight-Seven didn't wait to see how many cadets had survived the instructor besides him. He took off, now in the middle of the group, trying to ignore the carnage behind him, even as the instructor turned to face a new group of ambitious cadets.

A cadet, gasping and stumbling forward, came to a stop near Eight-Seven. "Who was that?" she asked, words squeezing out between pants. "I've never seen them before."

"A guest of the major," another cadet said, jogging up, one hand on his side.

"Major?" Eight-Seven asked.

The cadet pointed at the observation room high above the course. A tall man in black was watching the race. Eight-Seven couldn't make out his face, but there was no mistaking the fact that his eyes were on them.

Without warning, someone crashed into his side, sending him sprawling across the floor. Eight-Seven looked up to see FO-7155 looming over him. The bigger boy seemed torn between trying to finish off his quarry and winning the race. His dilemma was solved for him when three training instructors wearing robes and carrying durasteel-tipped quarterstaffs emerged from the shadows. Fifty-Five backed up, reluctantly giving Eight-Seven room to stand.

"What's the matter?" Eight-Seven said as he climbed to his feet. "Worried? You need a teammate now?"

A soft snarl was the only response. No way the boy would admit he needed help. Fifty-Five just balled his hands into fists and waited, ready for the instructors to attack. Eight-Seven joined him, leaving some space between them.

"Stay out of my way," 7155 said.

Eight-Seven sent him a mocking salute and then—without waiting—rushed forward. From their delayed reaction, the instructors were as surprised by this move as his fellow cadet was, but he didn't have time to allow a strategy to form. Sometimes the best plan was no plan at all.

Two lunging steps forward and Eight-Seven was among the robed instructors. They were still lifting their staffs as he punched, kicked, and kneed his way into the middle of their formation.

It didn't take long for 7155 to join him. The other boy used his forearms to knock aside swinging staffs, taking glancing blows to the shoulders in return, before finally reaching the instructors and raining crushing blows on each. Meanwhile, Eight-Seven ducked a staff, then hammered a white-gloved fist into the exposed ribs in front of him. A grunt of pain signaled Eight-Seven had found the right spot, and he sprang upward, both hands circling the back of the instructor's neck and pulling them in and down, straight into his knee.

Crack!

The instructor went limp. Beside him, 7155 had one instructor lifted in the air before slamming him to the ground. The robed man tried to lift himself, then slumped back down, limp and still. Fifty-Five stood, then pointed and shouted in alarm.

"Watch it!"

Shouts swelled behind them. Eight-Seven glanced back, but there were only a few cadets in the distance. He was turning back around when a whisper of movement alerted him. He ducked just in time, and 7155's fist swung harmlessly overhead. The other boy held several comlinks in his other hand, and his helmet shook from side to side as he backed up.

"Lucky," 7155 said. "But then you were always the lucky one."

"Give me a comlink," Eight-Seven said, forcing calm into his voice while he mentally kicked himself for falling for the trick.

"What? These?" The other boy held up the devices. "No. Get your own. Everyone for themself, remember?"

Thrum.

Eight-Seven cursed and turned around.

The masked instructor stood behind him, cadets at their feet, mace in a two-handed grip. The droid clicked away behind them, lens aperture opening and closing as it recorded everything.

"Let's see if you're still lucky," 7155 called out as he ran on to complete the race.

Eight-Seven cursed again. He could follow, hoping to either steal a comlink from 7155 or just finish the race at the front of the pack. Or . . .

The masked instructor reached a hand into their cloak and pulled out a comlink. It dangled from their gloved fingers like a piece of trash before they tossed it into the middle of the floor between them and Eight-Seven. An invitation.

A challenge.

Eight-Seven glanced back at the finish line of the race. He could still make it and be fine. Surely the instructors would recognize his performance, even without a comlink, and elevate him in the mysterious rankings they discussed among themselves. He could jog across the finish line and continue on with his day, unmolested and in relatively good spirits.

Eight-Seven sighed, then turned and raised his fists.

He wanted that comlink.

Cadets were piling up in a queue behind the instructor, but one look at the hooded figure and no one tried to sneak past. Eight-Seven could see FO-1103 in the middle of the group, one arm hanging limp, and fury boiled in his chest.

Eight-Seven sprang forward without warning, trying the same trick he had with the other instructors, but his opponent was waiting for that. They swung the mace in a low arc, forcing Eight-Seven to leap back, off-balance, before throwing himself to the right to avoid a follow-up overhead swing that slammed into the ground, singeing the gray floor.

That was close, he thought. *Need to keep moving.*

He lunged forward, closing the distance to prevent the mace from being fully extended. Somehow he managed to chop down on the wrist with the mace before a well-placed kick crashed into his left knee, buckling him. He had only a second to raise his arm and block the knee that was aimed at his face. Even still it made contact, dazing him, and he just barely managed to keep his wits and push it aside.

Okay, maybe don't move into their attack.

Eight-Seven rolled forward, trying to knock the instructor off-balance, and kicked out at their feet. He made contact with their thigh, and this time it was their turn to stumble backward, but they used their momentum to swing the mace around, twirling it in a flourish before lunging forward. Eight-Seven twisted left, tucked and rolled forward, rose to his feet, and turned, fully prepared to block another attack. But the instructor just stood in place, hands gripping the mace, waiting.

"Well done," the instructor said. Their voice was surprising, and he flinched. It grated against the ears. No wonder they didn't speak much. But they disabled the mace, the electric blue sparks disappearing as the instructor clipped the weapon to their belt.

Eight-Seven straightened. "That's it? No more fighting?"

"You have what you wanted."

He nodded, pulling the comlink from where he'd palmed it during his roll. "You saw that." A statement, not a question, but the instructor nodded anyway.

"But you'd better hurry if you want to finish the race," was all they said.

Eight-Seven watched them closely as they stood there. The instructor raised a hand and made a beckoning gesture to the crowd of cadets behind them. Tentatively they stepped forward, and then it was as if the floodgates had opened. Cadets streamed around the instructor, still giving them space, and even though they all had helmets, it was no secret they hungered for the comlink in Eight-Seven's hand.

He turned and began to run.

Before he rounded the corner and crossed the finish line of the obstacle course, he glanced back, and his last view of the masked instructor was of them standing still in that strange crooked stance, a stone in a river of white, the droid recording everything.

CHPTR - 5

The base of operations for TZ-1719—and her squad—hovered hundreds of kilometers above Hadne 3's surface, drifting in orbit around the luxury planet like a bloated beetle. The *Scarab* was a *Star Galleon*–class escort frigate that had—for some reason that bothered Twelve to no end—been converted from its more traditional role shuttling huge amounts of ore across hyperlanes to its current ill-suited job housing a rotating complement of stormtrooper squads. Squads that tried their absolute best to avoid patrol duty.

1719 relished the assignment. Away from the violence and slaughter of her last mission, she finally felt like she could breathe. She still got recurring headaches that the officers in the medbay labeled as normal, despite her constant complaints, but they were a small price to pay.

For the most part, their job consisted of occasional patrols and scrubbing the scrap ore containment wing that senior staff had converted into a training center. The accumulated rust and mineral deposits combined with sweat to make fumes so potent many a trooper had emptied the contents of their stomach on the floor seconds after stepping inside. Which, of course, only formed a united stench that could curdle durasteel. Still, Clamps continued to remind 1719 that containment scrubbing was always an option as they walked to their quarters.

"Look, boss, all I'm saying is we have no idea what sort of mission they could be giving us. Better the gutter drake we know than the scav worm swimming in the melon milk." The boy was walking backward down the corridor. They were on the command deck to deliver their report, then off to the mess to scrounge together dinner since it was after hours.

"What does that mean?" 1719 asked.

Clamps pivoted, nearly bumped into a cleaning droid, and fell into place beside her. "It means if we—and I really mean you—request ship duties before we can get ordered off to the next backwater patrol they probably have in the queue for us, boom—we're in the clear."

"Boom?" She wasn't really paying attention. She was still grappling with the stranger's words back on-planet. *Captain Phasma spoke highly of you.* What did that mean? Was she telling the truth? And if so, when did Phasma say that?

"Boom," Clamps repeated, slamming a gloved fist into his open palm.

"Boom?"

Twelve appeared as they crossed an intersection and elbowed Clamps out of the way so the smaller boy could be next to 1719. "Why boom?" he asked.

"Where'd you come from?" Clamps asked, puzzled. "I thought you were heading to morale session?"

"Unfortunately no. Well, I was, but I got orders to report and . . . well, here I am."

They passed a turbolift and an officers' lounge before they reached the *Scarab*'s briefing room. The former was out of order, while the latter contained a single officer sitting at a table with his hat off, his head in his hands, a cup of caf steaming in front of him.

"Ominous," Clamps muttered, more to himself than anyone else.

They rounded the corner, and somehow 1719 wasn't surprised to see TZ-214 leaning against the wall next to the briefing room's door. She nodded at them, but her attention was on the angry voice coming from inside. 1719 tried to listen, but as she drew closer, she was nearly knocked over by a staff officer practically running out, face red and pinched with embarrassment.

"Get in here," snapped a voice from inside, and 1719 led the others into the briefing room.

"Foot Patrol Twenty-Two-A—" she began, but was immediately cut off by the man standing in front of a holotable. Lieutenant Niashar was short and stockier than most officers she'd met, with tanned skin that was red with anger as he leaned forward into the table's current projection, Hadne 3.

"I know who you are," he growled. "Useless troublemakers."

"Sir?"

"Your orders, like every other patrol sent down to the surface, were to patrol the mansions, check around a corner or two, and hightail it back up here and file a report. 'Nothing out of the ordinary, sir! Nothing to report, sir! No mynock-sucking exogorths made it on-planet, sir!' "

Clamps cleared his throat. "No mynock—"

"Shut up!" Niashar roared. He slammed himself into the seat behind the holotable and rubbed his temples furiously. "I just had a planetary governor call and complain for the last quarter hour because—and I quote—an alarm was tripped in their third vacation house here on Hadne Three. Now she wants to come visit to make sure we're doing our job properly, a job—need I remind you—that has been done perfectly by EVERY OTHER SQUAD EXCEPT FOR YOU!"

1719 stepped forward. "Apologies, sir, it was my fault. As squad leader I instructed the team to enter the garden palace. We had reason to believe an unidentified pilot—"

"What pilot?" Niashar grunted.

"The pilot of the starfighter?" She glanced at her squad, who were just as puzzled as she was. "It descended around—"

"No ship entered or left atmosphere other than your shuttle, so I don't know what game of blame shifting you're trying to pull, but I advise you to cut it short and not waste my time."

Twelve began to speak, but a nudge and the tiniest of head shakes cut him off before he could get them into more trouble. Some strange puzzle was being revealed, and 1719 didn't like the missing pieces. Best not to show how little they knew.

"Yes, sir," was all she said.

Lieutenant Niashar glared at her, as if daring her to offer any more excuses, and when she remained quiet he seemed almost disappointed. The *Scarab*'s commander collapsed back against his seat and sighed. The hum and beeps of the escort carrier's outdated equipment filled the silence. Finally, Niashar waved a hand at the door.

"Report to the training room. Cleaning detail. Don't let me remember you exist for at least two ship cycles, understood? Dismissed. TZ-One-Seven-One-Nine, you wait."

This last comment caused everyone to turn around, but at the furious expression on the lieutenant's face, the other three troopers left the room. 1719 waited at attention, unsure of what she'd done to merit this additional conversation, but Lieutenant Niashar didn't speak for several seconds. Then he stood, dismissing the projection on the holotable, and clasped his hands behind his back.

"Your talents are being wasted as their squad leader," he said. "I know what happened during the Uprising. I read the reports. But this team you've taken under your wing . . . their performance metrics are last among the other troopers on the *Scarab*, and only your ability as a leader and your evaluation scores keep them from being shipped off to a front line somewhere. But, mark my words, eventually they're going to drag you down with them."

"They're my squad, sir," 1719 said, trying to keep any emotion out of her voice. "We'll get better. Just give us one last chance, sir."

"This is the *Scarab*, trooper," Niashar said in a wry tone. "This *is* your one last chance."

"They're good soldiers, sir."

The lieutenant began to count on his fingers as he spoke. "One of them has an explosive temper he can't control and a mouth to match. Another, according to his transfer docs, can't remember how to march in a unit but can recite the acceleration parameters of a speeder bike ten years out of production. And the last—if she cared about anything, she could be good. Really good. But that's the thing . . . she doesn't care. And her apathy, the other's absentmindedness, and the third's temper will eventually send you crashing and burning into a backwater system with them. Is that what you want?"

It took a minute for 1719 to respond. "I don't, sir."

Lieutenant Niashar breathed a sigh of relief. "Good. Very good. There's an assignment that—"

"Sorry, sir," 1719 interrupted. "I mean I don't want them to crash and burn, but we're a team. A squad. Whatever happens to them should happen to me."

The lieutenant threw up his hands, and she thought his face was going to explode, that was how red it turned. "Fine," he said. "I tried. It's your future, trooper."

He slammed a meaty fist on the holotable, bringing up

a sector 1719 didn't recognize. He zoomed in toward a space station operating on the outskirts of an asteroid field and jabbed a finger at it.

"Locke Station. Mineral mining hub from the nearby asteroid field has requested assistance because apparently there are pirates in the area. Normally command could care less about an unaffiliated space station begging for aid, but these pirates are becoming bolder. And I suppose access to that mineral hub wouldn't be such a bad thing, but you didn't hear that from me. Anyway, they want a few warm bodies to walk patrol and stop anything that doesn't look First Order. Make a little noise, flash some armor, impossible to foul up. Those three dregs of nutrient paste were on the docket to ship out no matter what, but you could've stayed here. Moved up the ranks. I take it you're not interested."

"No, sir," she said, clear and firm.

He snorted. "Your funeral. Since you want to stick with your squad, you all can do what you do best and walk a few klicks. More orders might follow, might not. Maybe you're stuck there until you muster out. In either case, I'm washing my hands of all of this. Now get out of my sight and go help your patrol team clean the training room. Your shuttle leaves in three hours because I don't need you doing anything to make the governor upset when she arrives. Dismissed."

1719's legs moved automatically. She was out the door and down the corridor by the time her brain caught up with what had just happened. Locke Station? She'd have to ask Twelve about it. She'd only been on a few missions since leaving the *Finalizer.* The Merchant Uprising on the planet Brel under Captain Shikra being the biggest. Their next mission wasn't in Wild Space like Brel, but it was just a hyperspace jump away. It felt surreal, being only a few hours away from where . . .

She pushed the memories of the massacre away and thought about the other missions. Well, not really missions. They'd been training runs or simple patrols, like on Hadne. Or what was *supposed* to have been a simple patrol on Hadne. And maybe there was nothing particularly complex about an escort run. They were practically babysitters. Most important, they weren't being split apart. No way they could mess this up, not even Clamps and his temper.

"Would you watch where you're aiming that thing, Twelve? You nearly got me!"

"Sorry, this stuff is really caked on."

1719 stopped outside the training room entrance to find her three squad mates in the middle of the space, cleaning droids puttering nervously nearby as Twelve desperately clung to a massive scrubber extending from the wall. The training hall was one of the few places troopers could remove their helmets without fear of reprimand. Apparently the fumes corroded the internal filters. She took a second to observe the raven-haired 214 and the tan-skinned Clamps, who held the scrubber hose attachment that was supposed to collect the grit and grime the scrubber dislodged. A sheen of sweat covered Twelve's dark brown skin as he wrinkled his nose and held on tight for dear life. They didn't notice her standing there, and 1719 watched, a small smile on her face. It was easy to forget that none of them were over the age of seventeen. Helmets and voice modulators obscured the fact. Twelve was the youngest, having just turned sixteen according to his bio data. 214 was the oldest, the only one of the squad to escape a Clamps nickname due to her seniority . . . and the memory of when Clamps had tried it and found himself in an arm-bar submission hold that took four troopers and a droid to dislodge.

"AAAH!"

A nasty bit of gunk brought the scrubber to a grinding halt and it jerked to a stop, leaping out of the short boy's hands and clattering to the floor. Flakes of—well, she decided to just assume it was metal flooring and not someone's snack—pelted the others, causing 214 to laugh and Clamps to chase

Twelve with the scrubber as the cleaning droids beeped in dismay and got to work.

1719 smothered a smile, then headed inside to reveal their assignment.

"New mission," she said, her voice carrying in the vaulted room.

Clamps whooped, dropping the scrubber, while 214 helped Twelve untangle himself from the hose that Clamps had tied him in. "Where to?" she asked.

1719 relayed the mission briefing. "So a patrol mission aboard a space station, pretty simple. It's assigned to a new unit we're being attached to, and since we're the closest, we'll take care of it. Once we finish we're to report in."

"No more *Scarab*?" Clamps asked. "Count me in. I'm tired of scrubbing the same filthy spots in here."

"Me too," Twelve said from behind him, lunging forward with the scrubber and knocking the larger boy to the ground. He laughed maniacally as Clamps shouted and struggled beneath the spinning heads, and 214 shook her head in mock annoyance.

"So a new unit?" she asked. "Do we know which one?"

1719 pulled off her helmet, scratching the short brownish-black curls she'd recently cut, and shrugged. "Not familiar. I did a little research, but I thought I'd put Twelve on it once he's done torturing Clamps."

214 nodded. "He'll probably have the task group ID before we even launch."

"Not a task group," 1719 said. She popped her helmet back on. "It's bigger. Company Seventy-Seven."

CHPTR - 6

"FN-Two-One-Eight-Seven?"

The cadet serving as messenger was from the younger cadres. She stood stiff as FN-2187 looked up from where he'd been sitting outside the training center's observation room.

"Yes?" he answered.

"They'll see you now." The cadet performed a textbook 180-degree turn and marched off to carry out the rest of her duties. Her left wrist bracer dangled from a thin arm, and Eight-Seven stood and watched her go, remembering when he was that age. Nothing had fit right, the bruises piled on top of each other, and every night seemed to stretch out in front of him as he tried to listen to the soothing whispered recordings of morale sessions that played in the bunks. They would get news from across the galaxy edited into the daily morale mantras, reports on planets he'd never heard of, much less visited. Politics, wars, famine—briefings kept the cadets up to date on the galactic pulse. He shook his head, stood, and marched through the doors of the observation room.

He actually wasn't quite sure what to expect. The immediate aftermath of the obstacle course had been an emotional jumble of triumph and chaos. There were still duties to be performed and routine to be followed, like showering and reporting for shift work and patrols. But then the message had come that he was needed back at the training center.

His immediate thought was that he was in trouble. One of the instructors wanted payback for how he and FO-7155 had taken them out. Or the strange masked instructor didn't like how he'd retrieved the comlink. Thoughts of punishment detail and panic swirled in his head. His knee had been bouncing as he sat outside the room, and now that he was standing it was hard not to squeeze his hands into fists. But training took over as he stepped smartly through the door and waited at attention.

"FN-Two-One-Eight-Seven reporting as ordered," he

snapped out, and saluted, eyes forward on a spot on the wall, then waited.

And waited.

And waited.

Finally, after several minutes, he let his eyes drop to the single desk in the observation room. A man stood behind it. He wore a nondescript teal uniform, a hat on the desk. With one hand he scrolled through a datapad as his lips pursed in concentration. Tanned skin peeked from between his gloves and the wrists of his uniform, and a single curly ringlet of black-brown hair escaped an otherwise swept-back hairstyle. He didn't wear any medallions or awards, but an armband with the word TARKIN stretching across it circled his left bicep. Whoever he was, this guy was important.

Eight-Seven continued to wait, his curiosity building to the point that he couldn't think of anything else. Was he in trouble? Was he being congratulated? Was he going to be made an example of? Or was he being granted a choice of specialist roles? *Was* there a choice? Or was it decided for him? He guessed he didn't really care, though being a snowtrooper was definitely his lowest choice if he had the option.

His eyes roamed as he continued to wait. The observation room jutted out from the vaulted walls of the training center, and they were surrounded on three sides by floor-to-ceiling windows that looked out over the training center floor. He could see all of the obstacle course from here, including the spots where he'd fought with FO-7155 and against the masked instructor. Several rows of auditorium-style seating stretched to the back wall, and he wondered what the instructors who'd observed the race had felt as they watched the competition. Pride? Concern? Cold detachment and brutal honesty?

"In your fight with Shroud, you chose to roll closer to her rather than increase your distance." The man spoke in such a low and calming voice that he was nearly done speaking before Eight-Seven realized he was being asked a question. "Explain yourself."

No wasting time. The command was confusing, but he knew better than to stall or stumble. "It seemed like the wisest option at the time, Major."

The major looked up. His eyes were warm and inviting, crinkling at the corners. "Ah, I see you know who I am."

"Only your rank, Major."

"Understood. You say it *seemed* wisest. Why is that?"

Eight-Seven struggled to keep up. "My balance, sir. Too much time would be wasted trying to enter a different position, and the instructor—"

"Shroud isn't an instructor, she's one of my personal . . .

guards," the major said, flapping a hand at Eight-Seven. "But continue."

"The—Shroud—is fast. Very fast. If I would've taken time to stand, or retreat, she would've had me in her sights and attacked. So I did the only thing I could from that position, which was to roll forward and attack unconventionally. It worked."

The major dropped his eyes to the datapad again, scrolling for a few pages before sighing and turning to face the window, hands clasped behind his back. He was a short man, slender even, and completely at odds with the other instructors. He didn't have Phasma's imposing size, or Cardinal's force of will. The major seemed . . . normal. Whatever that meant.

And yet . . .

The major turned back around. "I need to be sure," he said, almost to himself.

Eight-Seven remained silent. Stormtroopers didn't speak to officers unless spoken to or commanded to; that was a hard lesson driven into the cadets from their earliest days in training.

"Need to be sure," the major said again. He checked the datapad one more time, then looked at Eight-Seven. "Report back here immediately after dinner. And I would eat light—someone has requested you as a second."

Eight-Seven hesitated. "Second, sir?"

"For a duel. Between a . . . yes, between FO-Eleven-Oh-Three and FO-Seventy-One-Fifty-Five."

The slender girl and the large boy popped into Eight-Seven's mind. A duel? And he had been requested? He had trouble wrapping his head around it. Would that reflect badly on him? Could he refuse?

He cleared his throat. "Understood. It's just . . . that's during morale session, sir."

The major raised an eyebrow. "And?"

"I haven't missed a morale session, sir. Ever."

"It's important?"

"Yes, sir."

"You're committed to the cause of the First Order then?"

Was this a test of some sort? Had some loyalty flag been raised in his metrics? Eight-Seven racked his memories to try to find some sort of slipup he might have made but came up with nothing.

"Of course, sir," he said.

The major studied him. Then he turned back to the datapad. "We shall see, FN-Two-One-Eight-Seven. We shall see.

Report back here one hour after dinner. *After* your morale session. We'll postpone the duel until then. Dismissed."

Eight-Seven saluted, pivoted, and marched out the door. Only after the hatchway had hissed shut and he was back on the turbolift, heading for his assigned duty schedule that he was already late for, did he allow himself to relax and exhale.

A duel? What is that about? And why does it seem like that isn't the only thing the major wants from me?

But it wasn't until he was mid-patrol, somewhere near one of the many supply rooms scattered on each deck of the *Finalizer,* that he realized he still didn't know the major's name.

▮▮▮▮▮

Stormtrooper training regulations expressly forbid intra-corps duels. Cadets risked severe discipline, up to and including demotion and decimation, whether the duels were unarmed or not. This wasn't the old Empire, where cutthroat tactics were ignored or, worse, encouraged in the barracks. No wonder it had fallen beneath its bloated weight. And this definitely wasn't the New Republic, with its inflated sense of justice and moral superiority. Instructors cracked down harshly on troopers caught fighting, oftentimes using them as examples for the rest of the Corps of how the First Order did *not* operate. No. Duels. Period.

Unless an officer sanctioned it. Cadets gossiped (in bunks, never anywhere they could be reported) about underground fighting rings or instructors setting up cadets in shadowy corridors to "toughen them up." But Eight-Seven didn't believe it. Sparring matches, however . . . that was a different thing altogether.

As Eight-Seven walked out of the turbolift at the appointed time several hours later, he was thankful—once again—for the helmet he wore. The data streams were invaluable, oftentimes removing obstacles before they could become a problem. Mission confusion? Need to locate a particular cadet? It was taken care of. Stormtrooper armor was more than protection; it was an extension of their senses. Removing any of it—especially the helmet—felt like removing a limb.

And it also helped that the helmets covered a stormtrooper's face, meaning no one could truly see what someone else was feeling. Ideally, everyone was the same.

Right now, Eight-Seven valued the fact that his expression was hidden.

His steps echoed off of the polished floor of the corridor leading to the stormtrooper training complex. He passed multiple gyms, firing ranges, and simulation ranges, all filled with cadets of various ages, training under the watchful eyes of their instructors. All of them dedicated. All of them following the rules.

Eight-Seven felt a flicker of pride, then brushed his emotions aside as he stepped onto the training room floor. The helmet he wore might mask his face, but his body could betray his emotions just as well. He nodded at cadets on cleaning detail, then headed over to the sparring mats, where another trooper stood waiting.

"FN-Two-One-Eight-Seven," the trooper said by way of acknowledgment.

FN-0926, Eight-Seven's helmet informed him. Not that he needed the help. Only one cadet stood at ease like a proud parent surveying his brood. His hands were clasped behind his back as he rocked on his heels. As unworthy as it was to stand like that as a member of the First Order, 0926 was the only one who could get away with it. He was impossible to dislike. Still, there were regs for a reason.

"Where are they?" Eight-Seven asked.

"They?"

"Fifty-Five. Eleven-Oh-Three. Where are they?" He knew 0926 was aware who he was speaking of. The whole blasted Corps probably knew.

"Choosing their weapons for their sparring session.

Their perfectly normal, instructor-observed sparring session. You seem tense. Is everything all right?"

Eight-Seven took a deep breath before replying. "Just making sure the Corps are one."

The other cadet huffed. "Of course! We are a family." The last quoted a line from their morale sessions' closing mantra. "That's why I'm surprised the instructors sanctioned a duel. I guess this is one way to settle it."

"What are you talking about?"

He chuckled. "The final squad leader position. You didn't know? That's what the duel is about. There were two final positions left, and the instructors couldn't decide between Fifty-Five and Eleven-Oh-Three. Someone had the bright idea to make them fight for it. Some spoiled notion of gladiatorial combat or something like that."

Eight-Seven didn't answer. He scanned the room, searching along the walls where batons, maces, and other melee weapons were stored. The mats were crowded for the time of day. Normally the free hour cadets had after their first morale session of the evening was theirs to spend among their peers. Only the extremely dedicated would make their way to the training center after spending nearly all day in or around it. Today, however, the place was practically full to bursting, and ID after ID blinked in the corners of Eight-Seven's eyes as he searched.

FO-0624

FN-2625

FN-0449

FO-7155

There. Eight-Seven tensed. The hulking cadet who made no secret that he wanted a squad leader's pauldron. He wanted to command subordinates. Eight-Seven could think of no cadet who embodied the principles of the First Order less. The shoulder armor would be a mockery if given to Fifty-Five.

As if sensing his gaze, Fifty-Five turned, resonator mace in hand. The giant cadet faced Eight-Seven, and once again he had to marshal his emotions lest he flag the attention of others. Instead, he scanned the room for 1103. Where was she?

Red flickered in his peripheral vision. He turned and came to attention as an instructor clad in red armor stepped up to the mat next to 0926.

"Sir," Eight-Seven said automatically.

"Captain Cardinal," 0926 said.

"FN-Two-One-Eight-Seven," their former head instructor replied. "FN-Oh-Nine-Two-Six. All is well, I assume?"

"Yes, sir," they both answered as one.

Out of the corner of his eye, Eight-Seven admired the captain's armor. Each individual piece had been polished until the red gleamed beneath the training room lights, and his cape fell over his shoulder as if it had been poured.

Suddenly the captain's head turned to Eight-Seven. "It appears that I am no longer needed." At the lack of response, Cardinal chuckled. "I was supposed to serve as judge for a sparring match between cadets. But it seems that is not to be the case. We are less one competitor. One of yours, am I correct?"

Eight-Seven felt his jaw tighten at the admission that he'd lost the cadet he was supposed to keep tabs on. "Yes, sir."

"I was surprised to hear she'd agreed to spar with FO-Seventy-One-Fifty-Five. Top marks in hand-to-hand, that one, and second in melee, right?"

"I believe so, sir." The words squeezed through his gritted teeth.

Captain Cardinal waited for a few seconds, as if looking for something more, then turned back toward the mats. A few other cadets were sparring, light matches with no real contact. Eight-Seven squeezed his fingers into fists, then unclenched them one by one. He felt the weight of a gaze on him. He turned to stare across the gym, where FO-7155 lurked. His helmet was facing Eight-Seven, and he *knew* the older cadet was smiling beneath the helmet. It was in his stance. Or his posture. Like some six-legged scavenger that had just found a fresh carcass.

And that was when the realization struck.

Eleven-Oh-Three isn't coming, Eight-Seven thought. *Fifty-Five got to her somehow. Some way. Despite everything in the rules and all the instructors and all the punishment. Fifty-Five did something.*

Eight-Seven nearly snarled. Fifty-Five tossed the resonator mace in his hand and shrugged at one of his companion's comments. And like a switch that had been toggled, Eight-Seven made a snap decision. He knew what he had to do.

"Apologies, sir," he said, turning to face Captain Cardinal and saluting him. "But I forgot to mention that *I* would be taking the place of FO-Eleven-Oh-Three for the sparring match. As a way to demonstrate additional, higher-level hand-to-hand techniques."

"You forgot," Cardinal said dryly.

"Sir. It slipped my mind, sir."

"See that it doesn't happen again."

"Yes, sir. And, sir? If I win, would . . . cadet Eleven-Oh-Three make squad leader?"

"That's a matter for brains above your paygrade, cadet." Despite the words, there wasn't any heat in them, and Cardinal stepped onto the mat, drawing all attention with his hands raised and his cape swirling behind him. As Fifty-Five stiffened at the superior's approach, confused, 0926 stepped up beside Eight-Seven, hands still clasped behind his back.

"Forgot, hmm?" he asked.

"Like I said," Eight-Seven replied, "it slipped my mind."

"And the fact that the only cadet ranked higher than FO-Seventy-One-Fifty-Five in melee combat is you? When he was certainly expecting to pummel a novice?"

"A stormtrooper should be ready for any challenge," Eight-Seven replied, stepping onto the mat where Fifty-Five loomed, fingers clenching and unclenching. "To be prepared for a bigger fight is to be a stormtrooper."

"Another morale session quote?" 0926 quipped.

Eight-Seven didn't answer. He was done talking, and as crowds circled the mat where Captain Cardinal and Fifty-Five waited, he was once again thankful for the helmet covering his face.

He didn't want anyone to see his hungry smile.

CHAPTER 7

Coy was in over his head.

He paced back and forth behind a clump of bushes twice his size near the far end of the Resistance base. Only a few ships were back here, cargo transports and speeders, and he felt safe enough to let his frustration show. Safe enough from sentient eyes at least. Ajan Kloss was doing its very best to kill him, what with swarms of whining insects and strangler vines both trying to drag him away into the jungle. Still, those were the *minor* annoyances he could brush away. Coy's actual biggest opponent was himself.

"I've got a ship," he repeated for the hundredth time.

Finn and Jannah were wrapping up mission parameters. Whatever that meant. The protocol droid, C-3PO, had taken Niila to get checked out in the medbay. And Coy . . .

"I've got a ship," he said again in a mocking tone. "Right. I don't have a ship. I've got a rust bucket strapped to a podracer's engine. What were you *thinking*, Tria? You weren't thinking. You never think."

A chorus of laughter echoed from nearby. Coy paused, but it was just a group of mechanics arriving to sneak a break from refueling ships and running diagnostics. So much for privacy. They took turns trying to one-up a loading droid, heaving crates of tools onto the rear of an old speeder while egging each other on. Coy watched them for a bit before his thoughts drifted back to his immediate problems.

The simple fact was Coy was a tea farmer. That was it. Not a hero. Not an ace pilot. A tea farmer. Someone wanted a three-year-aged Sineesian brittle-leaf with notes of citrus and smoke? Easy. Steep an overnight energy brew for factory workers on the early shift? No problem. Escort a Resistance task force on a critical mission?

Coy shook his head. He needed to take back his offer. He could blame it on confusion, maybe fatigue, and say he needed to get back for the harvest, which was at least partially true. Maybe they would laugh at him, maybe they'd say good riddance. But it would be better than making a fool of himself and possibly endangering the others.

Back in the clearing, the mechanics were rooting on the loading droid.

"Look at Buford!"

"Get it, B!"

The droid was beeping enthusiastically when a whistle pierced the air. An officer marched over, shouting and waving his arms. Groaning, the mechanics gradually went back to work. The clearing emptied as a few transports lifted off, leaving the speeder and one last ship.

Coy caught his breath. Not just any ship. An X-wing.

A black X-wing.

His feet carried him across the clearing before he could think about what he was doing. Now *this* was a ship. A fighter, the T-70, with twin long-range laser cannons, a custom ferrosphere paint job for scattering sensors—it was incredible. No, more than that, it was iconic. Tremendous. It was—

"*Black One.*"

The voice came from behind him. Coy turned around to see General Poe Dameron leaning against a nearby tree, peeling a piece of fruit. His sleeves were rolled up, a helmet tucked beneath his arm, one boot propped up on a tree stump.

"Sorry?" Coy said, embarrassment heating his face as he backed away.

"That's the name of the ship. *Black One*."

"Oh, right. Sorry. I wasn't going to mess with it."

"Relax, kid. I feel the same way. Can't *wait* to get it flying again. Go ahead, take a look."

He went back to his fruit, but instead of approaching the X-wing, Coy took the opportunity to study Poe, trying not to be obvious about it. The general was geared up in his flight suit, clearly on his way somewhere. Probably his own secret mission. As if to confirm, Poe's droid, BB-8, whizzed by, beeping in annoyance as it passed Poe, prompting a snort and an eye roll from the pilot as he shook his helmet at the droid.

Coy latched on to the helmet. The bright crimson symbol of the Resistance blazed in the light, while the yellow-tinted visor sent light scattering across the underbrush. Putting that helmet on *had* to be exhilarating. The rush of adventure, the call to the stars, defending and attacking, overtaking and barrel-rolling.

"You ready for this?"

Poe's question dragged Coy from his thoughts. He'd been light-years away, and coming back to the present was disorienting. "Sorry," he said. "Ready for what?"

Poe grinned. "For your first mission for the Resistance, kid. I mean, no offense, but you didn't think running messages and doing sensor sweeps was all there was to being a pilot, did ya?"

"No, I guess not, but . . ." Coy shrugged.

"Let me guess. You got a case of the first-seat shuffle."

"The what?"

"The first-seat shuffle!" Poe started shimmying in place, which was slightly uncomfortable to watch and yet strangely hypnotic. "Happens all the time to pilots on their first big mission. First time in the pilot's seat. All that nervous energy gets you wiggling."

"Oh. I guess." Coy was 94 percent sure he'd never shimmied or wiggled when he was nervous, but then again this was *the* General Poe Dameron. And right now he *was* nervous. Maybe shimmying was a good thing. He could shimmy. Was it the left foot out, then a hip wiggle? Or a hip wiggle and then the left foot?

"Kid." Coy looked up to find Poe shaking his head in disappointment. "What is that?"

". . . A shimmy?"

"That's not a shimmy."

"But . . ."

"No. Not a shimmy."

Coy hesitated, one foot raised in the air. "If I do left foot first—"

"Still not a shimmy. Stop it. Whatever that is, it hurts to watch."

"Sorry."

Poe smiled. "Forget about it. But a word of advice, kid, shimmy or no shimmy. At some point you're just going to have to strap yourself in and lean on the throttle, understand? Everyone eases in with supply runs or simple sweeps. Lots of sweeps. They think that's the height of adrenaline. But then when it's time to do an escort mission? Or a blockade run! *Especially* the blockade runs. I remember one time I had to skirt along a trio of pirate cruisers with a container of shaak fertilizer, which is actually—"

Rustling in the jungle behind them interrupted whatever Poe was about to say, and Finn and Jannah emerged, the former shaking his head in disgust.

"Come on, Poe, not the shaak story," Finn said. "I just ate."

Poe shot him a mock glare, then turned to Jannah. "Clearly this is a story for refined people. Have I told you the shaak story?"

Jannah hid a smile. "I've heard of it."

"Not like this, I promise. There I was, with a cargo hold stuffed to the shields with shaak straight from Naboo, and when I tell you those things smelled like the underside of a—"

BB-8 whistled shrilly, cutting Poe off.

"Thank you!" Finn said loudly, holding his stomach. "At least someone understands decorum around here."

"Those shaak dumped their decorum all over the cargo ramp," Poe whispered. When BB-8 fired off a series of ear-piercing whistles again, he winced and raised a hand in apology. "Fine, fine, I'm on my way. I'll finish this story next time, kid. Until then, why don't you get General Squeamish over there to tell you how badly *he* messed up when he sat in a pilot's chair."

Coy looked at Finn, confused. "The escape from the *Finalizer*? I heard about that."

"Everyone's heard about that one." Poe climbed aboard *Black One*, slipping on his helmet and dropping into his seat. "I mean the *other* one, the one he doesn't like to talk about. Trust me, if he can survive that, you can ferry these two characters wherever the mission takes you."

With that, he fired up the X-wing's engines, and Coy backed up to join Finn and Jannah. He stared desperately at the elegant ship as it carved its way up into the atmosphere above Ajan Kloss. One day. One day that would be him. Today . . .

He turned to see both Finn and Jannah staring at him. "Ready?" Jannah asked.

This was it. He could back out. Come up with an excuse,

escape to his old ship, and fly it as fast as it could go back to Myoca. Easy. Simple. Everything back to normal.

But . . .

Coy swallowed his trepidation and looked at her. "I guess I'm not feeling that confident. I know I volunteered. Still not sure why. I think my brain was sightseeing and left my mouth in charge."

To his surprise, she didn't laugh. Nor did Finn. Instead they exchanged looks.

"Maybe Poe was right," Jannah murmured. "You *should* tell him."

"Poe just wants more people to laugh at my pilot skills," Finn said, grumbling.

"No one laughs at your pilot skills."

Finn stared at her.

"Not since the speeder crash."

He continued to stare.

"Or was it the shuttle crash."

Finn turned to walk back into the jungle, shaking his head as he went. Jannah winked at Coy, and shocking himself, he grinned back. He *could* head back home. But if the general could overcome whatever he'd gone through, maybe there was hope for a junior tea farmer from Myoca.

What was the worst that could happen?

CHPTR - 8

Captain Cardinal stood at the edge of the mat and stared at the two fighters. Even though his bright red helmet shielded his face, it was easy to tell he wasn't thrilled. At least from FN-2187's perspective. The captain's right hand was in the air, arm straight, as he prepared to signal the duel to begin, and yet it seemed his gaze flipped back and forth between the two boys, waiting for one of them to back out.

It wasn't going to happen.

FO-7155 rocked from side to side, the collapsed resonator mace in his right hand. He opted to forgo the shield, which was his choice and meant Eight-Seven had to follow suit. The bigger boy never glanced at the captain and instead kept his focus squarely on his opponent.

Eight-Seven stared back. According to the readouts inside his helmet, 7155's vitals were slightly elevated. He was excited. Meanwhile, Eight-Seven felt nothing. No fear. No thrill. Maybe he'd felt anger at some point, fear even, but he'd tried his best to shove it down to where it wouldn't impact him. He was a statue, had to be a statue, and his emotions were carved from rock as they both waited for the signal to begin.

Cardinal's arm dropped.

Before the captain could retreat completely off the mat, 7155 shot forward, mace descending in a devastating sweep that would shatter Eight-Seven's bones if it connected. So he skipped backward, only to raise his own mace to defend against the spinning follow-up attack. The impact rattled his arms and he shoved his opponent away, kicking at the inside of Fifty-Five's knee with the heel of his boot. Fifty-Five grunted and staggered sideways. Eight-Seven stepped forward and sent his mace whistling down, aiming at the bigger boy's helmet. Sparks flew as 7155's mace rose just in time to block the attack, and then he was rising to his feet, his fist colliding with Eight-Seven's jaw.

The match proceeded like this for several minutes.

Give and take.

Punch for punch, kick for kick, blow for blow.

Eight-Seven staggered his opponent with an elbow but had his legs swept out from under him. He rolled away from the follow-up attack that would've crushed his skull, buckling his opponent's knee with the handle of the mace. Neither one of them could take the upper hand, instead trading advantage when their defenses showed cracks. Eight-Seven tried to maintain his composure, keeping his breathing steady, but his opponent was just so frustrating. He tried to use his mace to knock Fifty-Five's out of his hand but got his own wrist batted aside and a blow to the ribs in response.

Both boys took a second to recover their breath. In the corner of his eye, Eight-Seven saw someone else watching from the periphery. It was the major. He stood a few paces behind Captain Cardinal, who was watching the fight, his fingers tapping his thighs with concern.

The major, however, looked pleased.

Something in that expression flipped a switch inside of Eight-Seven. What was this all for? Amusement?

Eight-Seven was the first to launch the attack this time. He dashed forward, sweeping the mace low toward his opponent's ankles. When 7155 stepped back, Eight-Seven rose smoothly, swinging upward. There was nothing his opponent could do but try to block, and he managed to do so, holding his own mace with two hands as Eight-Seven's attack nearly lifted him off his feet.

"Too slow—" 7155 snarled, intending to say more, but the rest of his words were cut off. Eight-Seven had continued to rise, leaping into the air and ramming his knee into the bottom of his opponent's chin. Fifty-Five grunted, his helmet knocked askew as he fell backward. Eight-Seven landed and lunged forward.

"Enough," Captain Cardinal shouted.

The club end of the mace crackled with energy centimeters away from 7155's helmet. After a moment, the purplish-blue electricity disappeared and the mace withdrew. The match had lasted seven minutes, but it had felt like an eternity.

Eight-Seven held out a hand. Fifty-Five snarled a wordless response and stood on his own. The two boys turned to face Captain Cardinal, who surveyed them for what felt like ages, so long that Eight-Seven began to worry. Had he taken it too far?

The major had his eyes back on the datapad he carried with him, and he was murmuring to the droid hovering at his shoulder. Had he even seen the end of the fight? Eight-Seven's shoulders slumped. Had it all been a waste of time? Other troopers around the mat were whispering among themselves, and once again he was thankful for the helmet that shielded his embarrassment from the others.

As if noticing the chatter, as well, Captain Cardinal turned on his heel to face the crowd. "The spectacle is over," he snapped. "Back to your duties, or get put on report."

Seconds later, the training floor was empty except for the officers and the two boys. Captain Cardinal lifted a hand as if he wanted to say something but dropped it as the major stepped up beside him, datapad clutched in both hands behind his back. He nodded at the droid, who zipped away, before smiling.

"My name is Major Chetachi Gohl."

Eight-Seven felt 7155 stiffen next to him. The major noticed and his smile grew even wider, though less warm.

"Some of you," he continued, "may have heard of me. And some of you"—his gaze flicked to Eight-Seven—"may have heard of my work. I am the head of the First Order Security Bureau. It is my responsibility to ensure the galaxy is aware of the atrocities being committed in the name of false governments and to share the First Order's message with those under and outside of our protection."

It finally clicked. "The mantras," Eight-Seven blurted. He immediately flushed with embarrassment as the other three turned to stare at him. Interrupting a senior officer was an infraction punishable by . . . well, by however the senior officer chose to punish him. Captain Cardinal seemed disappointed, but Major Gohl didn't demand reprisal. In fact, he beamed.

"Exactly," the major said. "The Bureau is also responsible for the words you hear every day, words meant to inspire and motivate. So I was thrilled when you asked to postpone our review earlier, just so it wouldn't conflict with your morale session. Why did you do that, if I may ask?"

Eight-Seven glanced at Captain Cardinal, but the red-armored instructor didn't say anything, so he licked his lips. "Sir. It's because the morale sessions remind us of who we are, sir. United. No matter where we came from or what we look like beneath the armor. The First Order gave us a home, and now we have the chance to do the same for the rest of the galaxy."

He could feel 7155 bristling next to him, but he didn't care. It was true. And when Major Gohl grinned—not smiled but grinned—and clapped his hands, he knew he was right.

"Brilliant, son. It's what we at the Bureau love to hear." The major turned to Captain Cardinal. "He'll do perfectly. Have him packed and prepped for an immediate morning departure."

"Packed?" Eight-Seven repeated.

The major nodded. "I need you, son. The exposure of the galaxy's deepest betrayals of their citizens doesn't make me popular. The complete opposite, I'd say. But it comes with the job, and believe me, I *love* my job. Right now, something's happening in the Sardich system that needs light shined on it, and quickly, before the scav rats behind these injustices scurry back into the darkness. I need *you* by my side to protect me while I shine that light. Can you help me do that?"

Eight-Seven's thoughts whirled inside his head. Again, thank the Order for his helmet so his confusion didn't embarrass him. A bodyguard? It wasn't a squad leader position, and it certainly wasn't a specialty assignment like a mountain trooper or snowtrooper.

Then again, wasn't it? Didn't FO-1103 say she heard troopers who worked with the major moved on to greater things in more prominent positions? Fifty-Five could keep his coveted pauldron. There were other ways to rise in the Order, and he'd just been given a turbolift of an opportunity.

"Yes, sir," he barked, coming to attention. "Will I meet your other bodyguard, sir? Shroud?"

The major frowned. "No, I had to send her on a separate mission. Perhaps in the near future I can arrange a more . . . proper introduction. But focus, son. Consider this the last step of your training. Execute this correctly, and your path to a desirable command in an even more desirable destination is inevitable."

He paused, and his expression grew grim and cold. "Fail, and the galaxy will never know you existed."

Eight-Seven licked his lips. "Understood, sir. I'll get packed right away, sir."

"Excellent," the major said, the smile returning. Then he glanced at 7155, his smile fading somewhat. "You too."

Both boys froze.

"Me too?" 7155 asked.

"Him too?" Eight-Seven said at the same time.

The major nodded. "If the two of you fight like that against each other, I can't wait to see what you'll do against the perpetrators of injustice we're going to face." And with that, he nodded at Captain Cardinal, spun on his heel, and walked briskly off the training room floor. His droid zipped down to hover at his shoulder, and Major Gohl began murmuring to it again.

Eight-Seven stared in disbelief at the retreating officer's back, then glanced at 7155. The large boy was practically shaking with anger.

"This is your fault," he hissed before turning, throwing an absentminded salute at Captain Cardinal, and stalking away.

Captain Cardinal didn't seem to take it personally. Instead, he stepped forward and clapped a gloved hand on Eight-Seven's shoulder. "Good luck," was all he said, and then he, too, walked off. "Try not to kill each other," he said over his shoulder.

Eight-Seven stared after him, then at the resonator mace still in his hands. Bodyguard to one of the most important members of the First Order. Not a captain on the front lines but, still, important.

CHPTR - 9

Locke Station dangled on the outskirts of an asteroid field whose name had so many letters and numbers, a droid had to have been the one to discover it. Like a deep-ocean predator trawling for prey, it waited for tugs and haulers to deposit ore-rich rocks within reach, and then it struck. Its central hub rotated inside of docking and refinery rings, while monstrous manipulator arms and tractor beam field projectors trailed beneath and alongside it, ready to snare mineral-rich rocks and feed them to high-temperature extractors. Cargo ships of different varieties buzzed around the facility, like feeder fish around a behemoth. They landed, took off, or drifted safely in a queue away from the danger of collisions while an assortment of TIE fighters and other models in the series patrolled the nearby space. TZ-1719 was sure there was some sort of order, but from her vantage point, it all looked like chaos, especially when they entered the station and found it swamped with people.

"This is chaos," Clamps muttered, as if reading her thoughts.

He stood against the wall with his arms folded, in one of the many cargo bays located on the station's docking ring. Twelve stood beside him, while TZ-214 and 1719 checked the IDs of as many people in the crowded bay as possible, but it was no use. Ships with their cargo doors wide open waited like gutted acid whales on the fishmonger's table, ready to be loaded or unloaded as crews swarmed around them. One such ship, coincidentally shaped like a fish and dwarfing the other transports, waited at the end of the bay, doors sealed and armed guards (not stormtroopers, interestingly enough) patrolling outside.

But if the areas around the ships were crowded, the rest of the docks were stuffed to bursting. It was almost impossible to walk. 1719 saw civilians sitting, standing, and even lying down next to piles of luggage and cargo. A few merchants set up makeshift stalls, selling food, drinks, and refurbished comlinks for people desperate enough to pay the exorbitant prices. School was even being held in a corner sheltered by old ship parts. A short woman with a gaggle of kids sitting around her taught reading lessons from an old Star Destroyer tech manual, and 1719 found herself mouthing the answers to a pop quiz. The teacher, her red hair streaked with silver and pulled back into a ponytail, laughed at something one of the students said, and she looked up, her eyes meeting 1719's helmeted gaze. The smile faded, but the amusement remained.

"He's not here," 214 said, dragging 1719's attention away from the class.

"Who were we supposed to report to?" Twelve asked, pushing off the wall to join them.

"Captain Tracian of the *Khamsin*," 1719 said. She looked back at the class, where the teacher was now trying to demonstrate how to put on a space helmet. It wasn't going well. One kid was sitting in his helmet, while another had hers in both arms and was using it to trap scav rats.

"Well, with the network slammed like this, it'll take weeks before we can do a proper search," Twelve complained. They were speaking on their squad comm channel, private, and the crowd around them couldn't hear them. Not that they were paid any attention besides the odd look that 1719 couldn't quite place. There was a buzz in the air. Something that hovered between excitement . . . and a riot.

Interesting.

Locke Station wasn't a First Order military installation. She'd had Twelve run down the basics about their next stop while on the transport. It was, to his inexplicable excitement, jointly controlled by several interstellar merchant corporations, and in exchange for protection patrols and piracy prevention—like the mission 1719 and her squad had been assigned—the First Order operated a small garrison complete with several docking bays. On the one hand, that meant fewer superiors to navigate, but on the other hand, it also meant situations like this—when larger numbers would have been useful—were made more difficult.

Their orders were to find and report to Captain Tracian as soon as their transport landed. Lieutenant Niashar hadn't offered much in the way of goodbyes, but he did mention that the aid request was weeks old, and it was possible that it—and maybe even the good captain—was a forgotten thing on Locke Station. Still, the squad had made it on schedule, but station logistics were in turmoil. A new asteroid the size of a small moon had been identified as being mineral rich, and several corporations, independent contractors, and even family-run mining groups had all come to lay claim to the transport rights. There were also several hundred refugees camping in public spaces, but so far no one could identify which war they were running from.

All in all, finding Captain Tracian when the comms system was bogged down with all the new arrivals, transfers, and departures was borderline impossible.

"Boss?" Twelve asked.

She shook her head to clear it. "Find the nearest relay and see what you can do to get the comms at least semifunctional. Then find all cargo transports leaving in the next two days."

"All? Commercial and military?"

"All."

"Because I see a couple GR-Seventy-Five haulers right here, but all of them . . . I mean you're talking *Baleen*-class, light freighters, heavy freighters, and that's just for the Order, not to mention old Imperial—"

1719 sighed, and Twelve cleared his throat.

"Right," he said. "I'll get on it."

She patted his shoulder. "Good trooper. Twenty-One-Four, get me gossip."

"Gossip?"

"For a space station with a lot of piracy nearby, there sure are a lot of wealthy merchants still lingering around. We need to know what the unofficial word is and why people are still risking their business."

The other girl nodded, and she and Twelve walked off. From an outsider's perspective, they were just two troopers conducting a routine patrol. But it didn't escape 1719's notice that several people seemed to do a double take, as if their presence was a surprise.

Really interesting, she thought.

Clamps shuffled his feet. "What about me?" he asked.

1719 nodded at the poster on the wall next to him, and he stared at it, recognizing it for the first time. A stormtrooper with impeccably clean armor and an aggressive stance pointed out at passersby. It was an FOSB poster calling for local security and staff personnel. An arrow pointed the way to the nearest garrison, and 1719 started walking.

"We're going to talk to someone in charge."

▮▮▮▮▮

"This has got to be a joke," Clamps said.

1719 didn't comment.

"No, seriously, this is the galaxy's idea of a joke, or Lieutenant Niashar is somewhere back on Hadne Three laughing into his caf because he pulled one over on the poor lunar worms of Foot Patrol Twenty-Two-A, and now we have to go scuttling back across hyperspace before we're declared deserters."

1719 still remained silent.

"Boss?" Clamps asked. "I can complain for days, but this is usually where you cut me off."

"Hmm," was all she said.

"Hmm? Hmm?" Clamps's comm abruptly went out, but 1719 knew he was muttering to himself in frustration, and she smiled. Her smile faded, however, as she resumed her examination of the barricaded shop at the end of the corridor they stood in, because, truthfully, there wasn't much she could say that would, one, be productive and, two, keep Clamps from short-circuiting. She felt like she was one malfunction away from a meltdown herself.

Locke Station's First Order garrison was a converted tavern. Actually, it looked like the tavern had been abandoned, raided for supplies, abandoned again, and then haphazardly plastered with First Order recruitment posters before it opened for business. The entrance hatch was propped open, the automated entry mechanism missing (probably stolen by another shopkeeper on the station), and the smell of old grains and curdled cream wafted through. It swamped her helmet's filters and clogged her throat. It was all she could do to prevent herself from gagging. Add to that the interior lights—those still working—which flickered with every footstep, sending shadows tumbling everywhere, and her senses were on high alert.

"Hello?" 1719 called out.

One of the shadows on the old bar top shifted and grunted.

Her blaster rifle was in her hands, the power cell whining as she peered down the scope.

The shadow belched, then began to snore. Clamps and 1719 looked at each other, and she noted with approval how he'd automatically rotated to cover her. She motioned with her off hand, and they approached the bar together. The taps had been removed and replaced by several vidscreens and computer terminals, while one of a few stacks of datapads collected dust in the corner. The other two stacks served as a head and footrest for a partially uniformed noncommissioned First Order officer with no boots or hat in sight. Their gray uniform top was unbuttoned to reveal a hairy chest, while the black pants they wore were stained with every condiment a cook could come up with.

1719 glanced at Clamps, then nodded. The tall trooper

saluted, then turned and began to walk back to the entrance. He was nearly at the warped door when suddenly he tripped and stumbled, bringing an entire stack of disassembled shelving clattering to the floor.

"Get it together, soldier," 1719 barked, and Clamps leaped to his feet, back ramrod straight.

At the same time, the shadow on the bar jerked upright and fell off, scattering datapads and dust everywhere. By the time Clamps marched back to where 1719 waited, the sleeping stranger had straightened and clicked on an overhead light, revealing a gray-haired man in an NCO's uniform, squinting at them.

"What? Who is—what's all this then?" he asked, watery eyes blinking rapidly.

"Captain Tracian?" Clamps asked.

"Who?"

1719 stepped forward. "Sir. Foot Patrol Twenty-Two-A reporting for duty as requested, sir. We have orders to report to Captain Tracian of the *Khamsin* and assist in the piracy problem. Can you direct us to him and his ship?"

The noncom—and she repeatedly reminded herself that he was her superior as he cleared his throat and spat on the floor—scratched his head, grunted, then leaned beneath the counter to pick up the datapads that had fallen. He took his time stacking them, sorting them, and replacing them on the bar top before retrieving a pair of glasses from a pocket and setting them on the tip of his bulb-shaped nose. He squinted and leaned in, the light gleaming off of the metallic name-plate pinned to his rumpled uniform.

Sergeant Onatha.

"You're here for them there pirates," he repeated.

"Yes, sir," 1719 said.

"And a captain?"

Assuming he was referring to Captain Tracian, both Clamps and 1719 replied in the affirmative. The sergeant glared at the two of them and removed his glasses, tucking them back into the same pocket he'd pulled them from, and then grabbed his hat and sat it on his head.

"Well," he finally said, "what in the blue skies of Corellia took you so long? Just like the Corps, slower than a knot of swamp leechbats wriggling in molasses. I been telling them that we need to get these relays fixed, but no, does anyone listen to the sarge? No! It takes weeks to get a maintenance request through. Of course it takes months for help with those filthy ore goblins."

He continued to complain like this without taking a breath, his face growing redder by the second, to the point she was sure Clamps was about to poke him to see if he'd deflate, but 1719 stopped him. "Sir—SIR!—does that mean these orders are old? The mission is out of date?" she asked.

"I told you," Clamps muttered on their private channel.

But Sergeant Onatha flapped a hand and shook his head. "Old, yes, but not out of date. Been sending requests up the chain for months now. The captain, not me. Only been here a month or so and already my workload is cut in half. He says, 'Sarge'—that's what he says—'you're working too hard. Let me put some of my grunts on it.' And I appreciate it, sure I do."

Of course you do, 1719 thought.

"In fact, just last week the captain told me not to worry about sending another request, because he's one of the good ones. Said he'd take care of it himself. Good leader, that's for sure. But then on one of my rounds I spotted, clear as a viewport in a dry dock, some riffraff with their hands on power packs, sticking their dirty fingers inside to strip 'em for parts! Hoarding a pile of old grips and sturm dowels. Like scav rats! So I said to myself, I said, 'Onatha, let's just send out a request to the nearest garrison instead of Corps staffing. That may get the captain what he needs.' I didn't let him know, because no one ever responded, but I guess that's where you all come in."

Clamps seemed dazed with the barrage of words, so 1719

nodded. "Yes, sir. If you can point us in the right direction, we'll liaison with the captain and get to work."

"That's the spirit. But I can do you one better. I can give you the exact berth. The Order has the two landing pads reserved for routine business as a part of the agreement ironed out with Locke Station, but the captain doesn't like to use them on account of the station traffic making docking a hassle. He doesn't know I know, because a good sergeant anticipates what his superior officer wants, but I tracked down the berth he likes to launch from a few months back. Guessing it keeps the pirates confused if they don't know where the Order's patrol is coming from. Here, there we go. Pad seven-oh-two-delta. I'd let him know you're coming, but the dang network's been down for the past few days. That muckglucking new asteroid they found is bringing all the get-rich-quick folks from across the galaxy."

1719 saluted, which seemed to take Sergeant Onatha by surprise. "Thank you, sir! I'll be sure to tell the captain how helpful you were."

Onatha saluted back before rubbing his nose. "No need, no need. For duty, you understand, not the glory. Always for the duty. But I suppose a good word could never hurt. It couldn't."

1719 nudged Clamps, who was clearly confused beyond belief, and saluted again. "Yes, sir. Will do."

They left the converted base, ducking through the hatch, and sucked down deep breaths of the cold recycled station air. Outside, 1719 commed the others on their private channel, tapping her foot impatiently.

"Boss?" Twelve responded in her ear.

"Anything?"

"No *Khamsin*, no Captain Tracian in the station logs at all. Managed to get a local comm array humming again, so I can do a wider search if you want."

"No need, at least not yet. I need you and Twenty-One-Four to do a physical check for me. Take a stroll down-ring and see if there's a ship docked in berth seven-oh-two-delta."

"On it, boss. We're heading that way to check it out now."

"Copy that."

Clamps kicked a crumpled flimsiplast and fidgeted with the vambrace on his left arm. It was what he did when he was conflicted about something, or working through a problem, and so 1719 began to search the nearby corridor wall for a data port. When she found one, she downloaded the station schematic and studied it on the HUD of her helmet.

"I don't get it," Clamps finally said. "There have been pirate reports for the last few months and apparently the station has requested assistance, but Lieutenant Niashar said this was the first communication he'd seen from Locke Station in a while. Then the station is stuffed to the cargo bay with merchant trade, nobody's afraid, and the garrison on-station is one stormtrooper and a missing captain? It just doesn't make sense."

"Maybe they're keeping the reports under wraps, just so there isn't a panic." 1719 shrugged. "Once we find Captain Tracian we can clear it up and help however he sees fit." What she didn't tell him, just in case she was wrong, was that another possibility was that there was no Captain Tracian.

If she was right, they were in for a galaxy of trouble.

As if right on cue, the team comm channel chirped. They waited for Twelve or 214 to say something, but the channel remained silent. 1719 frowned.

"Twelve?" she asked.

Nothing.

"Twenty-One-Four, Twelve, come in."

Still nothing. Then static crackled and background noise swelled through the helmet speakers.

"—ou doing here . . . is private . . . aren't allowed . . ."

"Twelve?" Clamps said, confused.

1719 held up a hand. Comm channels didn't open by accident. This was a message. Twelve wanted them to hear something, something he couldn't speak directly to them about. But the only thing that was coming through was garbled speech and crowd noise. She was getting ready to try to send a silent alert to the squad's helmet comm channel when Twelve began to speak.

"We're looking for a Captain Tracian," he said. "Do you know where we can find him?"

". . . do you know . . . Tracian?"

1719 strained to listen, and from his posture, Clamps was doing the same. The voice that filtered through the speakers sounded aggressive.

Suddenly blaster fire erupted through the speakers, followed by screams, and then the transmission cut out. 1719 didn't even look at Clamps when she started running, instead just barking, "On me!" as she rounded a corner. He was there, too, right on her hip, as they raced through corridors that grew more and more crowded the closer they got to the public docking pads. She could see the vitals of Twelve and 214 in her helmet's display—they were still breathing at least, though Twelve's heart rate had spiked. But who knew how long that would last. They had to get there, and fast, and somewhere in the back of her mind she was thankful she made the squad do the hours of routine drills to escape boredom back on Hadne 3.

Because as they rounded the last curve and saw what awaited them, 1719 slowed to a stop, Clamps right beside her.

Landing pad 702-delta was the one with the giant fish-shaped cargo transport, the one she had noted earlier. There were fewer crowds around the loading area, but people still lingered, the ones that were hoping for a last-minute summons for a contract. But they weren't mingling or conversing like before—no, all eyes were pinned to the boarding ramp leading up into the transport's main cargo hold, and the group of mercenaries bristling with weapons standing on it.

But 1719 had eyes for someone else. A wave of fury swept over her, though she forced herself to remain calm. Others depended on her, and from here, at the edge of the crowd, that fact was being driven home. She stared, helpless and angry, as Twelve and 214 were marched inside the ship.

"Well," Clamps said, "I guess we found the pirates."

CHPTR - 10

Captured.

TZ-1719 wanted to shoot something. Hit something. Hit something and then shoot it. She had to consciously take her finger off of her blaster trigger and forced herself to stop and take a breath. To be calm. Her head throbbed, however, and showed no signs of letting up. Unfortunately, there was no time for rest. She needed to focus. Yes, two members of her squad had been captured, and yes, the odds that they could be rescued were overwhelmingly bad, but they weren't zero, she reminded herself.

They weren't zero.

Occasionally, in between her thoughts racing to come up with a plan before discarding it just as fast, her mind would toss up the fact that they weren't *just* members of her squad but TZ-214 and even Twelve—her friends, no matter what Lieutenant Niashar suggested. They were family. Her only family.

And they were in trouble.

"Boss?"

Clamps was looking at her, even as his blaster rifle was aimed down into the crowd. Her own rifle had, somehow and on its own, lifted its barrel and was aimed at one of the mercenary guards on the boarding ramp, the only one still in sight. She guessed he was the lookout, watching for trouble. Watching for her and Clamps. The sight's crosshairs were lined up perfectly over his forehead, and something inside of her seemed determined to pull the trigger and take him out. Who cared about consequences or plans; her team could literally be facing death right now, and strategy seemed to elude her.

But when she zoomed in one more click, 1719 couldn't help noticing that the pirate was practically the same age as her, a smooth-faced Rodian with an ill-fitting uniform filled with holes and frayed around the edges. He practically cradled his pistol like a baby, at least until someone from the crowd still milling about the transport wandered too close, and then he held it in both hands, and she could hear his shouts from here.

She frowned. Every superior she'd trained under had made sure to emphasize they were just that—superior, when it came to other species in the galaxy. They talked about purity, about being human and how the Order's mission, among others, was to reestablish human dominance throughout that same galaxy. Clamps said when they spoke like that, they sounded like the mantras echoed during the evening morale sessions.

"Like droids in a feedback loop," he'd said one day after the training sims were done and they were lectured on their results. "They can't help themselves."

Well, not all of them were like that.

Captain Phasma never contradicted the Order's stance on nonhuman species, but she never reinforced it. Like disagreeing in silence. That was how 1719 always thought the captain carried herself. Once, during a weapons training session, the captain had drawn her aside after she'd been the last to choose a weapon and the blaster pistol she favored had already been claimed.

"Use the tool in front of you, not the one you are most

comfortable with," Phasma had said. "Here, and out there. The galaxy isn't a training sim—you can't tweak it in your favor. Make do with the resources you can find. There is an advantage in every scenario. A weak point in every trap. Press it. Find the upper hand and use it."

Her words echoed in 1719's ears now as she lowered the rifle.

"Boss?" Clamps asked again. She could hear the nerves in his voice. "What should we do? Call for backup?"

"We are the backup," she said. "Who are we going to call, Sergeant Onatha? No." She eyed the Rodian, then stared at the transport, at its size, and mentally counted the pirates she could recall from memory. There couldn't have been more than a dozen, right? "No," she repeated. "We're all there is, and we don't leave each other behind. Here's what we'll do."

Jharo wished he had woken up on time that morning. He'd forgotten to set an alarm, and he still wasn't used to the physical labor of loading and unloading cargo crates. Now he was stuck with guard duty while the others went back inside to cups of hot caf and the warmth of the ship. He shivered. Locke Station was freezing. No one had mentioned that taking down the station network would impact the heat circulation systems. And since the restart was on a timer scheduled to go off after the cargo transport was long gone, he'd just have to suffer the cold in silence.

A family bundled in multiple layers of clothes and pushing their belongings in front of them walked by. Jharo squeezed the blaster rifle he was cradling and tried to look intimidating. The father of the family met his eye, then hurried the others away. Jharo nodded to himself, but he was unable to prevent the feeling of shame after that brief display of importance.

He sighed. When he'd followed his friend Dal and joined up with the Xen Runners, he was expecting a whirlwind adventure. Something like what he'd seen when they'd snuck into Dal's family pub and watched the holos Old Ba had brought with him on one of his trips from the capital. Jharo thought they'd join the crew, earn enough credits to get their own ship, then start their own transport business, where no one could tell them what to do. When Dal had stumbled on the ship filled with supplies, they'd thought the Xen Runners would welcome them with open arms and calm antennae, as Old Ba used to say. Dal had been angling to join their crew for months, and handing over the cargo they'd stolen along with the hauler it came in seemed like the perfect opportunity. But instead of adventure, they quickly realized they'd signed up for something completely different. Instead of open arms, they were welcomed into something more sinister. Something more dangerous.

Something violent.

The Xen Runners were nothing like the smugglers from Old Ba's holos. Now Dal was dead after trying to make a run for it and Jharo was alone, his fingers aching from holding his friend's old blaster rifle. It was built for humans, not Rodians, and he wanted nothing more than to toss the rifle into an airlock and disappear.

But where would he go? Nowhere that Kesh, leader of the Xen Runners, wouldn't find him.

"Your friend got ideas," Kesh had said when he finally came to Jharo's bunk yesterday. His friend had been missing for twelve hours at that point, and the pirate captain's hands were sticky and wet. Jharo still felt hot shame vibrating his antennae when he remembered how he'd cried. "Big ideas. You came from the same planet as him, same city. You got the same ideas? Let's find out."

Someone yelped, bringing Jharo crashing back into the present.

A droid had been toppled over by a gang of unruly kids, and in its fall an elderly Twi'lek had been hurt. But Jharo only had eyes for the stormtrooper currently assisting the Twi'lek, and his antennae quivered nervously.

More stormtroopers, he thought. *Where are they coming from? Do they know about the two Kesh just took into the ship? Are they here to investigate?*

Jharo squeezed his blaster tight as he scanned the docking ring. No flashes of white caught his eye. Just the crowd gathering around the fallen droid and the injured Twi'lek and the lone stormtrooper. A large hovercart packed with crates and supplies floated near the boarding ramp, and the driver muttered to himself as he kicked at the stationary vehicle. But as far as Jharo could tell, there were no threats. Just the First Order. He took a step down the ramp, then hesitated. Kesh had instructed him to keep lookout as they *interrogated* the First Order troopers they'd captured. And you didn't go against Kesh. Dal had, and look what had happened.

Jharo gulped.

But then the stormtrooper helped the Twi'lek up, checked on the droid, and began to address the crowd.

"Don't worry, the First Order will have the systems up and running shortly, and then the heat will be back and ships can resume their departure." The trooper repeated it several times, even going so far as to have the droid translate it from Basic to local dialects.

This wasn't good. Not good at all.

Jharo stepped down the ramp, torn between alerting Kesh on the comm, despite the order not to disturb him, and taking the initiative himself. Come to think of it, if he could bring in a stormtrooper on his own, he'd prove once and for all that he was a Xen Runner. At least for the near future. He nodded, straightened his shoulders, and stepped onto the docking ring.

The cold barrel of a blaster pistol pressed against his neck.

"Back into the ship," a soft voice murmured.

Jharo glanced to his left to see another stormtrooper partially hidden by the overloaded hovercart. She reached over, snatched Dal's rifle from his hands, and nodded at the boarding ramp.

"Quickly," she said.

She escorted him back up the ramp, and his antennae flushed with embarrassment as no one on the docking ring tried to stop her or tried to help him. They all watched, a few even whistling in appreciation or laughing at his situation. All in all, Jharo's stint as a pirate and potential smuggler was looking more and more like a temporary lapse in judgment. Maybe Old Ba would let him work in the pub back at home.

If I make it back alive, that is.

CHPTR - 11

W*e don't leave each other behind.*

Only her need for information kept TZ-1719 from pulling the trigger. Right? She would definitely pull the trigger, but she needed more intel. She pressed the barrel of her blaster harder into the Rodian's neck as she peeked around the interior of the room at the top of the boarding ramp. Her hostage stayed between her and the hatch, just in case anyone walked by, but the area seemed empty.

"Who are you?" she snapped.

"Jharo," the Rodian said, his voice barely above a whisper. "My name is Jha—"

"Not your name, your gang."

"Oh, um . . . the Xen Runners. That's what . . . that's what they—I mean, we're called."

"How many of you are on board?" she hissed.

The Rodian whimpered as the blaster pressed harder. "Eighteen," he said, almost whining. "I mean seventeen, including me!"

"Keep it down! Is it eighteen or seventeen?"

"Seventeen! Dal—my friend—is dead."

1719 switched to the internal comm channel. "Did you get that, Clamps?"

"Roger, boss. I already passed it along to Sergeant Onatha. Good thing Twelve got the station network back up just before . . . well, he got the network back up. The sarge is calling in reinforcements as we speak. Should be here within the hour."

What he didn't say, and what 1719 didn't dare think, was that Twelve and TZ-214 might not have an hour.

Switching back to her external speaker, she pulled the Rodian to the bulkhead, then retrieved her riot restraints and cuffed his arms to a pipe fixture to keep him from wandering. Then she dragged the pistol from his neck to a point just between his eyes, making sure the barrel never broke contact with his skin, noting with grim satisfaction how he trembled.

"You *will* stay here until I come back and get you. If I even think you tried to move, or if I hear the faintest whisper of you warning your scummy friends coming from this hatch, my squad mate will send a thermal detonator in here to keep you company. Got it? We will turn this compartment into an oven. You will fry. Understand? Good. Now, where are they keeping my troopers?"

"I don't know," the Rodian whispered.

The blaster pistol whined as she stepped back and took aim.

"I swear! They could be in one of the compartments near the officer's pod—that's where Kesh, our leader, is set up. Or they could be in one of the cargo pods at the front of the ship. That's where Kesh likes to do his interrogations. That's where . . ." His voice trailed off.

1719 leaned in close. "That's where what?"

"That's where Kesh put my friend after he killed him," the Rodian said, tears welling up.

1719 stood. She tapped the blaster against her thigh armor, then pivoted and stalked to the hatch. She peered into the main corridor, both ways, and then glanced back at the imprisoned pirate.

"They'd better still be alive," she warned, and then left.

So, cargo pod or officer's pod? She had a fifty-fifty chance of finding the rest of her crew. And that was only if they hadn't been separated. Ugly thoughts flapped around 1719's mind, and she stamped on them as fast as they popped up. Her team was together, and they were alive. She had to keep thinking it to believe it.

Unbidden, thoughts of Captain Phasma singling her out for extra training popped into her mind. Grueling workouts in the training room, hour after hour, dismissal after dismissal as Phasma rejected her efforts.

"You are thinking too much," the captain had told her during one session when 1719 collapsed, too weak to continue. "You are slow because you are not letting your body do what it has been trained to do. Stop thinking and perform!"

1719 took a deep breath. The cargo storage area—that was her decision.

She slipped into the corridor. The interior of the cargo transport was dimly lit, the dingy gray durasteel plating sending shadows dancing into corners and bends. It was an old ship, probably floating around since before the old Empire's fall, and the dents and scrapes covering the surface emphasized its age. But it was sturdy and apparently still capable of hyperspace transit, which meant until the pirates stole it, merchants on Locke Station had rented space in cargo pods to send their goods to other hubs.

That explains the odd collection, 1719 thought.

Cargo containers of all shapes and sizes and colors were stacked and sorted in towering aisles. Bright orange, green, black. Angular, spherical, cube-shaped. They sprouted up into the air like manufactured trees, filling the space above her and blotting out the few remaining lights.

She crept forward.

Her helmet's heads-up display flashed, and she paused. An alert popped up—a crate highlighted in orange off to the left. Something had triggered the sensors. Noise? Some other irregularity? 1719 gripped her blaster and continued moving. When she reached the corner, she burst into motion. She lunged around it, blaster aimed at what would be the center mass of most beings in the galaxy.

A still form sprawled in the dark corner of the crate. No armor. No bodysuit. Unrecognizable tattoos up and down both arms. Some small creature skittered out of sight through a hole near the back. She ignored it and leaned closer, holding her breath.

The barrel of the blaster lowered.

Not Twelve or Twenty-One-Four.

The ship rumbled beneath her feet, throwing her sideways into a stack of crates. Lights flickered on, and 1719's lips tightened.

"Boss," Clamps spoke through her earpiece. "You're going to have company soon. Comms chatter—Twelve was so much better at this—comms chatter says there's a First Order ship inbound."

"Copy that," she whispered. "Sounds like these guys are going to cut out and run."

Clamps swore. "We gotta get them out, and you, too, boss."

"Working on it. Give me a sec."

1719 moved quickly but quietly retraced her footsteps, blaster gripped in both hands. The transport's engines rattled walls as they warmed, and she increased her speed. They were going to take off soon, unless she could do something.

The command pod was located at the rear of the transport, and that was the other location her squad could be, according to the Rodian. 1719 was practically running now, breath echoing in her helmet as she raced to a ladder and climbed it two rungs at a time. She peeked out on the next floor, blaster sweeping around her in a circle, and then she was up and through. The blaster rose as she passed intersection after intersection. Climbed deck after deck. She was in the main hull now, and someone had thoughtfully copied arrows and destination names on the walls, which made it easier to navigate.

Finally, she reached the bottom of the command module. Her legs burned with effort, and she gulped down ragged breaths as she slowed to a stop several dozen paces away. A few Xen Runner guards in rust-red armor, carrying blaster rifles stood on patrol near the ladder. Not good.

“Clamps,” she whispered into her comlink, dropping to a knee.

“Yeah, boss?”

“I need a distraction. A loud one.”

She could practically hear the smile that crossed his face. “Yes, boss. Loud nap interrupter on the way. Damage limit?”

“Try not to break the ship. We do still need it for evidence. Try to get it as forward as possible. We probably only have one shot at this.”

“Minimal damage, got it. On the way. Clamps out.”

1719 squeezed the blaster butt, rising to her feet and peeking around the corner of the cargo pod she was hiding behind. The guards were still there. Time was running out—the transport’s automated protocols were starting. Safety messages echoed in the halls; the ship’s hatches were locked down and secured. At any second now—

KRAKOW!

An explosion nearly knocked 1719 off her feet. She barely managed to keep hidden, even as the Xen Runner guards shouted in alarm. She squeezed back into her hiding space as the guards sprinted past while barking commands into comlinks. A smile crossed her face. *I said a loud distraction. That one could've taken out the whole station!* She counted to ten, then slipped out, tucked her blaster in her belt, and sprinted to the ladder leading up to the command pod. Hand over hand she climbed. At the top she eased open the hatch, peeked out.

The command pod was an egg-shaped room with sloping ceilings and a single viewport stretching nearly halfway around the space, the rest of the walls covered in displays and controls. Four Xen Runners stood huddled around a holodisplay in the center of the room, arguing in low voices. One, tall and wide in the shoulders, scowled as the other three grew more animated.

"And I'm saying we can't wait," said one of them, a human. He tugged on the stringy ponytail extending over his shoulder and scowled. "He's just going to have to deal with what we've got."

Another shook his head. "He won't like it."

"I'm not getting shipped to a labor camp in the Outer

Rim because *he won't like it*. Either he deals with what we have or there's no deal."

At this, the largest member of the gang, who appeared to be the leader, straightened and approached the holotable. Where the others wore mismatched armor, he was the only one with something resembling a uniform. In fact, 1719 was sure she'd seen that uniform before. She just needed a better look. All four had their backs turned to her, and she gently, carefully, eased the hatch open and climbed silently into the room. She pulled out her blaster and aimed.

"Enough," the leader snarled. "We're on a deadline. Once the bucketheads get here, it'll be too late. Toss anything not strapped down and find a seat. We're leaving."

The fourth Runner jerked his head at a corner behind him. "What about them, Kesh?"

1719's heart skipped a beat as she saw the huddled forms of Twelve and 214, both with their helmets off and cuts on their faces, slumped in the darkness. But her blood ran cold when the leader, Kesh, flapped a hand in dismissal.

"Dump them in an airlock. We'll vent them when we're out of the system."

He turned to head toward the airlock and froze as 1719's blaster hovered centimeters from his face.

"Release them," she ordered.

Kesh's face, scarred and vicious, broke into a smile. "Come to rescue your fellow bucketheads, hey? Look at you. Regular bounty hunter, tracking us all down."

"Release. Them," 1719 said again.

Twelve's head lifted. One eye was swollen, and from the way he'd fallen, it looked like he was trying to shield 214 with his body, even though his hands were tied behind his back. His one good eye swiveled to 1719, and he tried to smile. She turned away. If she lost focus now, they were all as good as dead.

Kesh shrugged. "It's four of us to just . . . you. More on the way." As he spoke, several more of his gang members climbed into the pod, their faces twisted into scowls. "Odds say you can't blast all of us in time before we get you, honey."

"I don't need to shoot everyone. Just you." She studied him, then looked past him to the other Xen Runners, including the newcomers. "A First Order light cruiser will arrive in orbit in under seven minutes, complete with two dozen TIE fighters and three squads of stormtroopers. Your . . . captain . . . is right. I can't hold all of you. But I'm not going to. I just want him. Because if I'm not mistaken, that's an old officer's uniform. Something from the old Empire. And I bet a few of my superior officers will want to talk to you about it, because there never was a Captain Tracian, was there?"

"Boss?" Twelve looked confused.

"I'm guessing Kesh here pretended to be First Order, made false promises to merchants that they'd be protected, and then turned on them once they were out in deep space. The only reason we're here is because Sergeant Onatha saw people stripping old parts to make their own weapons, and in his desire to get into Kesh's good graces, actually—and accidentally—did the right thing and bypassed procedure to send us a help request. All of that to say, you're in trouble now, Kesh. The rest of you can go, provided you're out of sight before reinforcements come."

She looked Kesh straight in the eye. "After that no one leaves."

For a moment, no one moved. 1719 thought she might have overplayed her hand, or forced the rest of the smugglers into a corner, and she was working on a way to distract the others, take out Kesh, and keep the rest of her squad alive when Ponytail suddenly threw up his hands.

"I'm *not* going back to a labor camp," he muttered, and practically threw himself down the hatch to the main deck below. After that, the rest followed, some muttering apologies to Kesh, the others ignoring him in their haste to escape before the rest of the First Order arrived. The last cut the restraints on Twelve and 214, muttered an apology, and left.

"Clamps," 1719 said into her comm.

"Go ahead, boss."

"Meet me in the command pod."

Kesh glared at her as she flicked her blaster to back him up. As Clamps climbed into the pod, shouldering his rifle, she tossed him her weapon and crouched beside Twelve.

"How is she?" he croaked, his frosted blond curls matted and bruises purpling his face.

1719 helped him up into a sitting position, then checked on 214. The slim girl was still unconscious. 1719 shook her head. "She'll need a medbay. Just sit tight. We'll get you ready for another patrol in no time. You're not checking out on me today."

"Thanks, boss," he mumbled before closing his eyes.

"Boss?"

She turned around to see Clamps staring at the blaster she'd tossed him.

"Your power pack is damaged. One more shot and it might've exploded."

Kesh's face twisted in rage, and he began to splutter. 1719 shrugged. "Guess it worked out."

Just then an alert popped up on the still-active holotable.

Twelve limped to his feet and, holding his side, made his way to check the display. "Ship just arrived in-system. First Order."

1719 smiled at Kesh, who spat on the deck and looked away. "Time to go home," she said.

But Twelve's next words lanced through her, pinning her to the spot.

"Boss," he said, "he's saying he's here to collect us, too. But that can't be right, can it?"

"What do you mean?" Clamps asked. "Who's here?"

"Company Seventy-Seven," Twelve answered.

"I guess they were in the area and came when we called. It's fine," 1719 said. "We've got our orders. Might as well join them now. It'll be good to get back to the *Finalizer.*"

But something in his expression gave her pause. "What?" she asked. "What's the matter?"

He stared at her in concern. "We're not going to the *Finalizer*. We're heading to . . . to the *Supremacy*."

CHPTR - 12

What have you gotten yourself into? FN-2187 thought.

The bulk freighter the *Loxodonta* drifted in orbit above a gray-green planet. *Hovering like a carrion bird waiting for its prey to die,* Eight-Seven thought. The ship was lopsided and ugly, and he really, really wished he was the one flying toward it.

He also really, really wished he knew how to fly.

The freighter's stabilizing thrusters fired, keeping it steady, as FO-7155 piloted their shuttle toward an open bay door. An automated voice issued docking commands while Eight-Seven studied the vessel from his seat in the copilot's chair and sighed. The major was in the back, dictating to his

PR droid, so Eight-Seven was supposed to be watching the readouts.

Fifty-Five glanced over from the pilot's seat. "Don't worry, you'll get your chance to fly . . . in a training sim." He laughed, and Eight-Seven scowled.

Major Gohl had informed them that part of their duties was piloting him to his different destinations, but one little inconsequential docking mishap and suddenly Eight-Seven was restricted to observation only.

"Easy now." Fifty-Five was whispering to himself. Eight-Seven began to comment, but they entered the shadow of the ship they were about to board and he swallowed his words. He couldn't shake the feeling they were entering the bloated belly of some monstrous creature out of a holo-sim.

Multiple landing bays dotted the exterior of the *Loxodonta*, with ugly bulges protruding from either side, and the vessel ended in a rounded stub, like a grotesque thumb, with a command center poking out of the top. If it was an animal, it would've lived in the deepest parts of the darkest oceans, dredging silt or feeding on the carcasses of other animals.

It was hideous.

It was grotesque.

And it was their next stop.

The three had been on a whirlwind tour of systems,

planets, and the major's contacts. Contrary to what he and Fifty-Five had been led to believe, Sardich wasn't their first stop. Actually, had he not heard that planet's name straight from the major's mouth, Eight-Seven could've believed they were on nothing but a media tour for the First Order. As soon as their shuttle touched down on the next planet on the agenda (and there was always an agenda), a steady stream of visitors funneled in and out of whatever building the major chose to be his headquarters, delivering reports and gossip the way small-time crooks paid tribute to crime lords. Except instead of credits, the major only dealt in information.

"What system is this again?" 7155 asked after Major Gohl had retreated to his private quarters. His droid had faithfully trailed after him at his shoulder.

Eight-Seven checked the navicomputer's readouts. "The Amosu system. Three planets. That big one down there, Tamo'Akora, is the largest by far, and the only habitable one." He looked up. "If you call constant lightning strikes and rainstorms habitable."

The other boy grunted, always eager to play contrarian. "Different people call different places home."

"The locals call it the thunder planet."

Fifty-Five hesitated, clearly not ready to concede the point. "How long has it been raining? I might like it."

"Records say it hasn't stopped in forty years."

They both studied the planet on the shuttle's small holodisplay.

Fifty-Five cleared his throat. "It could grow on me."

"I'm staying up here," Eight-Seven said at the same time. Fifty-Five grunted in annoyance and moved to the exit at the rear of the shuttle. Eight-Seven watched him go, then grabbed his blaster rifle and checked it, even though he'd done it a dozen times since boarding. The major didn't tolerate sloppiness or mistakes, and one reprimand was one too many. Neither boy had escaped his fury, and neither wanted to face it again.

The duel with 7155 seemed like it had happened ages ago. Strange enough, the animosity between them had mellowed into something more . . . tolerable. They weren't friends. Eight-Seven didn't think they could ever be friends. Truthfully, he still didn't like the other boy. He remained the large, arrogant trooper who thought he was better than everyone else. Unfortunately, the past month had shown that he wasn't entirely wrong. Partially wrong, but not entirely wrong. And if Eight-Seven made mistakes, 7155 didn't exactly gloat, or slip in backhanded compliments when something went right.

Which—he sighed—seemed to happen less and less.

There was the incident with the senator and the jammed

turbolift. That definitely had been Eight-Seven's fault. Then the drink mix-up over Kuat, and also the luxury liner debacle on the way back. *But* that had been more of a uniform issue than anything else, and 7155 was completely at fault. If he hadn't—

At that moment Major Gohl emerged. He'd changed from his standard all-black uniform to the more traditional gray of the First Order, and he glanced at his bodyguards, firing off instructions while fastening the buttons on his cuffs.

"Second to last stop on the training tour, cadets. A venture that, if I'm being completely honest and transparent, didn't start off to my expectations." His eyes swept over Eight-Seven, who stiffened. That felt like a rebuke. Then the major smiled. "But we improved, and while I hold our stormtroopers to a strenuous caliber of expertise, we are all citizens of the galaxy, and the First Order—like parents to the newly born—must demonstrate the excellence we wish our children to emulate."

He motioned Eight-Seven to join 7155 by the exit and hit the button to lower the ramp. "That is to say, you have both progressed admirably, and when we return to the *Finalizer*, it will be my recommendation that you both are promoted to squad leaders."

The major clapped them both on the shoulders, and his smile was infectious. Eight-Seven could feel his own cheeks aching as he grinned beneath his helmet, and from the sheepish way 7155 bowed his head, it was clear the large boy felt the same.

"Now then, let's collect our delivery and be off."

They followed Major Gohl down the ramp in lockstep, blaster rifles cradled in their arms like they'd stepped out of a recruitment poster. They took up positions just off the major's shoulders, heads on a swivel, scanning the environment while the major commed his contact.

"*Loxodonta*, this is Major Chetachi Gohl. Can you read me? Over."

Squad leader! Eight-Seven had never dreamed of that. Him? It was mildly terrifying, but in the way all new things were. He squeezed the butt of his blaster, then forced himself to take a deep breath and calm down. He wasn't there yet, and the last thing he needed was a misstep when the training tour was nearly complete.

Still.

Squad leader!

"*Loxodonta*, this is Major Chetachi Gohl. Can you read me? Over."

Would he be able to pick his squad? Or would it be assigned? Would FO-1103 want to join his squad? And where would their first mission be?

Someone cleared his throat.

Eight-Seven snapped back to the present. Major Gohl wasn't looking at him, but 7155 was shaking his head, and Eight-Seven flushed. *Right,* he thought. *Focus.*

". . . isn't answering," the major was saying. "I'm going to get on the shuttle's comm to try a few other contacts that should be on board. You two sweep the cargo bay and check for our supplies. They'll be marked for the Sardich Labor Union in green containers. Also . . ."

The major did turn to face them this time, and his cold stare pinned them in place. "Stay clear of the restricted areas. The security measures are still active, and I'd hate to explain to your commanders why their troopers are returning to them in pieces."

Eight-Seven gulped. Was that an exaggeration? It had to be. Right? The flat, emotionless expression on Major Gohl's face didn't indicate he was joking, but . . . come on, right?

The major turned and continued to hail different comm frequencies, tossing one more bit of advice over his shoulder. "And keep your eyes open—none of this is normal."

Fifty-Five joined Eight-Seven as they stepped off the ramp onto the metallic floor, and the major sealed himself in the shuttle behind them. The cargo bay stretched off into the distance, the very ends of it shrouded in darkness. Lights flickered on as they stepped forward together, but not nearly enough to make Eight-Seven feel comfortable.

Cargo containers were stacked in haphazard piles between the odd shuttle or hoverlift, creating islands of durasteel in what would otherwise be an enormous empty cavern of a space. Shipping labels from locations across the galaxy plastered the area, stuck on everything from trash cans to fuel containers. Binary load lifters stood in neat lines, like they were waiting for their next instruction. A few of them were idling, as if they'd just finished loading a ship. Carrier platforms—short-distance gravity barges used to ferry load lifters on and off planet—waited beside them. Apart from that, the cargo bay was empty.

"You take that side, and I'll start over here," Eight-Seven said. Fifty-Five just nodded and split off to the right. Eight-Seven shook his head. "Great idea, partner. Good thinking, chum. Way to strategize, big guy. Is that so hard?"

His speaker crackled in his ear. "Way to strategize, big guy."

Eight-Seven rolled his eyes and continued his patrol. The light on his blaster sent a cone of brightness sweeping left to right and back again, stopping on anything that seemed out of the ordinary. But, try as he might, the only things he could find were empty containers and idling load lifters. He doubled back, eyes peeled just in case he missed something, but the results were the same.

"Anything?" 7155 asked when they crossed paths back near the shuttle. After Eight-Seven shook his head in the negative, the larger boy hefted his blaster so it rested on his shoulder and blew out a puff of frustration. "So the ship is empty then? What sense does that make? Either the major's contact got his dates mixed up, or everyone's off partying, or—"

"Or they knew we were coming," Eight-Seven said.

"What?"

But Eight-Seven had pivoted and walked quickly toward the containers and load lifters he'd seen before. He kept his eyes on the floor, searching for something.

Fifty-Five lifted his blaster and swept their surroundings. "What is it? Where are they? Eight-Seven! Now what are you doing?"

Eight-Seven had backtracked and was staring at the load lifters, and when his partner joined him, he pointed the barrel of his blaster at the base.

Fifty-Five shook his head. "And? They're just load lifters. There's a bunch of them. We're in a cargo bay where things need to be loaded and/or lifted."

"But why are they idling?" Eight-Seven asked. "And not

even all of them. Just these, as if these were the only ones to finish a recent job of loading and/or lifting, as you said."

"You think they loaded up the major's supplies?"

"Someone had to."

"But why? And where would they go? The restricted holds?"

They'd passed the entrance to one near the middle of the cargo bay. Thick gray doors were guarded by pivoting turrets that homed in on the two troopers as they walked by, tracking them with eerie precision.

"No," Eight-Seven said, pointing out the shielded bay exit toward the black of space and the planet below. "Tamo'Akora."

The shuttle ramp hissed as it descended, and Major Gohl leaned out and raised an eyebrow. "So what are we waiting for?" he asked impatiently. "I still don't have my supplies, and every second we waste up here is time spent failing the First Order."

Eight-Seven glanced at 7155, who waved him ahead. "You wanted to fly, so here's your chance."

CHPTR - 13

In her dream, TZ-1719 zipped through the *Finalizer*'s training garage on a speeder bike. She'd had the same dream before. Many times before. Her hair, freshly cut again, didn't itch beneath her helmet. Why that detail seemed important was a mystery. But normally, as that thought appeared, the display in her helmet would flash . . . now, and three rectangles rapidly grew in size. Her targets were approaching. There, on the right. Exhilaration swept through her, and she nearly laughed as she gripped the butt of her blaster pistol.

Now.

She squeezed the brakes on her handlebar. Whipping the

speeder bike to her left, she drew the blaster and aimed to her right. She squeezed the trigger.

Three shots. Three targets down. It was almost anticlimactic. She exhaled, then holstered her blaster pistol and turned back toward base. She'd pulled into an open stall in the vehicle hangar and was securing the speeder when she realized she wasn't alone.

"You missed," an instructor said. Sometimes it was Captain Phasma; sometimes it was Captain Cardinal. But the thing that never changed was the anger in their tone. The vitriol, as if 1719 had disgraced them by assuming that her good was good enough.

1719 would ask, "I missed?"

"You missed. Head back out and try it again."

That was where the dream turned into a nightmare, and even if she wanted to skip the next part, even if she knew it was a dream, and no matter how hard she tried to wake herself up, the events unfolded the same way every time. She would climb on the speeder bike and ride back to the course. She'd take every turn perfectly, accelerate when required, and brake when necessary. And when the targets swiveled into view, she'd pull her blaster pistol up and aim.

Except now the targets had faces.

Three shots.

Clamps.

Twelve.

TZ-214.

Three targets down.

"You missed," the instructor would say. "Head back out and try it again."

She woke, her skin clammy with sweat and the feeling of a heavy weight on her chest. Her right hand twitched. She could still feel the butt of the blaster pistol as she squeezed the trigger. After a few seconds contemplating going back to sleep, 1719 muttered a curse and got up to pull on her armor.

▮▮▮▮▮

The medbay of the *Supremacy* hummed quietly as 1719 walked inside. It was first shift, early, and only the droids moved about. She eased her way around a medical droid checking on a cadet in a bacta tank, ignored a limp hand dangling from beneath a sheet on a gurney, and stopped next to a medical bed that beeped every so often.

The cadet currently being treated was asleep. Her vitals seemed normal on the display, so 1719 just watched the person instead. Slim, shorter than the average cadet, and with her hair cascading around her, she seemed almost peaceful. Content. Not like the deadliest sharpshooter, who broke more accuracy records in her first year than the previous ten cohorts combined. The one everyone avoided because they feared her cold gaze. And yet, she was the same cadet who, when they were juniors, sang every night just loud enough for a struggling bunk mate to calm down and fall asleep after a brutal day of training.

1719 sighed, then checked the time. She'd been up for a couple of hours. Actually, she hadn't really slept, period. Not since *that* message had come through her comm. Sleep had been the last thing on her mind; instead, thoughts raced and collided and separated, keeping her tossing and turning until she finally gave up and got dressed. Now, as she stood in front of her squad mate, one of two who were too injured to resume active duty, the message flashed in front of her eyes again and again.

Report to all staff briefing for troop realignment.

She clenched a fist. *We don't leave each other behind,* she thought fiercely.

214's eyes blinked open and focused on her. "You're thinking too loud again," she whispered.

1719 smiled—briefly—then leaned over to check the medical bed's vitals. It just so happened that she put her body between the cameras and the bed, and she slipped her hand into the other girl's and squeezed.

"Cadet," she said.

You okay?

"Boss." 214 squeezed back, though with not as much strength. *Been better.* "How's Twelve? And Clamps?"

"Twelve is back on his feet, moving around fine and should be cleared for training soon. Maybe a few more days. Clamps is . . . well, he's Clamps. Complaining. Wanting to get back on patrol."

214 quirked an eyebrow. "Are we heading out soon?"

But 1719 shook her head. "No. Not yet." At the frown crossing her squad mate's face (former squad mate, she had to remind herself), she sighed. "The patrol—our foot patrol—has been folded into Company Seventy-Seven's mission status. Orders came through overnight. There's supposed to be a briefing later this morning to discuss . . . realignment."

Realization flickered across 214's face, though she did her best to put on a wry smile that didn't quite reach the worry in her eyes. "They won't split us up. The med droid says I'm cleared to return anyway, so good luck getting rid of me."

1719 smiled, a genuine one this time. "I wouldn't dream of it." At the word *dream*, she remembered the one she'd experienced during the night, and her smile faded and a shiver rippled up her spine.

214 noticed. "They're happening again, aren't they?"

"I just need another morale session or two," 1719 lied, "and everything will be fine." She hated having her team worry about her. She was supposed to be the one they relied on, not the one they cared for.

As if reading her thoughts, 214 maneuvered herself into a sitting position. "You're not going to leave us behind. We won't let you. *I* won't let you. Let me get dressed, and then I need something to eat. Then we can see what our new team is preparing for. Whatever it is, Company Seventy-Seven won't know what hit it when FP Twenty-Two-Alpha shows up."

1719 laughed, as her squad mate had intended, and felt her resolve harden. She'd keep them together, and she wouldn't hurt them, whatever her dreams might say.

The *Supremacy* was massive. Orders of magnitude larger than the *Finalizer*, which 1719 had thought—until last night—was the largest ship she would see. But as she exited the medical bay and followed rows upon rows of stormtroopers filing toward the ship's internal tram system, the sleek black walls of the corridor stretching and expanding to accommodate the thousands of personnel moving through it at any one point, she couldn't help shaking her head at the constant reminder of just how small she really was.

"I prefer not to think about it," came a voice from her left.

Another trooper waited in line next to 1719. They wore a white shoulder pauldron, as well, and their ID tag pinged them as FL-4980. 1719 glanced at their helmet, then looked forward, keeping time with the troopers in front of her.

"That obvious?" she asked.

Her neighbor laughed. "You can always tell which trooper is new on board because of how often they look up. I get it, it's a large ship."

"It's improbable," 1719 murmured.

"Trust me, you'll get used to it. Until then, do what I do and shove it down beneath your other concerns, worries, and this-is-going-to-get-me-killed fears, and you'll do just fine. Better alive and inconsequential beneath the *Supremacy*'s gaze than dead and on solid ground."

An image of a dead pirate stuffed in a cargo pod flashed in 1719's mind. "That's the truth."

The line ahead of them shuffled forward, and suddenly they were boarding the tram, funneling in to stand in approximate order as the magnetic troop transport slowly picked up speed, barreling toward what FL-4980 called the staging area.

"It's where all the briefings and meetings are held," they

said. "That way they can load us onto shuttles or kick us out airlocks."

The trooper on the other side of them snorted. "Who needs airlocks when you've got executions?"

"Stuff it, Knives." Then 4980 turned to 1719 and shook their head. "Ignore him. He's going to find himself on the wrong end of a laser ax if he doesn't *shut up*."

Executions? They hold executions?

The other trooper shrugged and looked ready to argue, but their stop was approaching and the tram alerts cut off whatever he was about to say. 1719 and 4980 followed everyone else as they filed out of the tram cars and entered the staging area, a massive hangar-like space that she was told could hold a Star Destroyer. And she could see it, too. Maybe even a few palaces from Hadne 3, as well. The ceiling of the cavernous space was practically nonexistent. She knew it was up there, but it was shrouded in the unlit gloom of the rafters and hidden behind the glare of the lights mounted much lower to the floor.

The troopers filed into ranks, organized by squad, company, and battalion.

"Boss!"

1719's face split into a grin when she saw Clamps and Twelve waving at her from a spot in line near the rear of the staging area. She waved back, then turned to thank FL-4980 for their help, but she stopped when she saw how the other trooper's gloved hands were squeezed into fists at their sides.

"You're with them?" they asked.

1719 glanced back at her squad. The two were obviously arguing over who would stand next to her, much to the annoyance of the troopers around them, until they finally used their collective intelligence and made space between them. "Who, those droid heads? Don't let their idiocy fool you . . . they're actually even worse. No, they're good—"

"Not the troopers. The company."

Now several others had stopped to watch, but 4980 didn't notice. If they did, they didn't care. And it didn't make sense. But something was happening here; some miscellaneous information that was common knowledge had become relevant, and others had it, while 1719 didn't. So she did what she always did—pressed forward.

"Company Seventy-Seven. Just transferred in last night, straight from Locke Station."

Another trooper—the one they called Knives, and her helmet identified as FL-8007—pressed forward. "Heard about you all," he said. "You're the ones who held out against those pirate gunrunners. Makeshift weapons and all. Not bad."

More troopers gathered round, order forgotten as they asked questions. "I heard there was a huge firefight and the station exploded."

"Impossible, we just got a morale report on them a day ago."

"That's right! Heroic of heart and courage, or something like that."

1719 flushed hot under her helmet, thankful no one could see her face. They were on the morale report? Clamps would never let them hear the end of it. The boy got a big head when his accuracy at the blaster range was a percentage point higher than hers. . . . This would make it impossible for him to pull his helmet off. She was smiling until she saw how stiff 4980 still stood. How their fists were still clenched.

"I heard something else," the trooper said. The voices around them gradually fell silent. Obviously 4980 was someone they respected. "I heard your squad leader killed a pirate and used his body as a lure to shoot the others in the back as they went by."

1719's jaw fell open. "That's—"

"It was on the morale report," 4980 interrupted.

She closed her mouth. That was a lie. She hadn't shot anyone. She'd done her best to make sure she wouldn't have to. So why would the morale report say that she did? Was this

Sergeant Onatha's doing? Or someone else? Why would they embellish?

Before she could ask those questions, and more, a tone chimed over the staging area speakers and the other troopers began to muster out into formation. But FL-4980 continued to wait, their head slightly tilted, and it seemed like they were studying her. Finally, the trooper turned to walk toward their own formation. "Be careful," they tossed over their shoulder. "If you're used to death, good. From the morale session's portrayal, you should fit right in with your new company."

"Why?" 1719 called after them.

"Because they're bloodthirsty. Those executions Knives mentioned earlier? Seventy-Seven is the only company to volunteer. Killing pirates is one thing, but them . . . they kill other troopers. Hope you know what you're getting into."

CHPTR - 14

Storms raged across the surface of Tamo'Akora as FN-2187 watched FO-7155 fight to hold the shuttle steady. It had taken all of three minutes for the other boy to take over, and Eight-Seven still felt the heat of embarrassment on his face. He'd barely had a chance to fly! Did he scrape the hull on the way out of the docking bay? Sure. Did he reverse backward into a loader? That wasn't important. The important thing was, once again, 7155 hadn't given him a proper chance. And it wasn't like he was doing much better! Winds howled as they battered and bullied the ship during its descent, while rain drummed against the hull and made visibility practically zero.

"Do you have the spaceport coordinates yet?" 7155 shouted.

"Calm down," Eight-Seven muttered, even as he squeezed the armrest on the copilot's chair. "One second."

"We need them—"

"One second!" His fingers flew across the display, and then he held one up. Finally, right before he could be yelled at again, Eight-Seven tapped in the last few characters and pointed. "Go!"

A location popped up on the display in front of 7155 as the storm tried to wrestle the control of the shuttle from his hands. "There? In the middle of the canyon systems? That's impossible!"

"You wanted the coordinates, those are the coordinates. Scanners are picking up something, too, something big. It must be the ship that took the major's supplies."

"Which means they'll be waiting for us."

Eight-Seven grimaced beneath his helmet and nodded. "We'll be walking into an ambush."

Silence fell between them. In the pause in conversation, the major could be heard in the rear practicing another holo-display narration with his droid. It sounded like a somber one, and Eight-Seven wondered what he was reporting on. Had another planetary system fallen under the control of terrorists? What horrors had they inflicted on the population? War? Bombings? Or were they just starving the system of resources, hogging them for themselves.

"Hey!"

Eight-Seven snapped back to the present to find 7155 staring at him. "What?"

"I said what are we going to do? Walk right into their trap, whoever's behind this? Time's running out. Pretty soon we'll be on their scann—"

The ship jolted.

Eight-Seven was hurled forward, and his helmet cracked into the controls. Pain exploded in his side as the ship shook violently again and again. He could feel himself rising in his seat, the harness cutting into his shoulders the only thing keeping him in place. They were falling, dropping out of the air like a stone, alarms blaring and someone shrieking. They were also spinning. His arms banged off the controls as they whipped right and left.

The ship slammed to a stop.

Alarms went off as Eight-Seven slumped over, ears ringing. Someone was shouting, but it sounded like it came from far away. Spiderweb cracks covered the surface of his helmet. He couldn't see. He blinked, then slowly lifted his head and pulled off the helmet, sucking down a deep breath of burning metal and smoke. Sparks popped from one of the control panels to his left.

Someone shouted again.

He turned his head slowly. It was hard to stay upright. His body felt a hundred times heavier than it had when they left the *Loxodonta*. Something large and white moved in front of him, but it was blurry at best. He blinked again, then squeezed his eyes shut and opened them once more.

"You okay?"

The ringing had stopped. His vision was clearing, too. Fifty-Five stood over him. He held his blaster rifle over one shoulder and extended an arm. Eight-Seven squeezed his eyes closed again, then reached out and accepted the assistance. Thankfully he didn't fall when he was hauled up, though he took a minute to swallow down the bout of nausea threatening to rebel inside his throat before he shoved his helmet back on.

"The major?" he croaked out.

Fifty-Five shook his head. "Unconscious. I left a blaster within reach and used a couple medpacs. He's stable, and the droid is monitoring our comms."

Eight-Seven nodded and made his way, slowly, to his equipment. He grabbed his blaster, several thermal detonators (thank the Order those hadn't exploded during impact), and a hand scanner. Then he tossed a camo poncho to his partner, who snatched it out of midair and glanced at it.

"What's this for?" 7155 asked.

"What do you think?" Eight-Seven slipped his on, strapped on his gear, and made his way over the cockpit wreckage to the ship's door. He slammed the button and waited for the boarding ramp to descend, frowning when it paused halfway down. "The major is stable, so we're going to get those supplies."

The ramp shrieked as he hit the button again, but it didn't move. Eight-Seven frowned. "And a new ship."

The storm made visibility very low even with perfect gear, so Eight-Seven's cracked helmet wasn't doing him any favors. From the little he could see, the world of Tamo'Akora consisted of canyons, gullies, and the flora and fauna that called them home. They'd landed—crashed—at the top of a cliff system covered in spiny purple and red bushes that rattled when they passed by. Other than that, however, there was nothing as far as the eye could see. Just rain, cliff tops, and the dark cracks in the ground leading to the canyons below.

Speaking of rain, it pelted them as Eight-Seven swept the scanner across the landscape. Fifty-Five kept an eye out for hostiles—two-legged or otherwise—as they waited on the results. When the unit beeped, Eight-Seven tried again. After it beeped a second time, he shook his head.

"Don't tell me you broke that," 7155 said, groaning.

"No, I didn't. It's just giving me a faulty reading."

"So you *did* break it."

Eight-Seven rolled his eyes. "Must be some sort of interference," he said. "I'm getting multiple life-forms."

Fifty-Five turned around, arms wide, pointing at a nearby rattling bush. "Where? The plants? The rain? It's got to be the rain, since that's the only thing I can see in any direction." He ended up shouting at the end, but the words were washed away—along with some of the dirt beneath his feet—in a flash of lightning and booming thunder.

Eight-Seven waited until he was finished, then tossed him the scanner. "If you can get something different, have at it."

"This training mission is scrapped," the other boy grumbled, smacking the unit and glaring at it. "Completely scrapped."

"We can still finish it. Get the supplies, commandeer a ship from the locals—"

"The ones who shot at us?"

"—and report back to the major. Easy."

Fifty-Five snorted. "Always the optimist."

Eight-Seven ignored that. A bush rattled next to him. He stared at it, then turned toward the nearby canyon crack.

Streams of rainwater burbled their way to the many such openings across the cliff top, some as wide as he was. Finally, he kicked one of the spiny plants. Immediately it began to rattle again, and Eight-Seven backed up as several multi-legged creatures with bright green spots and bony ridges running from between their eyes down the lengths of their whiplike tails dropped to the ground. They chittered at him, then took off. He followed them as they hissed and skittered through mud to the closest canyon crack, a particularly wide one that stretched out into the distance for kilometers, and dropped inside.

Eight-Seven squinted. He followed, then dropped to a crouch alongside the canyon crack. He started to pull out a glow rod and aim it inside, then hesitated. Instead, he stood. "Let's go back to the ship and call for help. My boots are soaked, and if I spend one more blasted second on this forsaken slog of a planet, I'm going to fry a circuit."

He raised a hand as 7155 was about to comment, then switched to the internal comm. "Smart, right? That's called subterfuge."

"Uh-huh," the other boy grunted.

"Your enthusiasm aside, I think I found the locals." He waited, then turned. "Come and look. What are you waiting for?"

Fifty-Five joined him after a muttered curse, and something in his voice made Eight-Seven pause. But then the boy shoved him aside and peered over the edge into the crack in the surface. A few meters down, the crevice walls transitioned from the rust red of the rocky surface to gray and beige, and 7155 let another curse slip. No wonder the planet's surface seemed empty—it was because the inhabitants were *under* the surface. The crevice's walls had been reinforced and strengthened, and elaborate funneling systems carved into the rock channeled the rainwater down and away. Beams were mounted every few meters so additional structures could be bolted to them. A platform with railings and a built-in seat was one such structure, and Eight-Seven pointed at it.

"Lookout post," he said. "Can't have that many occupants. How much you want to bet somebody just left, probably to report our landing."

Fifty-Five hefted his blaster rifle. "And our movements. Which means now is the time to get out of here."

"No."

"No? What do you mean, no?"

Eight-Seven hesitated, then checked the scanner again. Fifty-Five was right. The smart—and safe—thing to do would be to hightail it back to the shuttle and report to Major Gohl.

There was no telling what, or who, waited for them below the surface. At best they'd have to do a lot of explaining. At worst it was a trap.

But they'd already come this far. Besides, he wanted to prove he had what it took to be a squad leader.

The scanner beeped. He lifted it so the screen was visible, including the bright green dot pulsating close to the center. "No. The supplies are right there. Right *there*! I say we go down, put eyes on them, and then call for backup."

Fifty-Five threw his free hand in the air. "We *are* the backup! Who else is even in this system besides us, underground pirates, and the . . ."

His voice trailed off, and Eight-Seven nodded. "The *Loxodonta*. All those pretty load lifters just waiting to stretch and flex."

"You can't be serious."

"Why not? You and me will go down, tag the cargo, and use the remote carriers to bring down those idling droids. The answer was staring us in the face all along. Imagine what Major Gohl will say when we not only find the supplies but bring them back to the *Loxodonta* without calling for help! Forget squad leaders, we'll both have our own battalions by the time we exit hyperspace."

Fifty-Five stood there motionless, trying to parse everything he'd just heard. "Have you been slurping droid oil? That's a terrible idea."

But his words met the stormy surface of Tamo'Akora, as Eight-Seven had already shouldered his blaster and was descending to the lookout platform via cleverly disguised handholds.

"Come on," he called.

"No!"

"Do you want to be squad leader?"

"I want to live!"

"Live later. Come help me get these supplies!"

Fifty-Five stared for a moment. Then: "This is why no one likes him."

"I heard that."

"YOU WERE MEANT TO!"

CHPTR - 15

"This is a historic moment. An *important* moment. We stand on the brink of a changeover, a period of time where the destructive days of old, filled with corruption, degeneracy, and chaos, are replaced with the firm guiding hand of the First Order. You all are the carriers of a new strain of governance, inoculating the galaxy against fear, against weakness, and against tyranny."

The officer speaking from his podium in the middle of the staging area continued, but TZ-1719's brain was spinning in her head. What sort of group had her squad been assigned to? Bloodthirsty? Troop killers? And if that wasn't enough, she had to contend with the morale session that painted her in a similar light.

"Boss?" Twelve pinged her on their private comm. "You okay?"

"Fine," she said. "And should you be talking on here like this? Can't they still monitor this channel?"

"Negative. I think. Pretty sure I updated the coding to automatically scramble our frequency every five minutes. Or did I only think about doing that?"

"Twelve," she and Clamps said at the same time.

"Got it, on it, understood."

He faded into a mutter that briefly amused 1719 before her somber mood returned. But more internal fretting had to wait, because Clamps spoke up next, the tone in his voice questioning.

"I checked on Twenty-One-Four before you got here, boss. She said you were having the dreams again. That true?"

"Dreams?" Twelve broke in. "What dreams?"

Twelve was the last member of the squad to join—214 and Clamps had been in a unit with 1719 by then, with several training missions and patrols under their belts. Twelve had missed the early days, the panic of those missions during the Merchant Uprising in the Tsevuka system, and the nightmares afterward.

"Nothing," 1719 finally said. "It's nothing."

"Boss," Clamps began, but then they all had to be quiet, because something was happening.

They were moving. The entire company. It took a few seconds, but it soon became clear that they were shifting position, rotating along one corner of their formation until they were facing the rest of the troops, the officer who'd been speaking from the podium earlier now marching toward them. Another stormtrooper followed, his pristine white armor interrupted only by the red pauldron worn on his shoulder, captain's honor.

"Boss, we're moving," Clamps hissed. The formation had continued to pivot, but 1719 was so shocked at the sight of the captain and the ID tag that had popped up on her display that she'd momentarily stumbled. She quickly regained her footing and stepped back into place, but the damage had already been done. She could feel the captain's gaze as her motion, irregular and out of place amid order, had drawn his attention.

Please, she thought. *Anyone but him. Don't let it be him.*

The officer hadn't noticed her mistake, and he stomped to a stop just in front of the company. He waited for the captain to join him, then beamed proudly as he spoke, his voice carried by a hidden mic to the entire staging area.

"The First Order is pleased to announce that Company Seventy-Seven has volunteered to spearhead our next phase of operations, securing intelligence leaks and capturing those responsible and bringing them to a swift and final justice. In that I am more than satisfied our forces will prevail, especially under the command of one of the Order's most dedicated and fiercely protective defenders—"

1719 closed her eyes, the images of the aftermath following the Merchant Uprising seared into her memory, the man who had ordered the destruction standing right in front of her.

"—Captain Shikra."

▮▮▮▮▮

She was studying blasters as her squad complained.

"Boss."

"I know."

"This isn't good."

"I *know*."

"First Strike Shikra? We're dead!"

"N.O.T." No old troopers. It was a saying they'd learned as cadets from older peers. Basically, there was no stormtrooper retirement plan, so there wasn't any use griping over survival odds.

"That's not funny," Clamps muttered.

The conversation paused as a trio of officers strolled by, datapads in their arms as they discussed troop movements and battle plans. 1719, Twelve, and Clamps stood with a group of troopers near the cargo section of the *Supremacy*'s staging area, the other companies and battalions dismissed nearly a half hour before. Truthfully, 1719 should've been alone, since usually squad leaders and other enlisted officers were briefed before the rest of the company, but Clamps refused to leave her by herself, and Twelve lingered out of curiosity, despite her demands that they leave. Which, if she was honest, she was thankful for. She wasn't looking forward to this squad leader briefing Captain Shikra had called. She wasn't looking forward to anything involving him. So to distract herself, she was studying blasters.

Containers of ammunition packs, blaster rifles and pistols, and even explosives waited to be loaded onto transport shuttles and drop ships. 1719 was staring at a container next to her that had been partially opened, probably to take inventory. Ever since this morning's assembly, more and more cargo skiffs had dropped off supplies, everything clean and in pristine condition. No rust, no warped plastic or scorched metal, no burning smell or parts that spit sparks when not held in a specific way. *Sonn-Blas Corporation.* The manufacturer, stenciled in bold silver letters on the black container, listed the batch and lot numbers along with the manufacturing date of the weapons. 1719 reached in and pulled out a brand-new blaster. Flipped it over.

"Why's the power pack missing?" Twelve asked.

Clamps snorted. "You want to hand a loaded blaster rifle to an itchy cadet?"

"Oh. Right."

The ammunition power packs were stored in a separate compartment in the same container. 1719 grabbed one and studied it. She could faintly trace the seams where the hardened plastic had been sealed together, small circular openings revealing the sturm dowels inside. She never would have dreamed of attempting to separate the casing to reach them, not with the safety briefings and controlled demonstrations every trooper was forced to attend before live weapon training. But if she was desperate? If pirates were extorting her family—well, she didn't have a family, not in the traditional sense. But if they were threatening her squad? Her friends?

The Xen Runners entered her mind, and she saw the sneering face of their leader as he hurled threats at Twelve and TZ-214 back on Locke Station.

"Boss?"

Clamps was staring at her. She was squeezing the trigger of the blaster rifle. If it had been loaded . . . She forced a laugh and returned the blaster and power pack to the container. "I guess I'm one of those itchy cadets, huh?"

"You okay?" Clamps asked.

"Just thinking about Locke Station," she said, which wasn't a lie.

"Oh, yeah. I guess if the stationers had five or six of these blasters, or better yet, a fully staffed garrison, the Xen Runners wouldn't have been able to extort them for so long." Clamps nodded at the container. "Just one of those might've made a difference and kept Twelve out of harm's way, not to mention Twenty-One-Four."

It was exactly what she'd been thinking. Then again: "At least now the stationers know how to defend themselves with whatever they have."

Twelve piped up. "Give that Sergeant Onatha you mentioned some of these and turn him loose. I bet he would have given the pirates a fight, boss."

Clamps snorted. "More likely accidentally—"

"Enough!" she said, cutting him off before he said something that would get them all in trouble. The others fell quiet, though she could feel Clamps chuckling beside her. Fortunately, at that moment Captain Shikra appeared, with a familiar figure by his side, though 1719 couldn't place where they'd met.

"TZ-One-Seven-One-Nine!" the captain exclaimed. "You are a delight."

"Sir!" She saluted but stared over his shoulder. She could feel his gaze as it swept every centimeter of her, and she fought off an unpleasant shiver. It was like she was a tool, an object being assessed for usefulness, and she swallowed a sudden lump.

"I was pleasantly surprised to see your ID pop up in our briefing report," the captain continued. "You've been quite busy since the last time you were under my command. I like to think I had a hand in this, you know. Your first mission came while under my tutelage, isn't that right?"

"Yes, sir."

"Keep this up and you'll be commanding battalions, mark my words, or one of my special shock trooper squads."

"Company Seventy-Seven has shock trooper squads?"

"No, they don't. They're a special detachment, really, outside of the . . . traditional chain of command. Never know when you might need to instill fear and decorum amongst the lesser mortals, right, Corporal?"

"Yes, sir," she managed to squeeze out.

The captain's companion shifted in place, and Shikra

turned as if he'd forgotten he wasn't alone. "Ah, yes. I thought you two would like to meet before the company briefing. This is Lieutenant Shroud. Forgive the theatrics, but she insists on the silly mask and her superior unfortunately approves."

1719 nodded. "We've met. On Hadne Three."

The slim lieutenant nodded back, her amber eyes twinkling. Her mask, which resembled the oxygen mask of a TIE pilot, glinted in the light. "You remembered. And again, my apologies for the mask, Captain, but space . . . has irritants."

Captain Shikra flapped his hand with impatience. "Well, good enough. The lieutenant's superior is responsible for the glowing recounting of your . . . heroics on Locke Station during the most recent morale report. I was delighted to find your detail reassigned to the *Supremacy* and Company Seventy-Seven. You will be an inspiration to the troops for this next mission."

The lump in her throat reappeared. Despite the transfer to the *Scarab*, despite putting distance between her team and the horrors of the Merchant Uprising, despite everything, they were back under Shikra's command.

The captain was still speaking, and she forced the terror in her throat down. It didn't help that Lieutenant Shroud was watching her with narrowed eyes. Could she tell 1719's heart rate had spiked? Or was it something else?

"—do you think?"

Too late, she realized the captain had asked her a question.

"Sir?" she barked, hoping her confusion didn't leach through the voice modulator. But he didn't seem to notice, his attention on a datapad one of the quartermasters had just hurried up to hand to him.

"You'll be working together for the first part of this next mission," he said, signing off on something before handing the datapad back. "Major Gohl was gracious enough to grant us the privilege of his experience."

"The mission, sir?"

"We're going hunting, trooper. Gather your squad and form up. Details in five."

"Yes, sir." She saluted, then paused. "If you don't mind me asking, sir, what are we hunting?"

Captain Shikra, in the process of turning away, his hands clasped behind his back, glanced at her. 1719 suddenly remembered the glint in his cold gray eyes when he sent them off to slaughter civilians.

"Traitors, One-Seven-One-Nine," he said. "We're hunting traitors."

CHPTR - 16

The lower FN-2187 climbed, the more Tamo'Akora grew . . . well, not beautiful but something close to it. Veins of some sort of green-tinted metal rippled through the walls of the crevice. Bioluminescent flowers of every color, what he'd mistaken for mounted lights, clustered on ledges and outcroppings. They closed as he descended past them, then slowly unfolded when he'd gone, sending a soft blue and silver glow over his shoulders as he peered down. The air grew warm, and the sound of the storm runoff trickling through cleverly cut channels in the rock was almost soothing. By the time he reached the lookout platform, Eight-Seven was convinced that he could lie down here and sleep for days. And from the look of the pile of blankets and assorted pillows, someone probably had.

"This is a bad idea," FO-7155 muttered as he climbed down. It was taking him twice as long as Eight-Seven, and he hadn't even reached the halfway point. Each movement was forced. Jerky. Every time he reached for a new handhold, or felt with his boot for something to support him, it was like he was moving through mud. He was clearly not a fan of tight spaces. There was only so much a simulator could prepare them for.

Eight-Seven watched for a second, then peered over the edge and checked the scanner. He checked again, then grinned and looked below him at a spot where the crevice widened and exposed a cave in the cliff wall, the entrance beneath an overhang. If he wasn't mistaken, and he triple-checked just to be sure, a pilot could carefully navigate into the crevice through a wider opening farther away and then maneuver into the cave, using it as a natural landing pad. As if confirming his suspicion, more light, this time artificial and not from any of the glowing flowers, flickered at the cave entrance, just out of reach.

"Look," he said. "There's a large plateau about twenty meters down. I bet you that's where the supplies are. Look."

"I can't."

"Just look. They're not that far."

"I said I can't!"

It was his rapid breathing over the mic that grabbed Eight-Seven's attention. He turned to see 7155 frozen on the wall, still clinging to the same handhold a dozen meters off the platform. He was staring straight ahead, and his breath came fast and ragged, as if his oxygen supply had been cut off.

"I can't . . . do this," 7155 said.

Eight-Seven snorted. Laughed. Almost started to needle him, then stopped when he noticed a tremble in the boy's arm. He was barely clinging to the handholds. If he wasn't careful, he'd slip right off and fall straight down to collide with the platform. And there was no way Eight-Seven was hauling him back up, *could* haul him back up, not to mention dealing with the injuries afterward.

And the complaints.

And the disappointed expressions of Major Gohl.

"I can't do this," 7155 said again. Almost in a whisper.

The Order will always find mountain troopers. It needs leaders.

Eight-Seven cleared his throat. "Okay, just hold on. I'm going to talk you down. Just hold on."

"I'm holding on!"

"Okay, calm down."

"I AM—"

"Look, there's a handhold just below your right boot. You can step down to it." Eight-Seven waited, and when the other trooper didn't move, he licked his lips and tried to lower his voice. Talk calm, like Captain Cardinal did to the younger cadets when they were nervous. "Trust me, there's a handhold right below your boot. Your right boot. If you keep your weight on your left foot and ease down, you'll feel it straightaway. It's wide and you can't miss it."

Slowly, 7155 moved his boot from its current position and lowered himself to the next handhold.

"There you go. Do the same thing with your left boot, but your next mark is even closer. Right there. You got it. See?"

Fifty-Five visibly slumped with relief. "Don't tell the major," he said, embarrassed. "I don't need this on my report."

"Of course not," Eight-Seven said. "I'll tell him you're a regular Corellian low-grav performer. Now tighten up. You're only halfway down."

Fifty-Five muttered something.

"Ouch," Eight-Seven said. "Definitely reporting that. All right, there's another one a meter down, but you should be able to reach it."

"Yeah, I see it." Fifty-Five took a deep breath. Then another. He didn't move, and Eight-Seven frowned. He was still trapped inside his head and needed a distraction. Something to peel his mind away from his current predicament and allow his body to take over.

"Tell me why you want to be squad leader so bad," Eight-Seven said.

"What?"

"Squad leader. Why do you want it? You're already bossy enough as it is. Do you need the official label, too?"

Fifty-Five started to turn his head before seeming to remember where he was and jerking it back to face the wall. "You're asking me now?"

"Why not? You can't go anywhere. And I want to know."

Silence followed, and it went on for so long, Eight-Seven was about to give up and try something else when 7155 spoke.

"What are we?" he asked.

"Soldiers?"

He shook his head. "No."

"Stormtroopers?"

"We're more than that. You listen to the reports during morale sessions, right?"

Eight-Seven nodded. "What about them?" he asked.

"Somewhere out there, at any given second, something has gone wrong, will go wrong, or is presently in the process of going wrong. But because somebody got greedy, or lazy, or maybe even tried their best but just wasn't good enough, another person is going to suffer. Did you hear the latest news? About Locke Station? That space station that was being run by pirates? Pirates! The people were suffering until the First Order came in and cleaned everything up."

"So? That's what we do, right? You're proving my point."

Fifty-Five shook his head, and—Eight-Seven noted with a small smile—had started to feel his way down the cliff wall while he was talking. "But it's what happened afterward that really hit me. The troopers helped repair the station, distributed supplies the pirates had stolen, and made sure the people living there were back on their feet before leaving them. That's what I want to do. I want to lead a team that doesn't just stop people from destroying what the First Order wants to build, but stays behind to help fix what was destroyed."

Eight-Seven whistled. "That could be a quote for the major right there," he said.

"Shut up," 7155 said, but there was no heat in the words. He continued to descend. "When I get down there, I—"

CRACK!

A large section of the cliff face splintered off from the handhold he'd just stepped on, showering Eight-Seven and the lookout platform with rock debris and glowing flowers.

Eight-Seven ducked, covering himself with his arms, only to hurl himself to the edge when 7155 shouted.

"LOOK OUT!"

The triangular cliff section plummeted down, striking the platform and nearly sending Eight-Seven over the edge. As it was, he scrambled for a grip as the blankets and pillows slid past him, tumbling down into the dark. He finally managed to grab a broken railing as his legs slid out over empty space. He tried to haul himself back up, but the platform groaned ominously. It was going to give, and probably take more of the cliff face with it.

". . . okay?"

He was being hailed. Had he gotten hit in the head? There weren't any damage readouts.

"Eight-Seven, are you okay?"

"I'm fine," he said, squeezing his teeth together as he tried to reposition his grip. "Just . . . hanging in there."

Fifty-Five ignored the pun. "All right, let me get you out of there. I'll be down in—"

"No!" Eight-Seven said sharply. "Don't. This platform is about to go, I can feel it. Any more weight and we'll be nutritional paste at the bottom of the cliff. Just . . . go back. There aren't any more handholds you can reach anyway."

Fifty-Five looked around and finally realized he was cut

off. Unless he planned on jumping to the lookout platform, which was a *terrible* idea, there was nowhere for him to go but up. He let loose with a string of profanity so impressive, a Hutt somewhere was blushing. "Fine," he finally said, "what am I supposed to do?"

"Get back to the shuttle," Eight-Seven said. "If it'll fly—"

"If?"

"If it'll fly, take the major back up, and then start bringing the load lifters down on one of the carrier platforms and wait for my signal. You send the carrier in, and I'll ride it out on the last shipment."

Silence followed, and it was clear 7155 didn't care for the plan. But as the increased groaning of the lookout platform indicated, the time for debate was short. Actually, Eight-Seven decided, it was done. He grabbed the handholds used to descend to the cave and slowly shifted his weight.

A long, tortured groan began to echo, and this time it was his turn to swear. "Go!" he shouted. "This whole thing is going to fall."

He began to descend, hand over hand, as pebbles showered his helmet and arms. There was no time to test for stability anymore. He just had to have faith that they would support him. Hopefully 7155 was doing the same on his way up and out.

CRAAAAACK!

Eight-Seven didn't look up. Refused. He knew what he would see, especially as larger sections of rock began to fall. One the size of his fist slammed into his right shoulder and he grunted, his grip slipping off the handhold. It was only through sheer luck that he accidentally grazed a different one, and he managed to stop himself from panicking as he sucked down air. He risked a glance down, then up, and neither filled him with confidence.

The cave was still a good ten meters below.

Cracks in the cliff face had stretched past him. The entire thing was going to go, handholds and all. He had to move.

He threw himself down, not worried about grip, only pausing for half a second to gauge distance to the next handhold. The cave was eight meters away. Seven.

A rock the size of his helmet barely missed crushing his hand, instead bouncing off the wall and tumbling away.

Six meters. Five.

The bolts anchoring the lookout platform to the cliff launched like missiles, pinging off of the walls. One clipped his back just as he began to drop to the next handhold, and it threw him off target. Eight-Seven slammed into the wall, arms flailing. At the last second his fingers wedged into a crack in the cliff and he shouted in pain as they were smashed.

"EIGHT-SEVEN!" 7155 shouted over the comm. "You all right? Did you make it?"

Three meters. But his hand was stuck. Eight-Seven glanced up again, just in time to watch the entire cliff face separate into fragments bigger than he was, blotting out the stormy sky as they dropped toward him. He was out of time.

Eight-Seven yanked his fingers free and jumped.

CHPTR - 17

"The mission area is located on Rive, an ecumenopolis moon orbiting a mineral-rich super planet in the Butler system."

Sergeant Calcon, the briefing officer, was one of Captain Shikra's subordinates. Short, fiery, and no-nonsense, she barked out mission details as if daring anyone to ask questions. More than once TZ-1719 had observed her biting off the head of a trooper who'd interrupted her. Now she stood in front of a portable holodisplay as she went through the briefing, highlighting the sectors of interest so they expanded in the air in front of them as she spoke.

"Ecumenopolis?" whispered a trooper with a yellow pauldron. Artillery squad leader. Interesting.

"City-planet," 1719 answered.

Sergeant Calcon's helmet turned to them, bristling at the interruption. "Correct. Though, in this case, a city-moon. Its residents are landowners loosely organized into a group called the Rive Collective, with stakes in the uninhabitable planet below."

"Uninhabitable," Lieutenant Shroud broke in, "but extremely vital."

The sergeant clearly didn't appreciate the interruption but—since Shroud technically outranked her—chose not to complain. She cleared her throat and continued. "Yes. Well. The cumulative output of the Collective contributes a significant amount of raw material for critical ship components, like hyperdrive transpacitors, and weapons manufacturing. The First Order provides several garrisons of troopers for protection from pirates and thieves, and the Collective provides metals and ores to our partners. Partners who produce the very blaster rifles you're carrying. Needless to say, the Supreme Leader is *very* interested in all matters concerning Rive."

"Especially when intelligence indicates some shipments from the Collective designated for the First Order have gone missing." Captain Shikra stepped forward, replacing Sergeant Calcon, who gracefully retreated. "That's where Company Seventy-Seven comes in. Our goal is to provide additional troopers to patrol Rive and track down those shipments."

1719 was raising her hand before she could think about what she was doing. "Sir?"

Captain Shikra didn't seem fazed. "Yes, trooper?"

"Are our forces currently garrisoned there overwhelmed? The sergeant mentioned several garrisons for a planetary moon that's less populated than a Star Destroyer."

He nodded approvingly. "A good question. Sergeant?"

Sergeant Calcon stepped forward again, and the holodisplay refreshed to show a large dome structure erected over the center of one of the moon's recreational districts. "Every ten years the Rive Collective opens Rive to noncitizens and corporate representatives and their families as a way of advertising through a citywide celebration. This go-round they're playing host to the Galactic Bazaar, a yearlong circus and festival. That means the moon has nearly ten times the foot traffic when compared to normal years."

"Which means more opportunity for theft and smuggling," Captain Shikra added. He surveyed the stormtrooper squad leaders. "Make no mistake, I don't care about petty theft, civilian robberies, or anything of that nature. Let the local garrisons take care of that. Someone is stealing from the First Order, and *that* is unacceptable. Find them, bring them in, and make an example out of them, no matter the cost. Is that clear?"

"Yes, sir!" the assembled troopers barked.

"Dismissed."

So she was going back on patrol. 1719 felt like she'd withstood a barrage of blaster fire and come through unscathed. Foot patrol she could handle. *They* could handle. Even if their patrol beat was a citywide circus. She'd have to make sure they were up to date on all riot-control protocols. And then they'd need a local liaison, someone preferably young, not too cynical yet.

Her mind whirred as she made her way back to the tram, and from there to the medical bay. Clamps and Twelve were waiting along with TZ-214. 1719 paused, surprised by the squad's sharpshooter being on her feet and fastening her armor. The other two looked on helplessly.

"Boss," 214 said.

1719 pressed her lips together. Finally, she said, "All good?"

"It will be once you tell Twelve to sign off. There's no way you're leaving me behind. Not with Shikra. Either he does it, or I do it and then end up in the brig. Is that what you want?"

Ah. 214 wanted Twelve to use his technical prowess to alter her medical clearance and give her record the all-clear stamp. Everything inside her told 1719 that bringing 214 along was a bad idea. The smart thing to do would be to pull rank, keep her in medical for her own safety, and endure the overwhelming feeling of guilt. That was what leaders were supposed to do. Bear the brunt of the successes and failures, the pride and the guilt.

But she also knew what it would do to the trooper's mental state to be left behind. It would be abandonment all over again, and 214 was strong, but she wasn't invincible. No one was.

"Boss, I got something you might want to see," Twelve said.

1719 pulled herself out of her thoughts. "What?"

"I started cross-referencing First Order reports from Rive with other reported piracy thefts from First Order networks around the galaxy, and I found something. Seven different reports filed on behalf of three different shipping agencies."

"Speak Galactic Basic, data boy," Clamps said. He folded his arms across his chest. "What does all that mean?'

Twelve ignored him. "In each instance, even though the cargo was stolen from different shipping agencies, the shipments originated from the same member of the Rive Collective: a corporation called the Jaliss Group."

"So they're terrible at picking someone to ship their stuff," Clamps said. "If I got a credit for each time someone I knew chose a bad partner, I could start my own fancy collective. The Clamps Collective."

"And if I got a credit each time one group's cargo was targeted by the same group of pirates and something *was* suspicious about the scenario, I'd . . . well, I'd have some credits."

1719 stepped in before the argument could grow. "You think the pirates are specifically targeting the Jaliss Group?"

"No. No, I'm saying I think they're working together."

214 whistled. "The pirates and the interstellar corporation?"

"Skim some weapons, make some profit, split the loot." Clamps actually sounded impressed. "If that's true, that's pretty bold, even for some bloodsucking corpos."

But Twelve still looked unsettled. No, it was more than that. He looked afraid.

"Why do you think that?" 1719 said quietly.

He shook his head. "Because one of the ships *not* declared missing is the same ship we were held prisoner in on Locke Station."

214 went still, and 1719 didn't blame her. Her mouth had gone dry as she realized what Twelve was saying. No wonder his vitals were skyrocketing.

"I still don't get it," Clamps complained.

"If the ship wasn't declared missing, it means someone sent it there on purpose," 1719 said, "and Twelve is right. Someone in the Jaliss Group could be working with the Xen Runners."

▮▮▮▮▮

1719 slipped to the back of the stormtrooper transport, squeezing into formation to the left of Clamps. She felt the beginnings of one of her headaches coming on as she nodded at him, then keyed the private squad channel and made sure Twelve and 214 did the same before speaking.

"Good news and bad news," she said.

"Bad news first," Clamps replied.

"Please no," Twelve said. "Good news. I definitely need good news." 214 nodded her agreement.

"Cowards," Clamps muttered.

The four stood in the middle of the troop transport, one of five assault landers being used to ferry Company 77 down to Rive's surface. The plan was to link up with a deployment of troops already in action, suppressing a riot in progress, and once completed, deploy into smaller groups to continue with their search for the pirates at known locations.

1719 hadn't shared her concerns about the Jaliss Group with any of the company's leadership. After all, she only had a handful of suspicions, Twelve's possibly illegal data scraping, and a chest full of knotted panic to go on. That wasn't enough to accuse a very wealthy mining company of possible collusion with pirates, and even if it was, she'd probably still hesitate. She didn't want Captain Shikra's attention any more than necessary, and Sergeant Calcon was an unknown, but from what 1719 had gleaned from trooper chatter, she was fiercely loyal to the captain. And that left Shroud.

To be honest, 1719 wasn't sure what to make of the lieutenant. She was cordial. Nice, even, at times. Yes, Shroud was working with Shikra, but on orders, not by choice; so that had to count for something, right? Right. But then again Shikra could be pleasant, and everyone knew the cold, calculating personality hidden behind the captain's pleasant attitude. The man could issue orders—had issued orders—that would end the lives of dozens while whistling a melody from a popular holodrama. Couple that with the fact that Shroud's boss, Major Gohl, was responsible for the morale session contents, and 1719 couldn't shake the feeling of unease that grew in her chest when the lieutenant was nearby. No, no matter how friendly or nice Shroud seemed, 1719 would keep her at arm's length, as much as possible with a lieutenant who could still give her orders. She could only hope to stay far away from the entire command structure of Company 77 until the mission was finished.

"Boss?" Clamps said.

She shook her head. "Sorry. Good news, right. They're not splitting us up. Apparently we're late to the party and patrols have already been established, and since we have experience working as a squad, it was convenient just to keep us troublemakers in Twenty-Two-Alpha together."

Twelve's relieved exhale was audible. Clamps jostled him with an elbow. But 214 didn't react.

"The bad news?" she asked.

The other two fell silent, and 1719 hesitated, then sighed. "When the sergeant said there was more foot traffic due to the Galactic Bazaar, what she *didn't* say was how nearly a third of that traffic is from the workers flown in to help keep the festivities running. Indentured workers."

214 and Clamps groaned at the same time. Twelve looked back and forth between the two, but he had to wait until a particularly rough bout of turbulence was done shaking the troop lander before anyone could explain.

"It's what the higher-ups," Clamps said, "in their wisdom and foresight, would call 'civil unrest.' I call it a riot, and those never go away on their own. Bad for business, too. Makes the people we're supposed to be protecting on our patrols angry at us."

He continued explaining the differences in techniques in riot control, waiting until the landing officer was occupied with another stormtrooper and then using Twelve as an unwilling partner in his example. 214 ignored them both. When 1719 glanced away to check if any officers were watching and turned back, she found Twelve studying her.

"Yes?"

"Just wondering if you've ever done riot control outside the sims."

The screaming crowds of the Merchant Uprising echoed in her ears, and she had to squeeze her eyes shut to get the voices from her head. "We all did. Once."

Clamps butted in, muttering as the lander shook again. "Well, playing nurse droid for some rich miners and their hired help doesn't sound bad at all. It'll be just like Hadne Three, and you'll all be complaining about boredom by day two."

The viewscreens inside the lander flickered on as they approached the ground, and all the chatter disappeared.

Every trooper fixed their eyes on the scene unfolding below.

Crowds hundreds thick swarmed around a large spherical dome constructed of glass and metal. The plaza, where they were supposed to touch down and rendezvous with the rest of the company, was packed with bodies pressed so tightly together they seemed to move as one, like some giant beast prowling in the forests on the outskirts of downtown Rive. Captain Shikra had decided to land the company at night, so they'd have to rely on the hanging prisms dangling above the plaza and the odd lantern pathway leading to the residential neighborhoods.

That and the occasional fireworks display.

As the lander made its final approach, neon flowers bloomed high in the night, erupting with brilliant precision. So brilliant that the lander had to course correct several times. By the time the transport had touched down, half the stormtroopers inside were recalibrating their helmets to account for both the occasional glare and the deep pockets of shadow. As they filed out, the noise swamped them, a combination of automated bazaar advertisements and the chants echoed by the protesting workers.

"Fresh kona juice!"

"Credits, not scrip!"

"Get your bazaar memento here!"

"No more wage slaves!"

The sight of the troop landers touching down on the rooftop landing pad south of the plaza sent the crowds into a frenzy. There were already several fires burning on the marble stone as workers stripped off their uniforms and set them ablaze.

"This is seconds away from turning into a bloodbath," 1719 muttered.

Someone stepped up beside her, but where she'd been expecting Clamps, it was actually Lieutenant Shroud. The masked officer stared grimly down at the scene. "You're right. This needs to be handled carefully."

"TZ-One-Seven-One-Nine!" A shout rang out over the rooftop. It was Sergeant Calcon. "Get your squad geared up and form up on the western edge of the plaza. Push into the dome, link up with the security inside, and escort the VIPs there south."

"There are still people in there?" someone asked.

"Cut the chatter! The rest of you, form up. We need to get this plaza clear."

"Why us?" Clamps muttered. "Why do we get the escort duty?"

1719 could feel the eyes of Shroud on her back as she turned to grab the hefty riot shields and several Z6 batons, testing the charges of the latter before passing them to her team. "Because you said playing nurse droid didn't sound bad, Clamps."

Twelve grabbed his shield and baton. "Now who jinxed the mission?"

"Shut up," Clamps said with a scowl.

214 took her shield without comment, but 1719 noticed the grimace when she fitted the straps to her arm. She was about to offer to let the sharpshooter hang back and scrounge up more information on the Jaliss Group and any additional connections with the Xen Runners when someone else stepped up, hands out.

"Lieutenant?" she asked.

Lieutenant Shroud raised an eyebrow. She'd removed her polyweave cloak but still had on her gray armor and mask. "Mind if I tag along? No orders for me yet, so I might as well help. And you seem to get the interesting jobs."

"But this is grunt work."

"Muddy work still needs to get done. Besides," she said, powering on the baton, testing it by swinging it through the air in a complicated pattern, and then powering it off and returning it to her belt, "my observation isn't complete."

1719 swallowed her complaint and instead nodded. That ever-present knot in her chest tightened even further as the rest of the squad watched in silence. She gritted her teeth. They would have to make sure everything was by the book if the lieutenant was lurking in their shadow. Their private channel was out of the question, not with how the lieutenant had breached it back on Hadne 3.

"Let's go!" she called out, and she couldn't help feeling a momentary sense of pride as her team fell into position smoothly, even as squads around her grappled with equipment and deployment orders.

Fine. Shroud wanted to tag along? Play mind games? Get down in the mud? Then they were going deep.

CHAPTER 18

Coy spent the first few hours of their journey to the Sardich system apologizing.

"Sorry," he said, brushing dried tea leaf flakes from a seat just before Finn sat down.

"Let me get that," he said, blushing as Niila bumped into a stack of his old respi-vaps.

"This bucket of rust is so old," he muttered when Jannah couldn't find the right toggle for a comm alert. "Probably the toilet overflowing again, or the fuel tank alarm. It's had a foot out the airlock for the last few trips. Let me just . . ."

The harsh chiming filled the cockpit as he scrambled to disable the alarm, refusing to meet anyone's eye when the noise finally stopped. Coy was positive they were only humoring him by not complaining. To be honest, he didn't know what had gotten into him when he volunteered—the *Harvest* wasn't a particularly fast ship, or a stealthy ship. He should've just kept his mouth shut and prepared to head home. That would've been smart. But for some reason, when the others had been making plans and discussing strategies, Coy had gotten this nagging feeling he was going to miss out on what his grandfather would call a life-rearranging opportunity. He had been a part of something, even if only for a couple of hours, and surprisingly, he didn't want that feeling to go away. So he'd opened his big fat mouth and volunteered his big fat ship. Now he was scrambling around like Aunt Melodina during First Bloom's tasting parties. It was a wonder they hadn't laughed him off the ship yet.

As if reading his mind, Jannah laughed softly. "I've been on older ships," she said. "This one is wonderful."

He glanced up at her, trying to determine if she was making fun of him. But she was reclined in the copilot's seat, one foot tucked beneath her, eyes on the streaming blue of hyperspace outside the *Harvest*'s viewport.

"Thanks," he finally said, collapsing into the pilot's seat after making sure it was clear of dust. "It's been in the family for generations. Pretty sure every Tria newborn has been flown in this to the hospital that doubles as a spaceport on my planet. My grandfather taught me to fly it, and I guess I'll teach someone to fly it when I have children. *If,* I mean. Not that I do. Or will. I want to. Not yet! But—" He cut himself off as Jannah smothered another laugh, but there was no malice in it, and he slowly grinned.

The alert chimed again and Coy sighed. He moved to flip the toggle to silence it, then paused. "This isn't the fuel tank," he said. "Or the toilet. This is the emergency channel."

Jannah looked up. "Proximity?"

He nodded as he rushed to switch the output to the cockpit speakers and cut off the alarm. Finn walked in at that moment, yawning.

"What's going on?" he asked.

"There's a distress call coming from somewhere close by," Coy said. He muttered under his breath as the communication panel blinked several times, then punched a few buttons and leaned back. "Playing it now."

A tinny voice echoed through the cabin. "—again if you . . . hear this, our ship . . . by pirates . . . and running out of oxygen. Please . . . need help."

The message looped two more times before Coy leaned forward and shut it off. Silence filled the cockpit as the three looked at each other, and then he licked his lips and adjusted a valve on his respi-vap. Suddenly it was getting harder and harder to breathe.

"We have to help, right?" Coy asked.

Jannah and Finn glanced at each other. Jannah raised an eyebrow, and Finn nodded. Coy gulped as Jannah straightened up in the copilot's seat and Finn leaned over the controls.

"Can you locate the source of that distress call?" he asked.

"I think so," Coy said. He tapped in a set of commands, then brought up the results on the display. "Here it is. The *Oasis*. Mining vessel."

Finn clapped him on the back. "Good man. Reset coordinates and let's loop back around and take a peek. Drop us out of hyperspace early to make sure no more *pirates* are lying around waiting."

"I can do that," Coy said.

"Do what?"

They looked up to see Niila in the cockpit hatchway. She'd changed into a clean pair of overalls and a spare shirt Coy kept for emergencies. Guess this was technically an emergency. She'd rolled up the sleeves of the shirt and tied the shoulder loops on the overalls like a belt around her midriff, and Coy felt his face redden when she saw him and smiled. *We're still on a mission, Tria,* he thought.

"Thanks for the change," she said, and Coy ducked his head, shaking it furiously.

"Of course, no problem, I've got more. Not here, but they're . . . well, I've got them."

But she'd turned back to Finn. "What are we doing?" she asked.

"Distress call," he said, nodding at the display. "Going to check it out."

Niila frowned, glancing at Coy. "But what about Major Gohl? Shouldn't we let nothing get in our way to stop him? Every second we lose is a second that he can use to get away!"

"Trust me," Finn said, "I want to find him just as badly as you do. But we can't let innocent people suffer if we can help them. Once we start doing that, we're doing Gohl's job for him."

"And whatever he's planning will be done by the time we get there if we stop!" Niila stared around the cockpit, then took a deep breath. "Sorry, it's just . . . I can't rest and act like everything's normal when I know there are more of us out there, maybe in even worse shape than we were on that disgusting shuttle, being herded to the stars know where just to satisfy that madman's desire!"

She broke off, chest heaving, cheeks flushed. Jannah

opened her mouth to respond, but surprisingly it was Coy who spoke first.

"Through the cracks."

Everyone turned to look at him, and he flushed, but he continued to speak, keeping his eyes on Niila.

"This is how it starts. That's what my grandfather always said. Once you let someone fall through the cracks, it gets easier and easier to do it again."

Jannah nodded, a smile ghosting across her face. "Your grandfather sounds pretty wise."

Coy shrugged, hiding the rush of pride he felt at her words. "I guess so, yeah."

It looked like Niila wanted to continue to argue, but the *Harvest* dropped out of hyperspace and she bit her tongue and nodded as the others gathered around the viewport. The streaming blue and white faded to the black of space and the stars within. A small emerald-green-and-white planet hung in the distance, two moons chasing each other in its orbit.

"Looks like the distress call came from the other side of the planet," Coy said, studying the display.

Finn nodded. "Loop around the back, and let's make sure no one's lying in wait."

Jannah left for a brief moment and then rejoined them, her bow on her back and her hair under a fresh scarf. She and Niila watched as Coy guided the *Harvest* on a wide path that would keep them at a safe distance from the planet and its moons while also allowing a thorough search to be performed.

But no matter their search pattern or duration, they didn't find the *Oasis*. Not on the larger moon and not on the planet, not as far as the scans could tell. The distress beacon was still active, but so far nothing they'd seen indicated that there was someone out there who needed—

"There!" Coy shouted. He stabbed a finger at the display, then at the surface of the smaller moon and a dark spot located just below the equator. "That's got to be it, right?"

They all fell silent as the *Harvest* flew closer. The old ship punched through the weak atmosphere and curved down to the moon. Blue-green ice covered much of the surface, while huge mounds of ice and snow sparkled like mountains of precious gems in the light of the distant sun. It was harsh yet beautiful.

The console chimed as a more thorough scan finished and an external damage report started generating on the screen. Coy winced as he read the data aloud.

"It's a merchant freighter. That's the *Oasis*, all right. Two crew members and four droids aboard. Emergency beacon has been active for over thirty hours now. The life support system . . ." He frowned. Stopping had *definitely* been the right call. "The ship is leaking atmosphere like a battle-drunk droid warrior leaking oil."

Finn tapped the screen. "Probably because of the giant hole punched through the rear of their hull."

"Whoever that is," Coy said quietly, "they need our help. We've got an emergency patch system and several relay droids in a repurposed missile launcher. We probably shouldn't take anyone with us to . . . to find the major, but we can get their life support back up and then launch a droid to the nearest comms buoy and get help here quicker." He looked up, suddenly realizing that he was making plans for generals of the Resistance. What was he thinking?

But Finn and Jannah were nodding along as if they agreed. Niila still looked uncomfortable with the delay, but she forced a smile and nodded, as well. Still, Coy hesitated.

"This is just something we, me and my grandfather, cobbled together in case of emergencies," he muttered. "I'm sure—"

"It's a good plan," Jannah said, smiling. "Take us through this patch system again."

Finn anchored the final corner of the patch system, then waved his hand. Coy gave him a thumbs-up, then turned on the small generator they'd bolted to the outside of the *Oasis*, fastening it to a bare section of the hull. The machine rumbled to life, and fragments of semitransparent rock skittered across the moon's surface.

The patch system expanded into a semirigid membrane, like a giant balloon, across the hole in the ship. It was basically a larger version of the respi-vap Coy wore on his hip, preventing harmful particulates from clogging his filters while also keeping the interior where it belonged . . . on the interior. When it was finished, there would be two entrances connected by a tunnel, like a portable airlock. Coy made sure the seams were completely sealed, then slipped inside and double-checked there, as well. He glanced at the readout on his wrist, then pulled off his helmet and took a deep breath.

"All clear inside the patch," he said into his comm. "Checking the interior of the ship."

"Roger that," Finn replied.

It had taken them several hours to repair the *Oasis*. The moon, which Coy had taken to calling Celadon because of its unique color, didn't make things easier. Its surface was hard and sharp, easily ripping into fabric and softer materials if he wasn't careful. But they were finally done, and he slipped inside the second patch entrance into the ship, where Jannah and Niila had already taken off their helmets and were treating the two passengers.

"Shock and low oxygen levels mostly," Jannah said as he approached. "Both of them, though the younger one seems to be the worst affected."

The owner, a Twi'lek male with drooping eyes, thanked them over and over as he held the hand of his young daughter, to whom Niila was slowly administering a medpac. "You've saved us," he kept whispering, his voice hoarse from hours of not using it. "You've saved us."

Finn entered and held up a scanner. "Relay droid away. Should make contact with the comms buoy within a couple hours. From there, a rescue tug should be out to collect you and the *Oasis* and take you home."

The Twi'lek nodded, his eyes dropping to his daughter. "She wanted to bring some of the moon to her mother. She's been so sick. She thought the beauty would cheer her up. But I misjudged. It's my fault. It's—"

"Shhh," Jannah said, reapplying a medpac as Niila positioned the younger Twi'lek in her father's arms. The two rested as Coy followed Finn out into the patch.

"Will they be okay?" he asked.

Finn nodded. "We'll swing by again when we're done with the major, but I suspect they'll be picked up before we even reach the Sardich system."

Niila and Jannah exited, and all four returned to the

Harvest, stripping off their gear and preparing for takeoff. As Finn and Jannah discussed increasing droid efforts in the Resistance rescue sweeps for situations like this, Coy dropped into the pilot's seat and began running through his preflight checks. Someone moved into the seat beside him, and he assumed it was Jannah, only to pause when Niila put a hand on his.

"You were right," she said.

He was so flustered from her touch that it took him a second to parse what she'd said. "What?" he asked.

"About falling through the cracks." Niila sat back and chewed her lip as she stared at the *Oasis*'s damage readout, still on the screen in front of her. "It was a good thing we stopped."

"Oh. Well." He hesitated, then shrugged. "You can thank my grandfather for that."

"You're so dismissive of yourself. We'll have to fix that. Your grandfather didn't do this. You did. So thank *you*." She squeezed his arm quickly, then let go and hugged her knees to her chest. "Sometimes I get so caught up in finding the people who hurt my family that I forget other people out there are hurting, too. I won't forget that again."

Coy glanced at her, then looked away. "You're welcome," he said quietly. Then: "Ready for takeoff."

The *Harvest* rose into space, leaving the jeweled moon behind, and seconds later, blasted back out of its atmosphere.

Other people are *hurting,* he thought. *Maybe this is why Grandfather wanted me to join the Resistance. To see that there's more at stake than just a successful harvest.*

Coy thought about that for a few seconds as he engaged the *Harvest*'s hyperdrive. Then he sighed.

I hope you know what you're doing, Coy Tria.

CHPTR - 19

I'm not alone.

That was the first thought in FN-2187's head when he came to his senses. The second thought was a little less dramatic but equally important in his estimation.

Everything hurts.

Keeping the first thought in mind while trying to take care of the second, he gingerly lifted himself from his face-down position on the rocky floor of the cave and surveyed his surroundings. He'd landed just past the lip of the cave. His blaster rifle was on the floor a meter away, and the flood of comfort he got when he picked it up and squeezed it to his chest was embarrassing.

Good thing Fifty-Five wasn't here to see that, he thought.

Lights flickered where they'd been hastily mounted, and more metal scaffolding and beams had been installed to reinforce the sloping ceilings and slick walls. From the reflected light, Eight-Seven took stock of everything inside the cave and swallowed nervously.

It looked like a smuggler's hideout.

It also looked like a battle had taken place.

Scorch marks covered everything, and a distinct odor of charred metal wafted through his helmet's filters. Eight-Seven pressed himself against a stack of three barrel containers and glanced around. No one immediately in sight. But several large crates were lined up against the back wall of the cave, and all of them had been opened. He was willing to bet those were the supplies Major Gohl was looking for. The major wouldn't be happy that the contents were gone.

Stacks of smaller boxes and cartons stood with no particular organization throughout the cave, like a small forest, and many of them had been covered with camouflage netting. Eight-Seven stood, then frowned as he realized that the cave was deep enough to land a small ship in, and in fact he could see an area off to his left that had been kept clear for takeoff and landing. He prepared to flag it and call FO-7155 to tell him not to worry about the load lifters, just to send the carrier, when he heard a noise.

Right, I'm not alone.

Something buzzed back near the large supply crates. Eight-Seven hefted his blaster rifle, luckily undamaged in the fall, and crept forward. A shadow slipped across the ground to his left and he froze. He couldn't hear any footsteps. No chatter, either. Whoever it was, they were either extremely cautious or completely oblivious. He hoped for the latter and prepared for the former.

The buzzing grew louder as he kept to cover, moving from stack to stack swiftly and keeping his eye aimed down the sight of his blaster. Something thumped to his right and he froze. Held his breath. The buzzing never stopped, and after a moment he continued. A three-stack-wide tower was the last bit of cover before the open space in front of Major Gohl's supply containers, and he paused, took a deep breath, and stepped around, finger on the trigger.

"This is the First Order," he shouted. "Nobody—"

Three spherical droids, about half a meter in diameter, rotated to face him where they hovered in midair. Their photoreceptors focused on him, and ports that looked suspiciously like the barrels of blasters slid open near the bottom of their frames.

Marksman-X combat remotes.

"—move," he finished.

The droids fired, and Eight-Seven dove back behind the stack of crates. Blaster fire ricocheted off the rocky floor and left smoldering scorch marks centimeters away from his boots. He hastily pulled them closer to his body, then levered himself up. He peeked around and fired off a shot that sent a droid spinning away, then yanked his head back out of the return fire.

"Guess that explains the other damage," he muttered to himself. He keyed his comm and huddled over, occasionally returning fire as he hailed the shuttle. "FO-Seventy-One-Fifty-Five, this is FN-Two-One-Eight-Seven. Do you read me? I said this is FN-Two-One-Eight-Seven. Do you—"

"Yes, I read you. I heard shots. Are you okay? Is it the smugglers?"

"No, no smugglers, just—"

"Some other locals?"

"No!"

"Then what are you doing down there, fighting the flowers?" Fifty-Five's voice sounded amused. Way different than the scared cadet from earlier.

"Never mind that. Just send the carrier to the location I'm sending you." Eight-Seven marked the clear area of the cave, then whipped around and fired several shots at a remote that was getting too curious for his comfort.

"Copy that. And how many load lifters?"

"None. Repeat, no load lifters. The supply containers are empty. They're empty! Somebody got here first."

Silence fell, during which Eight-Seven managed to tuck and roll across the cave floor, slide up against an overturned barrel, and let off a three-round burst that sent a remote spinning into a stalagmite. He grinned, then yelped as the third remote flanked him.

"Fifty-Five!" he shouted.

The remote whined, and the end of its barrel began to glow fiery red.

"Oh, you Hutt-humping lodaworm," he muttered, and dove aside. The remote fired, and the crate Eight-Seven had crawled behind crumpled into plasteel shards.

"Anytime now!"

The remote began to charge up again. Eight-Seven was out of nearby cover options. Only empty space remained between him and the remote. He rolled, firing off shot after shot as the remote answered fire with blasts that took divots out of the rock. If one of those hit his already damaged armor, he'd be at best making a date with a bacta tank and at worst . . . well, 7155 wouldn't have to worry about squad leader competition, after all.

A one-in-a-million shot tore the blaster from his hands, and he yelped. He tried to reach for it, only to recoil when a scatter of shots pelted the ground centimeters from his hand. He was defenseless.

The remote charged up, and Eight-Seven winced.

A single shot fired.

After several seconds, he opened his eyes. The remote lay on the ground in front of him, shattered into several smoking pieces.

Fifty-Five stood on the deck near the controls of the short-range cargo carrier, shaking his head. He hopped from the hovering vehicle to the cave and walked over.

"That shuttle has one good flight left before it falls apart. Didn't want to leave you stranded." He held out an arm, and Eight-Seven sighed and took it.

"You don't tell anyone about begging the droid to spare me," he said, "and I'll forget all about your claustrophobia."

Fifty-Five cocked his head. "What claustrophobia?" he asked.

"Exactly," Eight-Seven said, nodding. "Now come on. Let's report back to Major Gohl and finish this."

"Go ahead. I want to see the containers we flew all this way for."

Eight-Seven shrugged, then slowly made his way to the hover carrier. He groaned as he hopped on board, stretching out a leg that had become cramped from one of his maneuvers.

Maybe it was the tuck and roll. Or the sliding dive. Neither of those were standard moves the trainers encouraged. He was in the middle of checking the damage on his armor when 7155 hopped on board and began to guide the carrier out of the canyon and up into the still-raging storm. They got off, sent the carrier on its way, then hurried through the rain and up the shuttle ramp, kicking out the stray wildlife that had taken shelter inside, and began takeoff procedures to return to the *Loxodonta*. Fifty-Five was right: The shuttle was flashing so many warning lights it was hard to focus. Hopefully they didn't come apart in atmosphere.

"Did you look inside the containers?" 7155 asked suddenly.

Eight-Seven glanced at him from the pilot's seat (he'd rushed to claim it, only to find autopilot still engaged) and shook his head. "No. I thought they were empty?"

But 7155 didn't answer. Not right away. It wasn't until they were punching through Tamo'Akora's atmosphere and nearly at the *Loxodonta* that he spoke again.

"I did."

Eight-Seven looked up from monitoring the autopilot's landing routine. "What?"

"I looked in the containers. Back in the cave." Fifty-Five looked up from the copilot's seat, where he'd been brooding the whole journey.

"And?" Eight-Seven went back to the controls. "What'd you see?"

Just then, the automated voice of the *Loxodonta*'s navigation control crackled through the speakers. Eight-Seven grinned as he punched in the access code and slowly took the shuttle in. This was where he was supposed to be. Squad leader was fine, but being a trusted member of a high-ranking officer's security detail? Top class. He'd see things, go places, and meet people far above his security clearance. Rub shoulders with important decision-makers.

As the shuttle began docking procedures amid the chatter of the autopilot and the hum of the engines, and as the pale blue glow of the *Loxodonta*'s atmospheric shields spilled over the inner pressurized cargo bays, Eight-Seven was lost in the activity of shepherding Major Gohl to the medbay. It wasn't until much later, when he was tucked in his temporary sleeping berth in one of the cargo ship's many bunks, and just before he drifted off to sleep, that Eight-Seven remembered 7155 had never answered the question.

What had he seen inside those containers?

CHPTR - 20

Rive was tidally locked to the planet it orbited, which meant one side was always facing it, the other eternally hidden. The Galactic Bazaar, however, stretched into a terminator zone, a middle ground between the two that also served as a temperate refuge from the brutally hot days and the chilling nights. The size of the complex and the credits necessary to maintain it were a testament to the wealth it generated. The main attractions—gladiator duels, something called orbak racing, and many more extravagant competitions—took place in the heart of the Bazaar, where moderate temperatures allowed the Rive elite to mingle in comfort. This zone included the Plaza Solarity, where Company 77 had landed, and the Grand Prism, the dome TZ-1719 and her squad currently aimed for.

As they pressed through the crowd, ignoring the glares and scowls and brandishing their batons at the more overt displays of hostility, the city reminded 1719 of Hadne 3. Not in style, or even looks really. Where Hadne 3 mostly consisted of garden palaces and water features, glamorous and extravagant fountains with rare plants and flowers floating in the middle, Rive was a city of glass and metal. Statues and art fixtures that gleamed in the morning and twinkled at night. Buildings rimmed in silver or capped in gold, or one of several other precious metals brought up from the planet by the Rive Collective.

Was it functional? No. It was pretty, and that apparently was important enough. And that was where the similarity appeared. Both Hadne 3 and Rive spent extravagant amounts of credits on the grandiose displays, the unnecessary features. And 1719 figured that was what struck her as odd—one paid obscene amounts to keep visitors away, the other to bring outsiders and tourism in, and yet both seemed . . . *unnecessary*.

"Careful, boss." Clamps's warning brought 1719 out of her thoughts. They were nearly at the doors of the Grand Prism. This close to the subjects of their ire, the crowds in front of them had grown increasingly agitated. The shouting was more personal, the shoving more aggressive.

"Shields," she said.

A young man in miner's coveralls with a bandanna tied around his head shoved his way to stand in front of 1719, blocking her path to the doors.

"Stand aside," she ordered.

"You scurry at their beck and call, buckethead?" He practically spat the words out as he folded his arms. A young boy ran to his side and mimicked his stance. "They got you on their payroll, too, just like all the administrators. No credits to pay for the hell we dig in or to replace the trash they give us and call it tools, but they can transfer some money and get a standing army? Or they can pay a circus to come and entertain their mistresses? Well I say we've had it! We're tired of being shuttled around like cargo. We have families we haven't seen in months, and now they won't pay to keep us safe?"

"NO!" the boy shouted.

The miner raised a fist. "No more!"

The crowd, who'd quieted some to hear the confrontation, roared their agreement. More shoving, more shouted insults. 1719 curled her fist around the handle of her Z6, then let the baton go. Once fighting began, there'd be no stopping it. Not with the ugly mood that currently hung in the air, hot and thick. And if violence was to break out, she didn't want to be the one who started it. Especially not with the lieutenant breathing down her neck.

So she took a deep breath, then pointed at the young miner. "What are your demands?" she asked.

The question seemed to take him by surprise. "What?"

"You didn't set up out here just to hear yourself scream. What do you want? Or do you just like the sound of your voice?"

He flushed. "We have demands. Lots of them."

"Are you in charge?"

"I don't know if I—"

"Someone has to be in charge. Or is everyone in the plaza going to march inside and start shouting at once?"

Someone behind him nudged him, nodding their head. "Go ahead, Vilo."

The miner, Vilo, glanced around, then straightened. "Fine. I'll be the voice."

1719 nodded, trying to stand at ease while inside her armor, her heart pumping so fast and loud she was sure everyone else could hear it. She licked her lips and tried to emulate Phasma again. "Be more than that. Be realistic. The Collective doesn't deal well with threats and intimidation. That's when they call us. But negotiation? They understand negotiation. But the first step in any negotiation is to present what you want, knowing that all of your demands might not be met."

She couldn't believe channeling Phasma actually seemed to be working. The crowd immediately around her squad had grown quiet again, listening to the exchange. The young miner's expression had changed from fury to consideration. The shoving had lessened, and she could feel Clamps relaxing slightly beside her.

And that was when the lieutenant struck.

With a speed that startled even 1719, Shroud lunged forward, shoving the miner back into his peers and snatching the young boy by his collar. Before the crowd could react, her Z6 was activated, the pulsing vanes at the end of the baton crackling with its electric current.

"Vilo!" the boy shouted.

"Manny!" Vilo's face twisted with fury as he turned on the lieutenant. "You backstabbing bucket—"

"Now, now," Shroud said, bringing the humming vanes of the Z6 closer to Manny's neck. "This is a negotiation, right? So here's *my* demand. We're going in, getting the city admins out, and we're going to exit the plaza without a care in the world."

"You Hutt-spawned piece of—"

"And," she said, leaning forward, "we're going to do that

because young Manny here will be coming with us. Call it . . . your part in the negotiations. Now. Do we have an agreement?"

1719 glanced behind her. The crowd had gone silent, but the tension was so thick she could feel it pressing down on her. Clamps had his own baton half drawn, and Twelve and TZ-214 had pivoted so that no squad member's back was exposed. 1719 was proud but also furious.

Lieutenant Shroud lifted the Z6 even higher so everyone could see it dangling just above Manny's head. "I said, do we have an agreement?"

Vilo stared at her, teeth gritted and hands clenching and unclenching, but eventually his shoulders slumped. "You're just another bureaucrat using us to get what you want."

"Bureaucrats are like scav rats," Shroud said, "and the only good scav rat is a dead scav rat. But I have my job and you have yours. So. Do we have an agreement? Last chance."

The two stared at each other, but it was Vilo who looked away first.

"Get your leeches out of there. But if you hurt him, if even one hair is out of place, we will tear this city apart, stone by scummy polished stone."

The lieutenant's eyes twinkled. "Oh, never fear. Consider it a field trip! Manny will have the time of his *life*." With that, she backed up, tapping on the glass of the Prism's doors until they were opened.

Vilo turned to 1719, his eyes filled with hatred. Hatred and disgust.

"Squad," was all she could say in reply, and then she turned and went inside as her team followed, her own fists clenched.

Her headache was back.

1719 shoved through the Prism's interior doors. "Lieutenant?"

They'd followed the officer into the grand foyer of the Prism, and somewhere in the back of her mind, 1719 could appreciate the consistency of the Rive Collective. If there was a way their wealth could be displayed, they had done their very best to find and exploit it. From the vintage bottles of wine imported at great cost to the exotic appetizers 1719 was pretty sure were still moving on the iridescent pearl platters. It was hard to keep focused, because every step farther inside was designed to attract attention. Even the walls were lined with so much glass and silver, she caught distorted reflections in the corner of her eye.

The center of the grand foyer was dominated by multiple giant sculptures, cleverly constructed out of steel and ice.

They were sleds, 1719 realized, giant sleds pulled by frozen sculptures of the orbak creatures they'd seen outside, with sculpted piles of ore and minerals colored and polished to resemble the real thing heaped in the back.

A tribute to the ore haulers of old, the giant plaque floating in the center above the sculptures read.

"I always wanted to go sledding," Clamps muttered.

"Looks like they still work," Twelve said. "Maybe there's a tour around here we can visit."

"Cut the chatter," 1719 said. "We have a job to do."

The Prism was actually an egg-shaped building dotted with hundreds of skylights so that when the light of the sun or the moon glanced off of it at an angle, a kaleidoscope of colors bathed the Plaza Solarity. And while the top of the Prism curved brilliantly upward in the center of the plaza, the bottom half extended underground. The builders had carved deep into the surface of the moon, excavating a large chamber unlike any other, and they called it the Gravitorium. Visitors entered on the ground floor, which was technically the structure's equator, and either traveled up or down along the curving interior wall to their seats. From there they could observe one or all three performance rings that floated up from below, powered by repulsorlifts, along with the different set designs and props that were needed. From heart-pounding orbak races to death-defying gravobatics, the Galactic Bazaar had pulled out all the stops to entertain its wealthy clientele.

Their job could have been made even easier were this a normal evening. All of Rive's elite appeared to be in attendance, the opportunity to show off, network, or just be seen too powerful to resist. In fact, she realized Twelve's scanning protocol might have identified the members of the Jaliss Group in under a minute, leaving them the rest of the night to determine the extent of the group's connection to the Xen Runners. Unfortunately for them, the demonstration outside must have started midshow, cutting the event short and throwing a spanner into the works. Now chaos ruled, parties had scattered, and 1719's job was infinitely harder.

A chorus of screams cut into her thoughts.

Two of the three circus rings in the Gravitorium were still hovering in the center of the dome, while the third had begun to list wildly. Two orbaks snorted and tossed their heads as they stamped back and forth on the nearest ring. They were stuck in midair. The rest of the circus performers were all huddled on the main floor, trying to get the emergency cables to release as the orbak handlers tried—unsuccessfully—to coax the riderless beasts to safety.

1719 wanted to press on her temples amid the confusion. Nothing was going right. But she inhaled, spared one glance to take all of it in, then continued pushing her way through onlookers crowded near the entrance, following her superior. "Lieutenant?"

Lieutenant Shroud stalked forward, one hand clasped around the miner boy's wrist, the other stabbing with the baton at clusters of guests milling around in robes that probably cost more than the shuttle the stormtroopers had arrived in.

"I want teams of two escorting each group of VIPs out the back and toward the eastern entrance to the plaza. More troopers will be waiting. Secure the VIPs, lead the reinforcements back, repeat until everyone is secure."

"Lieutenant?" 1719 asked again.

Shroud glanced at her. "Not now, trooper. Unless the dome is collapsing, you've got your assignment. Get them out of here."

1719 slammed her shield down on the floor in frustration. "But, Lieutenant! Snatching the child?" she asked. She barely, just barely, managed to keep any anger or insolence out of her voice, but Shroud still lifted one eyebrow in reproach.

"I'll forgive the insubordination this time, TZ-One-Seven-One-Nine. Your adrenaline is spiking. But I did what was necessary. You managed to calm the rioters down, and I merely extended our advantage."

"But taking the boy like that—"

"The younger *rioter* is just a precaution, something to ensure our mission is completed." Shroud still held Manny by the collar of his shirt, and 1719 couldn't help staring at the defiance warring with fear on his tear-stained face. "And that's what we will do. Because that's our job—completing our mission. Or have you forgotten?"

1719 struggled to keep the anger out of her response. "Yes, Lieutenant."

"Good." Shroud pushed the boy toward Clamps, who grabbed him almost out of reflex. "You. Keep him on ice until we've secured all VIPs and transported them to a safe zone. If I learn he was prematurely released, even if he accidentally escaped, I will have you strung up in front of a court-martial so fast the medical bay will be treating you for whiplash. And I *will* be pushing for decimation, soldier."

Her eyes burned into Clamps, then the rest before she finally turned on 1719. When she was satisfied, she nodded. "The rest of you, pair up and perform sweeps. The sooner we grab them all, the sooner we can get the plaza cleared and any troublemakers dispersed."

The lieutenant stalked away, snapping orders and directing traffic, leaving 1719 staring after her in frustration. When she turned around, the rest of her squad milled about in quiet tension. Finally, Clamps broke the silence.

"I don't like it, boss," he spoke aloud. There was enough noise that his words were lost to anyone who wasn't standing within a meter of them, and using their private comm channel was too risky. Who knew if the lieutenant was listening?

"It's fine," 1719 finally said. She pointed at the nearest cluster of attendees still in their seats, many of them yelling into their own communicators for help, or to complain, or both. "Grab them. Let's go."

"Not talking about the VIPs. I'm talking about the kid."

Twelve shuffled his feet, unsure as he glanced around. "Is . . . is this allowed? Taking him like that?"

"Just keep on the scanning protocol," 1719 said. "A lot of guests scattered, but we might get lucky and get a hit. Soon as we can get them out, we can try and dig up some info in the confusion."

214 was on one knee, checking over Manny, and the boy was nodding as she murmured something.

"Is what allowed?" Clamps asked. "Kidnapping? Probably not, but who's going to tell her? I'm telling you, boss, I don't like it. We never should have joined up with this group."

"Did we have a choice, Clamps?" 1719 could feel the tension in her head swelling. She was coming apart again, cracking under the pressure. She knew he was right, knew this was her fault, that she had to make sure Manny got out of this unscathed. That they all made it out of this. It was just one more thing to take care of, one more thing to navigate, one more trap waiting to spring shut on her hand if she wasn't careful, and she was always trying to be careful, always trying to care, always trying—

"HEY!"

1719 whirled around to see Manny sprinting away and 214 hopping up and down in pain. "He has nails in his shoes or something!" she shouted. "They got through my boots!"

She swore under her breath. "Stay here," 1719 commanded.

"Boss!" Clamps shouted. "What about the lieutenant?"

"I'll take care of her. Just keep scanning! And get those VIPs out!"

With that, she tore off after the kid.

CHPTR - 21

FN-2187 woke, scrambling for his blaster. Something had dragged him from his sleep, some noise or disturbance or alarm that put him on high alert. He rolled off the bed, toggled the glow rod on his blaster, and swept the cone of light across the room.

Nothing.

Why was his heart racing? What had startled him awake? He could hear his breath echoing as he reached for his helmet and could feel his heart beating through his armor. He took a couple of deep breaths, steadying his nerves and his aim, as he continued to search the bunk. Where was his helmet?

"Fifty-Five, wake up. Something's wrong." Eight-Seven

kept low as he worked his way backward, keeping the berth he'd been sleeping in between him and the door. Unwilling to turn on more lights, he finally gave up on his search and forced himself to take several deep breaths. Panic wouldn't help anyone at the moment.

The *Loxodonta*'s bunk rooms were laid out with rows of sleeping berths stacked in threes and storage units lining the walls. The night before, after taking an unconscious Major Gohl to the medical bay and transmitting an incident report, Eight-Seven and FO-7155 had crashed in the first bunks they'd found. The astromech units in the hangar would take at least a day to repair the damage done to the shuttle, and they'd both looked forward to some rest.

Speaking of which: "Come on, wake up," Eight-Seven said, reaching back to shake 7155 while still keeping an eye on the door. Only . . . no one was in the berth.

Eight-Seven turned and ran the glow rod over the empty bed, then muttered a curse. Where had the boy gone? To the hangar to check on the ship? To check on the major? That was a terrible idea. Maybe he couldn't sleep and was wandering the *Loxodonta*, which was an even worse idea, since the major had explicitly warned them about exploring where they shouldn't. For a few seconds, Eight-Seven thought about letting 7155 get into trouble on his own. It would serve him right.

He sighed. Except they were supposed to be working together, and if one of them failed in some way, the major had made it clear that the other wouldn't survive the fallout. Which meant, unfortunately, Eight-Seven had to break the same rules to find 7155 and bring him back before they were discovered.

"This is why I wanted to be a mountain trooper," he grumbled as he crept toward the door, peeked out, and then plunged into the darkness outside.

Once in the corridor, it was hard for Eight-Seven *not* to find possible culprits for what had woken him up. The *Loxodonta* was an old ship, and whoever the owners were, it had been poorly maintained. The metal floors creaked, and the fabricated walls rattled if someone stepped too hard in random spots. Lights flickered, sending shadows rippling and flitting across the stacks of boxes and crates piled high in the walkways. Trash flew around whenever the feeble air scrubbers got their act together and forced air to recirculate as the vents coughed and choked.

It was *delightful*.

The blaster stayed glued to Eight-Seven's shoulder as he crept forward. The years of drills beaten into the cadets' heads made each room clearing a routine exercise, but rather than help him feel at ease, the lack of answers only confused him more. Where was 7155?

By the time he'd reached the end of the current deck, which terminated at a turbolift, the confusion had morphed into annoyance, then anger. Major Gohl was going to have them on janitor duty until they were using their blasters for canes. What was that boy thinking? And where could he be? If Eight-Seven was a giant meathead with no brains and a superior attitude, where would he go?

After a second, Eight-Seven snorted and stepped inside the turbolift, punching in a destination. Minutes later, the doors opened to the cargo bay. He swept his glow rod around, checking for company, as he navigated toward the middle, trying to retrace his steps, until he finally came to a stop and stared. Warning bells were going off inside his head.

The doors to the restricted holds were open, and the turrets were offline.

I hate being right, he thought as he lifted the blaster and stepped into the one area that was supposed to be off-limits. *It's a curse. Why do I have this cursed ability to figure out where the problem is? Why can't I—*

A light flickered inside. There was someone ahead.

The restricted holds were connected to the general cargo bay by a single dimly lit corridor lined with noise-dampening panels. His footsteps made no sound, and he could make out towering shadows just beyond the exit ahead. Eight-Seven crept forward as electric-blue lighting washed over him. He slipped out into the hold, recognition twisting his lips as shadows resolved into crates similar to the ones on Tamo'Akora. He was debating whether or not to look inside when more light flickered ahead. Another glow rod. Eight-Seven swiftly cut off his own and ducked around the side of a container, pressing himself tight against it.

"Not here," someone said. A comlink crackled, but Eight-Seven couldn't make out the words, only the reply. "The senator needs to relax. Nothing can be traced back to her."

More chatter.

"Well, that's between her and the First Order, though I'm guessing they won't be happy with the senator's sudden reluctance. I really hope she's sure about this."

Whoever was on the other line had started to shout, and the intruder growled a warning.

"I'm just the messenger, and I'm about to deliver the message. The fallout is between the senator and everyone else. Got it? I'm going to do one more sweep, set the charges, then get out of here."

The voice was getting closer, the light accompanying it flooding the small hold. Eight-Seven was cut off now—if he tried to get back into the corridor, he'd be spotted. He squeezed the blaster in his hands. What should he do?

"No one's here," the voice said. "One of the loaders must have tripped it."

The speaker was just on the other side of Eight-Seven's hiding spot! If they looked to the right when walking out, he was going to be seen. What now? Panic? Of course, but he also had to do something productive. Could he bluff his way out of this? Pretend to be lost?

"Understood," the voice said. "On my way."

Eight-Seven closed his eyes. This was it.

Click.

A hand closed on his shoulder, yanking him backward *into the open container*! A gloved hand clapped over his mouth, and a familiar voice hissed in his ear.

"Shut up. Do you want to die?"

Fifty-Five stood behind him. The boy, like Eight-Seven, didn't have on his helmet or chest armor, and it was the first time his face was clearly visible. Dark hair, dark eyebrows that seemed permanently furrowed, and tanned skin that looked almost silver beneath the blue lighting. The boy was also completely made of muscles. His biceps had triceps, and his triceps had biceps. It was ridiculous.

"What do you do, eat your trainers?" Eight-Seven asked. He couldn't help it. Fifty-Five had more definition in his jaw than Eight-Seven had in any muscle group. Maybe Eight-Seven needed to do more push-ups.

"What?" 7155 glanced up. He was holding a datapad—where he got it from, who knew.

"Nothing."

"Can you be quiet for once? Listen."

The chatter of the intruder's comlink was fading. They must've entered the noise-canceling corridor. Fifty-Five held a finger to his mouth and pressed an ear to the container hatch. After a few seconds he relaxed and turned.

"What are you thinking? Are you trying to get us killed?"

Eight-Seven scoffed. "What am I thinking? What are you thinking?"

"What am I thinking?"

"What are *you* thinking? Breaking into the restricted hold. Do you want to get us court-martialed, or worse?'

Fifty-Five smirked. "One, I was securing the hold from an intruder. They disabled the security first."

"Securing the hold from inside of a container?"

"I had a plan."

"Right."

"Anyway, what about you? You're here against the major's orders, too!"

Eight-Seven threw up a hand in disbelief. "Because I was following you!"

"Aha!" Fifty-Five grinned and hefted his blaster over a shoulder. "So I am your leader."

"Oh, please, you couldn't lead a scav rat into a junk hole."

The blaster was off his shoulder now. "How about I shoot you in your junk hole?"

"How about you tell me why you're here in the first place, and why there's a senator looking for these supplies, and why this ship is going to be blown up with us on it if we don't hurry?"

The smirk finally disappeared from 7155's face, and he grew serious. He heaved a sigh and scratched his head. "The thing is, I'm not sure. Nothing makes sense! I couldn't sleep, so I went for a run and a quick workout—"

"Of course," Eight-Seven muttered.

"Shut up. I ended up near the secondary communications center and started digging through the logs. I didn't find much, but what I did find I transferred to this datapad to read. Apparently this ship was abandoned *years* ago. Something about the drive system being too dangerous, and rather than paying to get it fixed or even towed to a scrapyard, the owners just abandoned it. But there were some messages I found buried in old system files where normal scans wouldn't locate them. . . .

Someone's been using the *Loxodonta* as a drop point to offload or pick up goods. Two containers here, a shipment there. And then, a few months ago, everything goes dark except for a couple of system notifications about security measures."

Eight-Seven squatted down and scratched his head. "And now there's a senator who's backing out of a deal with the First Order. With the major?"

Fifty-Five shrugged. "I don't know. I *do* know we don't want to be here when those charges go off. Come on."

"Aht-aht, me first. I'm the leader this time." Eight-Seven rushed out, cutting off 7155 and beating the bigger boy to the soundproof corridor. Which, it turned out, was perfect since he could jog backward and watch the boy yell at him and not hear a single word. He cupped a hand to an ear, feigning confusion, and laughed as 7155 pointed angrily at him.

No.

Behind him.

He stumbled out of the corridor, and his hearing returned, just in time to hear the whine of a blaster pistol as the end was pressed against his temple.

"What have we here," the owner said. The voice from the restricted hold. "A couple of First Order grunts on vacation? Drop the blaster, nice and easy. Come on out of there!"

Eight-Seven couldn't see the person currently holding

him hostage, but he could see 7155 crouched in the tunnel, blaster trained on the intruder.

"I will not ask again," the intruder said. The barrel of the blaster pressed harder against Eight-Seven's skin. "The Order will need another grunt soon."

"He can't hear you," Eight-Seven squeezed out against the pain, making sure his hands were raised and in plain view.

"*Tch.* The soundproofing. Thought I disabled that."

"No, sir. Ma'am. Person."

The intruder tapped the pistol as if they were thinking. "I hate killing kids, but there's no other—"

Light flashed.

Heat scorched Eight-Seven's head, and he dropped to the ground, reeling as he shouted in pain. Somehow he managed to turn his fall into a roll, scrambling along the ground to get to cover while clutching the right sight of his skull.

He wasn't the only one suffering.

The intruder was screaming as they dropped to the floor and scrambled to find cover, too. From what Eight-Seven could see, they looked Kupohan, though he couldn't be sure. To be fair, the way they clutched their face and writhed in pain, the only thing they'd be looking for in the near future was a bacta tank.

More shots emerged from the corridor, and Eight-Seven

dug at his ears, trying to figure out why he couldn't hear them. But then, he could hear the Kupohan still screaming insults in their native tongue. So his ears were fine. Fifty-Five was still firing, but . . . wait, the soundproofing! It was muffling the noise. Only the tracers of light indicated he was shooting. Another three-round blast slammed into the container the intruder hid behind, and Eight-Seven took the opportunity to reach for his blaster, only to yank his hands away when a shot—one he could hear this time—ricocheted off the ground just in front of him. The Kupohan was glaring at him from one eye while crouching behind a binary load lifter. They raised the pistol again, and that's when Eight-Seven realized he was on the wrong side of cover and the Kupohan had a clean shot.

Blaster fire sprayed the cargo hold just as a trio of binary load lifters rammed into Eight-Seven and the container he crouched against, driving him ten meters before crashing into a wall.

Nothing moved . . . then:

"Are you dead?"

Eight-Seven groaned. Everything hurt.

"Is that a yes?"

Fifty-Five emerged from the secure corridor, glanced at the destruction, then stepped over Eight-Seven's twitching legs to make his way to the Kupohan. The intruder was . . . well, he wouldn't be shooting at them anymore. Actually, from the scattered position of his limbs, he wouldn't be doing much of anything anymore.

"I wonder if he was having a good day before this."

Eight-Seven snorted from his position face down on the floor. Then, to his surprise, he was laughing. And 7155 was laughing, too, as he dropped to a seat nearby. It was only after several seconds, when they were both sniffing and wiping their eyes, that Eight-Seven frowned.

"Are you going to help me free myself?"

Fifty-Five smiled. "Not until you admit I'm the leader and you're a follower."

"Oh, come on."

"Nope, that's the deal."

"What would the major say if he knew one of his subordinates was a power-hungry dictator?"

A cold voice cut through the cargo bay. "He would congratulate that subordinate before sending their bloated corpse out of an airlock. He has no use for mindless ambition."

Major Gohl stood in the middle of the cargo bay, a bandage wrapped around his forehead. One arm was up in a sling, and the other clutched a small blaster pistol pointed in Eight-Seven's direction.

CHPTR - 22

Manny was fast.

"Twelve," TZ-1719 panted as she dodged rich and *very* upset patrons inside the Gravitorium. She could see the kid's dingy orange cape fluttering behind him as he hopped over rows of seats, heading upward. "Send the scanning protocol to my helmet."

"Boss, you sure?"

"I might as well have it running while I'm moving through the crowd."

"Roger that."

Clamps clicked on, the worry in his voice obvious even

as he feigned nonchalance. "Boss, I don't want to be court-martialed. It's bad for the skin."

"Get those VIPs out of here. That's all you need to worry about," 1719 said. She clicked off as she paused on top of a cushioned chair, searching the Gravitorium for Manny. There were fewer guests up here, so it was easy to spot the boy. Unfortunately, that didn't mean it would be easy to catch up to him.

She groaned.

"Boss?" Twelve asked. "Did you find him?"

1719 watched as Manny climbed onto one of the Gravitorium's support struts and shinnied out into space, aiming for the nearest still-operable circus ring and group of orbaks on top of it. "Unfortunately. You all keep working."

She dashed to the closest aisle and sprinted down, racing toward the circus staff beneath the rings. They'd finally gotten the cables to release, and 1719 shouldered by to grab one.

"Hey!" a uniformed Twi'lek shouted. "It's not stable! They can collapse any second!"

"Stand back," she ordered, then muttered a prayer under her breath and began to climb, hand over hand, sliding her feet up before pinching the cable between them for support. It reminded her of physical training back on the *Finalizer*. The obstacle course, the constant desire to be in the top ten, to gain Captain Phasma's approval. Back before the disaster during the Merchant Uprising. Back before the headaches. And the nightmares. She shook her head, realizing she was at the top of the cable, and she transferred her grip to the edge of the circus ring and pulled herself on top.

Manny stood with his back to her as he comforted the orbaks. They responded almost instantly. Too quickly, 1719 realized, as if they recognized him. As if he was an orbak handler, which meant . . .

"Hcy!" 1719 shouted. "Manny! Stay right there! Don't—"

His head whipped around, and his eyes widened in fear. He lunged for the reins, and 1719 swallowed a curse. The boy was up on the back of one of the orbaks in seconds, and the beast stamped once, then broke into a run straight at her.

At the last second she dove aside, rolling to her feet in a smooth motion to find Manny struggling to control the beast as it slowed to a stop near the edge of the ring. It reared once, twice, trying to throw him off as he shouted commands, but it was no use. He was too small and couldn't control it.

1719 keyed a command, switching her helmet speaker to broadcast. "Oy!" she shouted, her voice echoing. "Here! Here!"

The orbak shook its head at the command, digging with its hoof at the ring. It reared, skipped forward when it landed, then began to gallop toward her. She licked her lips. She had to time this just right.

The orbak was ten meters from her.

Captain Phasma's instructions rang in her ears. *Dislodge the rider, dispatch him, then take his vehicle. Three shots, three targets down. Now!*

Five meters.

Two.

She stepped right. The beast swung its tusks, trying to impale her, but that was what she was waiting for. She dodged left, then turned and sprinted alongside the orbak. She grabbed the tusk closest to her and used the beast's momentum to bounce off her feet and swing up onto its back behind Manny. The boy's eyes were closed as he hugged the orbak's neck, and she peeled the reins from his hands. He sagged back against her in relief as the beast began to slow from a gallop to a canter to a trot.

"I'm sorry," he whispered.

"That was very foolish," 1719 said. "You could have been hurt, or worse."

"I know. I just wanted to get to my brother."

"Vilo?" she asked, and when Manny nodded, she sighed. "Stay with us, let us do our job, and you and your brother will be fine. Now, let's get you—"

"Boss." Twelve's voice was sharp, almost excited. "We've got a hit."

1719 froze. "Go," she commanded.

"Northeast of you, in one of the box seats. The scanning protocol flagged . . . um, a high-priority VIP."

One of the Jaliss Group. Finally. 1719 wheeled the orbak around. The box seats sat midway up the Gravitorium. Bright silver and glass framed the hazy blue security shields that in turn enclosed groups of couches and divans. Motion fluttered behind one of the shields, and 1719 honed in on it.

"Got it," she said. "I need the codes to the shields, Twelve."

"On it."

Suddenly the orbak lurched beneath her. More screams echoed, and the circus ring surged upward by several meters. The orbak snorted and stamped. The other two rings were malfunctioning without the counterbalance of the third, and the repulsorlifts weren't enough to keep it steady. They would either fall into the side of the Gravitorium and slide gently down to the bottom, or they would rocket upward to smash into the seats above them.

The ring began to rise. The other orbaks chose that moment to leap to safety in the seats below, but 1719 had a different idea in mind.

"Hold on!" 1719 shouted, and she gripped Manny tight with one arm before snapping the reins. "GO!"

"HYAH!" Manny yelled, and the orbak responded, surging forward as the two clung desperately to its back. The ring had begun to rotate on its axis slowly, like a flipping coin, and they raced up along the perimeter of the high side. Another shudder from the repulsorlifts sent them rising again, and as they approached the top edge, the row of box seats appeared.

"Running out of time, Twelve!" she shouted. When Manny shot a fearful glance back at her, she pointed at the Jaliss Group's box and the gap between them and it. "We're going to have to jump!"

"But," he began, but she just whipped the reins faster.

"No time! Get this creature to jump!"

They were at the edge.

"HUP!" shouted Manny.

"TWELVE!" shouted 1719.

The orbak screamed a challenge but leaped into the air, black hooves stretched forward as the shielded box raced toward them.

A fraction of a second before impact, the semitransparent blue shield flickered, then died. The orbak crashed into a polyweave divan, smashing it to pieces as it slid across the floor, sending a group of tables covered in appetizers and wine glasses crashing. Paintings rattled against the wall, and silverware clattered on platters.

"Boss?"

Twelve's voice barely registered over 1719's heavy breathing. She gulped down a shuddering breath, then keyed her mic. "Here. Great timing."

"Do you see them? I can't get a read on who it is, but Clamps thinks it's one of the brothers who run the Jaliss Group. Vik, or maybe Tomas. And from the sound of your arrival, you might have to put on the charm. But you have to hurry—Twenty-One-Four says the lieutenant is looking for you."

"Understood," she said. She switched to her external speaker. "Hello? This is TZ-One-Seven-One-Nine, Company Seventy-Seven of the First Order stormtroopers, here to get you to safety. Is there anyone here?"

Silence. The orbak nickered, its attention preoccupied with the platter of vegetables overturned at its feet. Manny didn't seem to be in any hurry to get down. She guessed he'd learned his lesson trying to run the first time. She patted his shoulder to reassure him, then slid off the broad back of the orbak and patted its shoulder, as well.

"Hello?" she said again. Her boots crunched as she stepped into the center of the box.

Something squeaked.

She paused. Then she straightened and made sure to keep her hands away from her baton. An overturned couch rested against the far wall, just a pace or so away from where the orbak and Manny waited. She eased her way forward, careful to make no sudden movements. Keeping a good distance between herself and the end of the couch, she crouched down.

A young human woman—mid-teens, maybe Twelve's age—in an emerald dress crouched beneath the cushions, a small knife in one hand, the train of her dress clenched in the other. Tear tracks stained her face, though the blade she held didn't quiver at all when she sniffled. She tensed when 1719's helmet dropped into view.

"Twelve," 1719 muttered, sending her helmet's view to the team. "This doesn't look like Vik Jaliss."

"On it," came the reply. "One more second. Aaaaand . . . got it."

"Go."

"Endayi Jaliss, second daughter of Vik. Listed as a senior member of their community outreach and public relations team. And . . . oh. She's also the heiress to the Jaliss family fortune, including mineral rights and the Jaliss shipping fleet."

"Senior member?" 1719 muttered. "She's so young! She looks like Twelve."

"Twelve years old?" Clamps asked. "Like a junior cadet?"

"No, like she's Twelve's age, who's probably about to brain with you his baton for the misunderstanding."

"I was going to use the riot shield," Twelve interrupted.

"Got it. Both of you, stall the lieutenant for me while I figure this out."

"No promises."

"N.O.T."

1719 switched her comm again, making sure the external speaker's volume was dropped to a gentle level. The girl, Endayi, tensed as 1719 held up both hands to show they were empty.

"Endayi? I'm here to get you to safety."

The knife never shifted as the girl spoke for the first time. "Prove it."

"Prove it?"

"How do I know you're not a kidnapper, looking for ransom payments before you kill me and stuff my body in an alley or drop me out of a vehicle on the skyway?"

1719 hesitated. "I'd probably just feed you to the furry monster currently eating your plate."

She backed up, giving Endayi space to crawl out, which the girl eventually did, though she held the knife with an ease that made 1719 think she had some form of self-defense training. That training went out the window when she stood up and saw the orbak eating a fuzzy green appetizer that had spilled out of a bright golden bowl onto the floor. Manny waved sheepishly from his perch atop the animal.

"Oh," Endayi said, waving back in confusion. "Oh."

"Agreed," 1719 said. "Can we give you a ride to safety?"

The orbak snorted, then stamped, crushing a decorative melon carved to resemble the Gravitorium beneath its hoof before eating the rind.

"Or we can walk," 1719 added.

Endayi nodded quickly. "Walking sounds good."

"Boss," 214 said over the comm. "We have a problem."

"Lieutenant Shroud? I know, we're on our way back with—"

"No, it's worse. Shikra is attacking the demonstrators."

CHPTR - 23

"Tell me everything."

Major Gohl sat in the shuttle's pilot chair as if it was a throne, his spine stiff and the hand clutching his left side the only sign that he was suffering. His uniform jacket was draped over his left shoulder, as it had to be cut away to treat him, and his droid buzzed anxiously overhead, beeping with worry.

The shuttle was currently on a slow acceleration away from the *Loxodonta* to a destination that the major had keyed into the navicomputer in secret. From the man's grim expression and the way the hand still holding the blaster pistol didn't waver, there was no guarantee FN-2187 or FO-7155 would live to see where they ended up.

The two teens stared at each other, and then 7155 shrugged as if to say, *After you.* Eight-Seven glared at him but turned back to the major and cleared his throat.

"When I woke up," he started to say, but a twitch of the blaster pistol cut him off.

"Before that," the major said. "Start earlier."

"From the crash, sir?"

"How about the moment we arrived in-system, just to play it safe, hmm?"

Again, Eight-Seven glanced at his fellow trooper, then racked his brain. The major was clearly searching for something, something specific, but he didn't know what. He *did* know that he would be as thorough as possible in recounting whatever details he could remember, down to the most boring and minute ones.

"Well, once we approached the *Loxodonta* and docked, FO-Seventy-One-Fifty-Five and I began a preliminary sweep of the general cargo holds. We noticed that several of the binary load lifters . . ."

Eight-Seven swiftly recounted the events following the descent of the shuttle to Tamo'Akora and their crash, including the hidden supply outpost built beneath the planet's surface. Major Gohl watched, his face cold and emotionless, with only the flicker of an eyebrow serving as his reaction to the discovery of the powered supply crates.

"Were the containers unlocked?" he asked. "And did you look inside?"

There was something deceptively calm about the question, and warning bells began to nag at the back of Eight-Seven's mind. Still, he couldn't see what the major was angling toward, so he was about to respond when 7155 cut him off.

"No, sir," the boy said. "They were powered on and locked when we found them."

Luckily, Major Gohl wasn't looking at Eight-Seven, because his jaw immediately fell open. A lie. Fifty-Five had lied. Why? Telling the truth was basic trooper instruction, right after you learned how to salute and to never take off your helmet outside of approved scenarios. And 7155 knew that. He had to know that.

Major Gohl narrowed his eyes. "And yet somehow the containers in the restricted space were unlocked?"

Fifty-Five nodded. "My guess is the intruder, sir."

"The Kupohan." It took a second for Eight-Seven to realize he'd even spoken, that's how concerned he was about lying to the officer. Fifty-Five had to cough to alert him, and Eight-Seven flushed beneath his helmet as the major waited.

"Sorry, sir, I was saying the intruder was a Kupohan—I got a look at him before . . . well . . ."

"Before the load lifters turned him into an assortment of fluids and viscera," the major finished in a dry tone. The blaster disappeared with a flourish into a hidden holster in his uniform, and with it, so did some of Eight-Seven's tension. Was it over? Did they pass? The major sighed, then winced and smiled. Eight-Seven blinked. How could he just . . . turn off that cold-blooded personality like that?

"Well, boys," Major Gohl said, "you've had quite a training mission, haven't you? Your captains will hardly believe your transformation from bickering schoolyard hooligans to a coordinated bodyguard duo. You have my thanks. Without your quick thinking, we all might be drowning in the forever storms on Tamo'Akora. You did good."

The major stood with another wince, and both boys came to attention, saluting even as Major Gohl limped to his private quarters in the rear of the shuttle.

"At ease," he said, "at ease. Rest up. You've both earned it. We have one more stop to make, and then you both will be fighting off accolades from your peers and instructors."

Eight-Seven was preparing to sink into a crash chair and count his blessings, but 7155—surprise, surprise—couldn't keep his mouth shut. "And where are we heading next, sir?"

The major paused and considered the both of them. The smile returned. "I have to go see a senator," he said.

Eight-Seven swallowed a sudden lump in his throat, and from the way 7155 stiffened, it was apparent he'd made the connection, as well. The Kupohan had mentioned a senator doing business with the First Order. That wasn't strange or new. What *was* strange was the news that the senator was backing out of a deal. Even Eight-Seven knew you didn't back out of a deal you negotiated with the First Order. He'd seen the morale reports of the Order going in to liberate planets and stations where local governments had become too heavy-handed and thought themselves above the rule of law. Was that what this was? The senator going back on a contract to deliver supplies?

"Sir," Eight-Seven said, "what about the Kupohan? Do we need to alert anyone about him, or get a cleanup crew to . . . pick all of him up?"

The hatch to the major's private quarters hissed open, but the officer stopped to look back at them before going inside. "That won't be necessary. After all, he took care of it himself, remember?"

With that, the major ducked into his quarters and the

door hissed shut. Eight-Seven was still confused but knew better than to continue to pepper his superior with questions. He'd just have to wait until—

The shuttle shook violently, and alarms went off on the control panel. Fifty-Five dashed to the front of the vessel, then paused.

"What is it?" Eight-Seven asked. "Are we under attack?"

The other boy didn't respond. Instead, he stared at something outside the viewport before disabling the alarms with a grim expression. Eight-Seven joined him at the front, concerned.

"What—" he began to ask, but the answer became clear as soon as he looked out the viewport. In fact, it was scattered all around them.

The *Loxodonta*, or what remained of it, was in pieces. Larger remnants of the ship drifted down, on their way into Tamo'Akora's orbit, while twisted bits of metal hurtled after the shuttle, as if chasing them, demanding answers. The last thing Eight-Seven saw before the autopilot jumped to hyperspace was the warped top half of a binary load lifter, a gash in its chassis giving the impression that it was screaming.

▮▮▮▮▮

Fifty-Five left the cockpit, and after a few stunned seconds, Eight-Seven stormed after him.

"What are you thinking?" he hisspered, which was a whispered hiss and to him sounded like a perfectly reasonable term. "Hey. Hey! No, don't walk faster. I'm trying to talk—"

He never got to finish that sentence, because as he followed the other stormtrooper down the ladder to the shuttle storage rooms, 7155's oversized paw of a hand grabbed him by the back of the armor and yanked him into a corner where a portable armor repair station had been bolted to the wall. The station's many cords, cables, and automated brushes rattled at the impact.

No one person should be this strong, Eight-Seven thought, just before he was yanked forward again and slammed into a crate.

"Shut. Up." Fifty-Five held him in place as he took a half step back and peered up the ladder. Satisfied, he turned and flipped on the armor repair station's power. There was a cleaning routine programmed as the first option, and he yanked off his helmet and fit it into place. A whirring sound filled the cabin, and then and only then did 7155 seem to relax.

Eight-Seven shook his head. "Are you that dirty?"

"I said shut up." This time there was no heat in the words but more weary exasperation.

"Seriously, what is wrong with you?"

Fifty-Five finally backed up, leaning against the repair station and folding his arms. His brow was furrowed in concentration as he stared at the floor, as if he was struggling for words. Eight-Seven hesitated, then took off his own helmet, flashing a worried glance at the ladder. This wasn't an approved circumstance to shed armor, and they were already aggravating the major.

Finally 7155 looked up, his eyes filled with worry. "Did you see him?"

"Who?"

"The major. Did you see him?"

Eight-Seven had to step forward, because he could barely hear the other boy over the noise of the repair station. "See him? Yeah, he was injured. Ruined his uniform, which must've hurt more than the actual injury, because I've *never* seen him so disheveled. I thought he crawled out of bed every morning with a freshly pressed uniform."

"No," 7155 said, shaking his head. "The blaster."

"The—"

"He pulled a blaster on us!"

Eight-Seven shifted, uncomfortable. "I know. The pain and the drugs from the medpac must have had him on edge or something."

"Oh, come on! Open your eyes!" Fifty-Five surged upright and began stalking back and forth in the tight space. "You can't possibly be this blind. He was going to shoot us!"

Shoot them? No. The blaster was just protocol. Right? Right. Shooting them didn't make sense at all. It was so outside the realm of possibility that Eight-Seven actually laughed. "You're in shock or something. That's ridiculous. It was just . . . I don't know, more like he was on edge. Why would he shoot us?"

Fifty-Five shook his head. "Why? Because we learned something he doesn't want us to know. Something about those storage containers."

"The containers you lied and—"

Fifty-Five lunged forward, again slamming Eight-Seven against the wall. This time Eight-Seven was prepared, swiping down with his forearm to knock away the bigger boy's hand. He ducked an elbow but caught a rising knee, the air driven out of him as he went limp. But as 7155 pulled him upright, Eight-Seven used the helmet he still held as a club and rammed it forward into the other boy's face. He stepped forward, only to realize it was a ploy. Fifty-Five batted the helmet away, then slipped behind and managed to put Eight-Seven into a headlock.

"Will you," he said, hissing between breaths, "shut up?"

"You . . . you've lost it," Eight-Seven squeezed through gritted teeth. "I'm—"

A shadow drifted across the wall in front of them. The

light from the main cabin in the shuttle . . . someone was there. Fifty-Five shoved Eight-Seven aside and quickly turned to stand in front of the armor repair station.

Major Gohl's droid floated down, antennae waggling back and forth as it twisted in midair, photoreceptor tightening first on Eight-Seven, then on 7155. Eight-Seven pretended to check his helmet, rotating left, then right as he watched the droid out of the corners of his eyes. The recorder droid floated there for another few seconds until 7155 turned around, then acted startled.

"Whoa, didn't see you there, little guy," he said, patting the droid and nearly sending it spinning out of control. He pulled one of the brushes from the repair station and pressed a button. The roller heads began to spin, and a noxious green foam squirted between the bristles. "You need a polish, too?"

The droid beeped in indignation before hastily floating back up through the hatch. Fifty-Five waited a few seconds, then replaced the brush and shot a glare at Eight-Seven. "See?"

"See what? The droid?"

"He's *watching* us!"

"Who? The major?"

"Yes." Fifty-Five rubbed his face. "Listen. What do you think would've happened if we'd admitted to peeking inside the containers? Or that they were unlocked?"

Eight-Seven shrugged, his stomach folding in on itself. He didn't like the territory this conversation was heading toward. "I don't know."

"Yes, you do. You saw the blaster. Don't act like it was just for show."

"The major wouldn't shoot us. Do you hear yourself?"

"Do you hear *yourself*? Are you still living in the fairy tale those morale sessions try to download into our minds? Wake up, man, the galaxy isn't like that."

Eight-Seven rubbed his eyes. He was starting to get a headache, either from this line of thought or repeatedly being slammed into the wall by his supposed partner. "You're telling me the major is doing something . . . the Order doesn't know about? Something he'd *kill* us for if we discovered what it was?"

"I'm telling you the major has his own little thing on the side going on. Smuggling, probably, and somehow he has big players involved."

"Like the senator."

"Exactly."

"And it's not just a couple extra cases of fancy wine?"

Fifty-Five glared at him. "You don't shoot your subordinates over wine. Besides . . ." He hesitated, then closed his eyes. "I told you I looked inside those containers."

"And?"

Fifty-Five reached inside of his chest armor, pulled out a small item, and tossed it over. Eight-Seven snagged it in midair. It was a credit chit. No identifying markers or anything, but definitely a chit.

"I think whoever was on Tamo'Akora was paid to deliver something from the senator to the major. Maybe the senator backed out at the last minute and took back the items from the containers. That's why the outpost was deserted. Now the major is on his way to see the senator."

"That's . . ." Eight-Seven was at a loss for words. "That's a stretch, isn't it?"

Fifty-Five got defensive. "I'd rather believe a stretch than follow along blindly. Did you hear how he was interrogating us up there? One wrong answer and the same thing that happened to the Kupohan would have happened to us. Or do you think I turned on those load lifters just in time to save you?"

Eight-Seven looked up, and 7155 stared back at him with a grim expression. That was exactly what Eight-Seven had thought. That he'd been saved because 7155 had, at the last moment, engaged the powerful droids and sent them to the rescue. But the other boy was shaking his head.

"No way I could do anything like that in time. That was the major's droid. *It* sliced into the load lifters. It was protecting its boss from whatever that Kupohan could possibly reveal. The only reason we're still alive is because we're useful to the major *and he thinks we don't know his secrets*."

Eight-Seven was reeling. Inside and out. He stepped back, leaning against the wall for support as his mind raced.

"Look," 7155 said, his voice softening. "Officers don't usually pull blasters on their subordinates. We're the First Order, not a street gang. We *saved* him, remember? Did everything we were supposed to do, but all he was worried about was whether or not we saw what was inside those containers."

Eight-Seven felt like his thoughts were walking through mud. He felt sluggish. "But why even bring us if there was a risk we'd learn something classified? It doesn't make sense."

An alert began to chime throughout the ship. They were dropping out of hyperspace soon, which meant they'd reached their destination.

Fifty-Five switched off the armor repair station and, with the last bit of noise, grabbed his helmet and began to put it on, pausing only to offer one last thought. "I don't know, but just . . . keep an eye out. That's all I'm asking."

He slammed his helmet on and began to climb the ladder. Eight-Seven remained downstairs, his thoughts racing. The Order expressly forbid smuggling, and quite a few stormtrooper training sims revolved around the objective of stopping smugglers. During briefings, awards were handed out routinely to squads who confiscated illegally transported goods. Most of the contracts he saw assigned were requests from allied systems for aid against thieves and smugglers. It just didn't make sense.

But as he headed back up to the main cabin, he once again remembered the look on Major Gohl's face as he sat in the pilot's chair, blaster pistol aimed in their direction. What if 7155 actually was right? The major would be watching them closely on this final stop of the mission.

Eight-Seven just hoped it wasn't their last.

CHPTR - 24

Manny sobbed.

Endayi pressed her lips thin but didn't speak.

TZ-1719's head was splitting in two. Captain Shikra didn't bluff. If he was attacking, the only question was how long the demonstrators would be able to hold out.

Her squad had to get the VIPs away before that happened. If they were gone, there would be no need for Shikra to hang around.

At least that was what she hoped.

The trio raced back to the grand foyer of the Gravitorium, choosing to take the long way this time instead of leaping out of the shielded window. They careened down the long, winding exterior hallway, the stuttering bursts of blaster fire and brief glimpses of the growing violence outside spurring them on. The orbak snorted with all three people—one an armored stormtrooper—on it, but maybe the brief buffet it had consumed had improved its mood, because it seemed to put on even more speed as Manny encouraged it with *hups* and *has*.

They burst out of a sapphire-carpeted hallway into a side entrance of the grand foyer. A few VIPs, already on edge, screamed at their appearance. Several stormtroopers whirled around, riot shields raised and Z6 batons in hand, only to lower their guard at 1719's barked command.

"Stand down!"

She counted the troopers still inside and winced. Including her squad, she had around sixteen stormtroopers. Twelve and Clamps had taken up positions on either side of the main entrance, their postures stiff and the vanes of their batons crackling with electricity, while TZ-214 ushered the remaining guests to spots of relative safety beneath stairwells and in insulated side rooms. All of them looked relieved to see 1719's return. Even now, with tensions elevated and emotions running high, she couldn't help feeling some sort of sarcastic amusement at the way she could read her squad's emotions from their stance. Armor and helmets—it didn't matter. She could tell when they were tired, when they found something funny, and when they were angry. She couldn't explain it. It was how they gripped their weapons, how they shifted their weight, how their heads tilted, swiveled, and drooped.

Right now they were scared.

1719 took in a deep breath. They were allowed to be scared. She wasn't.

"Situation," she said, her voice firm.

Clamps's shoulders drooped in relief now that the squad leader was back. Technically he was in charge when 1719 was away, and right now it seemed it was the last position he wanted to be in. "It's bad, boss. Real bad."

As if to punctuate that statement, she heard a noise that had her sprinting to the door to peek out. "Is that blaster fire?" she asked.

"Yes," 214 answered grimly. She pointed at Endayi. "This her?"

1719 nodded. "Endayi Jaliss, this is Twelve, Clamps, and Twenty-One-Four, all members of Foot Patrol Twenty-Two-Alpha. And Manny, our newest recruit and orbak handler. Give me one second, ma'am, and we'll get you to safety."

The heiress quirked her lips, looking amused, then flattened her dress with the palms of her hands. "Sergeant, was it?"

"Corporal, ma'am."

"Well, Corporal, I can assure you that I know how to stay

out of the way, and you have more pressing items on your agenda than to babysit me."

"Manny, get our furry troop transport somewhere quiet. We may still need him. Anyone seen the lieutenant?"

When 214 shook her head and no one else spoke up, 1719 bit back a complaint. What was Shroud playing at? She turned to Endayi and cleared her throat. "With respect, ma'am, we'd still better keep you close. This isn't the time to throw caution to the wind, and unfortunately we have our orders."

"You technically give the orders here," Clamps said. When 1719 turned to look at him, he shrugged. "S'the truth, boss. With the lieutenant gone and Sergeant Calcon out there with the captain, that just leaves you."

1719 wished her helmet could go transparent so he could see her glare, but she took two deep breaths and turned to the assembled stormtroopers. No one disagreed with him.

"Fine," she snapped before turning back to Endayi, who was watching the whole thing with a faint trace of amusement still on her face. *Let's see how long that lasts.* "Then, again, with respect, ma'am, we're going to have to keep you safe until this blows over."

The amused expression disappeared, replaced by a practiced look of studied disapproval. *They must teach that to heirs and heiresses*, 1719 thought. Endayi lifted her chin and crossed her arms in front of her chest.

"Corporal, I refuse to tell you how to do your job. But I am one of several dozen civilians currently stranded here while your . . . troops shoot and arrest, maybe arrest before they shoot, unarmed protesters."

A nearby red-faced Zeltron elder puffed out his cheeks in indignation. "They're ruffians, is what they are! Intoxicated slime with no regard for proper society, and they need to be dealt with."

"They're *dying*," Endayi snapped back. "For *your* profits."

"Of which your family rakes in their fair share," someone else shouted.

"And yet I don't recall seeing your face at the mediation table for better mining safeguards. Or your face, Mr. Jemes, at the safety review where the drills of Silvum Industries were found to be the cause of more injuries than any of the so-called intoxicants you abhor so much, sir. But that's not the issue right now. The Rive Collective wouldn't exist to make your family or my family richer if it wasn't for the *miners*. The people out there facing down blaster fire just for the right to the bacta tanks you were just complaining about. I know my family's past, as does everyone here, but I—we—have to put that aside for the moment and get. Our. People. Safe."

214 keyed the squad's private channel. "Is it just me, or does the young heiress seem to be the odd one out in the Rive Collective?"

"She's very . . . passionate," Twelve said, his voice more dreamy than 1719 would've liked.

Clamps must've felt the same way, because he dropped his riot shield on the other boy's boots. "Down, boy."

1719 studied the Jaliss heiress. "So she doesn't match her father's ambition. But do we think she's passionate enough to undermine him and the rest of her family?"

Everyone, stormtroopers and civilians, fell silent, watching as the tiny teenage girl squared up against a group of blustering elders, ignoring their insults and firing back with her own salvos. More of the guests had begun to gather around them, a few standing with Endayi to show support, but more either chose to lurk in the background so as not to pick a side or gathered behind Mr. Jemes and added their own glowers to the Zeltron's. Endayi was outnumbered by many of her father's peers, powerful movers and shakers with a lot of influence, but her stance never wavered.

She redoubled her efforts, not allowing anyone else to speak as she badgered, bellowed, shouted, yelled, and stomped her feet to drive her points home. By the time she finally took a breath, the crowd around her stood with their jaws hanging open and their eyes wide.

"I think that's your answer," 214 said.

1719 grunted. Maybe. But something wasn't adding up. Endayi was arguing on *behalf* of the lower-class protesters. Yes, maybe she could attempt to undermine her family's operations, but associating with pirates? Hutt scum who killed with no warning? 1719 bit her lip. No, something didn't make sense.

Clamps, who was keeping an eye on the violence outside, straightened. "Boss, they've stopped firing warning shots."

Everyone froze.

Twelve peeked out the window. "I think Captain Shikra is up to something."

Knowing him, it wouldn't be anything good. "Any sign of the lieutenant?"

"Negative."

Where was she?

"Boss," 214 said, the word slow and contemplative. "What if we brought the VIPs to the miners?"

▮▮▮▮▮

The grand foyer went silent. Even the orbak seemed confused. "Explain," said 1719, but Endayi had already grasped the meaning.

"No, that's brilliant. Corporal," she said, turning to 1719, "if you're here to get us to safety and your troops won't fire on us, if we forge a connection with the miners and broker our own agreement, surely your captain would cease his bombardment."

Her voice grew in excitement as she spoke, and she pivoted and stalked over to where the Zeltron, Mr. Jemes, was listening while rubbing the underside of his chin.

"Mr. Jemes," Endayi continued, "think about it. How much profit are you losing by the work stoppage. Millions?"

"Billions," he muttered, but there was a bit of thoughtfulness in his voice.

"Exactly! And I assume it's the same for the rest of you?"

More grumbles that leaned to the affirmative echoed Mr. Jemes's response, and Endayi nodded. "As I thought. And none of this is made any better by trigger-happy soldiers leveling our moon, right?"

"Far from it," Mr. Jemes snapped. He glared at 1719, as if it was her idea to bombard the area. "Any more destruction and there won't be a Rive Collective to negotiate with."

1719 pursed her lips beneath her mask. "So get you to the miners without anyone getting hurt or either group getting into another scuffle, and Captain Shikra can't order any more strikes and will be forced to pull back because an agreement will have been made."

Mr. Jemes nodded, as did the others around him. Endayi folded her arms. "You do realize that means there will have to be some concessions. From *all* of us, the Jaliss Group included."

There was some more grumbling, but ultimately everyone agreed.

Endayi turned to 1719. "Corporal. I believe the floor is yours."

For a split second, 1719 wanted to drag the heiress to a corner and ask her plainly if she was doing business with pirates. Get the information out into the open once and for all, since she couldn't reconcile the bloodthirsty Xen Runners with Endayi Jaliss. But there was no time to ponder, only to act, and 1719 pushed aside the mystery of the Jaliss Group connection and hefted her riot shield.

"Boss, how are we going to get all these civvies across the plaza before Shikra launches his next strike?" Clamps asked.

1719 smiled and pointed at the glistening steel-and-ice sculptures in the center of the foyer. "You always wanted to go sledding," she said. Then: "Manny, bring me His Highness. And someone round up the other trainers and orbaks."

CHPTR - 25

The Sardich system.

FN-2187 read the info about their destination off the navicomputer as the shuttle curved around a giant red star. Three planets orbited it, the farthest being a gas giant with multiple moons and the middle planet an uninhabitable desert wasteland. It was the closest planet to the star and the one the system was named after, Sardich, that they were heading toward.

FO-7155 stood next to him, helmet on, at rigid attention. He stared straight ahead at the gray-and-brown land mass growing in the viewport. Eight-Seven glanced at him. The huge trooper hadn't said anything since emerging from the shuttle's storage room, which was fine with Eight-Seven, as it left plenty of empty silence he could fill with his thoughts.

The major, a smuggler. And willing to kill to keep his secrets? The voice of the First Order's morale program, completely undermining everything the First Order stood for?

"Ah, here we are."

The words, breaking the tense atmosphere in the ship, came from the man himself. Major Gohl had informed them that he would fly them in-system to their rendezvous. If he noticed the thick, heavy silence, he didn't comment. He also took care to make sure only he could see the coordinates he punched in, which seemed odd since Eight-Seven could see the massive city the major took them toward out the front viewport.

The capital of Sardich, Cluost City, was an industrial-quarry mining city built into the natural terrain of the planet. Every citizen was also a miner, often living in the very rock they carved. Failed farmland crowded the edges of the city, decaying stalks of grain wilting on the rooftops of abandoned homes that lay partially underground. The land was dead, or dying, in the older parts of the city, while newer mines carved the ground hollow. Everything grew dry and more sparsely populated the farther north they traveled, with previous quarries and the villages surrounding them buried beneath dust and sand. Empty shells of mountains lay exposed to the winds, while bare valleys gathered nothing but ghosts.

It was toward the northernmost and highest mountain that the shuttle flew, passing over ore-loaded automated trains, partially buried bazaars, and a seedy entertainment district built around a small desert oasis. People milled about as orange-and-black-armored troops patrolled the streets.

Sweeping up into the clouds, the shuttle headed toward a fortress carved into a mountain made of black rock. Turrets and autocannons in the foothills tracked their arrival for several seconds. Major Gohl smiled as Eight-Seven inhaled in alarm.

"Relax, trooper," he said. "You worry too much."

"It's my job, sir," Eight-Seven said, to which the major laughed.

"Yes, it is, isn't it."

"What's that?" 7155 suddenly asked.

Eight-Seven looked where 7155 was pointing out of the starboard viewport. Another abandoned quarry village passed beneath them, but this one bore the telltale signs of bombing. Scorched rock and piles of rubble dotted the ground. A major battle of some sort had taken place there, and from the looks of it, there had been very few survivors. Now construction had started on a large building, though he couldn't make out exactly what it would be used for.

"That, boys," Major Gohl said, checking his readouts, "is a lesson in bringing the right tool to do the job. Now pay attention. Our business is above the clouds, not down there." The major was so busy studying the instrument panel and keying in the comm channel that he missed the glance the boys shared. He continued fiddling with the controls until he nodded in satisfaction. "Got it."

The speaker crackled. "Unidentified vessel, you are flying in restricted airspace. Turn around immediately or we will—wait, what?"

Major Gohl smiled but said nothing as the autocannons that had been tracking them suddenly disengaged. Instead, he pushed on the flight controls, taking the shuttle straight toward a landing pad extending from the topmost portion of the fortress. The shuttle dropped onto its landing gear, and the major swiveled around in the pilot's chair. His gaze swept over the two of them, and Eight-Seven barely restrained himself from flinching as the cold flat eyes examined him.

"You two have performed admirably," Major Gohl said. "One final stop and your futures will be set. Come now. Let's announce ourselves, shall we?"

Eight-Seven followed as the major strode off the ship and

onto the landing pad. High winds greeted them as they made their way to a door cut into the fortress stone at the other end of the landing pad. Three figures waited for them. The middle one—an older human with silver hair and expensive robes to match—walked forward with arms outstretched while the two flanking her stood watch. They looked like soldiers of some sort, and he recognized the armor: The troops patrolling the bazaar and oasis had been wearing the same. More important, he noticed the wicked-looking vibrosword each carried in a hilt at their waist. He filed away a mental image with the intention of checking it against the *Finalizer*'s databases when they got back.

"Major," the woman said. "Had we known you were coming, we would've extended the quarry festival by another day. You just missed the festivities."

"Excellent, Senator Reat'ha," Major Gohl replied. "I'd prefer a more inconspicuous meeting."

"Is that why you scrambled your ship's signature?"

Eight-Seven glanced at the major in surprise, as did 7155. The senator noticed, and her smile stretched even wider, perhaps with a trace of honesty sprinkled in, as well.

"You know perfectly well why and how I've chosen to come here, Senator. I'm in no mood for banter," Major Gohl said.

The senator sighed. "Then come inside and let's get down

to business. There's a performance down in the oasis tonight and it's supposed to be phenomenal."

Inside, a luxurious office furnished with expensive furniture opened up to an indoor fountain with divans scattered around it. Flower pads floated on the surface, and jeweled aquatic creatures cut through the shallow water. The rough rock exterior of the walls gave way to marble polished so smooth Eight-Seven could see his reflection. Gold sconces held flickering lamps above a desk on the far side, and that was where Senator Reat'ha sat, folding her hands on the ancient surface and smiling, waiting. If the senator appeared welcoming, her two bodyguards gave off the exact opposite aura. Their hands never left the hilts of their vibroswords, and though he could only see their eyes, Eight-Seven could feel the animosity when they looked at him.

"So," the senator said, breaking the silence and staring expectantly at the major.

The major sat in one of the chairs on the opposite side of the desk and crossed one leg over the other. "I believe you know why I'm here."

"And you know my answer."

"Unfortunately, Senator, I can't accept that."

Senator Reat'ha's lips went thin. "We agreed that the First Order would provide infrastructure assistance to aid in the recovery after the attempted coup, and that you would also provide temporary shelter for the many displaced children who lost parents in the violence."

Major Gohl brushed a speck of dust from the hem of his pants. "And that agreement—"

"What we did *not* agree on," the senator continued, her voice growing louder, "is the First Order *kidnapping* our children and forcing them to join up as child soldiers in that recruitment facility you're building in the old quarries. Yes, we knew about that. Your power over my people is not as complete as you like to think it is. So no, Mr. Gohl, our agreement is off, the people of Sardich will *not* subsidize the inflation of your army, and we will not be conducting any more business with you or your superiors."

The major's face had gone a vibrant red, and he honestly looked like he might explode. Eight-Seven glanced at 7155, who had his eyes trained on the senator's bodyguards, and he quickly did the same. The mercenaries hadn't shifted position, but the tension in the room had ratcheted up several notches.

After a few more silent seconds, the major stood, straightened his uniform, and walked over to the fountain. A crystal bowl filled with breaded delicacies sat on the marble edge, and he plucked one out and tossed it into the pool. There was a flurry of activity and splashing as the jeweled creatures fought over the treat, and the major sighed.

"Such artificial constraints," he said. "More than enough food exists just out of their reach, and yet they're forced to squabble over tidbits. It's almost as if they live in squalor instead of a veritable paradise."

Eight-Seven shifted. The major's tone had hardened, and it reminded him of the interrogation at blaster point back aboard the shuttle. Cold. Sharp. And yet the senator's body-guards didn't pay him any mind, so maybe they'd had this same argument before.

"Here's what will happen," Major Gohl said, finally turning back toward the senator. "The people of Sardich *do* want to send their children elsewhere. I'm expecting to hear exactly that during the oasis performance tonight. And do you know why?"

"Why?" the senator asked through a brittle smile when it became obvious the major was waiting on her.

"Because they know the opportunities the First Order can provide will be near limitless. And you will make sure they understand that. Because if they don't, and if I don't receive the credits we initially agreed upon"—he paused, cocking his head as if thinking about something—"plus a small five percent increase, for administrative fees, of course."

"Of course."

If the major heard the senator's mocking tone, he didn't acknowledge it but instead continued speaking. "Because if that is not paid, then there will be another outbreak in violence, Senator. More children will lose their parents. More parents will lose their sons and daughters. The devastation will be so utterly complete, so violent and sudden, that the so-called attempted coup will look like a birthday party by the time the smoke clears and the blood—that will be on *your* hands—drains away."

Senator Reat'ha's face had gone pale, her eyes wide. "You can't."

"You mistake me for one of your subordinates, Senator. I can and I will. The credits. By the end of the night. Or your next population census will happen when you collect the names of the dead."

The senator slammed the palms of her hands on the desk. "I will *not* be bullied, Major."

"No. You will be convinced."

The major snapped his fingers.

For a second, Eight-Seven stood frozen in confusion, not understanding if that was supposed to be a signal for him and 7155 to do something. That was until the sound of humming metal echoed throughout the hall and the senator's bodyguards unsheathed their vibroswords. Eight-Seven began to raise his blaster, only to pause as the mercenaries turned and extended their blades so the tips hovered centimeters away from the horrified expression of Senator Reat'ha.

"I've taken the liberty of renegotiating the contracts of the *soldiers* you employed," the major said, plucking another treat from the crystal bowl and tossing it into the fountain. "These men are now contracted with the First Order for . . . security. In fact, why don't we give them the official title of Sardich Planetary Security. They will continue guarding the VIPs here in the city for as long as . . . our interests align."

The message was clear, and Eight-Seven swallowed. But to his surprise, the senator only smiled.

"And here we see the true colors of the Order," she said. Her gaze flicked over to Eight-Seven and 7155. "Unwilling to get the hands of your own soldiers dirty? Or . . . they didn't know, did they?"

The smile faded from the major's face. "I advise you to worry about your own fate, Senator."

Senator Reat'ha flapped a hand, ignoring the vibroswords centimeters away. "My fate was set when I hired the agent to take back our credits and destroy you aboard the *Loxodonta*, Major Gohl. I had to protect my people. Everything else is as the universe wills."

Her smile grew wider, and she actually reclined in her seat.

"So . . . what now?"

Eight-Seven had never seen the major so angry. So furious. His face, red before, was now twisted in hatred so raw Eight-Seven actually thumbed off the safety on his blaster. The whine of his blaster's power core echoed throughout the hall.

Fifty-Five shifted beside him, raising his own blaster.

The major snapped his fingers.

The mercenary closest to Eight-Seven pulled his vibrosword back, dropped into a crouch, and lunged forward. Senator Reat'ha's head stayed attached to her body for one whole second before it toppled off.

"No," Eight-Seven whispered.

The mercenary stood just as three blaster shots caught him full in the chest, knocking him backward to join the senator's severed head on the floor.

Fifty-Five was breathing heavily as he kept his blaster trained on the other mercenary.

Major Gohl spun around, snarling in anger. "Fool! Who told you to fire?"

The second mercenary had paused, obviously confused, and Eight-Seven didn't blame him. But that confusion turned to anger as he shifted his target and leaped onto the desk, sword descending in a vicious cut aimed at 7155.

The older boy tried to fire again but ended up raising his blaster to block the vibrosword. The blade sliced nearly all the way through, rendering the weapon useless, but 7155 just twisted it, wrenching the blade from the mercenary's hands. Spinning, he backhanded his opponent so hard he flew backward, colliding with the desk. The merc spat a curse in a language Eight-Seven didn't understand, then pulled two knives from behind his back and sprinted forward.

A blaster shot ricocheted off the marble at his feet, and the merc skidded to a stop.

"Drop the knives," Eight-Seven said, blaster aimed at the merc's head. "Now."

"Just shoot him!" 7155 shouted. The giant boy had pulled his own knife from the holster all troopers carried on their belts, though it was more of a utility blade than a weapon. "I got this handled!"

The merc shouted another curse, then flipped both knives so he held them by the blades. "You should listen to him."

"I'm warning you," Eight-Seven said, edging closer to the merc's left while 7155 circled to his right. The merc flipped his head back and forth, trying to keep both troopers in view.

"Please stop talking," 7155 said calmly. "Shoot him."

"I've got this," Eight-Seven snapped. It was a lie—he was barely holding on to rational thought, everything was moving so fast. But the senator was dead, and the other mercenary, and if he thought about it for too long, the lights began to get too hot, too bright, and sounds began to get too loud, his chest too tight, and . . .

"Shoot him," 7155 repeated.

Eight-Seven lifted the blaster and adjusted it, and his finger hovered over the trigger.

"He's not going to stop attacking. Just—"

"I said I've got this!" Eight-Seven turned his head just a fraction to glare at 7155, and that was when the merc made his move.

One blade flickered through the air, forcing Eight-Seven to duck aside, and he lost his balance. A shot rang out, and he scrambled up from his hands and knees, raising his own blaster to sweep the room.

The merc stood still. At first Eight-Seven thought it was because the soldier couldn't believe he'd been shot, but the merc started to back away.

And then 7155 collapsed to the floor.

Major Gohl stood behind him, his own blaster in his outstretched hand.

"Foolish children," he said with a sigh. "It's like I said,

there's a lesson here in bringing the right tool to do the job. You two were not the right tool, unfortunately."

The major glanced at the senator, grimaced, then turned and headed for the exit at the other end of the fountain.

"Kill him. Quickly. I need to find where the senator stashed the credits and then depart this depressing rock." He looked back over his shoulder at the merc, then at Eight-Seven. "Training over, boy. The real lesson is this: Survive, at all costs."

CHPTR - 26

Sergeant Teena Calcon took pride in her command. It was an accomplishment she leaned on during the rougher missions, like an internal pillar. She never had the highest scores or best accuracy, but she was determined and unrelenting. A force, that was what her instructors called her, and right now that force was straining to be let loose.

She stood near the holoprojector built in the center of the forward command post. The aides and troopers avoided her aside from the occasional glance or hushed whisper. Her hands were folded. Her jaw clenched. Her left foot tapped impatiently. Everyone knew that stance. They feared that stance. She might have been young, one of the youngest sergeants in the Corps, but her reputation for dogged persistence in combat, armed and unarmed, was second only to her temper.

Sergeant Calcon was annoyed, and an annoyed sergeant meant heads would roll.

Company 77's forward command was located on the western side of the Plaza Solarity, tucked on the first floor of a palatial estate too gaudy for the sergeant's taste. All the topiary bushes and the stone fountains. Give her a cot and the hum of the *Supremacy* to lull her to sleep and she was perfect. But she couldn't deny the benefit of the location, as the elevated grounds gave company command an unobstructed view of the gathering riot, a fact that would have been immensely more enjoyable if not for the irksome approach of one Lieutenant Shroud.

"Lieutenant," she said as the officer stepped up to the holoprojector. Calcon was a soldier first, no matter what.

"At ease," the lieutenant answered in a quiet voice.

Shroud stood a few paces away, her masked face also turned toward the rioters. She'd appeared nearly an hour ago, smug and superior in her evasive answers about where she'd been, and Sergeant Calcon respected the chain of command too much to attempt to pry. Now both watched as

Company 77 assembled into formation, looking somewhat lackluster, Calcon noted. Probably, she admitted to herself, because they weren't being given the honor of subduing the rioters. That privilege was apparently going to the detachment of riot troopers standing stiff and alert to their left. Outfitted with M480 shock cannons, heavy-duty riot shields, and electrostaffs, the newcomers double-checked their equipment before the order to deploy commenced.

"So," the lieutenant suddenly said, "a holoprojector?"

The ghost of a smile crossed the sergeant's face. "Captain Shikra prides himself on thoroughness."

Shroud chuckled back before turning toward the display. "I'm surprised at all the efforts to subdue the aggressors with nonviolence. From my understanding, and his record, your captain's method of crowd control consists of blasters first, cuffs second."

A flash of anger spiked through Sergeant Calcon, but she prided herself on being a professional. On keeping cool under pressure. She inhaled. "The captain takes the preservation of life seriously, Lieutenant, and doesn't wish to cause additional strife for the Rive Collective," she said, then exhaled.

"Or their pockets," Shroud murmured.

"I can't speak to that, sir," Calcon said stiffly.

"Of course not."

At that moment, the man of the hour appeared, emerging from the darkness of the estate grounds like a wraith. Captain Shikra nodded at the trooper who saluted before passing him a datapad, which he studied as he joined the sergeant and the lieutenant near the holoprojector.

"Company ready for action, Captain," Calcon said, saluting.

Shikra nodded but turned to Lieutenant Shroud, who saluted him, as well, almost absentmindedly.

"I trust you were able to acquire whatever it is your commander sent you to retrieve, Lieutenant?" The captain's voice was smooth, but there was a sharp undercurrent to it, a frustration that whatever mission she was here on, the captain wasn't privy to it.

"I have, Captain," Shroud said. "The major will be pleased and grateful for your aid."

"Well, I couldn't really refuse, now could I? Not the First Order Security Bureau."

"I suppose not."

"Hmm." Shikra turned to face the Plaza Solarity, checked the time, then sighed. "Sergeant, have the troopers stand down and activate the shock trooper squads."

"Sir?" Sergeant Calcon wrinkled her brow.

"Change of plans. I've allowed enough of this mockery of order to proceed unchecked, and I'm not prepared to go any further. Have the riot troopers stand down, and form up two squads of shock troopers. They will advance after the cannons fire. I want those criminals off the streets within the hour."

"Yes, sir. But the Rive Collective—"

"Does not trump the rule of law, Sergeant. They are citizens, as well, and you can believe their inability to control a simple group of hired hands will be called into question during a board of inquiry."

"Yes, sir!"

Lieutenant Shroud tilted her head. Captain Shikra noticed, and the sickening sweetness in his voice was positively nauseating. "Will your major have a problem with you advancing with the shock troopers, Lieutenant? Your presence and experience would be . . . invaluable."

"I can—" began Sergeant Calcon, but Shikra cut her off. "I'm asking the lieutenant. I need you here, Sergeant."

"Yes, sir."

Shroud simply nodded. "Happy to be of service."

The captain almost seemed disappointed, as if he'd expected her to put up more of a fight, to protest the assignment and the risk it entailed. But the lieutenant only pulled out her own blaster pistol and checked it for readiness. Shikra watched her closely.

A stormtrooper ran up to the command post. "Something's happening, sir. The doors are opening."

"The rioters forced their way inside?" the captain asked sharply.

"No . . . I mean, I don't think so. Nearly all the vehicles and barricades from the exterior are still in place."

"Enough. Quadnocs."

Shikra took the offered tool, then swore under his breath. "Sergeant, get the troopers ready to fire on my command."

"Sir! Gamma Company, repel formation, on the double!"

As the shock troopers hustled into place, Sergeant Calcon retrieved her own pair of quadnocs and stared through them, eager to find out what had frustrated the captain. It took her several seconds, not because she couldn't find it, but because she simply couldn't process what she was seeing.

"What . . . are they doing?" she finally spat out.

She was so stunned that when Lieutenant Shroud held out her hand for the quadnocs, Calcon offered them up without question. It didn't matter, anyway, as the spectacle was now ripping across the Plaza Solarity and could be seen from here.

Three massive sleds—clearly ornamental and not practical—rocketed across the polished stone in the plaza, sparks and ice chips leaping in their wake. A pair of those massive circus beasts pulled each sled, snorting and stamping as they demolished decorative plants and landscaping in their demonic rush. Two sleds peeled away in the direction of the rioters, while the third turned and headed straight for the command post. The shock troopers, just now assembling into their squad formation, began to lift their blasters.

"I want a round of fire across the front of those sleds!" Shikra commanded.

"Hold!"

Sergeant Calcon turned her head at Lieutenant Shroud's order. She had her hand up even as she continued staring through the quadnocs. "Those are your own people."

Shikra continued as if he hadn't heard. "Sergeant?"

Sergeant Calcon licked her lips. She was speechless. Were those really Company 77 troopers? No, it couldn't be. The lieutenant was mistaken, of course. She had her own agenda.

"Steady now!" she barked. "Wait for it!"

The shock troopers leveled their blasters and aimed. Calcon glanced over at the captain, but he stood with his hands clasped behind his back and waited.

"Fire!"

Blaster fire roared, hammering into the sleds.

"Again!"

Splinters of ice shot off into the night, and one of the sleds swerved, nearly overturning. The second split off in the opposite direction, presenting the more heavily protected side to the troopers. Calcon paused, confused. That wasn't what a hostile force would do.

"Another round, Sergeant," Captain Shikra said.

"Sir, I think—" Calcon began.

"You aren't here to *think*, Sergeant, but to do as I command, and without hesitation. Now, I want those sleds charred ash, and I want it done yesterday!"

Sergeant Calcon straightened, her face hot with embarrassment, but before she could give the order, Lieutenant Shroud lunged forward, startling her. But Shroud had eyes only for the outpost's comm unit. She slammed her hand down on a toggle. A static-filled transmission crackled into the night air.

"—I repeat, this is Corporal TZ-One-Seven-One-Nine, Alpha Squad, Company Seventy-Seven, with the rest of Foot Patrol Twenty-Two-Alpha. Hold. Your. Fire!"

Sergeant Calcon stared in horror at the lieutenant, then turned to the captain. To her shock, Captain Shikra still looked unmoved. He glanced at the lieutenant, and some private conversation the sergeant wasn't privy to happened in an instant. Finally he turned and extended his hand.

"Sergeant, your radio." He took the comlink Calcon unclipped from her belt and passed over. "TZ-One-Seven-One-Nine, secure comms."

The captain paused, switched channels, then waited.

"Epsilon," everyone heard. The code word that a stormtrooper was secure and not under duress.

"Harbinger," Shikra responded. "Trooper, what is the meaning of this?"

Sergeant Calcon edged closer to be able to overhear the relieved trooper's reply. "Sir! Here to report that the Rive Collective has reached an agreement with the miners and a ceasefire negotiation is underway. Repeat, a ceasefire negotiation is underway!"

Shikra lifted a hand in mock surprise. "A ceasefire? There is no ceasefire between criminals and order, trooper. You should know that. There is justice, and it is punitive."

"Yes, sir." The stormtrooper didn't take the cue to shut up. "It's just . . . there's no more fighting, sir."

"TZ-One-Seven-One-Nine, your orders were to escort VIPs to safety, not to play hero peacemaker."

"Yes, sir."

"Where are the VIPs now, Corporal?"

"Sir, well . . . most of them are back with the miners, working on the details of the ceasefire."

Calcon thought the captain was going to explode. "Most?" he finally squeezed between his gritted teeth.

"Yes, sir. Lady Jaliss of the Jaliss Group and the patron of Silvum Industries, Mr. Jemes, are on the sled with me and the rest of my squad."

Gasps rang throughout the command post. Lieutenant Shroud turned to Sergeant Calcon. "Tell your troopers to stand down, Sergeant."

But Calcon barely registered the order. Her ears had filled with a deafening roar, and it felt like someone else was in control of her body. Her heart dropped into her boots, and her tongue was thick. Those were her allies! And she'd given the order to fire. She turned toward the captain, even as Shroud continued to talk.

"Sergeant?"

The captain stood motionless for several moments. Then, without a word, he turned away.

"Stand down," Calcon finally said, and the shock troopers lowered their blasters. She closed her eyes and exhaled. When she opened them, Captain Shikra stood in front of her, his face centimeters from hers.

"Never debate an order with me, *Private*," he snarled, then marched out of the command post. Calcon swallowed, then turned to see Lieutenant Shroud watching her, her expression unreadable behind her mask. Her gaze never faltered. But Calcon . . . Private Calcon couldn't bear it, and she turned away.

That pillar of pride she'd come to lean on was starting to crumble.

CHPTR - 27

FN-2187 felt hollow, as hollow as the empty quarry villages on the outskirts of the city. The sudden outburst of violence had shaken him to his core. Not only had a senator died—no, been killed, and on Major Gohl's orders—but so had FO-7155.

He hated 7155. Eight-Seven could honestly say that. He hated that 7155 had turned what might have been an easy assignment as a mountain trooper into this current position as the muscle for Major Gohl. He hated how 7155 knew everything, or at least acted like it. He hated that 7155 was a better pilot, that he was stronger, that if everything was different and they'd never competed and never fought in the training gym and never agreed to go on this stupid training mission and had remained on the *Finalizer*, Eight-Seven would have followed 7155 into the bowels of a fiery volcano. He hated him, and now he was dead, and it felt like his chest was on fire.

The mercenary flipped the blade in his hand.

"Nothing personal," he said. "This is only business."

Eight-Seven's breath rattled inside his helmet. He slowly dragged his eyes up from the body of his . . . his friend. "I . . ." he said, "I have a blaster."

"Do you?"

Eight-Seven lifted the blaster and squeezed the trigger, twice, the way he should have when 7155 told him to, and then maybe the other boy would still be alive. He was gasping for air at this point, panic gripping his chest in a vise, and those gasps turned to sobs when the power core whined, then fell silent.

He squeezed it a third time, yelling incoherently as he did.

Nothing happened.

The mercenary shrugged. "The First Order loves to claim it has the best military in the galaxy. It's all we hear about. How they're finely trained. Disciplined. Terrifying." He mimed shivering, then laughed. "Truth is, you're just a kid playing soldier. All of you. Don't even realize that your weapon is damaged."

Eight-Seven backed up, making sure to keep the desk—and

the beheaded body of Senator Reat'ha—between him and his opponent. He quickly glanced at his blaster, flipping it over, and a sinking sensation of dread washed over him.

The power core had a hairline cut that twisted its way along the bottom of the blaster, and the stench of acid began to waft up through his helmet. Eight-Seven dropped his arms in dismay, the blaster falling to the floor with a clatter.

"You don't have to do this," he pleaded, hating the whine in his voice.

The merc shook his head. "Don't do that. Die with honor."

Eight-Seven edged backward, circling around to the other side as the mercenary chased him. "You can let me go. I'll disappear."

The older man laughed. "See, that's the problem with you stormtroopers. You go for their blaster and without it they're useless. Well, son, I'm sorry to say, but the greatest lesson you're going to learn will probably—no, definitely—be the last lesson you'll ever learn. But don't feel too bad. I never got to take out a stormtrooper before. It's about time for me to get me a piece of that armor for my collection."

Eight-Seven bolted. He turned and sprinted toward the fountain, aiming for the door on the opposite side. He heard the merc swear and begin to give chase, sliding across the desk while scattering blood-splattered datapads everywhere, but Eight-Seven didn't turn around. He took the long way around the fountain. Angling past 7155's body, he leaped over it, dropping into a roll and grabbing the merc's dead partner's vibrosword as he scrambled to his feet. He whirled around, two hands on the hilt as he faced off against the oncoming merc.

His opponent laughed as he slowed to a stop, the knife flipping from hand to hand.

"I've got to give it to you, kid, you've got heart. No brains and half a sense of survival, but you've got heart. Too bad I'm gonna cut it out of you."

Eight-Seven didn't say anything. He just sank into a crouch, the blade extending out and up as he waited. All traces of humor disappeared, and the merc flipped the knife in his hand so he held it by the blade.

"Suit yourself, just don't—"

Eight-Seven lunged forward. The merc, not anticipating being on the defensive, hesitated for a split second but recovered in time to fling the knife low and hard. But Eight-Seven wasn't upright any longer. He'd allowed his momentum to carry him forward, tucking into a blend of a dive and a roll. He twisted as he rose to his feet, the vibrosword slicing upward—only for the merc to dodge it.

"Come on, kid, this is—*oomph!*"

Eight-Seven had never stopped rising. It was actually

all thanks to 7155 that he'd even tried this move. He surged upward, lifting his knee to slam into the underside of the merc's jaw as the bigger man's momentum carried him into its path.

The mercenary stumbled backward, tripping over the fountain lip and splashing onto his back in the water. Flashes of color darted away as he floundered among the drifting plants, tangled in their roots and vines.

"You piece of—" The man stood up, the water coming to his waist as he pulled his mask off and scraped leaves and flower petals off of his face. He wiped his mouth, then spat in the water. "I'm going to peel you like a targafruit and dry roast your innards, boy."

Eight-Seven slowly walked to the edge of the fountain as the man cursed and waded toward him, grabbing at the slippery edge. Behind him, beneath the surface of the water, a crowd of colorful fish began to gather in his wake.

"What are you doing? You should be running, because when I catch you—"

Eight-Seven used the tip of the vibrosword to tap the crystal bowl Major Gohl had left on the fountain lip. The mercenary's words dried up as his eyes widened, going from the sword to the bowl to the water, and then back up to Eight-Seven.

Who flipped the bowl of treats into the water.

The gentle waves turned into a frothing maelstrom. Flashes of ruby and emerald and sapphire glinted beneath the spray of water, and the mercenary screamed as he was swarmed, armor cracking as the feeding frenzy began.

Eight-Seven watched.

It didn't feel like he was alone, and even as the waters finally grew still and the mercenary drifted beneath the surface, Eight-Seven didn't move. It was only when a speaker crackled at the senator's desk that he looked up from the mess in the fountain.

"Ma'am, I have a Major Gohl here who says you authorized him to access the cargo storage outside of the oasis. Can you confirm that? Ma'am? One second, sir. . . . Ma'am?"

Eight-Seven stared at the vibrosword in his hand. He needed to get 7155's body onto the shuttle and leave. The First Order needed to know what the major was doing, and 7155 needed a proper burial.

"Ma'am, are you there? Can you—hey. Hey!"

A blaster shot sounded, and then the comm went dead.

Eight-Seven stared at the vibrosword, then at 7155 and sighed.

"I hear you," he muttered, and he headed toward the exit the major had taken. There was one more thing he needed to do.

CHPTR - 28

"He shot at us."

Clamps paced up and down the aisle of the assault lander. It was what he did. How he worked through his problems. The rest of the squad had found their own places to deal with the aftermath of Rive. Twelve sat near the front, keeping an eye on the instrument panels and letting the streams of data drown out his nerves. TZ-214, despite being told otherwise by multiple people, was doing pull-ups on one of the overhead storage racks. She was up to 230, or thereabouts.

And TZ-1719?

She cleaned her blaster rifle.

First, off went the power cell. Didn't want to discharge a shot accidentally. Then the collapsible grip at the front and the stack at the rear.

"Boss, he *shot* at us. His own company. We're on the same side!" Clamps rapped his knuckles on his helmet, the sound filling the interior of the lander. "Did I knock my brain crooked or something back there? Isn't that against the rules of being a stormtrooper? One of the first rules you learn as juniors? Don't fire on your own side?"

1719 unscrewed the electroscope from the top of the blaster, which allowed her to reach the housing underneath. But first she had to detach the main adhesion grip, and then—

"Boss!"

Clamps's distressed plea finally dragged her back into the moment. The blaster rifle was nearly completely disassembled, with screws she didn't even recognize collected in a neat pile. 214 whistled in appreciation as she continued to reel off pull-ups.

"If you're cleaning weapons, I think my baton got some orbak souvenirs on the vanes," she said.

1719 grunted, then leaned against the crate she'd converted into a makeshift workbench. They were the only four in the lander, though that wouldn't be the case for long, so it was best to let Clamps get his words out now.

"Yes," she said, "he ordered his personal squad of shock troopers to fire on us. To be fair, all reports say he didn't *technically* know it was us. He thought it was the miners."

Clamps threw up his hands. "Well, that makes me feel safer."

"Why does he have his own squad of shock troopers anyway?" Twelve asked. He didn't look up from his data streams, and his voice was quiet. "Isn't that, like, against protocol or something?"

"And they were conveniently the only troopers with blasters," 214 added in between pull-ups. "Don't think we didn't notice that."

"I didn't notice that," Clamps said, sounding stunned.

1719 looked around the lander, really looked. 214 resumed her pull-ups, pushing herself to the brink of body failure only days after leaving the medical bay. Clamps was straddling the edge of another eruption, one that she hoped happened without a weapon in his hands. Twelve had holed up inside of his helmet, rarely letting any of them into his thoughts. That was when she realized all the work she'd done to get them functioning as a unit, as a team, after the Merchant Uprising had nearly been undone. They couldn't keep going like this. Not for much longer. Not under Shikra.

"So we put in a transfer request," 1719 said.

The conversation in the lander stopped. Everyone turned to look at her. Even Twelve lifted his head from the comms panel at the front to stare at her.

"A transfer request," Clamps repeated. "Just like that?"

"Not all at once, and not a unit-to-unit request. Specialist requests. Twelve can qualify for a systems specialist easy. Data retrieval, network maintenance, that sort of thing."

"I could do that," Twelve said, perking up.

1719 continued, enthusiasm building as she started pacing. "Twenty-One-Four, with your scores, you could—"

"Pilot," 214 said, cutting her off. "Cargo pilot."

1719 stared at her, nodding slowly. She was actually going to suggest the sniper division, since the squad's best shooter had precision scores that made her instructors drool during training. But maybe the medical bay couldn't heal everything, and not all scars were visible.

"Pilot," 1719 said. "Perfect."

"What about me?" Clamps asked. "Where am I supposed to go? Or did you think old Clamps could just tough it out here while the rest of you head off to bigger and better things?

Just because I'm not that good with datapads or flying? I can fly. Where's our pilot? Tell him I'm gonna fly this lander back to the *Supremacy*. Rotate the thrusters. We're cleared to launch."

1719 was, once again, thankful for her helmet, because her eyes rolled so hard they would've bounced into the aisle. Instead she just patted Clamps on the shoulder.

"Easy, big guy. I thought you and I could check and see if the good lieutenant needs two extra soldiers."

214 paused mid pull-up. "Shroud? Can you trust her?"

1719 shrugged. "She's an officer. N.O.T., right?"

Everyone nodded.

"Besides, she seems to dislike Shikra as much as the rest of us, so that's got to mean something."

A new voice spoke up from the loading bay door. "I wouldn't count on that."

1719's pulse skipped as she, along with the others, whirled around. Getting caught talking about a superior officer was not taken lightly by Corps Command. A few troopers had gotten shipped off to backwater parts of the galaxy where Hutts wouldn't be caught leaving slime trails. But it wasn't an officer who stood framed in the entrance; nor was it a trooper. It was Endayi Jaliss.

"Lady Jaliss," 1719 said after taking a moment to recover. "What are you doing here?"

The young heiress stepped into the light of the lander, holding the hem of her dress off the floor. She paused, then pressed the button to raise the ramp, waiting until it closed completely before stepping closer. Lady Jaliss looked at each of them, almost as if she was measuring what to say and how to say it. Finally she pulled her shoulders back and inhaled.

"We don't have much time, and we are limited in who we can trust," she said.

Clamps glanced around. "We are?"

"I am," Endayi said. "And the group I represent. I have to admit that I wasn't completely honest earlier when you asked me about my family's shipments, but I didn't know if I could trust you. If I should trust you. The First Order doesn't always make it easy to do so, and our family has been burned by galactic governments in the past."

Twelve stiffened. "Your family's shipments? You're working with the pirates?"

Everyone started talking at once. Clamps shouted accusations, and Twelve listed off cargo shipments and the deaths of the crew members ferrying them after the pirates attacked, while 214 tried to calm him down. Finally, 1719 had to short-circuit her external helmet speaker, letting the high-pitched feedback squeal in the lander for several seconds, until everyone reeled in discomfort.

"Enough!" she shouted. "Whatever Lady Jaliss is admitting to, we won't understand unless we let her talk. So . . . let her talk. Lady Jaliss . . . I think you'd better explain."

The young woman nodded. "We . . . I . . . owe you an apology. I am deeply, deeply sorry. Had I known what I know now, I would've told you this when we first talked. But the protests and my own fears got in the way. So I tell you this now: First, the Jaliss Group is not working with pirates. At all, and unequivocally. It is all my fault. I, without my family's knowledge, have been funneling money and supplies to my sister-in-law. She and her children, my nieces, have been trying to survive on their own since . . . since my third brother's departure."

1719 and Twelve glanced at each other. *Third brother?*

"Third brother?" Clamps said, echoing their thoughts aloud, since the big guy wouldn't know what a filter was if it punched him in the mouth. "Didn't know you have a third brother."

"Had." Endayi smiled, but it was a sad smile, one filled with memory and regret. "Not many do, and my father likes it that way. My father and my brother had a disagreement, a major one, and my brother left with his wife and my nieces a year and a half ago to start a homestead on Brel. Father was livid. He had every record of my brother scrubbed from all of our systems and the ones he could influence. And if he couldn't use his influence, he used his money. Before long, any mention of my brother could get you blacklisted from contracts and employment."

That's why he wasn't listed in the records, 1719 thought. She was making a mental note to work with Twelve and some of the droids back on the *Supremacy* to update their data retrieval protocol when a sharp inhale broke her concentration. 214 was standing frozen, and she was looking right at 1719.

"A year and a half ago," she repeated. "On Brel."

Clamps glanced at her, then at 1719 before muttering several curses everyone was too preoccupied to comment on. 1719 was rooted to the spot. Unable to move. Her fingers were stiff, curling into hooks inside her gloves, and her mouth had gone dry.

Twelve looked around the lander. "What? What happened on Brel?"

"The Merchant Uprising," 1719 said, swallowing a lump in her throat.

Endayi flashed a small bitter smile. "Is that what they're calling it on the newsfeed?"

She doesn't know we were there, 1719 thought.

"It was more like a massacre," Endayi continued. "A bloodbath. Father didn't share all the details, but I overheard him talking about it with colleagues one evening after too many cups of wine. Apparently, though he didn't approve of his son and 'rightful heir' joining up with the merchants and protesting the First Order, he kept tabs on him. Kept updating the feeds, kept getting information from his sources."

Blaster fire rained downhill, churning up dirt and dust and clogging the air with as many screams as there was smoke. She couldn't see. Couldn't hear anything beyond the screams, and her hands kept squeezing the trigger on her own blaster even after the power pack whined its overheat alarm. She just wanted the screaming to stop.

"Boss?" Clamps whispered on their private channel.

1719 pulled herself back to the present. She hadn't slipped into an episode in months, and now she'd had two in a week. She nodded at Clamps and turned back to Endayi, who was still talking, unaware of the problem.

"—tried contacting my brother and his wife. He tried to get them to come back, and then when . . . when my brother was killed during the—what did you call it? The Uprising? Well, after the Uprising, my father kept trying to convince my sister-in-law to come back. Saying the kids needed a support network, but she ignored him. Months later, after he named me heir and I gained access to the family resources, I searched his secure files and got my sister-in-law's location. And . . . I started sending her supplies. Small things at first. Toys for my nieces. Clothes. Then I sent more. There were always more children needing something. Hundreds of orphans, no one to care for them. I wished I could bring them all here. Instead I sent what I could."

1719 squeezed her fingers into fists, then uncurled them one by one, forcing herself to calm as her mind raced. "And . . . and then she started telling you about the pirate problem."

"It was like the Uprising all over again," the heiress said, her voice filled with frustration. "Except this time no one was coming to help."

"So you sent weapons," Clamps said, catching on.

"But not the new ones," Twelve jumped in.

Endayi shook her head. "I found what I could. Old blasters from the guards, or barrels of old sturm dowels they could use to fashion their own weapons."

"Like the crossbows they had on Locke Station," 1719 said slowly. She looked over at the young woman, a few years younger than herself, yet taking on the protection of an entire space station when those in charge refused to do the same. And here she was, a stormtrooper corporal on the verge of a breakdown. Helpless.

No, not helpless. Not yet. There was still something she could do.

1719 walked over to the Jaliss heiress, stopping right in front of her. "You said you needed our help," she said. "Is it about the supplies? Or your sister-in-law?"

Endayi took a deep breath. "Both. After the last shipment got intercepted by pirates, Serah—my sister-in-law—said that she was taking matters into her own hands. She was going to pick up the next shipment herself."

"What's wrong with that?" Clamps asked. "Less go-betweens, less of a chance information gets leaked to the pirates."

"I know, and originally I agreed. Especially because of the confrontation today. It's been stewing for a while. Some of the older members of the Rive Collective didn't want to call in the First Order for the trouble on the horizon, so they managed to get brand-new blasters from their connections with Sonn-Blas Corporation smuggled in just in case something like today happened."

"You want to talk about a bloodbath," 214 said. She leaned over and snagged the power cell, turning it over in her hands. "Untrained rich people waving around blasters. No offense."

"I know, I know, and I agree. That's why I thought I would be helping when I arranged for a crate or two to go missing and be shipped to Serah separately. At least they could put them to better use. So I paid a crew to grab the first shipment, but when they didn't deliver, Serah said she would get the second shipment herself."

Twelve sat up. "Wait. Wait. They didn't grab just the shipment."

Everyone stared at him. Clamps bent over until they were helmet to helmet. "What are you talking about, Twelve? They did grab it, that's why we're dealing with this mess in the first place, remember?"

"No, they didn't just grab *a couple of crates*." He spun around in his seat and started tapping rapidly on the lander's comm console, then pointed at a stream of data that he quickly realized no one but him could really understand. "Remember the morale report? And the reason the Xen Runners were so eager to get away rather than continue to shake down the people on Locke Station? They grabbed the whole ship."

"The Rodian," 1719 slowly said. "Remember? The kid. He and his friend stole a ship filled with supplies. He told me they were allowed to join the Xen Runners because they let Kesh have everything they brought."

214 stopped messing with the power cell. "They bribed their way into a gang of pirates with enough guns to take over a small planet. Right under the First Order's nose. And that was only one of the shipments. No wonder Shikra wants those blasters back. It happened in his sector. He's the one who'll get the blame."

"Shikra won't be the only one hunting for that second shipment," 1719 said. "Anyone who found enough containers of next-generation F-11Ds to outfit a battalion would be pretty powerful on whatever local scene they were in."

"But they'd have to find them," Clamps said. He looked around. "You just said the only reason the Xen Runners got them was because two kids practically gave them away."

"And one of them got himself killed as a result," 214 muttered.

1719 ignored her and stared at Endayi. "I think that's what the heiress is about to tell us. Someone found the location of the pickup." She had a sneaking suspicion who but waited for the confirmation.

Endayi, to her credit, didn't shift any blame. "Someone broke into my files when the riot started. I shouldn't have had them away from my secure console, but I needed to get a message to Serah. Your Lieutenant Shroud was seen tampering with them while we were . . . occupied in the Gravitorium."

"And that's when the good lieutenant disappeared," Clamps growled.

1719 sighed, a weary exhale that seemed to leach away energy from deep inside her until she was scraped and hollow. "No old troopers," she whispered.

"Boss?"

She looked up. "We were used. We're always being used." When no one replied, she sighed again. "I guess that means we're not going to work for her, hmm, Clamps?"

He snorted. "No. No, probably not."

1719 turned to Endayi. "So what exactly do you want us to do?"

"Find Serah. She hasn't responded to my messages, and I'm afraid when she gets them it will be too late. She's heading for the second shipment of blasters. Get her out of there, any way you can." Endayi shook her head, her eyes wet, even though she kept the tears from falling. "She'll fight to the last, but my nieces have already lost one parent. They can't lose the other."

1719 glanced at her squad. Twelve, of course, was nodding along enthusiastically. The boy was infatuated. Clamps had his arms folded but was looking at 1719. He would follow whatever order she gave. 214 stood silently for several moments, then nodded, as well.

1719 hesitated. "Why us?" she finally asked. "We're stormtroopers, the people who killed your brother."

Her words were harsh. Maybe intentionally so. But if Lady Jaliss took offense, she didn't show it. Instead, the heiress smiled.

"The First Order says they are a force for change and peace," she said. "You are the first I've seen that made me believe that."

1719 swallowed. Those words . . . she wanted to—no, needed to hear them. "I . . . we understand. We'll do our best." She cleared her throat. "For now, you need to get back." She hit the button to lower the ramp, letting the cool breeze of the Rive night slip into the lander. As Endayi stepped down, Twelve stepped forward, a datapad in his hands.

"Lady Jaliss," he called.

"Yes," Endayi said, pausing on the ramp.

"Should we take a message to S—to your contact? From you?"

She smiled, then shook her head. "Just to get somewhere safe for a while. She knows where. She's the explorer. It was her idea to pick our drop-off location."

"Where is that, by the way?" 1719 asked.

Endayi frowned. "An archipelago on a planet in the Outer Rim. Lovely place, which doesn't surprise me, since she hates the cold. I think it's called Ansett Island."

CHPTR - 29

FN-2187 walked forward, one step after another.

The oasis was filled with color, from pennants and flags tied to the few trees to the outfits the Sardichians wore, long and flowing and forming a kaleidoscope of every color imaginable. Young children scampered around the lone pond with homemade kites on strings while adults cradled cups of something spiced that fizzed when poured. Vegetables and other delicacies roasted on spits, and pockets of musicians danced from crowd to crowd, bursting into song while they drummed furiously.

Eight-Seven weaved his way through the crowd, his helmet off, a colorful cloak draped over his armor. A few people glanced at him suspiciously, but he ignored them, even when they shot glares or huddled together in whispers. Then a couple of younger adults started to follow him, but a few theatrical twirls of the vibrosword—even when he continued to stare straight ahead—kept any sort of confrontation from occurring. He just moved forward. According to a stumbling lady with two friends supporting her, the cargo storage was in the abandoned quarry village on the other side of the oasis, and that was where he was headed.

That was where the major would be.

The vibrosword scraped against the ground as he walked. Eight-Seven had wrestled with the idea of bringing it. He'd never trained with swords. Not even something close to it. But he had no blaster rifle, no pistol, and the knives seemed like an even worse idea. So it was the sword that ended up being the only weapon he carried, the only defense he had.

That, and the beginnings of an idea.

Eight-Seven continued to put one foot in front of the other. The musicians had all gathered in the shallows of the pond, stomping and splashing as the crowds circled them, clapping in time. They sang along, some booming collective song that swelled and repeated in the night air.

The song continued to echo in Eight-Seven's ears long after he left the oasis behind. He moved slower now, more carefully, as the ground began to slope downhill. The quarry village unfolded in front of him suddenly, as if the foothills were slowly beginning to devour it. Tan homes carved out of rock were partially sunk, sand spilling out of windows and doorways. An old marketplace had become overgrown with sweet-smelling succulents, thorny plants blooming with flowers in the shade of an old repair shop and general store.

Eight-Seven put one foot in front of the other.

He heard the swearing first. Holding the vibrosword in one hand, Eight-Seven discarded the cloak—it would only get in the way now—and put on his helmet. He crept forward, peeking around corners as he listened.

"Slag-forsaken piece of junk. I would resurrect that senator just to have her killed again if I could. She's tormenting me from the grave."

A pause, then a sigh.

"No, don't record that. Strike that last bit, please."

Eight-Seven crept around the high wall of some sort of animal pen, peeking around the corner while holding his breath.

Major Gohl stood at the entrance of a boarded-up cantina, his droid hovering above his right shoulder. Carved into a flat section of reddish-brown rock beneath a large overhang, the abandoned business sported faded letters in a local dialect that curled over the windows, and it must've been a hub of activity when it was open. Now it played host to a corrupt officer of the First Order, a murderer and a traitor to everything the Order stood for.

Eight-Seven stepped around the corner. It took several seconds before he was noticed, and it was the droid who actually spotted him. It zoomed in and out, then beeped in alarm.

"What?" Major Gohl said, not paying attention. "Who?"

More beeps.

The major looked up, then turned around. For once, he appeared rattled. His jaw dropped before he recovered and straightened up, smoothing his uniform and adjusting his cape before producing his trademark smile.

"FN-Two-One-Eight-Seven!" he called. "My boy! You did it!"

Eight-Seven walked forward, vibrosword tip scraping the sand-covered rock at his feet.

The major shifted, the smile faltering. "Congratulations are in order, aren't they? You've finished the training! When we return home, your superiors will be pleased to learn of your progress, and how your new role as *squad leader* will slot in nicely with their troop deployments. You've done it, son. You're—"

"Don't," Eight-Seven snarled.

The major's smile faded. "I don't—"

"This was never about training. You used us, didn't you?"

"I am an officer with the First Order," Major Gohl snapped. "You don't question me. I am the one who asks the questions."

"Lies."

"Excuse me?"

"Lies, all of it." Eight-Seven stepped forward again, his right hand squeezing the hilt of the vibrosword so hard, it was cutting through his gloves. "Lies and more lies. You don't represent the First Order. You only care about your own schemes. The money. Your own little empire you're building."

"That's preposterous!"

"Is it? I've listened to every morale session. I've never missed one. I heard about 'the civil war on Sardich.' About the bombings. The killings. The violence. About how there was nothing left but refugees who were transported off-world to First Order–provided housing aboard a space station."

The major's face grew paler and tighter the more Eight-Seven spoke.

"But this doesn't look like refugees and violence, does it?" Eight-Seven gestured back toward the oasis, where the faint sounds of music and laughter could be heard. "Recovering, maybe. Struggling, sure. But not a lost cause, which is what you called it."

"Naturally there's a bit of embellishing," Major Gohl said, "but surely that's to be expected."

Eight-Seven gritted his teeth. "What was *expected* was aid. Help. Credits, supplies, and equipment to rebuild. You know, things the First Order is supposed to do. Our responsibility."

"We are building something," the major hissed.

"And it starts with the people! I saw the logs on the senator's desk. The requests. Food. Materials to build shelters. All sent to the First Order, all denied by one Major Chetachi Gohl. And now I see why."

"You don't see anything!" the major exploded. "You see the same thing everyone sees, which is what someone higher up tells you. You are a cog, and cogs don't lecture the builder on the blueprint. You hop when I say hop, you shoot when I say shoot, you go where I say go."

"And we die?"

The major paused, distaste flickering across his face. "Sometimes cogs need to be replaced. But one fault can bring down an entire operation."

"We are *not* pieces of a puzzle—"

"That's exactly what you are! You are a piece of the First

Order! Remember? There is no individual, only the unit. The squad, the team, the group."

"And you killed one of us."

Major Gohl flapped his hand. "FO-Seventy-One-Fifty-Five disobeyed orders, and the senator's bodyguard killed him."

"You mean you killed him. *You* did it! Why?"

"Oh, come on, son! Look around! Where are you? Light-years away from your home, which is a floating fortress in space. The galaxy is an enormous place, and we are expected to bring order to it while waiting on the chain of command? No! This is initiative! This is ingenuity! Sardich can become something great, a cornerstone of power!"

"With you in command," Eight-Seven said softly.

"Well . . . yes."

"And the mineral deposits crucial to the new blaster rifle variants are what? A bonus? Yeah, I saw those reports, too."

"Oh, come now," the major said, throwing up his hands in exasperation. "It's a simple mining venture."

"One that will mean a lot of credits for whoever controls it. Is that why you killed the senator? Because she wouldn't agree to putting her people back into servitude after they just finished fighting for their freedom from forced labor?"

"Senator Reat'ha was killed because she was a fool!" Major

Gohl shouted, fists balled. He pointed at Eight-Seven. "Now her people will suffer. I offered her a partnership. A respectable split. There were never any intentions to take over. But she, like you, couldn't see the vision from the clouds her head was floating in. We could've created a story to rival that of Corellia itself. A planet pulling itself up from civil recklessness with the help of the First Order, becoming the center of an economic powerhouse out here in the lawlessness of the Unknown Regions."

"But she cared about her people."

"She should've committed to them. Instead she forced my hand."

Eight-Seven couldn't believe this was the man he had idolized. Who he'd thought embodied everything good about the First Order. He felt disgusted. Used and unclean. He pointed the vibrosword at the officer, his voice trembling with barely restrained anger.

" 'We are of a singular mind,' " he said. "Remember? Those were your words. 'Without stability there is unrest. Without dedication there is corruption. Without order there is chaos.' "

"Don't parrot the creed at me, boy," Major Gohl said. "I wrote it."

"We are supposed to be heroes."

"And who do you think manufactures those heroes? *I* do! The idols you worship, the soldiers you champion, the history you commemorate—I create that! I build your adulation. I design your rage and thirst for vengeance. I am the First Order! Without my words, you would have no purpose! No motivation."

It was true in a sense. Eight-Seven shivered in disgust at the memory of how eager he'd been to attend morale sessions. To lie in the dark and visualize the battles occurring across the galaxy. How many of those were false, or embellished, or *designed* as the major said? How many people in the First Order had the major lied to? He gripped the vibrosword in both hands now, bringing it in front of him to point at the man who'd betrayed everything Eight-Seven believed in.

"You are *not* the First Order," he said. "I still believe we can do great things without betraying the code. It's people like you who need to be exposed and reported."

Major Gohl laughed. "And how—"

He didn't finish the sentence, because Eight-Seven had lunged forward, the vibrosword swinging. The major flung himself to the right, just barely missing being skewered. But he didn't have time to rest as Eight-Seven pivoted and lashed out with the sword again. It was ugly and ungainly, lacking any semblance of skill, but he didn't care. He just wanted to attack.

The major flapped his cloak, pulling his small blaster pistol from the hidden holster at his waist and getting off one shot before deflecting another attack with the bottom of the muzzle and punching the boy in the helmet, momentarily stunning him. The blaster hammered the side of the helmet again and again.

"Give it up, boy," the major panted as Eight-Seven grappled with him, struggling to avoid the hail of blows raining down on his helmet, which could only protect so much. "You will die here. I will craft a story from your death, too. Two stormtroopers die protecting the senator of a backwater mining planet from a rebel faction of the most recent civil war. In response, the First Order moves in, liberating the planet and vowing to protect it and the rest of the sector."

Major Gohl hurled Eight-Seven to the ground, and the stormtrooper rolled several meters before slamming into the boarded-up entrance of the old cantina. He lay there, hunched over and groaning, for several seconds.

The major laughed as he sucked down lungfuls of air. "Whew! Been a while since I sparred, boy. I owe you thanks—can't neglect my own training, now can I?"

Eight-Seven clawed at the sand, slowly rising to his hands and knees, only to grunt in pain as the major kicked him in the ribs. The major straightened, wiping his forehead and backing up.

"You would have made a fantastic agent for the Bureau," the man said. "I could have made that happen. Now you're just a statistic. A regretful line in a datafile no one will ever read."

Major Gohl laughed sarcastically again as he started looking around, checking his pockets and his cape. As he did, Eight-Seven slowly began to climb to his hands and knees again, then used the cantina walls to pull himself to his feet, swaying slightly as he cradled his ribs. He pulled off his helmet to reveal a bruised and cut face glistening with blood and sweat and spat in the sand before wiping his mouth.

"Missing something, sir?" he asked.

The major turned.

Eight-Seven removed the arm that had been cradling his ribs to reveal the major's personal droid, powered off and motionless. He flicked it on and held it up. "Replay previous recording, mark seven minutes ago."

The major's face pinched in fury as the droid played back a garbled recording of his own voice. *"Senator Reat'ha was killed because she was a fool! Now her people will suffer."*

"What do you think that will do?" the major asked. "You have no way of getting that off-planet, not by ship or by comm relay. I *control* all of the ships and comm relays in this system. I am information, I am the message, I am the news! You are a body with no brain, because *I* am your brain. You put on your armor when I tell you to, you aim your blaster where I tell you to, and you do what I TELL YOU TO DO!"

Major Gohl was shouting at this point, wide-eyed and nearly frothing at the mouth. His arms waved about, and veins popped out of his neck and forehead. Gone was the calm officer. He was rattled and only focused on Eight-Seven. As if he suddenly realized he was losing control, the major paused and inhaled. He smoothed his cape, took off his cap, and ran his fingers through his hair, then replaced it and brushed sand off of his pants.

"You are nothing," he said simply. "And you will be nothing. Now . . . hand over the droid before you do irreparable damage, more than you've already done."

Eight-Seven, in response, raised the droid and played the recording again. *"Senator Reat'ha was killed because she was a fool! Now her people will suffer."*

Major Gohl sighed. "What is the point of this? Why do you even care?"

Eight-Seven lifted his chin. The evening breeze whistled

through the abandoned quarry village, carrying the scents of wildflowers and spice. FO-7155 would have complained it was too hot, and Eight-Seven smiled and looked back at the major, ignoring the rustle of movement gathering in the square behind the officer.

"I care because a good friend—who you murdered—said that was the reason for the First Order. To care. I care"—he paused and pointed to the stone rooftop opposite the cantina—"because they care."

The major turned and froze.

Hundreds of Sardichians lined the street and the rooftops. They were silent, even as their colorful cloaks flapped in the wind. They were still, even as their faces twisted from confusion to comprehension to anger. No. Fury. They gathered, like a storm on the desert horizon, even as Eight-Seven lifted the droid high in the air and replayed Major Gohl's warning over and over.

"Senator Reat'ha was killed because she was a fool! Now her people will suffer."

"Senator Reat'ha was killed because she was a fool! Now her people will suffer."

The response, when it finally came, was harsh and inevitable. The Sardichians swarmed the First Order officer and demanded answers, anger boiling over as Major Gohl screamed for help. He briefly waved his blaster in the air, and the crowds paused momentarily, but when he tried to fire, the power core whined before cutting off.

Eight-Seven turned, holding up the vibrosword. "You go for their blaster and without it . . . they're useless," he muttered to himself. Then, with a vicious slash, he cut through the boards sealing the cantina and kicked the door open.

A stack of crates waited inside. Eight-Seven stared, then reached into a hidden pocket on his belt and pulled out the single credit chit 7155 had found on Tamo'Akora. He examined it, then turned and tossed it to a curious boy, whose eyes widened. Eight-Seven nodded at the now open cantina.

"Tell your leader it's all here," he said. As the boy called to his friends and rushed inside, Eight-Seven limped away, his thoughts far from the shouts of the Sardichians and the terrified screams of Major Gohl.

Later, when Eight-Seven had respectfully carried Senator Reat'ha's body to a place where her staff could find her, and after he'd lugged, pulled, and willed 7155's body aboard their shuttle and the boy's helmet sat atop the flight controls in front of him, Fifty-Five's body wrapped for transport in the back, Eight-Seven had a brief moment of regret. A flicker of worry. Should he have saved the major? Maybe he could've bargained with the Sardichians, taking him into custody after returning the credits. Transported him back to the *Finalizer* to face judgment.

But would he? Or would he escape punishment, allowed to retire somewhere without retribution?

And that flicker of worry disappeared. Let the major face the people he'd betrayed. Eight-Seven's responsibility lay in getting 7155 back to the First Order. He tapped in the coordinates, prayed they were accurate, and took the shuttle up from the mountain fortress, aiming for the stars.

"Let's go home," he whispered, glancing at the helmet in front of him.

The shuttle bucked as a thruster sputtered, and the ship nearly clipped a turret on its way to the clouds.

"Whoops," Eight-Seven said. Sheepishly, he toggled on the autopilot and slumped back in his seat, arms folded in disappointment that he still didn't know how to fly. The helmet stared silently, and he shook his head and turned it to face the other way. "Shut up."

CHPTR - 30

Halfway to Ansett Island everything went wrong.

Actually, the mission—their mission—had gone sideways before that. Clamps and TZ-214 got pulled into a different platoon. One second they were loading up as a squad, the next, two officers clad in gray were dividing troopers into sections, sending some to one lander, others to a different one. She didn't even have time to react. They were gone.

Doesn't matter, TZ-1719 thought. *We're heading to the same place. We'll link up on the island. Find Serah, get them away from Shikra's reach, and if we get back to the* Finalizer, *maybe Phasma will take me on as a bodyguard. Maybe she can help the others get out of Company 77, as well.*

Those thoughts kept her from spiraling. Her plan, and the assurance of her squad's future—her friends' future—kept her sane.

Find Serah.

Make it back to the Finalizer.

Join Phasma.

She chanted the steps in her head like a mantra. 1719 glued them to the top of her mind as the assault lander descended through the charged storm clouds of planet Epo. She recited them as the troopers around her shuffled their boots nervously, or rocked in place, or whispered about the increased number of officers joining them on the mission. She pressed them so firmly into her thoughts, she could have sworn they left a mark.

Still, the fact remained Captain Shikra had left a skeleton crew aboard the *Culverin*, pulling several staff from the cruiser's flight crew to keep Company 77's three platoons on task and on time, in his words. No official reprimand had been given, but 1719 was pretty sure Shikra wasn't happy with their performance on Rive. Far from it. He was furious.

Yes, they'd done their job—tensions had eased and negotiators were optimistic. No more disruptions, no more delayed Rive Collective shipments for the First Order. Mission successful.

And yes, the captain had his traitor . . . somewhat. Before they'd taken off, Lieutenant Shroud had revealed Endayi's role in shipping supplies to her sister. If Shikra felt any remorse at the impact of the Merchant Uprising, he didn't show it. He absorbed the information that there was no betrayer sabotaging the First Order, only desperate relatives sending aid to a sector torn by violence. So mission accomplished, right?

From the outside, sure. But there was a thick tension in the lander. Something more than pre-mission jitters or descent sickness. The troopers were nervous. Anxious. And though they would never admit it, 1719 could sense it. Something Captain Phasma had drilled into her head hour after hour during her intense training sessions: Trust your instincts. In this case, her instincts were screaming that Shikra didn't trust them, and the proof lay in the presence of the six extra squads split up among Company 77's landers.

Shikra had brought his shock troopers, and finding Serah and getting her away unharmed suddenly became more important . . . and more difficult.

"Platoon Gamma," a familiar voice said over a comm channel, "our job is to secure the landing site for Platoons Delta and Theta. This is a rolling drop, so I want boots on the ground ASAP so our lander can clear out. Understood?"

"Yes, sir!"

1719 gripped her blaster. The platoon leader walked the line, barking orders and counting down. When they reached her, 1719 stared straight ahead. Sergeant (or was it Private now?) Calcon stared at her for several seconds, then continued on down the line, performing her as yet unchanged duties. Even though the helmet hid her expression, something in her tone, or maybe in the set of her shoulders, caught 1719's attention, pulling her from her thoughts. Something familiar. Something she herself had felt at one point while serving under Captain Shikra during the Merchant Uprising.

Calcon was still in shock.

1719 pursed her lips. She glanced back. Calcon had paused again, silent, and seemed to be staring off into the distance. When a nearby shock trooper shifted in place, Calcon flinched. It was tiny, so tiny 1719 nearly missed it, but the former platoon leader flinched.

1719's pursed lips turned into a full frown. She keyed her squad's private channel. Static burst in her ear, and she winced. The lights above her flickered, and she realized the storm was influencing the electrical systems. Her speaker still worked, however, and she began to turn.

"Clamps—" she said.

But before she could say anything else—not that 1719

knew what could be done about Calcon, maybe a warning to the team or just a plea to be careful—the lights in the lander flickered from red to green, and suddenly the front door was lowering into a ramp. Sunlight crashed inside. Wind hurled sand at their helmets, momentarily blinding them, but they stormed out regardless onto a misty gray beach. Frothy waves slammed into the base of giant sand dunes that stretched overhead. The coastline curved left and right, disappearing into the distance. Platoon Gamma split apart, fracturing into smaller squads that pushed outward in a circle, blasters tight against shoulders as they scanned for hostiles.

"Clear!"

"Clear!"

"Delta lander coming in!"

A hand landed on 1719's shoulder. "Boss," Twelve said.

1719 nodded in acknowledgment, still scanning the area. Serah would be farther inland. "Any signs of Clamps and Twenty-One-Four?"

"Not yet. Managed to grab a deployment order and a map before the equipment went haywire. South side, by the former sergeant. But the channel is down, so we'll have to go back and get them."

1719 paused, remembering the flinch, then shook her head. "They'll be fine," she said, as much to herself as to

Twelve. She hated the idea of not being able to communicate directly with her squad, not being able to shield them. It was like losing a bit of herself. She pushed her feelings down, locking them away, and focused down her blaster sight at the top of the dune in front of her. "They'll be fine."

He nodded at the blaster. "Surprised to see you carrying that."

"Don't worry," she said, twisting so he could see the riot baton dangling from its holster on her waist. "Your good friend is still tagging along."

Twelve snorted and she grinned, but the expression faded when he turned back around to survey the slope of the dune. The absence of the rest of the team nagged at her.

Platoon Delta's landing distracted her, and soon more troopers disembarked, the process repeating with Platoon Theta. Soon the beach was a hive of activity. Command posts went up, comm arrays were connected, and orders were dispatched. Techs argued, examined displays, and fiddled with the controls. A trooper with a mobile comm array on his back pushed forward, receiver in his hands, and Captain Shikra shook his head in disgust.

"The storm is jamming the comms," 1719 said, understanding dawning.

"Boss?"

She nodded at the trooper, who'd shrugged out of the array and was fiddling with the circuitry. "They can't get through to the *Culverin*. Just like our squad channel. The storm is naturally jamming us. The landers will probably have to stay here since they won't be able to call for evac."

Twelve groaned. "More guard duty?"

"Not us. Them."

Shadows emerged from the mist behind them. Shikra's shock troopers, with their repeater blasters and matte black armor, marched toward a clearing on the sand, creating a perimeter. They must have disembarked farther down the beach, creating their own HQ. The sand began to rumble and shift as the roar of thrusters joined the angry waves, and the three landers swept forward from the southern side of the beach, the opposite direction from where they'd departed.

They were scouting, 1719 realized.

Sure enough, an officer jogged from the nearest lander to Shikra, speaking rapidly into his ear and gesturing deeper inland, east, up the massive dunes. Shikra nodded, then turned to the platoon leaders. Orders began to travel up the line, but 1719 had started searching for Clamps and 214 again. She hated that she was worried, because a worried trooper was an unprepared trooper, and unprepared troopers found early graves.

"They'll be fine," she whispered.

"You say something?" Twelve asked.

1719 shook her head, then pointed up the dune. "Looks like we're moving. Get that map handy, and remember—"

"Find Serah, get her to safety. I know, I know. I've got this."

She tried to force a light tone into her voice. "And stay alive. N.O.T., remember?"

Twelve threw a mock salute before scrambling up the hill. 1719 glanced back to the beach, where Shikra stood, hands clasped behind his back, scanning the area. His gaze swept past her, then returned, and for a brief moment she could feel him studying her. He turned, nodding to someone just out of sight.

Three black-armored shock troopers stepped forward. She studied their stance, noting how they weren't protecting the command post, only the captain. Bodyguards. They all turned to look at her.

1719 turned and began to climb the hill.

CHPTR - 31

"According to reports, Lady Jaliss's information, and this map . . . we're lost."

Twelve stared at the holomap projected on the ground in front of them, twisting his head this way and that to somehow find a better angle where they weren't hopelessly astray, and failing. He was squatting, the projection emitting from his wrist display, which he'd continued to fiddle with for the past five minutes. Maybe this spot was the clearing they were in. No. Maybe . . . no, not there, either. The map expanded, zooming in on a section of forest, then zoomed out to show the island's entire topography before rotating and repeating the process. Finally he threw his hands up and turned off the holomap.

"I don't know, boss, maybe we should've went left at that last dune instead of . . . boss?" He turned to find the clearing empty. "Boss?"

Nothing.

They'd run nearly a quarter of an hour from the beach before stopping to catch their breath in this section of scrub. Ansett Island seemed to alternate between sand too soft to move about appropriately to dense scrub that . . . well, was also difficult to move around in. He was panting and wheezing when 1719 had paused, though now he wasn't so sure it was to check the map like she'd said but to give him a minute to catch his breath.

His neck flushed, and Twelve bit back a grimace. He knew he was out of shape. Knew the others held themselves back to make sure he didn't fall behind, physically or in the training scores. He knew it, hated it, and was grateful for them just the same. So he sighed, hefted his blaster rifle from where he (incorrectly, probably) had it propped against a particularly large bit of scrub, and cleared his throat.

"All right, boss, I'm ready."

The trill of some local fauna was his only response. Twelve frowned.

"You can stop pretending now. I know you don't need to catch your breath. I know you want to spare my feelings, but believe it or not, I'm not a kid. I can take care of myself."

Silence. Even the fauna seemed to have no reply to that. The heat of embarrassment switched to anger. "I said, I can take care—"

A hiss and a pop, followed by garbled chatter, cut him off. He knew that noise. He heard it all the time—it was a comlink. Someone was nearby, and they didn't want to be found.

Fear slithered down his spine.

Nothing moved. Nothing made a sound. Not even the wind.

He wanted to run. Wanted to hide. Too late he remembered his blaster, and Twelve fumbled with the strap, trying to raise it and aim when the clump of leaves to his left shifted.

The silver-and-black nose of a heavy repeater blaster emerged from the dense scrub. It stayed there, floating amid the green leaves and brown branches, and he swallowed, his mouth suddenly dry. For several long seconds, it floated there before suddenly withdrawing.

A shock trooper stepped through. Twelve closed his eyes in relief. Shikra must've sent backup. He opened them and started to make a joke when he realized the repeater blaster was still aimed at him.

A branch cracked to his right. Another shock trooper emerged from the foliage, blaster aimed at Twelve. Both troopers were tall, a full half meter larger than Twelve, and the matte black of their armor was jarring to look at, like an optical trick designed to confuse him right before . . . well, whatever was supposed to happen next.

"Found him," the first said.

The second nodded. "No sign of the other one."

More garbled chatter sounded, and the first pressed a hand to his helmet, as if trying to hear. Twelve noticed the barrel of the repeater never wavered. He needed to do something.

"Hey, guys," he said. "How's . . . how's the weather?"

Smooth, he thought. *Real smooth. You're never getting invited to their wing.*

The first trooper looked at his partner. "Roger that," they said. "Interrogating now." Both shock troopers aimed their repeaters at Twelve and took a step forward.

"Hey, whoa, whoa!" Twelve shouted. "We're on the same side!"

"Where's TZ-One-Seven-One-Nine?"

"Who?" He was genuinely confused, and it took a second for him to realize that he was so used to calling her boss that he'd forgotten her ID.

"I don't know. I don't know!" The last was shouted as the repeater's power core or whatever it was (Clamps would know the specific model and version) began to whine when the trooper thumbed off the safety. "We got lost in the scrub and I got separated. What are you doing? Does Captain Shikra know you're waving that thing around like that? You're violating about fifty stormtrooper regulations! I should march you back to command—"

The repeater whined as Twelve took a step forward, and he froze, arms lifted in the air.

"Okay, okay!"

"Where is TZ-One-Seven-One-Nine?" the shock trooper repeated.

"I said I don't know. I'm lost! I'm *lost*!"

"Down," one commanded as the other kicked the back of Twelve's right knee, sending him collapsing to the sandy ground. He was panicking. He couldn't breathe. This wasn't supposed to happen. They were on the same side. They were First Order!

"Restrain him. We'll put him with the others," the first shock trooper said. Disgust curdled the words. Twelve had heard disgust like that before as a trooper, usually when he was too slow, or too weak, or too different from the other cadets, or juniors, or pretty much everybody he ever encountered.

Except for TZ-1719, and Clamps, and TZ-214.

Wait . . . others. What others? The people they came to

find? Or other stormtroopers, like himself? He was so confused, so out of sorts that nothing made sense.

"Please," he said, "there's been a mistake."

"No mistake. Other than command letting runts like you into the Corps." The second trooper put his boot on Twelve's shoulder and kicked him onto his back. He landed hard, the breath whooshing out of his lungs and a searing pain shooting through his wrists. His vision blurred. He saw treetops swirling with the stormy gray sky, and the barrel of the repeater as it blocked everything else in his vision, like a violent eclipse.

"You should've just told us where your partner was," the shock trooper said.

"Here," came a voice from the scrub.

A surge of joy rushed through him when he heard 1719, and he nearly laughed, only for the sound to choke in his throat as an explosion of sparks erupted next to the shock trooper's helmet. 1719 had stepped out from behind the tall scrub and slammed the charged end of her riot baton into his head. The repeater landed on the ground with a thud, followed swiftly by the trooper.

Boss, he wanted to say, but she never looked at him.

1719 whirled, whipping the baton in a tight arc to bat aside the repeater blaster of the other shock trooper. Several shots went off, scorching the branches, and Twelve screamed, bile rising from his throat to fill his mouth as he scrambled out of the way of falling branches. When he looked up again, 1719 had lunged in too close for the trooper to aim properly. He snarled, dropped his blaster, and pulled a vibroknife from his belt, then ran forward. Swiped. 1719 dodged, then grabbed his arm and pulled him off-balance. Her elbow slammed into his wrist, and he yelled. The knife fell, but 1719 was still pulling. They were falling, tumbling, and 1719 rolled on top of the shock trooper. She held a rock in her hand—from where, Twelve didn't know—and she was hammering at the temple of her opponent. Once. Twice. Cracks began to grow from the steadily widening dent. The shock trooper struggled, kicking his legs and bucking his hips to get her off, but he couldn't. Her knee was on one arm, and she still held the other, improbably, and he was unable to defend himself as 1719 struck again. And again. And again, until he finally fell still, the side of his helmet caved in.

Then Twelve did throw up, pulling his helmet halfway off to let loose on the sand. He retched, wiped his mouth, and staggered to his feet as 1719 lifted the rock, made a disappointed noise in her throat, and hurled it aside. She nudged the trooper's helmet, then sighed.

"Useless," she said. Twelve watched her stride across the

clearing, drop to a knee, and yank off the helmet of the first shock trooper to reveal a slightly older male with a smear of blood on his temple. She reached inside the helmet, felt around, then yanked out a speaker and wires.

"Better comms," she muttered. "Not affected by the storms. Convenient."

"Jam-resistant processing," Twelve said, and he could barely hear his own voice. Shock. He was in shock. What was the proper protocol for that? "Spreading the spectrum to . . . to allow real-time decision-making on what frequency to use, thereby eliminating interference—well, reducing, not completely eliminating, that's a fallacy . . ." His voice trailed off. "Sorry, I'm babbling again, aren't I?"

1719 laughed. "I could listen to you babble all day, Twelve."

He didn't hear her. His eyes were on the bodies on the ground, and he swallowed. Took a step forward. "You killed them."

Her chuckle faded. "No."

"But—"

"They're not dead. Whether that's a good thing, we'll soon find out. But they're breathing. Which is better than how they were going to leave us."

"How?"

"How is that better? Because—"

"No, how did you do that? Take out two shock troopers without a blaster or anything."

"Training."

"Training! What training? I didn't get training like that!"

1719 shook her head. "Twelve, I promise I'll tell you everything later, but right now I need you to help me hide these bodies before someone else stumbles upon them, and then we need to go. She's waiting."

"She?" Twelve grabbed the trooper's boots as his squad leader lifted from the shoulders, and together they dumped the first trooper into a particularly dense section of scrub before grabbing the second. "And, not to be too paranoid, but aren't we going to get into more trouble for this?"

"She. Serah, remember? I found her. Well, them. I'll explain as we walk. Well, run. And no, we won't get in more trouble."

"Why's that?"

1719 finally looked up and stared at him. "These shock troopers wanted us dead. Can't get into more trouble than that."

CHPTR - 32

TZ-1719's right hand throbbed. She could still feel each blow of the rock bashing into the shock trooper's helmet, the jarring impact shooting up her arm and into her shoulder.

You killed them.

She pushed Twelve's accusation aside. No time for that now. Serah was just up ahead, and though she'd told him they were waiting, she hadn't actually made contact with Lady Jaliss's sister-in-law. She'd spotted the hidden cove while avoiding the shock troopers hunting Twelve, and now she hoped they didn't shoot first and ask questions later.

"Here," she called out. "Just over this ridge."

Twelve grunted something, either a curse that would make Clamps proud or some factoid about trooper armor's lack of aerodynamics.

"Hutt-slimin' piece of ferroceramic anchor-weight weighs more than—"

Okay, so both a curse and a factoid.

The rest of his tirade faded away as 1719 crested the ridge. Ansett Island was actually a caldera, an old volcano whose interior had collapsed, allowing the ocean to seep inside. It formed a sheltered cove, hidden from the exterior beach by the massive sand dunes and scrub forests covering the slopes. Perfect shelter for ships avoiding the constant storms.

Or smugglers avoiding the eyes of the First Order.

A small shuttle with more patches on its hull than undamaged duralloy stood on a large sandbar that jutted out from the inner edge of the caldera. A dozen or so containers were piled by the rear bay door, and several members of the crew hustled about, shoving them on skids and running them up the ramp. Steam wisped from the shuttle's vents, and the air hummed. The ship was ready to take off.

Good, thought 1719. *That should make this even easier.*

Twelve huffed to a stop next to her, stooping as his hands dropped to his knees. "Is that them?" he asked between wheezes and gasps for air. "I can't feel my chest. Is that normal? I need . . . boss, I need something. Oxygen. Water. Anything!"

He was spiraling. 1719 knew the signs. Shock. She had to talk him down, get him back in control of himself.

"We're in so much trouble," he repeated over and over. "So much trouble."

"Twelve, take a breath. It's going to be okay. *We're* going to be okay."

He turned on her, and she didn't need her helmet's heads-up display to tell her Twelve's vitals were all over the place. She could see it in the jerkiness of his movements. Hear it in the shallow breaths and frequent pauses he took between his words. "How do you know? I'm . . . I . . . How do you know? You can't possibly know that! How do you know?"

"Twelve! Breathe." 1719 took a step forward.

"I can't!" He started to claw at his helmet, trying to rip it off. "It's too tight! Everything is too tight!"

Without warning he turned and sprinted downhill, heading straight for the ship and its crew. He was ripping off his gloves and the vambraces on his forearms, then returned to clawing at his helmet.

A shout echoed from below. The crew had noticed Twelve's approach, and 1719 swore under her breath. A stormtrooper running at a group of smugglers? Blasters could start spraying at any second. She could already make out several crew members running into the cargo hold while the others spread out.

She swore again, then took off after Twelve.

The good news was that she was faster than him. Taller, longer, fitter. The bad news was that he had pure terror fueling his sprint, and so it took longer than it should have to chase him down. She flew downhill, leaping over hardened rock outcroppings left over from some eruption in Ansett Island's past and disturbing ground avians that hopped several steps before launching themselves into the air. They swept downhill, low to the ground, in a crowd of leathery wings and clacking bills. It actually worked out in her favor as they disguised her approach, and the smugglers must've thought the disturbance was due to Twelve's erratic dash.

1719 managed to make up two-thirds of the ground between her and Twelve before the avians curved up and away, finally gaining enough speed to lift their ungainly bodies above the caldera. She put on a burst of speed, trying to take advantage of the confusion before she was spotted, too.

Seconds later another shout went up, and she kept her arms up and away from her sides as she splashed through the caldera shallows, skidding to a stop and spraying water and pebbles everywhere as she reached Twelve. The young trooper was on his knees, helmet finally off, dunking his head in the turquoise water and gasping for air. Sand striped his face and the top of his head as he blinked and looked around.

"Boss?"

"Right here," 1719 said, lifting her hands into the air as the smugglers approached, blasters raised. They finally realized it was only the two troopers, not a squad or platoon. She needed to convince them otherwise. "Follow my lead."

"Wha—"

"Follow. My lead. Hey!"

The last was aimed at the three smugglers, assorted blasters pointed at the troopers' chests. They were cloaked and hooded, with scarves and goggles hiding their faces, wearing calf-high boots. No identifying features. In fact, she was pretty sure that Twelve's scanners, even with his "updates" and out of the interference of the electrical storm, would find the transponder on their ship either disabled or shouting a false identification.

"We're looking for someone," 1719 shouted.

"Where's the rest of your squad?" The one in the middle spoke, but their words were altered, modulated and pitched even more than the voices of stormtroopers. Another layer of their disguise.

1719 jerked her head back up the hill. "Three platoons, a full company, are on their way right now for those containers.

You have about three minutes before their island sweep finds this caldera, and then . . . well, you know what will happen."

The three smugglers seemed taken aback at her honesty, just like she'd hoped. They'd approached ready to leave the troopers lifeless in the caldera shallows, and the only way to prevent them from riddling their armor with blaster holes was to keep them off-balance by telling them the truth.

"She's bluffing." The smuggler on the left lifted their blaster as the trio waded closer, until they were only a few paces away. "I say we do the galaxy a favor and rid it of two bucketheads."

"She's not bluffing," Twelve snapped. He was still on his knees in the shallows, hands on his thighs as his shoulders heaved and sagged with each breath that seemed to drain him of energy. "It's true. We're here to warn you."

The one on the right grunted. "Make no sense to bluff. Also doesn't explain why these two are here by themselves? Two grunts out in the middle of a storm? Doesn't track."

"No," the middle smuggler said. "It doesn't."

1719 tilted her head. The way the others kept glancing toward them, how they stood in the middle, slightly ahead. This was the leader. Which meant . . .

"We were sent to you."

"Sent," the smuggler repeated.

"Yes."

"To find us?"

"No. To find you."

The trio of smugglers glanced at each other. Behind them, the others began to slowly filter out of the ship, resuming the cargo container loading. 1719 watched, then shook her head.

"You need to leave. Two minutes, maybe less, and assault landers are going to home in on your position. The island isn't that big."

"And how would they know where we were in the first place?" The smuggler on the left hefted their blaster, as if weighing whether or not to shoot them and ask for forgiveness later.

"Because her sister-in-law's datapad was sliced."

The smugglers froze for an instant, and then blasters hovered centimeters from 1719's face. Even the big calm one on the right gave a low rumble of a growl that sounded like thunder, their massive pistol resting on Twelve's temple. But it was the leader who stepped forward to put the barrel of their blaster beneath 1719's chin.

"What did you say?"

Twelve gulped. "One of the Bureau's spies sliced into a datapad your sister-in-law was using to communicate with you. The First Order's been trying to track down these blasters for months. And now they know they're here. And that you're here."

"Yeah," the smaller smuggler said, "well whose fault is that?"

"Ours," 1719 said. "Which is why we promised Endayi we'd warn you. To make up for our mistake."

The blaster pressed harder beneath her chin. "If you've harmed a single hair on—"

"Lady Jaliss is safe, Serah. Actually, if she can stop picking fights with her fellow members of the Rive Collective, she'll have them all eating out of the palm of her hand."

At her name, and the name of her sister-in-law, the smuggler leader—Serah—stepped back, almost on instinct, but her gaze never left 1719.

"She said you always fought to the last," Twelve spoke up. "But her nieces already lost one parent."

"You have . . . to go," 1719 said softly.

Serah pulled down her scarf. Slipped off her goggles and pushed back her hood, even as her two crewmates protested. She was a slim woman but older than 1719 had expected. Silver streaks shot through the top of her hair, which was pulled back into a ponytail, and the sides of her head were shaved. She wore a ring fastened to a leather cord around her neck, and a small tattoo peeked through the gap in her shirt: *Endal Jaliss,* it read, curling above her collarbone.

1719's eyes widened. "I recognize you," she said. "You're the teacher on Locke Station, the one with the kid who trapped scav rats in a pilot's helmet."

Serah sighed and pinched the bridge of her nose. "Asher," she said. "That girl. But yes. Teacher by day. Smuggler by night." She hesitated, then rubbed at the tattoo on her chest. "Endayi really sent you?" she whispered.

1719 nodded. "You have a minute. Maybe less."

Serah nodded. A woman of action, Lady Jaliss had said. She motioned at the other two smugglers, and after a second, they lowered their weapons. "Jerem, Glass, get the skids on board. Grab the . . . packages, leave everything else. I want us in the air in thirty."

"Serah?" the little one snapped. "Really?"

"S'lot of supplies we're leaving," the big one added.

Serah holstered her blaster pistol. "Greed doesn't drive us. Freedom does. And we have more than enough of what we need for the station. Let's move."

"Why?" the big one—Jerem—asked, aiming the question at 1719 as he slung his blaster over his back. "Why help us? Won't this give them a reason to execute you if they find out?"

1719 nodded at his blaster. "Maybe you can shoot us? In the leg, probably."

"Besides," Twelve said bitterly, "Shikra doesn't need a reason to execute anyone."

The three smugglers froze. 1719 winced at the expression on Serah's face. The way the blood drained away and her eyes widened. Twelve's smile slowly faded as he glanced around at the others. "What?" he asked.

"Shikra?" Serah said.

"The Bloodhawk?" Glass pulled his scarf down and spat into the waves splashing at their feet. He'd also raised his blaster again, and although it wasn't aimed at anyone in particular, his finger hovered over the trigger. "He's here? That bloodthirsty—"

"Shikra," Serah interrupted, stepping right in front of 1719. "He's here."

No use lying. No reason, either. "Yes."

"The man who had my husband killed. That's who your commanding officer is."

It wasn't a question, but 1719 nodded anyway, unable to stop the unease curdling in the pit of her stomach. She knew where this was going, knew that any hope of getting Serah and her crew away and safe was swiftly fading. All that effort had been for nothing. There was no chance they'd flee, not now. The only question that remained was how far they would go. "It is."

Serah looked at Jerem, then at Glass. Something unspoken passed among the three, and then Jerem was slinging his blaster over his shoulder and hugging the other two. "S'not fair," he mumbled.

"Never is," Serah said.

1719 took the opportunity to nudge Twelve, motioning him to get to his feet. Her hand was already loosening the riot shield on her back.

"What?" Twelve asked. "What is it?"

"Behind me," 1719 muttered. "Now. Quickly."

By this time, Jerem was running back to the ship. Serah and Glass watched, then turned to find 1719 with the riot shield on her forearm, Twelve behind her with his blaster out but aimed at the ground.

Serah smiled. "You're good. You would've made a good smuggler."

"We're going back up the hill," 1719 said calmly.

Glass shook his head and hefted his blaster. "Can't have you two warning the Bloodhawk. Why don't you drop the shield and follow Jerem to the ship? Better for all of us if this doesn't get out of hand."

She shook her head. "My friends are up there."

"And my husband is dead," Serah snapped. "Because of the man leading you and your friends. And it's about time the Bloodhawk gets his wings clipped. Permanently. Now . . . you won't get a second chance. Ship. Now."

She stepped forward, only to hop backward as Twelve let off a shot that scattered the waves at her feet. Glass snarled and fired his own blaster, the impact slamming into the riot shield. 1719 grunted as her shoulder bore the brunt of the force, but the shield held. This time.

"What would Lady Endayi say?" Twelve shouted. "We helped her! We came to help you!"

Serah locked her eyes on 1719, a flicker of understanding in her gaze before it turned hard and cold. "She would say 'Remember Endal.' "

She lifted her blaster as Glass did the same, opening fire, and the ground heaved beneath them all.

CHPTR - 33

The message came in while Captain Phasma was on her way back to her quarters. She'd just left a planning meeting where Cardinal had spent what seemed like the entire time obstructing all her plans, by denying training time in the multiple stormtrooper centers around the ship and poaching troopers under her command without prior authorization. And, as usual, his inability to discern the greater objective rankled her. No, it *infuriated* her, and a furious Phasma was a dangerous Phasma. So much so, the messenger tech who stepped into her path as she exited the turbolift yelped in terror when she whirled on him, the spearpoint of her quicksilver baton quivering centimeters from his throat.

"Speak," Phasma ordered.

The tech gulped. "A-apologies, Captain. Message for you, from a Major Gohl."

Phasma had already begun dismissing the tech before he'd finished speaking, taking the datapad he'd extended and turning to leave. But she paused at the name.

"Chetachi Gohl sent a message to me."

A declarative statement, and yet it seemed like a question, so the tech nodded. "Yes, Captain."

"Over a nonsecure channel?"

"Yes, Captain. Well, not exactly, Captain."

Phasma turned her full attention back on him, and the man shrank as the spearpoint grazed the tip of his chin, a line of blood beading up after a few seconds. "I am not in the mood to decipher your ambiguity. Explain. Now."

"O-of course, Captain. It's just . . . the message came from the shuttle registered to the major, and it was transmitted at the same time as the clearance code when it approached. Just, tacked on at the end, like an afterthought."

"And did you confirm with the pilot that it was, in fact, the major transmitting that message?"

The tech seemed bewildered. "No, Captain. He . . . he had the right codes."

Phasma stared at him for several seconds as traffic flowed

around them, no one daring to look at the confrontation unfolding for fear of becoming the next person struggling to answer questions at the end of that spearpoint. Finally she turned and strode off. She heard the tech exhale audibly behind her, which meant he thought he was off the hook and escaped reeducation.

But then the quicksilver baton flashed through the air, the spearpoint bursting through the remaining stack of datapads in his arms before burying itself in the wall next to the turbolift with a thunk.

Phasma marched back to retrieve it, yanking it from the wall and spilling the sparking datapads across the corridor floor. She engaged the baton's containment field and slipped it back onto the belt at her waist before moving to stand over the cowering comms tech.

"Report back to your superior," she said, committing his face to memory. "Tell them you are to retrain on proper communication protocols and data transfer procedures. And, soldier . . . I want you *personally* delivering my messages for the foreseeable future, and each day I will assess your progress. Do not fail me again."

She turned, cape flapping behind her as she marched down the corridor to her quarters. Within seconds the altercation was driven from the front of her mind, compartmentalized and stored away to be retrieved when the tech's face appeared in front of her again. At that point he would face judgment. Until then, this business with Gohl buzzed irritatingly at the top of her to-do list.

The message, when she played it in the secure privacy of her quarters, was frustratingly simple. Seven seconds long, plain speech, no code words—either First Order or Phasma's own that she created with her key subordinates. It was, to be frank, a puzzle that wasn't a puzzle at all.

"This is the FO shuttle *Conveyance*, returning two stormtrooper cadets from extended training on behalf of Major Gohl."

Phasma played the recording over and over again, her temper flaring with each listen. What was Chetachi playing at? The glorified comms tech had always reveled in his little games. She growled in frustration and was seconds away from deleting the message and ignoring it when she paused, her finger just above the console.

Two stormtrooper cadets on extended training.

She opened a different screen and scrolled through the list of identifiers, unsure of what she was looking for but positive it existed, the knowledge folded and organized in the recesses of her mind. There. Another communication, this one internal and flagged for her review *days after* it had been authorized.

By Captain Cardinal.

Two stormtroopers pulled from training regimen and assigned to Major Chetachi Gohl for extended training and evaluation. Training will *possibly include live fire and risk of injury, possibly death. Upon successful completion, training candidates to be advanced to the top of the queue for squad leader.*

Phasma stared at the note, then keyed an open line on her console.

"Yes, Captain?" came the voice of a tech.

"The shuttle that just docked, designation *Conveyance*—give me the identifiers of the passengers on board. And whoever is responsible for updating the logs in the system will report to me within the hour."

"Ah . . . yes, Captain. That would be me, Captain. However, there's been a delay in the log upload due to clerical issues."

"I'm not interested in the excuses, trooper. The identifiers."

"That's the problem, Captain. The manifest says the *Conveyance* left with three passengers, however only one returned."

The tapping paused. Phasma narrowed her eyes. "The

docking transcript recorded two stormtroopers returning."

"One is dead, Captain. And there's no sign of the major. We've held the lone trooper for questioning. Would you like to be present, Captain?"

"Yes," Phasma said. One trooper dead, no Major Gohl. "Yes, I would very much like to hear what this trooper—"

"FN-Two-One-Eight-Seven, Captain."

"Let's hear what FN-Two-One-Eight-Seven has to say for himself."

"Yes . . . one second, Captain. New communique flagged for your attention, priority security from one of our relay stations in the Unknown Regions, heading to your console."

Phasma scowled. What now? She selected the file and opened it, scanning its contents. Her scowl deepened into a mask of fury, and then she was standing, stabbing at a button in front of her with barely restrained anger.

"Yes, Captain?"

"A change of plans, trooper. Flag FN-Two-One-Eight-Seven for further monitoring. I will interrogate him later. In the meantime, meet me in my office. This correspondence you sent is faulty and needs to be reassembled."

"I . . . yes, Captain. Right away."

Phasma disconnected, then stared at the message again. After a while she deleted it, scrubbed it from her files, then erased the records of her talk with the comms tech. Message received and understood, as infuriating as it was. She then turned and stalked toward the door, disengaging the containment field on her quicksilver baton as she did, snarling as the words on the viewscreen hovered in her mind.

Light cruiser Culverin *destroyed during Battle of Ansett Island. No survivors.*

Phasma curled her lips. She was surrounded by failure and incompetence. She needed to hit something. Hurt something. She twirled the baton in her right hand. Luckily, there was one more loose end that needed to be taken care of.

The door to her quarters chimed. "You wanted to see me, Captain?"

Phasma let a savage smile cross her face as the door closed on the unfortunate tech. "Yes, trooper, come in."

CHPTR - 34

FN-2187 stood on the training room floor and watched a group of cadets scramble over an obstacle course simulating a ship-boarding maneuver. It didn't feel real, being back here as if nothing had happened. Actually, after the interrogation Captain Cardinal had put him through, he was surprised he could feel anything at all. Cardinal and several other officers had grilled him. Eight-Seven told them everything. He wanted Major Gohl—no, the former major—to face the punishment he deserved.

"And was the major alive when you last saw him?" Cardinal had asked.

"Yes, Captain."

Another officer broke in. "And you couldn't reach him?"

Eight-Seven remembered the Sardichians swarming the First Order officer. "No, Captain. And so we—I—returned for more orders."

The officer snorted, but Cardinal simply nodded. Eight-Seven had been dismissed after that, and several grueling and nerve-racking hours later, Captain Cardinal approached him outside the officer quarters with two bits of news. First, Eight-Seven wasn't in trouble. Second . . .

He rubbed his right shoulder and grinned, glad the helmet he wore obscured his marveling over the white pauldron recently installed on his armor by a grumpy quartermaster.

Squad leader.

The new label still felt unfamiliar. Undeserved, to be honest. The events over the past few months seemed like a blur, from the *Loxodonta* to Tamo'Akora to the fortress palace of Sardich. Even the times before that, when his biggest concern was becoming a mountain trooper. It was unreal.

The smile faded. FO-7155 should've received a pauldron, as well. Eight-Seven clenched his fists behind his back to ward off the rising sadness that threatened to engulf him. He snorted. The giant boy would be scoffing in his ear right now, saying something like, *I said care about someone other than yourself, not cry over them. Loser.*

"Squad leader?"

The hail pulled Eight-Seven from his thoughts, and he glanced at the junior cadet standing next to him, holding a datapad. "Yes?"

"Compliments from the head training instructor. It's your squad list, sir."

He took the datapad and nodded at the boy, dismissing him to join the others in training. Three identifiers blinked at the top of the display, and he tapped on each one, studying their scores, vitals, and comments from different instructors dating back to junior cadet days.

So it was to be four of them. A proper fire team. He studied the letters and digits, wondering what drove his future squad mates. Did they care about others? Were they passionate about the First Order? Or did greed and the hunger for power keep them clawing forward? Eight-Seven pursed his lips, trying to glean what he could from the little bit of data handed to him. He would find out. It was his job as a leader, and he took that job seriously. Not knowing put himself, his team, and the people of the galaxy they were supposed to serve in danger, and he refused to put someone else in danger before himself. He didn't know when that resolve had solidified inside of him, only that it was fused to the core of his very being now. He would lead this team the way 7155 would have done.

Well, except better.

Take that, he thought, shooting a final barb wherever the boy's spirit now traveled. *Loser.*

The troopers on the course had finished and were in various poses of fatigue. No, that wasn't true—one still hadn't finished. The remaining trooper labored past the final obstacles of the course, stumbling forward in a half jog while cradling their side. He checked their identifier, then glanced at his datapad.

FN-2003.

Eight-Seven frowned, then glanced up when laughter echoed. The others were watching 2003 struggle over the last hurdle on the course, a high wall coated with polyadhesive that simulated the sap found in many forested worlds throughout the galaxy. After several seconds of struggling helplessly, 2003 went still, exhausted.

Squad leader.

Eight-Seven found himself jogging toward the course. The other troopers at the finish line elbowed each other and straightened when he approached, only to stare as he jogged past them. Eight-Seven stopped by the wall and looked up at the stuck trooper, who started and resumed struggling when they noticed Eight-Seven's presence.

"Sir!"

Eight-Seven stared at the wall. “The trick,” he said, “is to use the adhesive to your advantage.”

The other trooper glanced down in confusion. “Use it?”

“Exactly. Anchor your lower half like this, using your hands, boots, and knees as additional points of contact to distribute your weight. Then twist to disengage. You won’t completely get rid of the sap, but it’ll actually harden and help increase your grip as you climb. Try it.”

FN-2003 fumbled about for bit.

“No, no, anchor, then twist. Yes, exactly, like that.”

Eight-Seven stepped back and watched as 2003 managed to free himself from the excess strands of sap clinging to him and made his way over the wall, sliding down the opposite side.

“Excellent,” Eight-Seven said. “Now hustle. Dig deep. Everything is monitored, so finish strong.”

He jogged alongside 2003 as they crossed the finish line, and a few of the troopers actually clapped and whistled. Everyone began to disperse, but Eight-Seven nodded at two in the middle of the pack.

“FN-Two-One-Nine-Nine, FN-Two-Zero-Zero-Zero?”

The two separated from the others and joined 2003 to gather around Eight-Seven, who studied them all. “You have been chosen to complete our fire team of four. FN-Two-One-Eight-Seven, squad leader. Take a look around, troopers. Find something to care about in each other, because we're the only ones obligated to have each other's backs. It starts with us. If we don't care, who will? That's what being a part of the First Order means. Never forget that. Now come on. Let's grab a bite and talk about how we're going to blow these other fire teams out of orbit with our scores. That Training Cup is as good as ours."

That got them fired up, just as Eight-Seven knew it would. Nothing pointed a team in the right direction in lockstep like a competition. As they left, Eight-Seven—the last on the course—paused. He felt like someone was watching, and as he turned, he saw the red armor of Captain Cardinal at the other end of the training facility. Cardinal nodded, and Eight-Seven nodded back.

A flash of chrome from above, high in the observation room near the ceiling, caught his eye. He squinted, but there was nothing. Eight-Seven frowned. For just a second, it had felt like Captain Phasma was also watching him.

He left, shaking his head. The captain had no interest in him, and he planned on keeping it that way. The fewer officers whose attention he attracted, the better.

CHPTR - 35

Phasma stood over her, which was impossible.

Right?

Right.

So that meant she was dreaming, hallucinating, or dead. Of the three, death was the easiest. Death was simple. Too simple, actually, and therefore the most unlikely. Especially since Phasma, or her ghost, was currently barking orders at her.

Actually she couldn't be dead. Phasma couldn't die—at least, that was what the junior cadets used to whisper as the metallic captain swept through the halls. So that left a dream or a hallucination. And really, weren't they the same thing?

Phasma continued to stand over her. "You will not die

a useless death. I cannot use a useless death. Do something. Accomplish something. Die with purpose."

TZ-1719 blinked the apparition away. She lay on a makeshift cot—every trooper battalion carried one in their medical kit—inside one of the assault landers. Along with a medpac, a portable medscanner lay on the floor beside her, a partial readout blinking on its display. She groaned as she rolled to her feet, ignored the medscanner's readout (more bad news, most likely), and snagged the medpac. The right side of her body, especially her ribs, ached like the time she'd tumbled off an airspeeder during training. Maybe that was why Phasma had appeared in her mind. The body remembers trauma, like cellular memories.

"Clamps," she croaked. She cleared her throat, then tried again. "Clamps, come in. Twelve. Twenty-One-Four. FP Twenty-Two-Alpha, come in. Anyone?"

Nothing.

1719 opened the medpac, stripping off her chest plate and slipping the device under the black body glove. She continued to cycle through channels before she thought to check her helmet, and then she groaned a second time. A giant crack ran along the base of the helmet, right where the comm circuitry was mounted, and she could smell the aroma of singed electronics.

"Great," she muttered, pulling it off and rotating it to stare at the damaged armor. Something caught her eye in the visor—a face. Her face. She stared at it, willing herself to remember the last time she'd examined her own eyes, the nose, the brown skin, the smirk on her mouth.

Blaster fire cut through the air, followed by shouts.

1719 was out of the lander, helmet forgotten as she grabbed a blaster in one hand while the other kept the medpac pressed against her side. Her aching ribs grew deliciously numb over time, and she was able to jog after a few seconds, rounding the third and final lander only to come to an abrupt stop.

The three stormtrooper platoons stood in formation, their backs to 1719, blasters at the ready. A few shifted their stances, clearly uncomfortable with something. She continued to move, closing the distance, and then she saw them.

Serah's crew, including Glass and Jerem, were on their knees in the sand in front of the assembled troopers. There were fifteen or so, all different ages, some no older than a junior trooper. Jerem was clutching his side, writhing in pain on the ground, and Glass leaned over him while holding his own face. Serah knelt to his right, her eyes defiant even as they flickered between someone 1719 couldn't see and her injured crewmates.

A commotion dragged her eyes away from the standoff to the containers several members of Delta were hauling down the dune on the grav skids, then bringing to a rest off to the side.

Someone stepped into the space between the two groups.

Shikra.

"I simply refuse to ask again," he said.

There. 1719 spotted Clamps and TZ-214 near the end of one of the rows. But where was Twelve? He'd been with her when the landers fired on the ship.

Panic surged.

Was he okay? He had to be okay.

1719 began to circle around the standoff. Protocol stated she should find a working helmet and rejoin her squad. Her training screamed at her to get in formation. But she ignored both, choosing instead to focus on the steady cooling numbness of the medpac and the need to find Twelve.

She'd circled far enough around the formation that some troopers had noticed her. They stared at her helmetless face and her torso covered only in a body glove and nudged each other. Clamps noticed, did a double take, and elbowed 214 hard enough to cause her to stumble. She was about to hammer him with the butt of her blaster when she caught sight of 1719, as well, and froze.

All good? 1719 signed, using Corps hand signals reserved for stealth scenarios.

Good, Clamps answered, his movements furtive and shielded from view. *You?*

Good. Where's Four? She twirled a finger in the air, then held up four fingers. In their patrol squad, she was One, Clamps was Two, 214 was Three, and Twelve was Four.

Clamps pointed, and she turned in that direction and groaned.

Twelve stood between two shock troopers, looking down at the ground, his blaster confiscated.

Shikra was still talking. "That was the first and only non-lethal warning shot you will receive, and I firmly believe it's one too many. Sets a bad example, you *must* understand. So, I am now going to order each and every one of your compatriots shot, in descending order of age, leaving you for last, so that you and your youngest scav rats can witness the end of this little crew of villagers. The bodies will be left here for the surf to dispose of, and those surviving will be sold into slavery in the deepest bowels of the galaxy. Is that understood? Open the containers and *give me my blasters*."

Many troopers were rustling now, clearly rattled by Shikra's threats. 1719 didn't blame them. This was their first mission under the captain. They weren't there for the Merchant Uprising, or the aftermath. Indirect torture wasn't in any of the training sims or the lectures. Aggravated interrogations weren't included in the classroom lectures.

How many will request foot patrols in quiet sectors this time? she wondered before shaking off the question, because Shikra was moving.

"That one," he said, stepping aside. Two troopers, after a moment's hesitation that earned them a withering glare and a raised eyebrow, took his place and raised their blasters. They were pointed at Glass. "Fire."

"Captain!"

The shout cut across the beach, and helmets turned as one toward 1719, who only just realized that she'd called out without thinking. She stepped forward, watching as Shikra tilted his helmet in disbelief.

"TZ-One-Seven-One-Nine," he said, her identifier dripping out of his mouth like he tasted something awful. "You are in violation of so many protocols and codes of conduct I don't know where to begin. Where's your helmet? And the rest of your armor?"

"The blasters, sir," she said.

"Excuse me?"

"The ones in those containers over there."

His posture stiffened. "What about *my* blasters, trooper?"

"I can get them open for you. Right now." 1719 held her breath. Sweat beaded on her forehead, dripping into her eye, and yet she didn't move. Couldn't move. She was making this up as she went along, and she was banking on Shikra's greed and desire for the blasters outweighing his typical solution of killing any living obstacle in his way.

"Please, sir." 1719 hated the desperation in her voice. The helmet's voice modulator would've taken care of that, smoothed it out so she sounded like everyone else.

And yet the helmet couldn't translate the feeling of the wind on her face. The salty smell of the ocean, or heat of the sun on her skin. This was new, untransmittable data. Information that couldn't be processed, packaged, and delivered in blips and sequences. That knowledge bloomed in her mind, doing more to calm her than any medicine the medpac could provide. Her shoulders settled. Her stance straightened, and she slipped her hands behind her back, clasping them, at ease.

Captain Shikra noticed, and perhaps that helped, because he didn't immediately call for her to be thrown into binders or hauled away by the shock troopers or, worse, her own battalion. Instead he nodded, a quick sharp gesture, and she stepped into the barren zone between the uncomfortable troopers and the smugglers who now stared at her with undisguised hatred.

"TZ-Twelve-Twelve," she barked. "With me."

Twelve was marching across the sand to join her before he—or the shock troopers who had been bracketing him—could do anything about it. His guards started to follow, but a raised hand from Shikra halted them, and 1719 understood. He was allowing her just enough room to pull this off.

Fail and she, Twelve, and Serah and her crew would be buried in the sand they stood in.

"I hope you know what you're doing, boss," Twelve said as he fell into step just off her right shoulder.

"Have I ever—" she started to say, but Twelve cut her off.

"No, you haven't, so don't start now."

And then they were walking in front of Serah's kneeling crew. Twelve slowed and looked at a girl no older than he was before hurrying to catch up. 1719 could feel their stares burning into her back, harsher than any concentrated laser fire from a training sim. Only Serah met her eyes, though.

"You can't," she whispered.

1719 tried not to glance at her as she walked by. She knew

what the smuggler was feeling. Being responsible for all those people back on Locke Station, ensuring their survival. But supplies could be scrounged up again; shipments could be restarted. If they all died here, what then?

"I have to," she muttered without looking. "It's the only way everyone lives. Those blasters aren't worth dying over. Twelve, I really hope you can crack them open."

"But you don't understand—"

"Gag her before I lose my patience," Shikra commanded. "And anyone else who makes a sound."

Whatever protest Serah was going to lodge was cut off when one of the shock troopers roughly placed a thin metal device in her mouth. The spiderlike object, called a silencer, expanded, locked spindly arms around its victim's head, and began to hum, negating whatever noise she tried to make. Several members of her crew, especially the younger ones, started to cry, but they were quickly shushed by the elders.

Twelve, to his credit, had begun to work. He mumbled to himself under his breath, and 1719 forced herself to turn away from the burning, tear-filled eyes of Serah to watch. She dropped to a crouch beside him, accepting the thin metal sliver he produced out of nowhere.

"Hold this," he said, running his fingers along the edge of the container. "I've seen chatter about this sort of thing in the archives. NadirLinks. Really expensive shipping container. Never thought I'd see one, though."

"Why?" 1719 asked, because she was supposed to, not out of any burning curiosity. That was just how Twelve worked. He needed to talk through the problem in order to solve it. "A container is a container, right?"

He snorted. "Try telling Clamps a blaster is a blaster. A repeater and an F-11D are the same thing."

"Okay, I get it."

"A container is a container. Honestly." Several seconds of silence followed. Then: "A container is—"

"We're kind of in a tight spot here, Twelve," she hissed.

"I'm sorry, you're right, you're right. Okay, enter a code into the keypad."

"What . . . ?"

Her voice trailed off when a virtual keypad appeared in the top corner of the container. 1719 glanced at Shikra, then swallowed and turned away.

"What code should I use?" she asked.

"Any code. Six digits will do. Here, give me that shiv. Okay, enter something."

"But . . ."

"Any code, boss!"

Gritting her teeth to bite back the words she wanted to

hurl at him, 1719 stood and stiffly stepped over to the keypad. After a second's hesitation, she hit it randomly six times, not really caring at that point.

An alarm started blaring, and the keypad transformed into a countdown in a language she couldn't understand.

"Twelve," she said, almost too calmly.

"I got it, I got it."

"Tweeeelve."

"Okay, wait, I thought I had it."

"TWELVE!"

"There!"

He shoved in the shiv, and something audibly clicked, even over the sound of the alarm. Instantly silence fell over the beach again and the keypad disappeared. A seam appeared along the edge of the container, and steam hissed out as it cracked open.

1719's jaw dropped.

"You're joking," Clamps muttered.

More exclamations rippled around the beach as 1719 pulled it open all the way.

"Funny thing I learned about NadirLinks," Twelve was saying as he packed his tools into his armor. "They're essentially tiny habitats. Self-contained atmosphere with air scrubber and oxygen tanks, complete life support actually. Supposed to be for terraforming projects and stuff like that. But, and here's the thing, the company that made them went out of business because slavers kept using them to transport . . ."

He stood and turned, finally seeing what everyone else was seeing.

". . . children."

Two sealed bassinets hovered amid a network of tubes, pumps, and monitoring devices. Hoses ran from them to a chamber bolted to the side of the container. In the corner, a small monitoring droid rested in a secure bracket. It whirred to life at the sight of the light, beeping and whistling as it dropped from the ceiling and began to putter around the container, checking the readouts and the interior of the crash bassinets, where two toddlers were sleeping peacefully. One slowly blinked their eyes, then shifted and began sucking their thumb.

Hundreds of orphans, no one to care for them.

I wished I could bring them all here.

She lost a husband.

1719 felt like the ground was exploding around her all over again. She clutched her ribs, her breathing erratic. There weren't any guns in this shipment. Locke Station was smuggling orphans from the Merchant Uprising, children the Order refused to acknowledge by their refusal to acknowledge the Uprising had happened at all. She whirled around to stare at Serah, who stared back, tear tracks running down her face even though her eyes were now dry.

Someone stepped up beside her, and she turned again.

"Those don't appear to be my blasters," Captain Shikra said in a deceptively calm tone.

"No, sir," 1719 answered.

"In fact, trooper, I would say that what we have here is a complete waste of the First Order's time and resources. Wouldn't you agree?"

The second toddler woke up and yawned.

"I said, wouldn't you agree, TZ-One-Seven-One-Nine?"

1719 swallowed. She didn't agree. Who could look at these two children and agree? But . . . what could she do? She opened her mouth to protest, to disagree, to argue. She closed it. Then tried again. Obedience. The chain of command.

"Yes, Captain." It came out no louder than a whisper.

Captain Shikra made a sound of disgust in his throat. Suddenly he pivoted and strode away, heading to the formation of shock troopers. He took two of their repeater blasters and returned, tossing one at 1719's feet.

"Pick it up," he ordered. Then, turning to Twelve, he pointed with the remaining blaster at the other containers on skids. "Get those open. Now."

Twelve jumped, startled, then saluted. "I, uh, need someone to—"

The repeater shot into the air, and Twelve froze. One of the toddlers began to cry at the noise. Captain Shikra glanced at it, then returned his glare to Twelve. "Now. If you please."

Twelve nodded, then ran to the nearest container, calling 214 and Clamps once he was far enough away from the captain. Together the three of them began to work on the other containers, and soon the air was filled with the ringing of alarms and the beeps and whistles of caretaker droids.

Meanwhile, Captain Shikra stared at the first container, almost wistfully. The repeater blaster was aimed at the ground, yet 1719 held her breath. This was when the Bloodhawk was at his most dangerous. When his next move couldn't be anticipated and he stood on the precipice of violence. She needed to look at him, to watch him, but she couldn't tear her eyes away from the droid puttering around the container, twisting nozzles and tapping controls. It was mesmerizing.

"It appears," Shikra said, "that you have once again found yourself the subject of my ire, TZ-One-Seven-One-Nine. We are back, once again, at a crossroads. You are out of uniform, out of compliance, and consistently—consistently!—out of line. Your movements are unaccounted for, your presence among known smugglers and terrorists unexplainable, and I find that I am *uninterested* in any more excuses. So, I offer you the same choice I did a few months ago."

1719 didn't have to guess at the choice she was about to be given. Maybe the Bloodhawk *was* getting predictable.

"Pick up the blaster, TZ-One-Seven-One-Nine."

She bent down, eyes never leaving the droid, and grabbed the repeater. Somewhere in the back of her mind, she noted that the alarms had stopped. All the crates were open, and from the rumble of conversation sweeping the beach, more children were inside them.

Captain Shikra turned, facing the troops. "First Order protocol requires the elimination of all insurgent communities in occupied territories of the First Order. Under said protocols, the crew members of the ship identified as"—a pause—"the *Bulwark* are classified as insurgents in the protected territory of Ansett Island. And since I see all ages and genders present, I'm willing to say this is a community. How about that, miss? You're a community leader now. Your own little village. Surely this makes you happy?"

He was talking to Serah now, who only glared daggers at him as the silencer continued to gag her. Shikra beamed, then turned back to 1719 while pointing at Serah and the containers in one sweeping gesture.

"TZ-One-Seven-One-Nine, I'm once again tasking you with eliminating the insurgents. Spare the children. We'll take them to Processing and make something useful of them. Improve upon the mistakes of the past."

She had known it was coming, but the words still fell like hammers on durasteel. It was Shikra the Bloodhawk at his worst. It would've been simpler to order his shock troopers to kill Serah and her crew. They stood behind him, a wall of armor and blasters. But Shikra wanted a statement. He wanted to send a message, and 1719 was his tool of choice.

The repeater blaster trembled in her hands, and her eyes were stinging. Roaring filled her ears, louder than engines, louder than storms. The captain was still speaking, and then he reached inside the container and yanked the caretaker droid from its berth. The droid beeped in alarm, but Shikra said something, then dropped it to the sand and crushed it beneath the heel of his boot in one swift stomp. What he said, 1719 didn't know. She couldn't hear. She couldn't feel anything but the weight of the blaster in her hand. She was back at the conclusion of the Uprising, staring at a defiant man with blood on his face and a tattoo curling above his heart. 1719 turned to stare at Serah. They locked eyes for what seemed like an eternity as her world unraveled into fragments, her brain trying to preserve itself before breaking down.

She raised her blaster.

Obedience.

Serah looked at her.

Except it wasn't just Serah.

It was 214.

It was Clamps.

It was Twelve.

Obedience.

It was Endal Jaliss. Endayi Jaliss.

It was Jharo, the Rodian.

It was Dal, his friend.

Obedience?

It was Manny, begging her for help back on Rive.

It was a faceless trooper, scorch marks on their armor, the helmet visor slowly retracting to reveal one of the babies from the container. It was everyone; it was no one.

It was herself, staring back at herself, eyes open and clear.

Obedience . . .

She lowered the gun, then dropped it. "I can't," she whispered.

Shikra stared at her. "You . . . what?" His voice was cold with fury.

"I can't, sir."

After a second, he whirled around and pointed at a shock trooper. "You. Put this traitor in binders. Looks like we'll be having a day of executions. And you! Code-breaker trooper. Front and center."

As 1719 was hauled away, feeling the bite of the binders snapping onto her wrists, Twelve, after looking around wildly only to realize that he was in fact the target of Shikra's command, walked, trembling, to stand near the captain.

Shikra pointed at the repeater blaster 1719 had dropped. "Pick it up and eliminate the insurgents."

Twelve opened his mouth.

Shikra leaned forward. "What?"

"I . . . I-I—"

"Is there a higher power here that I am unaware of, or am I still the captain? PICK UP THE BLASTER. AND. FIRE."

Twelve closed his eyes and inhaled. "N-n-no . . ."

"No?"

"N-no old troopers, sir." And he stepped back, moving to stand by 1719, in front of Serah and the rest of the crew.

Shikra started to laugh, though his voice held no trace of humor. "Oh . . . oh, this is unbelievable! Is there no one who understands a command when they hear one? For all the . . . how many people do I have to bury on this forsaken island before everyone understands the rule of order?"

Clamps and 214 stepped forward. Shikra, noticing, acknowledged them with a wave of his hands.

"Thank you, troopers. Please, show this—"

They tossed their blasters alongside the other one without a word and kept walking, eventually arriving to stand on either side of Twelve and 1719. Shikra's face twisted into something close to hatred.

"Private Calcon," he snapped.

"Sir!" Calcon stepped forward. Her helmet started to swivel toward 1719 but stopped as the captain continued to spit orders.

"This failure lies directly at your feet. I'm reinstating your rank of sergeant. Get them in line, or get in line with the insurgents."

Then Sergeant Calcon did turn to look at 1719.

"*Now*, Sergeant!"

She jumped, then straightened. "Company Seventy-Seven, all squads, fall in!"

Boots thundered across the sand. 1719 watched as the troopers she'd shared rations with stood across from her. Soldiers who'd had the same training she'd had lifted blasters aimed in her direction. She felt . . . empty. Hollow. There should have been some sense of betrayal, some bitterness at her fate, but she was surprised to find none of that. Like this was a bit of theater, a scripted performance where everyone knew the ending. She definitely did.

Sergeant Calcon stared at her. "COMPANY—" she shouted.

1719 stepped in front of Serah. She felt a hand on her wrist. Twelve, who followed. Then Clamps, her anchor, never letting go, and 214, a constant presence at her side. Her squad. Her family. All of them protecting the civilians kneeling behind them.

Shikra leaned forward as if he was hungry for the potential violence.

Sergeant Calcon pulled out her blaster pistol.

"COMPANY," she repeated. "About face!"

Then the sergeant stepped forward until she was face to face with 1719, pivoted, and tossed her weapon on the ground next to the others.

No one spoke.

No one moved.

Until another trooper stepped forward. Knives. He moved to his sergeant's side and dropped his weapon before folding his arms. And then FL-4980 followed. Then two more. Three. Five. 1719 stared in a mixture of relief and shock. Soon all of them, the entire company, had shifted, rotated, put their bodies between the civilians on the beach and the Bloodhawk snarling at them all.

"Cowards! Traitors!" Captain Shikra whipped his head left and right, roaring at the troopers defying him. "I will have you strung up!"

Twelve shifted behind 1719. She could feel a tugging at her wrist, and then the binders were off, and she nodded her thanks while not taking her eyes off of the near-demonic captain melting down in front of them.

"You have all signed your execution warrants." He stomped, beat his chest, even ripped off his helmet before finally turning and stabbing a finger at the milling shock troopers. "If you want to make it off this abysmal island with your heads still on your shoulders, I want you to open fire. NOW! OPEN—"

An ear-piercing, pulsing whine filled the air, and the troopers around 1719 stepped away to reveal Clamps walking toward Captain Shikra with a thermal detonator in each hand. He didn't speak or give any warning. Instead, he hurled them at the feet of the shock troopers.

Loud shouts echoed as Shikra's crack enforcers scrambled

to get out of the way. The whining increased in pitch and speed, rapidly counting down until the detonators merged into one shrieking sound and finally exploded in a loud *whumph.* The shock troopers fell to the ground and covered their heads, ready for shrapnel and flames.

Except only smoke billowed out.

1719 leaped forward to grab a repeater and plunged into the chaos. Shots were fired, followed by several shouts and the distinct sound of a helmet cracking. By the time the smoke cleared, Clamps, Twelve, and 214 stood over the stunned squad of shock troopers, and 1719 held a repeater rifle to Shikra's head where he lay on the ground.

When she glanced at Clamps, he shrugged. "I had a few left from Locke Station."

Sergeant Calcon stepped forward, staring at Shikra. "Sir, you are relieved," she said.

The captain—former captain—snarled something, but whatever words he wanted to say were muffled by the end of the repeater blaster 1719 shoved into his cheek.

The sergeant turned to 1719. "Well . . . now what?"

1719 glanced at her, then at the landers on the beach. They couldn't stay here. Nor could they let Shikra and his troopers go; they'd only report them at the first opportunity.

They needed to disappear, and fortunately, the First Order had trained her how to do just that.

"Twelve," she said, pointing at the shock troopers, "take a squad and strip all helmets of their comms. Clamps, grab all weapons and anything else useful and get it on the landers. Twenty-One-Four, I hope you're ready to pilot."

1719 turned back to Calcon. "If the Order learns about this, everyone here is dead. There's no going back. One wrong word from anyone, and we'll all be on the next morale report."

Calcon didn't like it, but she didn't argue. "So what, we disappear? A whole company? How? Where? And on what?"

"Leave the how to me. There's a cruiser right above us that doesn't know the details of . . . the Battle of Ansett Island because of the storms jamming our comms."

214 let a laugh escape. "Is that what we're calling this?"

"That's how we'll log it. If a company mutinied, the First Order would never stop hunting for us. But if we all died in battle? Who cares."

Shikra wriggled beneath her, and she dropped a knee onto his back.

Calcon whistled. "You want to hijack the cruiser because Shikra only brought a skeleton crew and we outnumber them?"

1719 nodded.

"Okay, but that still doesn't answer all of my questions. Where are we going?"

1719 didn't know. She was pulling this together as they went, the way Phasma had trained her. Use what's available. Never be predictable. The answer had to be out there.

"I know a place."

Everyone turned to see Serah, standing behind them, Twelve having just finished disengaging the silencer before dropping it in her outstretched palm. Serah rubbed her mouth, then stepped toward the closest open NadirLink container, the one with a missing caretaker droid. She stared, then turned and squatted beside Shikra.

"A moon," she said, not taking her eyes off the former captain, "off the map and with plenty of good hunting and cover. I'll copy the coordinates for you when I get back to my ship."

1719 stood, replacing her knee with a boot on Shikra's back. "You sure you should be saying all this aloud?"

"Oh, he won't be telling anyone." Serah yanked the man's head back, then shoved the silencer into his mouth, watching grimly as his screams turned to whimpers when the device locked behind his head and began to hum. "He won't be telling anyone anything. Ever."

A limping Jerem and Glass appeared at her shoulder, and together the two men hauled the former First Order captain up between them and began dragging him up the dune and out of sight. The rest of the shock troopers, their weapons now in the hands of Serah's crew, were herded after them.

1719 watched, a feeling somewhere between relief and nervous anticipation swelling inside her. She pivoted to Calcon, one eyebrow raised.

Sergeant Calcon pursed her lips, then drew her boots together and saluted. "You heard *Lieutenant* One-Seven-One-Nine, troopers! We have a moon to find and a ship ready to take us. Fall out!"

1719 jogged back to the lander she'd woken up in. Clamps was already by the ramp, and he tossed a helmet at her after she'd climbed aboard. Her helmet. Conformity. She snorted, then shook her head. No. Never again. She prepared to toss it into the sand outside as the lander's thrusters began to fire, then paused as something fluttered inside. She reached in and pulled out the now flattened flower she'd tucked away after their patrol on Hadne 3.

A small girl in a mechanic's jumpsuit too big for her ran up and handed Clamps a datarod. He waggled his helmet at her and she giggled before running off. Clamps moved up beside 1719, then tossed the datarod to her as the thrusters fired and they rose into the air. He noticed her helmet. "You don't have to toss it. I deleted the ID tag inside. We're going to have to get new ones, though."

1719 shook her head. "I don't want a new identifier. I want a name."

"A what?"

"A name! Like yours."

"What, like Clamps? I guess I can keep it, not like it's in the system anywhere. What are you going to choose? How about Boss? No? Okay, not Boss. Superior? Leader? Most Exalted Leader? We can call you Mel for short."

1719 stared at the flower. What had Twelve called it, what seemed an eternity ago? Carpet of Paradise? *Jannah al Sajada.*

"Jannah," she said.

Clamps pulled off his own helmet, frowning at her in confusion. "What?"

She—Jannah—smiled, then slammed a fist on the button to raise the ramp door as the lander began to climb, leaving Ansett Island behind. She sent a mental note of encouragement to Serah, then turned as the door closed to face Clamps and the others now looking to her for direction. "My name is Jannah."

CHAPTER 36

The *Harvest* dropped out of hyperspace in a wink of light. Coy bit his lip as he sent the lumbering vessel curving on a path that would put them in line with Sardich's orbit. He fiddled with the controls on his respi-vap, trying to regulate his breathing. This was it. His first action, first real action since Exegol, which had pretty much been over before he'd arrived. Sweet brittle leaves, why was it so hard to breathe?

A hand settled on his shoulder. Niila. Great, now his breathing would never go back to normal.

"Nervous?" she whispered.

Coy shook his head, then snorted. His forehead was practically glistening, he was sweating so much. Lying wouldn't help anything now. "Actually, yes," he said, shooting her an embarrassed look. "I don't know why, but I just . . . I have no idea what I've gotten myself into. I make tea!"

Niila laughed, and the sound did more to ease the tension knotting his shoulders than anything else he'd tried. "We all have talents and flaws. It's how we come together that determines our success. A good team is like a puzzle, and all of our odd shapes and quirks make sense when we work as one."

Coy nodded. "That was . . . a really good analogy."

She laughed again, and he smiled. He could really get used to that sound.

Niila swatted at his arm. "You know what I mean."

"I do." He grinned. "And thank you. I feel better."

"I'm glad. But . . . I think *I* would feel better if you stayed aboard the ship when we land."

He looked up. "What?"

Niila bit her lip. "It's my fault we're here, and I don't want anyone else to get hurt."

But Coy shook his head. "We're a team. I can't stay safe while everyone else risks their lives. Is it scary? Yes. Definitely. I am not excited about this. But I won't leave you alone to face it. You *all*! I won't leave you *all* to face it."

"Good," Finn said behind them. He walked up to the controls and leaned over them. Coy couldn't help feeling disappointed when Niila shifted, putting more space between them, but he was also surprised by the expression that flickered across her face. "Because we're here. Make for the coordinates I transferred to you earlier."

Coy nodded, taking the *Harvest* out of orbit on a sweeping curve down through a thick layer of clouds. Gray skies and a dreary landscape greeted them. Coy grimaced. Jannah, approaching the viewport, winced. Finn glared, and Niila bowed her head in apparent distress.

"What happened here?" Coy asked.

Finn turned, pulling his blaster pistol and checking it before slipping it back into the holster on his waist and heading toward the rear viewport. "The First Order got their hands on this place," he said.

The *Harvest* flew over a city-sized graveyard. It was the only way Coy could explain it. Craters the size of speeder bikes dotted the ground. Homes, which seemed to be built into the ground or the many hills and cliffs, had collapsed into piles of rubble. Other structures had shared a similar fate. Stores. Theaters. Schools. All mounds of debris and memory. Even the roads were nothing more than winding scars cutting through the land.

Jannah approached and stood behind Coy. "He was here, you know."

"General Finn?"

She nodded. Niila looked up, interested.

"How? When?" Coy tried doing the math, but failed. He normally had a droid to help him with calculations.

"When he was younger. Told me about it one time when we were swapping stories. A good friend of his died here."

Coy winced. "Should I not have asked?"

"How could you have known? Just remember that memories can be a sharp knife on soft skin. Especially in this place. Go ahead and bring us in." She patted him on the shoulder, then went to take her seat.

Coy, troubled, coaxed the *Harvest* to a landing pad that was relatively undamaged at the base of a giant mountain that seemed to double as a fortress. Several plateaus also served as more landing pads for cargo and personnel transport, and he could just make out the tip of a comms relay poking out from a cluster of trees on a slope. He found it strange that the entire mountainside was covered in black streaks and deep gouges, as if some animal the size of a city had marked its territory on the way through. It wasn't until he put the ship in an autopilot-assisted landing routine that Coy was able to examine the landscape more thoroughly, and he swallowed a lump of fear at a sudden realization. The streaks and gouges were from ship cannons. This place had been bombarded, too.

Coy lowered the ramp, glanced around the ship, then stepped outside. If the mood was somber inside, outside wasn't much better. The sky seemed perpetually gray, whether from the never-ending threat of storms or the smokestacks emerging from various peaks in the mountain. The scorched stone belched clouds of noxious fumes into the atmosphere, and Coy dialed up the intensity of his respi-vap, just in case.

"Was it always this . . . polluted?" he asked.

"No," Finn said, taking the lead. "This used to be the senator's mansion, though it doesn't look like much now."

"It looks like one of our tea oil refineries. Only angrier."

Finn wore a permanent scowl as he reached into a pouch on his hip and pulled out several scanners. He glanced back and found Niila, who lingered behind Coy and Jannah, her face turned to the ground. "The shuttle originated from the fortress, but there's kilometers of corridors and a thousand different rooms inside, so a room-by-room search will take forever, especially since Gohl's network could be anywhere. Here, take these scanners. I had a few techs work up a tracking algorithm for them. It should home in on them as long as you're on the same floor."

Jannah nodded. "So we'll split up."

"Right." Finn glanced at Coy, then Niila. "You even get a sniff of Gohl, you ping your position on the scanners and wait for everyone else to back you up. Got it? All right, Coy, you're with me."

Jannah tossed a scanner to Niila. "We will start at the top and work down, Finn and Coy will work their way up, and we'll meet in the middle."

"Stick to the service turbolifts and the maintenance tubes, stay out of sight, and stay safe," Finn said. "I don't know what Gohl's endgame is, but he'll stop at nothing to make sure it happens. Good luck, and may the Force be with you."

▮▮▮▮▮

The interior of the senator's palace—at any other time—would have been a jaw-dropping sight. Mesmerizing. Probably the grandest thing Coy had ever witnessed since the rare bicentennial pollinator migration descended on his home planet and brought a new species of microgravity pollen with it. (He really needed to get out more.) In fact, Finn had to continually whisper for him to keep up, that was how often he paused to examine the wonders of the palace.

Unfortunately, nearly everything had been destroyed in the bombardment, so most of what Coy examined no longer worked. Like the giant mineral maze that took up the entire first floor of the palace. Niila had mentioned during the flight that Sardich was a planet renowned for its valuable rocks and minerals, with over a hundred different types extracted from the quarry villages surrounding the capital. According to the glitchy holorecording playing on repeat, the maze had displayed them all. Samples of each had been collected, fused, and shaped into a decorative spiraling walkway that visitors to the palace could admire before heading to the upper administrative floors.

Now it was a crumbling pile of gravel.

"Come on," Finn said from the opposite end of the room. "Let's keep moving."

The next few floors were more of the same. Collapsed office walls. Destroyed meeting rooms. One stairwell was completely exposed to the air, revealing a mountainside hit so hard the ground had glassed over.

And then there were the bodies.

"Why didn't they leave with the others?" Coy asked, averting his eyes from two boots partially buried beneath a pile of rubble.

"Maybe they couldn't," Finn answered. He held the scanner, checking the signal, and Coy flushed as he realized he should've been doing the same. "Maybe they were helping others first. Maybe they had to organize the retreat from the ground. Maybe they just didn't have the speed or strength to flee fast enough. Whatever the case, it wasn't their fault they didn't survive. That distinction belongs to the First Order. Remember that."

The next few floors were relatively undamaged, and Coy soon found the reason why. They rounded a corner and discovered the hallway, as well as the two above and three more below, had been wiped completely from the palace. Just . . . gone. Gaping space yawned between two jagged remnants of mountain stone. But the interior rooms that the hallway connected had been left untouched, and Finn led Coy inside one.

Then he immediately paused.

"Something isn't right," he said, pulling his blaster from his holster.

Coy froze. His anxiety ratcheted up higher than ever. "What?" he asked. "What is it?"

"The signal originates from right here. According to the scanners, we should be right on top of it. Also . . . this seems familiar."

"Really?"

"Yeah. It looks like a detention center. Where you might keep troublemakers until they can be processed."

"Maybe the major is nearby?"

"Or maybe it's a trap."

Coy turned in place, examining their surroundings. The room they stood in was a bare rectangle, its walls a pearly white. A dividing wall that ran lengthwise was embedded with a reinforcing metal lattice. A lone security hatch waited partially ajar in the middle, and the windows spaced regularly on either side of it were so thick the view was distorted. The only other distinguishing feature in the room was a series of cylindrical bulges mounted to the ceiling. All in all, Coy had no idea what was supposed to be here.

"Maybe we should keep looking," he said, stepping farther into the room.

"Wait," Finn said, studying his scanner. "I think—"

He never finished the sentence. The bulges in the ceiling spiraled open, and out dropped multiple security turrets. Coy had a fraction of a second to gawk at the turrets' mounted blaster cannons before the barrels began to spin with a keening whine.

"RUN!" Finn shouted.

A hailstorm of blaster fire erupted, destroying the floor and shredding the walls as the two sprinted across the room. Finn dove through the partially open hatch, and Coy followed. He scrambled back on his hands and scooted up against the wall, which had so far stopped all the fire, but who knew for how long.

"Why are they still active?" he shouted over the noise. "I thought everyone left!"

"The security protocols must still be working," Finn said. "Or, like I said, it's a trap."

"Can we get out of here and figure it out later?"

"Not that way." Finn looked around, then pointed at a rear entrance. "There. Come on."

Without another warning, Finn scrambled to his feet and sprinted to the door. He fired twice with his blaster pistol, burning out the lock, and bashed it open. Coy followed, hands covering his head, only to slam into Finn's back, nearly knocking them both over.

"Why did you—"

"Because of that," Finn said, cutting him off. "Or rather, them."

Coy peeked around his back, only to flinch at the dozens of blaster barrels aimed at his head.

CHAPTER 37

Niila checked her footing, then climbed down a partially collapsed wall to the floor below. The stairs no longer existed, and the turbolift had lost power. She slid down the last few meters, paused to look around, then exhaled in frustration.

"How's the signal?" Jannah called down.

"Stronger," Niila said, looking around. "Not a hit yet, but definitely stronger."

Jannah grunted. Seconds later the former stormtrooper slid down the rubble. She made it look easy, and Niila had to chuckle at the irrational flash of jealousy spiking in her chest when the other woman landed on her feet, not even looking at her surroundings as she pulled out her scanner. Some people just had it, whatever *it* was.

"What?" Jannah asked. "Another conference room?" When Niila turned around, the former First Order trooper laughed at the disgruntled expression she was confronted with. "I'll take that as a yes."

"I just don't understand how one building, even a government palace like this, would need so many conference rooms. What are they discussing? How many meetings are they having? I've seen more conference rooms than offices. Did they just come to work to have meetings all day and then leave?"

"If there's one thing I know about data pushers," Jannah said, peering at her scanner and then pointing out the conference room door to the right. "It's that bureaucrats can never have too many meetings."

Niila snorted. "Bureaucrats are like scav rats, and the only good scav rat is a dead scav rat."

She was going to say more but kept her mouth shut because a cloud of dust billowed from the walls as she pushed a door open and stepped into the corridor. The palace had taken the bulk of its damage on the upper levels, so if they weren't wading through or climbing over rubble, the duo had their faces wrapped to avoid coating their lungs in dust and ash. Not for the first time, Niila wished for one of Coy's respi-vaps. He'd probably give her the one he was wearing in a heartbeat if he knew she wanted one. Silly boy. He was so cute when he was flustered.

She paused. Now why had she thought that? Was he cute? Sure. And she'd enjoyed her time with him, teasing him, just listening to him and how *honest* he was about everything . . . no cynical jests, no jaded biases. He was simple, which sounded like an insult when she first thought about it, but . . . simple was good. Simple was refreshing. Maybe, when this was all over, she'd ask him to show her if simple could work for her.

It took Niila several more seconds to realize that everything had gone silent.

Only for a moment.

Then the low thrum of a converted power core filled the air.

Niila had started walking again, but she stopped and sighed, staring off into the distance. "What gave me away?" she asked.

When she turned, Jannah stood near the beginning of the corridor, still by the conference room they'd recently exited. But instead of her scanner, she held her energy bow, the bowstring pulled taut and the custom arrow nocked and steady.

Jannah's expression was neutral, and she lifted her chin in thought. "We were always suspicious."

"Really?' Niila laughed. "And I thought I'd done really well."

"You did. I fell for it, and I'm the one who fought side by side with you. In fact, it was on Rive when I heard you say bureaucrats were scav rats for the first time, the second time being just now."

Niila groaned. "I *love* that saying."

"But even though I was fooled, Finn had concerns."

"Oh?"

"Yes, but I'll let him explain it. Matter of fact, let's all go reunite right now."

"But you don't want to track down Major Gohl?" Niila widened her eyes.

Jannah motioned with her bow, and Niila stepped away from the wall—a wall with a massive crack twisting its way down from the ceiling, she noted.

"There is no Major Gohl," Jannah said. "Is there?"

Niila smiled as she slipped a hand inside her shirt.

"Easy now."

But she only removed a curved bit of metal, waggling it to show it wasn't a weapon, then slipped it over her nose and around her jaw. She pressed a hidden button and inhaled with audible relief when the rest of the mask extended, obscuring the lower half of her face completely. Another press of the button, and embedded ocular units emerged, switching her view from the normal spectrum to an electromagnetic one. Live electric currents were illuminated in blue, of which there were only a few after the bombardment, while thermomagnetic hot spots showed up as bright orange or red. Several of those hot spots showed up concentrated in the wall with the crack next to her, but Niila didn't panic.

After all, she was the one who'd planted the mines there.

"Now there are no more secrets between us," she lied.

Jannah studied her. "It's amazing what a mask can do for confidence. You look taller"—she stretched the bow even tighter—"Lieutenant Shroud. But it's over now."

Niila, who hadn't used that identifier in years, smiled behind the mask. "We're just getting started," she said, and triggered the mines.

▮▮▮▮▮

Coy heard the explosion—rather, he felt it—but was too preoccupied to try to figure out what else was happening. Hard to investigate something like that when a dozen oversized shockballs with blasters bolted to them were trying to kill you. No, his only focus was on escaping. Unfortunately . . .

"What are we supposed to do?" he screamed.

Finn, who was crouched next to him, peeked out, fired a shot, then kicked one of said spherical attackers toward Coy. "Pick it up and start shooting."

"The ball?"

"Ball? What ball? It's a training remote. Grab its blaster and shoot something! I've fought these before. You just have to aim carefully. The blaster, not the whole thing, the—"

Coy didn't hear the rest because one of the balls—or training remotes, whatever—sped by on his left. He ducked as it circled overhead, trying to find a good angle, until Finn managed to clip it and it spiraled down to crash out of sight.

This was madness. They were crouched behind an overturned pillar made of the room's same dark panels. Finn had said this was a mercenary training facility, similar to the ones that the First Order used to run different training simulations. How one ended up on the inside of a senator's palace was a question for another day . . . provided they all lived to see it. Right now they needed to escape. The door they'd come in was on the other side of the squadron of training remotes, and the only other exit was a turbolift on the opposite side of the room. The only problem was there was no cover between them and it. They would be picked off before they made it ten meters.

A piece of panel split off of the pillar, nicking Coy's ear. Panicking and ducking as shots whizzed by overhead, he lunged for the remote Finn had kicked over and picked up the whole thing. He swung it like a club, shouting as the blaster slammed into a remote that had gotten too ambitious. Coy grinned as it careened off of another remote, sending both crashing to the ground in a shower of sparks.

"Hey, I got one! No, two!" he shouted.

Return fire sent him yelping back behind cover. Finn shook his head, popped up, and took out another remote, then dropped back down. "Rookie," he said.

Any response Coy wanted to make was cut off. The remotes, either by command or by collective intuition, increased their fire until a storm of energy bolts began to shred the pillar they were hiding behind. He shrank down as far as he could go, covering his respi-vap with his hand as he crawled to Finn's position.

"How long can we last like this?" he shouted. "We have to make a move!"

"Just be patient," Finn said, shooting down another remote.

"But we're trapped!" Coy was starting to hyperventilate. Panic tightened his chest, gripping his lungs in a vise and squeezing. He pulled out a miniature screwdriver and loosened a bolt on the respi-vap. The breathing apparatus began to inflate and deflate at a faster clip, and Coy inhaled deeply. There. Better. The old unit was working itself to death. Any more power draw and its circuits would overload. Now—

His gaze fell on the training remote with its blaster still extended. *That's it.* Coy pulled it closer and used his screwdriver to pop open the panel covering its control circuits. If he overloaded the targeting system . . .

"Just hang on a few more—What are you doing?" Finn shouted.

He was trying to be useful! But Coy's hands fumbled as more blaster fire encircled them, and the screwdriver dropped. Time was running out. He squeezed his hands into fists, then forced them to uncurl. He'd done tough things under pressure before. Flying through uncharted space. Sheltering stranded yearlings during a surprise winter dust storm. He could do this. His fingers searched the ground and found the screwdriver, and trying again, he managed to pop off another panel, then jerked out a wire and reattached it to a prong that was now exposed.

"Got it!" he shouted.

The remote whirred to life, sparks spitting from the open contacts, and rose into the air on wobbly thrusters. It beeped several times. More sparks shot out, and then, suddenly, it was spinning around and rushing over to the other remotes. But rather than joining in formation, it began to fire indiscriminately, knocking its former batch mates out of the air.

"What did you do?" Finn asked. The rogue remote was taking out targets before he could shoot.

Coy grinned. "Just a little technical recruiting."

Finn clapped him on the shoulder. "I like the way you think. Now—"

Another explosion rattled the training center. Only this one felt a lot stronger.

Coy and Finn flew backward as the floor heaved. The door to the ground floor entrance buckled inward before disappearing beneath the collapsing ceiling. The ground rose, then dropped, and they slid, weapons lost, all the way to the wall. Finn crashed to a stop first, and Coy slammed into him, both of them grunting in pain.

For a second all he could do was try to breathe. Pain wrapped his chest, and something dripped down his arm. Dust and smoke filled the air. Thankfully, however, the training remotes had stopped firing. Coy managed to push himself up to his feet, staggering back to lean on a broken pillar as he coughed.

Someone spoke amid the chaos.

"So . . . here we are again. FN-Two-One-Eight-Seven comes to Sardich."

Coy wiped blood off of his hands—there was a small gash on his forearm, and he ripped off a strip of his shirt to bind it. As he did, he looked around. No one else was here. But when he turned to Finn, the young general's face was grim. Whoever was speaking, they had history together.

"Who will it be this time, trooper? Sorry . . . former trooper. Who will you kill this time?"

Kill? Coy gulped.

"Once again," the voice continued, "he's going to leave a companion behind. When will you realize that everyone who follows you ends up dead? That, because of your selfishness, people *you* could've saved suffer instead."

Coy searched the billowing smoke for the speaker, but the echoes bounced all around him. A short distance away, Finn was searching for his blaster, a furious look on his face. Coy wanted nothing more than to ask him about the voice and what it was saying, but the general's expression didn't leave any openings for questions.

"How long has it been?" the voice continued. "How many cycles have you spent gallivanting across the galaxy playing hero? The Resistance freedom fighter! The defector from the

First Order who toppled their greatest weapon and stole all of their secrets."

Finn stiffened. He turned, finally, to look at Coy and spoke in a low whisper. "The turbolift is our only way out. We take it up to the docking pad on the upper levels, find the others, and put an end to this. Follow me and don't stop for anything. Got it?"

Coy nodded, a thousand questions bubbling up, but he pushed them down as Finn took off into the smoke. *They'll just have to wait,* he thought before sprinting after him.

The back of his neck tingled, and he expected a blaster bolt to knock him flat any second. A shape loomed up in the smoke in front of them. An undamaged remote. Finn pulled a knife from his belt and shoved it through the unit's ocular lens, and Coy caught it before it crashed to the ground. He jimmied a panel open, yanked out the power core, and ran to catch up to Finn.

Another cluster of remotes swept beams of light through the destruction, searching for them. Finn took the one on the left, silently bearing it to the floor before stabbing its control circuitry repeatedly, and Coy pinched the wires of the power core together before he slammed it into the body of the remote on the right, dispersing an electromagnetic pulse that dropped the unit to the ground. The third spun around, its blaster's power core beginning to whine as it got ready to fire, but a simultaneous knife thrust and EMP attack sent the remote smoking to the ground.

And then they were through to the turbolift.

"Are you still here, Two-One-Eight-Seven? Are you still alive?"

The voice continued to taunt them, but the speaker couldn't see them. Coy glanced back into the destroyed training room, hesitating. He looked at Finn. "Who is that?"

"An old friend," Finn said before the doors of the turbolift closed. Then, and only then, did the general take a deep breath. They hadn't made it through unscathed. At some point the general had been hit in the side with a laser bolt, and he clutched his ribs with a grimace. Coy's makeshift bandage had become soaked with blood, and he muttered a curse as he ripped off another strip of his shirt to rebind it. At this point he'd be lucky to be fully clothed when they confronted Gohl.

If we live through this, Coy thought.

A similar thought must've occurred to Finn, because he took another deep breath and straightened.

"Listen," the general began, "these next few minutes are going to—"

The lift shuddered to a sudden stop. A dull tapping sound, followed by a scrape, cut off whatever instruction Finn was going to relay, and Coy frowned. The noise reminded him of how his grandfather showed him the correct way to harvest mature tea leaves. Tap the stem to see if it was hollow, then swiftly cut . . .

"General!" he shouted, lunging forward and shoving Finn away from the turbolift door, which he was trying to pry open. Finn crashed against the far wall just as the first half meter of a vibrosword sliced through the door and into Coy's hip.

Pain lanced down his side, and wetness sprayed everywhere. Coy fell, his mouth open in a soundless shriek of pain. Agony locked his limbs and seared through every nerve as he slid down the turbolift wall.

An alarm blared somewhere in the distance. The lift doors split open, light pouring in. A shadow stepped inside, with eyes like embers before they burst into flame. Coy opened his mouth. He wanted to ask for help.

The tip of the vibrosword appeared in his vision.

Cold metal lifted his chin. The masked shadow stared at him, and the eyes appeared sad. The shadow held up their other hand, revealing a remote detonator.

"No!" Finn shouted, slamming into the shadow, sending

them both tumbling out of the turbolift. Sounds of a fight reached Coy. He fumbled for his respi-vap. He could help.

Then the shadow spoke:

"Another death on your hands," he heard. "You're good at letting people die for you, aren't you . . . FN-Two-One-Eight-Seven?"

CHAPTER 38

Speak of fairness to the orphans of war.

Pain.

Blaster fire.

Alarms.

Pain.

Wait, he noted that already. And the sound of blasters was interrupted by taunts and insults. Which meant he wasn't dying, not yet, just really, *really* hurt. In fact, his hip felt like it was on fire. But pain meant life, and life meant there was still a chance to escape back to a boring, but pain-free, existence surrounded by tea leaves. Right now, sorting tea leaves felt like the most important job in the galaxy. He wanted nothing more than to go home, banter with the droids, and do inventory on a bunch of brittle plants.

Coy forced his eyes open, gasping for air as his entire left side throbbed in agony.

Oh. My hip is actually *on fire.*

Coy disconnected his smoking respi-vap with a trembling right hand, gritting his teeth as he twisted to reach. The machine disconnected and tumbled to the floor. His lungs immediately began to burn, but the smoldering assistant breathing apparatus no longer seared his skin. He couldn't be too angry at it—there was a perfect gash about four centimeters wide on the outside of the unit.

Right where the vibrosword had stabbed it.

It was the only thing that had saved his life.

Fumbling around with his arms, Coy managed to sit up and look around, only to duck, wincing in pain, as another round of blaster fire splattered across the turbolift doors. He was still inside, and he could hear voices in the adjoining room. He dragged himself closer to the opening and peeked out.

The figure in the mask stood in the center of the ruins of what once was a large lobby. Some decorations still hung around the room, but more were scattered on the dust-covered marble floor, stained or shattered. A trio of old protocol droids stood frozen in one corner, with another two crushed beneath a pile of rock on the floor beside them.

Coy glanced up. Vaulted ceilings carved out of the mountain stone, and probably an incredible sight before the destruction, were pitted and scarred from the explosions. No windows had been installed, so it was all artificial light that sent shadows flickering and dancing, making the room feel more full than it actually was. A security door with a console flashing red next to it stood at the far end. Once again, he and Finn were trapped with someone who didn't like the fact they were breathing.

The figure laughed and muttered something. The cavernous space sent the words bouncing around the chamber, followed by the sound of their blaster firing as it hammered at a fountain in the middle of the floor. Carved in the shape of a flower, the stone it was made of shimmered in the light, sending rainbows rippling up and down the petals—those that were still intact. Every so often the masked figure would shoot a petal off of the fountain, sending fragments of chipped stone ricocheting everywhere.

That was when Coy saw Finn taking shelter on the other side.

"Come on, Two-One-Eight-Seven," the figure called. "You're making this too easy. Major Gohl raved about you in his reports. You should've heard him. Sickening, really."

Finn peeked over the lip of the fountain, then ducked as the blaster pistol singed the stone near his head. "You sound jealous, Shroud."

Shroud? Who was Shroud? And how did they know the general?

"Hardly," Shroud said, shrugging. "Just annoyed."

"Are you that loyal to the First Order?" Finn shot back. "You keep doing their dirty work for them even after they've lost the war?"

The argument faded in and out of Coy's attention. Finn seemed to be holding his own. The most important thing to do now was find Jannah and Niila, then get to the *Harvest* and flee while they were still able to do so. His eyes fell on the protocol droids still upright. Droids meant a programming station or console could be nearby, and Coy might be a terrible shot with a blaster, but programming droids to cause a distraction was right up his alley.

Shots cracked against stone, and he flinched. Shroud was gesturing wildly with the blaster. "I don't *care* about the First Order."

"Then why are you doing all of this? Why fly all that way

with a fake distress call and a made-up story about stolen children and a rogue army?"

Coy froze.

Fake distress call? Made-up story?

"You know why. TZ-One-Seven-One-Nine said as much. She said you knew who I was the whole time. Pity she isn't here to explain what she meant."

TZ-1719. That was Jannah's old First Order identifier.

Finn's face turned furious. Coy could actually see that from where he hid, so the general must've been angry. "Where's Jannah? What did you do?"

"The same thing you did to Major Gohl—buried him."

Cold shock gripped Coy's spine. Jannah . . . dead? No, that didn't make sense; it *couldn't* make sense. She'd just left with Niila. There had to be some mistake.

Finn peeked up again, then ducked back. "I didn't kill your father figure, Niila, if that's even your name. I left him with the people whose suffering he caused. Take your parental issues up in a therapy session. The Resistance has scheduled thousands. You can be next."

Niila.

Niila.

The name hit Coy like a sledgehammer to the chest. His already difficult breathing grew worse as he struggled to connect the dots in his brain. Niila was Shroud? Shroud was . . . trying to kill them? Because the general . . . did what exactly?

"He was my BROTHER!" shrieked Niila—or was it Shroud? The pistol in her hand fired shot after shot as she stalked around the fountain, sending Finn scurrying on his hands and knees, ducking and wincing as fragments of stone pelted his unprotected head and face. One jagged chunk slammed into his temple, and Finn grunted and fell sideways, scrambling for cover even as he clutched his head. Shroud stalked forward, and Coy realized that he would have no better opportunity to escape his current hiding spot and did so, crawling out of the turbolift and off to the left, where a series of toppled couches and divans surrounding an old desk provided a little bit of cover.

The desk also had a dataport. Coy peeked around, then pulled out his datapad. A quick scan showed him the security door on the other side of the room led to the upper docking pads that Finn had mentioned. It was locked, but it wouldn't remain so for long. He just needed—there!

Coy highlighted a subroutine for protocol droids greeting palace guests, added his own little suggestions, then synced it to a timer and began the data transfer. Now it was just a matter of waiting. Once it was done, he could go about sneaking past the confrontation unfolding in front of him unscathed.

Blaster fire sent more debris raining down from the ceiling, and Coy ducked. Sneaking felt more hypothetical at this point.

Shroud flailed about with her vibrosword as she spat out word after word. "He was my brother, and you might as well have pulled the trigger. You left him, abandoned him to a gang of filthy poverty-stricken beggars who wouldn't know rules of engagement even if they were paid to understand. You left him, knowing what would happen."

"He killed innocent people!"

"And your hands are clean?" Shroud laughed, a metallic sound that unnerved Coy with how at odds it was with the stillness of her mask. "Answer that, *stormtrooper.* Now that you're with the Resistance and your fame has stretched to the far reaches of the galaxy. General . . . what are you calling yourself now? Finn? General Finn, the former stormtrooper who saw the light and switched allegiances, helping to bring down his former masters. Do they think you have taken no lives? That your soul is pure and there is nothing haunting you in the late hours of the night, when the only thing standing between you and sleep is the weight of your conscience? Have you nothing to atone for? No sins to admit to?"

Silence fell after the questions. It looked like Finn was struggling to answer. Coy chewed at his lip, silently urging the datapad to finish the transfer. Ninety-eight percent complete. Ninety-nine . . . one hundred! It was done. He started to disconnect when he saw a file name at the top of the inbox. The sender was Major Gohl. He clicked on it and watched. Seconds later he was on his hands and knees, trying not to retch.

The datapad chimed, and Coy groaned as the noise echoed in the stillness.

Shroud/Niila whipped her head around, blaster pointed directly at Coy and ready to fire.

He panicked. "Wait!" he screamed, scrambling from behind the desk. "Wait, it's me. It's me."

"Coy?" The mask's voice filter couldn't hide the hesitation.

"Niila," Coy said. "Is that you?"

"You were supposed to stay on the ship!"

"Is this why? So you could do . . . this? I don't understand!"

Niila shook her head, though the blaster never wavered. "You should not have seen this. I didn't want to hurt you, only the traitors."

"But why?" Coy shook his head, limping away from the desk and farther from where Finn gently held the side of his head. It also put the protocol droids at Niila's back and out of her line of sight. "Why destroy this place with everyone in it?"

"You don't know what they've done." Her voice, low and filled with pain, trembled. "You have *no* idea."

But Coy shook his head. "I do. I saw it."

Finn peeked up, blood streaming from the gash in his temple. "Saw what?"

"A morale report." He held up his datapad. "The final one created by Major Gohl before he was killed. Sort of. His droid did it."

"I told you all, I didn't—"

"Kill him, I know. You left him with the quarry villagers. Apparently, after you were gone, all talk of a trial went out the window. They took vengeance on the major for killing their beloved senator. She was a hero to them. Well, Gohl left his droid recording as the crowd tore him apart, and when it was over, the droid's memory buffers were full and it sent the recording as a morale report draft to Gohl's second-in-command . . . his sister."

Finn and Coy looked at Niila. Slowly, she reached up

and pulled down her mask to reveal red, bloodshot eyes. "I watched," she whispered, "my brother being ripped apart every day for months on end."

The datapad chimed in Coy's hand.

At the other end of the room, the security door's lock changed from red to green. It opened, slowly.

"And you know what's ironic? The audio file immediately before that is one where he sang your praises as he worked on morale reports. You and the other trooper. 'Two-One-Eight-Seven could make an excellent squad leader. One-Seven-One-Nine has shown remarkable ingenuity.' Hour after hour, I would stare at that recording. The two troopers he swooned over, traitors at the very end."

Finn stood, slowly, arms raised. Coy raised his, too, trying not to look at that shadowy figure slipping in from the upper docks and creeping toward them.

"Niila," Finn said, "I never meant to hurt your brother. You have to believe me. Doing this—killing us—won't bring him back. I only wanted him to face justice for the people he hurt and was continuing to hurt. You would do the same thing."

Silence fell between them, broken only by the clatter of bits of stone falling to the floor.

Niila replaced the mask on her face, and Coy's heart sank. "You're right," she said, her filtered voice cold and emotionless once again. "I would. So it's only fair you face the same exact justice."

She lifted her blaster and aimed at Finn.

Coy tapped his datapad.

The three protocol droids near the wall straightened as one, turning toward the standoff in the center of the chamber. "Guests!" they spoke as one. "Welcome to the ha-hallowed halls of Sardich's sen-senatorial palace!"

Niila whirled and fired. The droid in the middle flew backward, a hole rimmed with molten metal glowing in its chest. She realized her mistake almost immediately and tried to turn around, but it was already too late.

Jannah lunged forward from the shadows.

Coy could've sworn nothing but rubble had been there previously. He fell to the seat of his pants and scrambled backward as Niila retreated under an onslaught of attacks. Jannah moved like a rictorfang covered in droid oil—one second she was there, firing a shot from her bow, the next she was blocking the vibrosword with that same bow, shifting, twisting, and spinning out of Niila's line of fire.

"Stay still!" Niila screamed, firing shot after shot as Jannah ducked away, then jabbed an uncharged arrow into the eye of the mask. Niila screeched, and Jannah rammed a front kick into her chest, knocking the other girl onto her back.

The blaster pistol went one way, the vibrosword another.

Finn leaped over the fountain and dove for the blaster.

Jannah nocked an arrow.

"WAIT!" Niila shouted, climbing to her feet. One arm was outstretched, and she clutched the remote detonator in her fist.

Finn and Jannah hesitated, and Niila smiled. Her mask was knocked askew, split in half by Jannah's assault, so it hung on either side of her face. The glowing ocular units gave her a terrifying visage, some droid/human hybrid programmed only to destroy.

"Yes," she hissed. "We'll all die here. Together. The way it should be."

Coy limped forward. "No," he said.

Niila looked at him, then glanced away. "If you want to live, leave. Go. You've had your adventure. You have your stories to tell. Fly back to your farm."

But he pressed forward. Slowly, so as not to tempt her into pressing the detonator. "I am . . . and you should come with me."

"What?"

"What?" Finn said at the same time. Anger twisted his face into a scowl. "After all she's done? Absolutely not."

Jannah didn't take her eyes off Niila. "Explain, Coy."

Coy inhaled, ignoring the pain in his side. "The warrior doesn't seek war."

"Come on, farm boy, speak plainly."

"That's what my grandfather told me right as I was leaving for Ajan Kloss, to join the Citizens' Fleet. He said, 'The warrior doesn't seek war, for fear the war returns to seek the warrior.' I get it now. It's a cycle. And we have the chance to break it."

Coy turned to Jannah. "You said she helped you, even when she had her own goals. And, General, she didn't kill your squad mate—that was Major Gohl."

He whirled to face Niila. "Where did those kids in the shuttle come from?"

Niila hesitated, then lifted her chin. "A slavers' vessel."

"You bought them?"

"I *rescued* them. Took them and gave them spare First Order cadet uniforms. Better than the rags they were wearing." She paused, weighing her next words, then shrugged. "They don't know anything about this, for what it's worth. But I thought you'd do a better job—the Resistance, that is—caring for them than some slavers."

Coy looked at Finn and Jannah as if to say, *See what I'm saying?* He pointed at Finn. "Let's not forget, you've known this whole trip that Niila wasn't who she claimed to be, and yet you let her live then. . . . Why not now?"

"Because," Finn stressed, "I am apparently *unintelligent*."

"Finn," Jannah said, her eyes still glued on Niila.

"Fine. I wanted to see if she would follow in the footsteps of her mentor, and I was right," Finn said. "Just look at all the destruction she's caused. She stabbed you! And you want to let her go home with you?"

"Maybe I'm also unintelligent," Coy said, flushing.

"Or hormonal," Finn muttered. "Lover boy."

"I think what *the general* is trying to say," Jannah said, cutting off Coy's embarrassed protests, "is that you need to think about this. Really think about this."

"I have," Coy said. He glanced at Finn. "You left the major in the hands of the people he hurt. Why not do the same for his sister?"

Jannah slowly nodded. Niila didn't say anything, though her arm holding up the detonator trembled, and a brief flicker of emotion crossed her face when she met Coy's eyes.

After what seemed an eternity, Finn huffed out a sigh and shook his head. "How do you know she won't turn on you? She already hurt you once."

Coy didn't look at him. He kept his eyes on Niila and took a step forward. He grimaced, and her eyes flickered with sorrow as she looked down. But he didn't look away. He limped closer, ignoring how Jannah and Finn tensed, even though they didn't stop him. He continued to walk forward, step by painful step, breath by agonizing breath, until Niila's hand—the one with the detonator—was pressed against his chest. If he took one more step forward, he'd set the charges off himself.

Coy stared at Niila until she looked him in the eye again, and—so soft he could barely be heard—he said, "I don't. But no matter how hurt I am, I'll never again forget that other people are out there hurting, too."

At those words, something else flickered in Niila's eyes. After a second, she turned away, a huge sigh heaving her chest and sending the fragments of her mask clattering to the ground.

"You're so dismissive of your own life," she said. She opened her hand and Coy caught the detonator as she dropped it. She then folded her arms across her chest and pretended to ignore him. "We'll have to fix that."

Coy grinned, even as relief flooded his muscles and he relaxed in a way he hadn't in weeks. "You'll have to help me."

"Great," Finn said, lowering the blaster pistol.

"Phenomenal. A real life lesson. Have we all figured out our true selves now? Can we go home?"

Jannah lowered her bow. "Stop whining and pull your body glove out of your—"

"I think," Coy loudly interrupted, "I'll go get the *Harvest* warmed up. I'm ready to go home, too."

He held out his hand, and after a second, Niila took it, and she helped him hobble across the destroyed lobby to the landing pad door.

Finn watched them go, then shook his head. "People need to stop falling in love on the battlefield. 'Rules of engagement' means something totally different these days."

"Mmhmm," Jannah said, falling in beside him.

"I'm serious! Though I guess marrying the enemy will save on torpedo costs."

"What do you know about marriage?"

"I watched a holo one time. By the way, were you really going to let her blow us up, or did you take care of the mines?"

Jannah smiled. "You think I was gone that long because I had faith in you?"

"Wow. Wow wow wow."

ACKNOWLEDGMENTS

Nearly three decades ago, a boy stood and stared in wonder at a poster hanging in a Blockbuster Video window. This book is for that boy.

But no book is made without its own support squad. (Strap on your body armor; there are tons of these references incoming.) Thank you to everyone involved with *Star Wars* publishing, especially super editor Jen Heddle, for giving this lifelong nerd a chance to tell this story. Furthermore, a big thank-you goes to the crew who joined me on this journey, and who deserve acknowledgment as well:

Mike Siglain, creative director
Pablo Hidalgo and Matt Martin from Lucasfilm Story Group
Megan Speer-Levi, copy editor
Jason Wojtowicz, designer
Jeremy Burton, production editor
Rodger Weinfeld, managing editor

Thank you to Wookieepedia. You know how important you are.

I wouldn't be doing this without my agent and co-pilot, Patrice Caldwell, and the Caldwell Agency. We're only just getting started.

As always, thanks to New Leaf Literary, agency extraordinaire:

Joanna Volpe, chief executive officer
Alaina Mauro, chief operating officer
Katherine Curtis, junior manager, film, TV, and media rights
Hilary Pecheone, director of Brand Development
Eileen Lalley, marketing associate
Joe Volpe, director of Business Affairs
Donna Yee, associate director of Business Affairs
Gabby Benjamin, Business Affairs assistant
Kim Rogers, accounting and royalties manager

I have to thank my family for humoring me and allowing me to include pieces of *Star Wars* in my day-to-day life, whether it's wearing a Jedi robe to cut the grass or collecting LEGO sets and hounding them to build with me. My wife, Mallory—I can't think of anyone I'd rather cruise to the stars with, and thank you for listening to my lore drops with extreme patience.

Finally, *Star Wars* is for everyone, so to everyone out there, may the Force be with you.